THE WICKED ONES

CHILDREN OF THE LOST

J.Z. FOSTER

DEDICATION

My parents.
I built the engine,
but you both helped me put gas in it.

Special thanks to:

Jordan Dube
Kurt (Sally) Frazier
Nicole Huston
Andy Pavlides
David Sorensen
Maria Townsley

PROLOGUE

DANIEL TANNER SAT HUNCHED OVER HIS DESK, CREATING AN ache in his back. A rough-edged notebook lay before him, a poor replacement for the leather-bound journal he had in better days, but he'd lost the taste for such things long ago.

He drew out his pen and tried hard not to scribble the next words.

They say that when you look into the abyss, it looks back into you. I never really understood what that meant.

The shaking of his hand made the words nearly illegible, but he found some power in placing them on paper. They were words for him, and no one else.

What you could become.

He stopped when the tears began dripping onto the paper. The pages swallowing his pain like so much else had. He closed his eyes and took a deep breath, then poured himself another shot and drained it. He needed the warmth that rushed down his throat and steadied his hand.

I thought I could handle it. I thought I wouldn't be like this. I didn't know I'd become like them.

Daniel stopped and squeezed his eyes tightly shut,

wondering again why writing always seemed to make things easier, as if it somehow made them certain, a thing no longer to be questioned. The pen dropped and his head slid into his hands. It felt heavy in his grasp, but surely another drink would make it lighter. It did.

When I've finished this drink, I'll go to that thing in my basement and cut it. I'll hurt it until it gives me what I want. What does that make me? When I stared into the abyss . . .

The next drink went down as easily as the others.

Did it stare back into me?

1

___

Daniel stared at the dirt pile, the spot where his son had been buried mere hours ago. A temporary grave marker sat above his son's final resting place. In a few weeks, when the dirt had settled, it would be replaced by a stone that read: Sam Tanner. Beloved son. He is missed.

But that's a lie, isn't it?

There was no holding the thought back. His gaze wandered to where his wife, Julia, had a seat; it was empty. His throat tightened at the thought of a mother who wouldn't even come to her son's funeral.

How could I have loved someone who grew so cold so fast? Someone who turned her back so easily when her son was sick?

Sam rested deep in the cold dirt, that part was true; but he was the beloved son of his father, not his mother. They found Sam that one dreadful morning, sickly and pale in his bed, barely able to form words.

"I don't want to go to sleep. I don't like the people in my dreams," Sam had said.

Daniel shushed him, read him a book, and rubbed his head.

"Monsters aren't real, Sam. Those were just stories people used to tell naughty boys. But you don't believe in those kinds of things, do you? You're a good guy, right?" Sam nodded, his eyes heavy for want of sleep. "So, you just go to sleep, and if you have any bad dreams, you come and wake me up, okay? Daddy will always come and help you when you need him."

That too was a lie, though, wasn't it?

Monsters are real. Sam's mother is a monster.

It all played back like a single blurred event. The memories raced in and out of his mind, giving him no relief. First, the doctors failed him by saying that they didn't know what was happening. But now, he remembered the phone call with Julia just after the consultation.

"They can't stop the fever, they don't know why." He barely choked the words out over the phone. "What is happening to our son?"

"That's not our son," Julia hissed.

"What the hell are you talking about? Your son needs you, Julia. You get your ass down here. He *needs* you."

She didn't come.

That wasn't their first argument, or their last. Over the next few weeks, Julia descended into madness, unraveling like a cut ball of string and howling about how it wasn't their son, all while poor Sam's brain cooked. In the end, Sam could only form rough, incoherent words or sounds more akin to a caged animal than a sick boy.

And he did—he did look like a caged animal. Daniel remembered Sam's eyes, that gaze that seemed to wander and look through him, like he wasn't even there anymore.

"He's doing terrible, Julia," Daniel whispered into the phone. "He . . . he doesn't have long. It would help him to see you one last time."

"No," she said. "I hope he dies."

I hope he dies?

Daniel couldn't recall what he said next, but those stark words ran through his head again and again. He couldn't believe them then, and they hadn't softened since.

I hope he dies? She's a monster, a cold-hearted bitch. Evil.

He couldn't live with someone like that. He left her before Sam had even died, and the divorce would be in order shortly. She barely resisted. It was strange—she did seem sad over it all, but devoid of any energy to do anything about it. There might have been a chance for her to change the tide, to come and pour her heart out, tell him how it was all too terrifying to deal with—he was scared too, after all. Maybe they could have gone to a counselor, worked through the death of their son together, been there for each other, healed one another.

But she never changed. And some wounds didn't heal, only festered.

And now I'm alone with this. Alone with thoughts of my son, my wife.

Standing over his son's plot of dirt, Sam's final place on Earth, and still the woman occupied his mind. Daniel's gaze drifted to her seat once more. Empty.

Just like that bitch's soul.

The thought made tears form in his eyes and his throat started to tighten with the awful reality that Sam died without a mother to hold his hand.

How could she do that to our son?

A crack in the sky opened and rain began, suitable weather for the miserable day. Daniel had stayed several hours after the funeral, just watching. He couldn't choke out more than a few words at a time to any of the guests. Daniel's parents stayed with him, silently watching their grandson's grave, before they too left. Even Julia's parents had shown up, but Daniel didn't dare make eye contact with them. He had no interest in speaking with the people who had raised that woman.

He thought only of his son—he had lost a beloved child and the man Sam would never become. Sam would never grow old, would never go to high school, or marry, or have children. He lost everything that he would be.

And so had Daniel. He would never see him run a race, teach him to drive, meet his fiancée, or bounce a grandchild on his knee.

What is left for a man who's lost his family? He was a novelist. He wrote comedies for God's sake, but he knew that he would never write another comedy. That part of his life was over now. He couldn't foresee any jokes in his future.

"Mr. Tanner?"

An older man appeared behind him, holding an umbrella to shield against the cold rain. The clean-shaven man had a hard jawline, and it was clear from his white hair and weathered face that he was well into his sixties.

Daniel nodded.

"I'm sorry to bother you. My name is Larry Maker, and I'd like to talk with you soon. How about you give me a call?" Maker fished a card from his pocket and held it out to Daniel. One glance at it showed only the name *Larry Maker* and a phone number under it.

Daniel reached automatically for the card and slid it into his pocket as he muttered just one word:

"Okay."

Larry's gaze searched Daniel's face. "I'd really like to talk with you. I'll be looking forward to it. My condolences for your loss." He gave Daniel a tilt of his head, then turned and walked away, leaving Daniel to the wind and his sorrow.

Daniel returned to Sam's grave, and any thoughts of Larry blew away with the breeze.

That's more than my son in the dirt. That's my wife. That's my career. That's my life. My God, that's my son.

That web of thoughts laced through his mind over and over, like a virus that corrupted everything it touched, then wound back like a circle to do it all again.

His son, his wife, his life, his son.

In the seven weeks since they found him in his room, the illness had run through his body, weakening his heart and dulling his senses. He'd been fine just the day before they found him, up and walking around, talking, getting ready for school. Then, in one night, he couldn't walk or even talk. It took seven weeks for his heart to stop, but they had lost their son in just that one night.

And now he was in the ground.

Daniel turned away and walked home, only because there was nowhere else to go. Each step felt heavier than the last. He left his car at the graveyard, as if walking would somehow clear his mind, would somehow break him away from it all.

He'd told Julia that he was leaving her, but she had cleared out by the time he came back from the hospital. He hated her, hated what she'd done to his son, *their* son. But even now, after everything that had happened, some part of him wanted her there. Wanted her to be there, to cry with him for their son, wanted her to be someone who could feel what he felt. But she wasn't.

I hope he dies?

A DEAD MAN'S stink crept up from the back seat of the car. It clung to clothing, seeped out through open windows and pierced the senses of those nearby. A cheerful whistle in the air said the pale man wasn't concerned about the smell; rather, it brought a tune to his lips. His feet were propped up on the dashboard as he enjoyed the glowing lights of New Athens.

"You know what I like about small cities?" he asked the dead man. "They just fit so comfortably, don't they?"

"He can't hear you," came a childish voice, as fingers dug at the dead man's flesh. "He's dead!"

"Heh, heh, heh. I always find the dead are the best listeners."

A thing prowled around in the darkness between the trees, snorting, followed by a low growl.

"Looks like we have company," the pale man said with a thin, gray-lipped grin toward the dead. He stretched up to his feet and stepped from the car, wiping a long, stringy strand of hair from his face and leaving the car door hanging open in the cool night air.

"Oh boy, oh boy! Does that mean I can see my family now?" The creature in the back seat climbed out through the window and hopped to the ground, barely able to contain its excitement.

"I think it does." The pale man patted the creature's raw, bald head. "You were always my favorite."

It looked up to him and smiled with a mouth full of needle teeth and pinkish, rubbery gums laced with purple veins.

The thing from the woods stalked out, heavy and large, a nightmare given form. It used its arms like an extra set of legs, and its neck snaked out several feet. It dropped large chunks of mauled meat into the grass before the pale man, a gift of submission to a greater beast. The meat was so torn and violated that it gave no hint to what it once had been.

Without hesitation, the small child leapt at the offering, tearing meat from bone with its pointed teeth. Nearly a half-dozen sets of eyes opened in the darkness, and their hungry mouths followed the scent of meat. The pale man took one last deep breath as he looked out over the city.

"Great city." His grin stretched even farther. "I think I'll take it."

2

THE HOURS TURNED INTO DAYS, BUT THEY ALL SEEMED TO burn together.

How long has it been since the funeral? Four days? A week?

Daniel was now afraid of the dark. Something about the emptiness of the house, something childlike inside him . . . It was the nightmares—they'd changed him.

Daniel's imagination was a powerful thing; accolades and awards hung on his wall to attest to that. He had made a career with the worlds he built inside his mind and grafted onto paper. He imagined characters so real that he didn't so much write them as listen to them speak. But it was torturous now. Now, his imagination constructed nightmares that plagued him.

In one, he sat in his house, alone in the dark. It was the same every time, but inside the dream it always felt fresh, and each began like it was the first. Laying in his bed and staring at the ceiling, soft steps just outside the open bedroom door drew his gaze to the hallway.

A misshapen hand reached out from the abyss of the hallway, and with fingers chewed by some painful disease it pulled itself forward, until a head came into view, eyes sunk deep into the skull. Its lips pulled back into a twisted sneer of yellowed teeth. Brown spots of rot dotted its surface, and small patches of hair grew from its scalp. It dragged itself on all fours across the wood flooring, slapping heavy hands down with each horrible pull. Its twisted face somehow resembled Sam's.

Has Sam rotted so quickly? Have Sam's teeth turned so yellow or his eyes sunk so deeply in just a few days?

Daniel wanted to get away from it, this horrid thing his son had become. But it came relentlessly, and left a sickening wet trail in its wake. Clinging to the posts of the bed, it pulled itself up into the glow of moonlight that cut through the bedroom window. Only when its rotted fingers sank into Daniel's flesh would he wake up.

Each time was the same—the dream and the waking, the shaking, the sucking in of deep mouthfuls of air as a cold sweat rolled down his face. And there, in the dark, he turned to his bedroom window that hung so precariously open with its curtains softly swaying. Daniel knew the fingers stretched toward him even though they were out of view. Those same rotting nails and that same flesh starting the nightmare once again.

He shut his eyes. Even as the floorboard creaked again and breath hissed in the air, even as he felt the tug on his blanket, he kept his eyes shut, told himself that he imagined things, repeated what he had told his son long before:

Monsters aren't real.

OPENING the chamber of the revolver, Daniel saw the six loaded bullets, the same as the night before and the night before that. Julia forced him to buy it a few years before Sam was born. He didn't think much about it then, but in the last few days, his mind drifted to it more and more.

Guess she was right when she said I might need it.

He didn't remember it being so heavy. He spun the chamber, listened to the *click-click-click* as it slowed, then thumbed the chamber into place with another reassuring *click*.

He wondered if there'd be room for his own plot of dirt next to Sam's.

Probably should have arranged that beforehand.

He had little energy to think about anything else. His face was stiff as he pulled the hammer of the revolver back, locking it into place. There was no fear when he thought of the gun. It had a sense of release to it, a remedy for the nightmares, six little antidotes for the pain.

Now, he only considered whether the temple or the mouth would be best.

Ring-Ring!

The sound of the house phone—he hadn't heard that in some time. No one called him there, only on his cell phone, and he had turned that off for the evening. He pressed the barrel of the gun into his head; the temple would be fine.

Ring-Ring!

There was something there, something that refused to be ignored. He lowered the gun and waited. Perhaps it was a wrong number? No one called the house phone anymore after all.

Ring-Ring!

Who the hell would call me this late at night?

He stood up, placed the gun on the nightstand, and made his way into the kitchen.

"Hello?" he said, his voice hoarser than he expected it to be.

A man took a breath on the other line. "Mr. Tanner? It's Larry Maker. I gave you my card at the funeral. I'm sorry to bother you so late, but I was wondering if we could talk."

It took Daniel a moment to remember the old man from the funeral. "Oh, Larry." His eyes shifted toward the bedroom where the revolver rested. "Can it wait until morning?"

"It could." The old man's voice sounded restless. "But it's important."

Daniel rubbed his forehead and sighed into the phone. "All right, what is it?"

There was a moment of silence on the other end, as if the man was considering his words carefully. "It's about your son. His death . . . I don't think it was an illness."

3

DANIEL ARRIVED AT THE RESTAURANT TEN MINUTES LATER than they had agreed. He'd forgotten that his car wasn't at home; it might have been towed from the cemetery lot for all he knew. The truth was he wasn't thinking too clearly. He hadn't slept well lately, and he certainly hadn't slept after the call last night.

Larry Maker told him that he was a retired detective, and he sometimes looked into strange cases. Daniel had already spoken with the police—there were concerns of poisoning, but the toxicology report came back clean. Everything came back clean. Nothing made sense. But, since that phone call the night before, he started to reconsider. Julia had certainly been acting strange.

Maker had insisted that they discuss the rest of it the next day, after Daniel had some time to sleep. It was important that he get a good night's sleep, Maker had said.

Did he really think I could sleep after he told me all that?

Now, inside the restaurant, he quickly found the old man in the corner booth drinking a cup of coffee. He nodded at Daniel and waved for the waitress. Maker ordered food for both of them; even after Daniel said he wasn't hungry. "You look like you haven't eaten in days, Mr. Tanner. Or slept, for that matter."

Daniel nodded; he hadn't. He'd lost his appetite, though he was pretty sure he gnawed on a cereal bar the day before. He even slept some, but the dark bags beneath his eyes said it wasn't much. "The days aren't going so smoothly."

"I wouldn't suspect so." Maker took another long sip of his coffee, set it down, and studied Daniel, weighing him with aged eyes.

Daniel coughed and took a sip of the coffee the waitress had brought him. "You said you know something about my son?"

"Yeah. Your son, he went to school around here. At Liberty Elementary?"

"He did." Daniel took a longer drag of the coffee. It helped to clear the fog in his brain.

"You attend many of the parents' meetings?"

"Yeah, but what does that have to do with anything?"

Maker nodded coolly. He kept his voice low to keep it from traveling far from the table. "I was at your son's funeral. I saw the other families there with their children. I assume they were friends of your son, went to school with him." Nothing was a question, only statements.

Daniel simply listened and started to consider whether he was wasting his time. He thought of the revolver back home. "What does this have to do with my son?"

The waitress brought their food to the table and disappeared again to other business. "I'd like you to eat a little first, before we get in too deep," said Maker. "I'd like your thoughts to be clear."

"I am clear," Daniel persisted, without so much as a glance at the food. "I'm fine."

"If it's all the same."

Daniel sighed and picked up his fork. Maker was clearly a man used to getting what he wanted, but Daniel wasn't in the mood for games. Still, he cut a piece of egg and began to eat. Maker nodded and did the same.

They ate their breakfast in silence, and only when they had both finished and begun their second round of coffee did Maker speak. "I read the toxicology report, and I spoke with the detective that investigated your son's death. Both came up empty. Even the hospital staff was clueless."

"You did?"

A silent nod, and Maker answered his question as if he could read his mind. "I know how to get things. I know the right people to talk to." The lines in his face did seem to imply experience. "Nothing is hard to get, so long as you know where to find it."

"The doctors said they didn't know what it was." Daniel tried to control himself as he spoke, but he could hear his voice wavering. "They said they've never seen anything like it, and the only cases that resembled anything like it came from Africa and the Caribbean. I wanted to move him to see another doctor, but it was already too late. They told me moving him at all might kill him." Daniel huffed. "Still, he died anyway."

"Why'd you dismiss an autopsy if there was all that confusion?" Maker asked flatly.

"Sam had already been through so much and..." Daniel had to take a deep breath before he could speak again. "I just didn't want to put him through anything else."

Maker waited for him to finish. "The detective said your wife had been acting erratically while Sam was sick."

Erratically.

That made Daniel laugh, that simple word. Like that was

enough. No one could possibly understand how she had changed unless they saw it.

Daniel took another deep breath. "She *refused* to go see him. She told me it wasn't her son. She told me she hoped he died." He laughed again, but not in any way that resembled joy. Daniel fought against the tears clawing at his eyes. "She lost her mind. I can't blame her. Now I feel like *I'm* losing *my* mind."

Maker listened patiently as Daniel stammered through it.

"But I was j-just so surprised at how f-fast she lost it all. It was only a f-few weeks, and she had been loving on him the day before he got sick." He sighed. "Did she have something to do with it?"

Maker stopped and smiled at the waitress as she came by to refill their mugs. When she left, he spoke. "No, she didn't. Don't blame your wife, Mr. Tanner. Some people fall apart in situations like this. I'm sure she loved your son in her own way."

"No, she didn't. You weren't there. Julia wouldn't even visit him in the hospital. You don't turn your back on someone you love like that." The shakes were coming harder now, rattling his hand against the table.

"Well, you would certainly know better than me." Maker didn't seem to want to push. "Enough about that. She didn't have anything to do with it either way."

"Who did? What happened to my son?"

Another long drink of the coffee, black and hot. It probably scorched Maker's throat, but he didn't seem to be bothered by it. "There's a man I've been investigating for the past few years. He moves from town to town—might be the next one over or might be a few hundred miles. Sometimes it's hard to keep up with him. He targets children, and I believe he was involved with Sam."

The words clawed their way into Daniel's heart. The thought of a man cracking open his son's window and slipping in during the dark of night shook him to the depths of his soul.

"No signs of entry," Maker said, as if reading Daniel's mind. "I know. He doesn't work that way."

"H-how?" Only the one word croaked out.

Maker glanced at his watch and then up at Daniel. The old man's eyes were heavy, calculating, searching. For what, Daniel didn't know. "I think it's best if you come with me. I'm renting a place nearby, a little out in the sticks. I can tell you what I know there. Some things are better said in privacy. You up for the drive?"

"Yes." Daniel knew he had little choice. Nothing else was as important as learning about what had happened to his son.

Maker left a few bills on the table, glancing up just long enough to make eye contact with the waitress. He seemed like a man who used words only when he had to, a touch unfriendly.

They took Maker's car, and he was right about it being out in the sticks—they drove a good twenty minutes outside of town. Daniel had lived here for years, but had no idea that Terrace Drive stretched so far out, let alone that a property out there could be rented.

Maker seemed to pick up Daniel's thoughts again. Maybe he noticed the confused look on Daniel's face. "Found a house out here for sale, did a little research, and saw that it'd been up for quite some time. I called the owner and asked if she'd let me rent for a few months. She wasn't so eager at first, but she agreed. All under the counter, of course. Gets her a few bucks and me a place to stay."

Daniel looked out across the looming trees that hurried past his window. It was a modest car that seemed to have the same aged appearance as Maker. And although the man was clean-shaven and his looks well maintained, the car was rough and damaged. There were several long tears in the cushions in the back seat, the longest with a piece of duct tape over it. Strange stains that resembled spilled coffee formed odd shapes on the seats and floor.

He couldn't imagine Maker had paid much for the car, or the house for that matter. "Why'd you come so far out here?"

Maker's eyes stayed dead ahead on the road. "Almost there." He made no further attempts at conversation.

Daniel looked away and stared idly out the window. He hadn't seen a house in some time. They pulled off the main road and onto a dirt stretch, then made their way to an old farmhouse with a sea of trees behind it. Long swaths of weeds showed that any real farming done here had dried up decades ago

Two other vehicles, a car and an old truck, were parked outside, both in a state of decay similar to Maker's car. "This is it. Mr. Tanner, could you put your cell phone in the glove compartment?"

"Why?"

"I'd appreciate it," was all the older man said, and Daniel found himself complying without even knowing why— something in Maker's voice made it hard to disobey. He stuffed it in the glove compartment on top of a pile of old letters.

With a nod of appreciation, and without another word, Maker stepped out of the car. Following him, Daniel felt the gravel of the weed-infested driveway crunch under his feet. The house was worn down and in desperate need of a new paint job. A barn stood not far to their left—one side had caved in, leaving a mouth gaping at the sky. The rest of it threatened to collapse at any moment.

"Come on in," Maker said, taking the lead and moving toward the worn patio steps. "You can meet the others."

"The others?"

Something was in the air; Daniel could smell it, in a way he couldn't describe. His instincts told him to leave it alone, to turn away now and take that long walk back to town. Something inside him cried against the unnatural breeze and the way Maker walked. Something told him it was wrong.

Maker didn't spare a glance back, and the door hung open, beckoning him to enter. To find out what little he could about his son.

Sam.

His feet met the old wood of the patio and, before his instincts could persuade him otherwise, he pushed the door open and stepped into the dimly lit room. The shades had been drawn, making it hard to see the three others until his eyes adjusted.

A black woman with a wide smile and a country twang in her voice stood up and introduced herself as Jenna. She was the youngest there, other than Daniel, in her mid-fifties by the look of it.

They went around. Another man, Greg, had rough hands that seemed to engulf Daniel's when they shook. He had arms that said he lived a life of labor, and that was surely his truck outside. His face was as stiff as a board, with an unshaven chin and the faint smell of alcohol.

The last was Rebekah, a thin, frail woman with short

gray hair and a muted black and white dress. She gave him a courteous smile, but it vanished the second it became unnecessary.

When Maker mentioned that they were all familiar with what had happened to Sam, Jenna interrupted. "God Bless you, son." No one else said anything.

"Well, now that you've met everyone," Maker said, "I'd like to get down to business. I've got something in the basement I'd like you to see, Daniel, but it's important that you remain calm."

The made Daniel hesitate. "What is it?" He glanced at the others, all stone-faced except for Jenna, who wore a perpetual smile.

"The man I told you about . . ."

"Yeah?" Daniel stood frozen, waiting.

The older man cleared his throat and looked up again at Daniel, his eyes once more weighing him, judging him, calculating. Preparing for what came next. No one else dared to speak.

"I've got him locked down in the basement."

4

———

With his eyes fixed on Maker, Daniel waited for something else, some kind of explanation—a laugh, even. The strangeness of it all wouldn't register in his mind. The bluntness of it only numbed him.

"What the hell are you going to do with him?" he asked, entirely confused.

"Well, right now, we want you to come downstairs and take a look at him." Maker's voice was steady, as if it wasn't a strange request.

"Why? Shouldn't we call the police?" Daniel turned to scan the room again. Except Jenna, their faces were empty and serious.

"No police," Greg croaked, his thick arms crossed in front of him, locked tight like stone.

"There might be a time for that," Maker said with a sideways glance at Greg. "But for now, we think it's best you see him. Before we turn him over."

Jenna stood up, her long, flowing dress kissing the floor as she stepped up to Daniel and lightly touched his arm. "Now, don't you worry." Her country accent was comforting.

"We're gonna be right here with you. It's important you see 'im."

Despite her comforting voice, Jenna's touch made his skin crawl and itch. He wanted to leave, but one more look at Maker told him that he wasn't allowed to choose. He considered darting toward the door, but he wasn't sure he'd make it before Greg or Maker was on him.

"All right," he said with a dry throat and a hint of a nod.

"Bless you." Jenna's fingers slid down to squeeze his hand.

Lights spun in Daniel's head. The dizzying rush of things threw him off and gave him tunnel vision as they descended into the basement, each step hammering loudly against the wooden stairs like nails into a coffin. A musky smell assaulted his senses. A low moan came from deeper within the basement.

There really is a man down here.

Maker stopped when he reached the concrete floor of the basement and pulled a string hanging from the ceiling. A bulb flickered several times before it came to life, casting a weak glow that was blocked by a sheet hanging between the joists. The sheet had a smiling sun and frowning clouds stenciled on it.

Something moaned again behind the sheet.

"What the hell was that?" Daniel said over Maker's shoulder.

"Who's there?" A child's faint voice, scratchy and dry, carried from behind the curtain. "Is someone there? They're hurting me, please, help me, they're hurting me..."

"Oh my God." Daniel turned and saw Greg behind him, the large man's fist balled tight. "You said you had a man! That's a kid back there!"

"Help me!" cried the childish voice.

"Ain't no kid," Greg responded, his lip pulled up to expose his dark, stained teeth. "Fucker ain't even human."

With one last glance back at Daniel, Maker pulled the sheet down; it came loose easily and fluttered to the concrete floor. A boy was there, chained by his wrists, ankles, and neck to the bed, with a blindfold wrapped around his eyes.

"They're hurting me!" he wailed. Dried blood caked around his shackles and green bruises dotted his arms.

Spinning to face Greg, Daniel tightened his fist. He'd have to go through Greg and make the first one count, right into his nose, enough that the bigger man would feel it. Then past the two women watching from the stairs before Maker could pounce on his back. If he could catch them fast enough, he might be able to get outside, get to Maker's car.

The keys.

"Settle down, Tanner." Maker stepped closer to the boy and grabbed one of the ends of the blindfold, tugging the boy's head weakly to the side as it came loose.

Yellow eyes with black veins and split pupils blinked and stared. Breath seized in Daniel's chest. His hands shook dumbly as he felt across the wall for something to grab onto as he sunk to the floor.

"What the fuck?" he said, unable to pull his gaze from the boy's eyes, though he desperately wanted to.

"Help me!" the boy shrieked as his eyes went wide, fixing onto Daniel. "Help me, they're hurting me!"

Maker shoved the boy's head back and stuffed the blindfold into his mouth. The old woman, Rebekah, spoke with a thinly veiled German accent, "No, no, we didn't do this to the boy. *Wechselkinder.* This boy is a thief in the night."

"More like a burning shit on your porch," Greg said as he descended the stairs. Daniel saw the hammer hanging from a strap on Greg's belt. He knew why it was there. He knew what Greg could do with it.

The boy's eyes grew more desperate still. His gaze wrapped around Daniel and held him there, tears watering from his eyes, pleading. And for a moment, if only just a moment, he looked like Sam.

Maker reached up and grasped a metal sheath that had been hanging from a nail above the bed. "This isn't a boy, Tanner." He waved the sheathed blade in front of the boy, whose gaze released Daniel to track the weapon.

Daniel gasped cool, stale air—he hadn't been breathing. The yellow gaze had cut into him and squeezed the breath from him like little fingers squeezing his lungs.

"This one is too weak for its guise," Rebekah said. "The iron." A thin finger pointed to the chain around his neck. "You see, it weakens him. The knife, it too is made of iron. His cloak will burn."

Terror burned out of the boy's eyes as something more sinister grew, a hatred for the thing in front of it, the knife waving before it. The boy growled and ripped at his bindings.

Daniel saw terrible bruising around the boy's wrists, dark and black. It had been trying to free itself for some time. Maker violently pressed the metal sheath of the knife to the flesh just above its temple.

Its back snapped loudly into an arch as its skin turned a deep green that was nearly black. Maker withdrew the knife and hung the sheath above the bedposts, then wiped his hands across the sheet as he turned to Daniel.

"Mr. Tanner, have you ever heard of a brood parasite?" Maker asked gruffly.

The thing that played as a boy writhed behind Maker. Daniel shook his head and stared at the thing's legs and arms, afraid to make eye contact with it again but unable to look away completely.

"Sometimes a bird, or an insect, or *some thing*, steals into the nest of a host and lays its brood there. It leaves the thing for the host to find and raise as its own," Maker said.

Daniel was still drawing in sharp breaths, each thick with the soiled smell of the basement. He couldn't move, and although he desperately wanted to be anywhere else, he watched. Even when it turned to him again, staring with those yellow eyes that said so much but nothing at all, he watched.

"Sometimes they'll kill the offspring of the host so that their young can be better attended to." Maker gave a muffled groan as he drew down on his haunches to meet Daniel's eyes. "Do you understand the point I'm getting at?"

Daniel shook his head again. "No." But that was a lie; a thought was forming in his head. A thought he was afraid he couldn't withstand, an idea that might kill him if said aloud.

Maker did not soften his words. "We believe this thing's progenitor stole into your house one night and killed your child, leaving its own with the hope that you and your wife would raise it to maturity. For whatever reason, the offspring left at your house didn't take. I'm sorry, I truly am. I'm sorry for your son's death, and I'm sorry to have to tell you like this, but you wouldn't have believed me any other way."

No. He's insane. They're all insane. Nothing like that happened to Sam. They're lunatics.

"No," Daniel insisted, rising to his feet, as if that somehow proved them wrong. "No," he said once more. "Sam got sick and died. He's buried . . ." The words caught in his throat.

"I understand. I do. I had a son a ways back. We all did,"

he said with a wave of his hand at the group. "A son or a daughter or a nephew or a friend. We've all been there, and we've all seen the same, all had the same reaction as you. Only the names are different."

Uneasy, Daniel moved past Maker and toward the steps, but Greg interceded. "Listen to the man." Greg uncrossed his arms, adding emphasis to his command.

"Here, child," Jenna said, coming close and grabbing his arm. "God has His ways, and He brought you here to us." She gave him a wide, innocent smile. "This is what He wants. This is where you're supposed to be."

Daniel wanted to pull away from her, rip her down if need be, and shove past Greg. But Maker spoke and he couldn't be ignored. "You wanted answers? We have them. Not the ones you wanted, certainly, but the truth. You gonna let them get away with it, Daniel? You gonna let them get away with what they did to your boy?"

Daniel's arm shook in Jenna's grasp. "Shh," she soothed, trying to comfort him. "We know, child. We know."

"H-how can I know that this th-thing had anything to do with Sam? How can I be sure it was a b-brood parasite?"

"We're going to ask him. He'll know a little. Not much, but a little." Maker stepped close enough that Daniel could smell the coffee on his breath. "Got a picture of Sam?"

Daniel found himself obeying without consideration. With shaky hands, he fished a picture of Sam out of his wallet. Maker gave a nod of thanks and stepped over to the boy with the picture. "See this kid?" Maker asked as he pulled the knife and sheath down again.

The boy's gaze fixed on Maker, then traced back to the knife.

Maker handed it to Greg. "There. Now, the boy." He held the picture again in front of its nose. The creature was covered in a thick, oily sweat now, with inky black tears. Its face had widened, its cheekbones stretching and cracking. Its face tightened into what might have been a smile. Its head tipped low as it let out a low, hissing chuckle with the blindfold stuffed in its mouth.

"Heh-heh-heh."

Maker dully fixed his eyes on it for a moment, and then held his hand back to Greg, who placed the blade and sheath there once more. "I'm going to ask you some questions. If I don't think you're telling me the truth, I'm going to hurt you."

The creature's guise collapsed and its body contorted into something still more inhuman and monstrous. With another crack, its jaw stretched down, growing another inch. It spit out the blindfold.

"How many are in your brood?" Maker seemed to be transfixed.

Its wicked eyes sized up Maker and the others. It said nothing, only pursed its lips into a smile. Maker reached out and pulled the knife from the sheath. "I won't ask twice."

The boy stayed silent.

The sharp edge of the blade slashed across the inside of the monster's arm. Its pink flesh tore apart like a stretched curtain, exposing what looked like spoiled meat. The creature bellowed in agony and Maker stopped. He waited, giving it a chance to catch its breath.

It huffed in air and giggled like a child between breaths. "So many this time, so many of my brothers and sisters are here." The creature's laughter broke like a jackal. "They have your scent, old man! They have you and the rest of your whores' scents!" It froze in place and spoke with wide eyes. "But if you release me, they won't defile you!"

Maker responded with the blade, opening a wound on

its palm–black tar leaked from it. It screeched again and burst into laughter. "He's dead!" It turned to look at Daniel between breaks in its hysterical laughter. "Your son is dead! We ate him as he cried! He cried for you!"

Daniel's stomach lurched, and he puked his breakfast onto the concrete floor. Its laughter, the maddening laughter, beat across the inside of his skull while horrid thoughts danced within.

"Get him out of here!" someone yelled. A pair of hands grabbed him and dragged him up the steps. He tried to stop, to catch his feet beneath him, but he turned to see its eyes. Those yellow cruel eyes, once more met his and dug into his soul. Vomit burst into his mouth, and he retched on the stairs as Greg dragged him through the open door.

With no power to stand on his feet, Daniel slid carelessly to the floor. Daniel's mind swam with lunacy and threatened to fail him. His head swirled with horrors and apparitions.

"Shh, it'll be all right," Jenna whispered to him as she cradled him against her dark skin; he hadn't heard her come upstairs. "It's all going to be all right."

He tried to form words to scream: "What was that? What was that!" but they spilled out broken, convoluted.

Upside down and inside out. A son that's a monster. A wife that's insane. Am I insane? Where's my son? Where's my son? Am I insane?

"Where's my son!" he moaned as he thrashed. "What was that?"

His vision blurred, his muscles went weak, and the fog of sleep gathered over him. The long tiring days now threatened to overcome him. Before it took him, he heard her whisper:

"Shh," she soothed in a sweet tone. "You stared into the

eyes of the devil—he's real. God help me, I wish he wasn't, but he is, Daniel. He's real."

He gasped for air as she whispered, and some of her words were lost to him.

The eyes, those yellow eyes.

"He's real," she whispered once more into his ear, "but we know how to kill him."

Then the dark took him.

5

———

THE NIGHTMARES CAME LIKE AN OLD FRIEND WITH THE KEY TO the door and no need to knock. There were the regulars: The dream where Sam broke like dust in Daniel's arms while he tried to scoop the parts back together, and the horrid thing that looked like him crawling down the hallway. But now there was something new and even more sinister than the others. It started in Sam's room. He begged a faceless man not to leave for reasons he couldn't comprehend, but the words wouldn't come out. His throat was dry, and the faceless man didn't listen closely enough, didn't bother to try to understand.

As the door shut, the room expanded and cruel shadows took shape along the walls: things with teeth and sharp nails that reached for him. He had to climb onto the bed to evade their reach. Then the window began to slide open, without so much as rattle on its wooden frame.

Slender fingers stretched out of the night and pulled the rest of its body into view, and it wore Sam's face. It came up with a curious smile. It reached toward the bed and then Daniel was there no more, only an observer to it all. He watched this thing that looked like his son stretch its arm out. Sam shook with terror, a deep, scarring fear across his face, as the creature grabbed hold of his ankle, and with a single, powerful jerk, ripped him from his bed and out the window into the black, into a place unknown.

Then it crawled the rest of the way into Sam's bed and curled into a ball, its smile fading as its eyes closed and it drifted to sleep. Outside the window, Sam was shrieking.

The screams carried Daniel into another place. He was young, and an injured bird laid flat on the ground with the occasional twitch. Daniel picked up a stick and prodded it, watched it squirm, not dead but knocking on the door.

Growing bored, he reached out and grabbed the broken wing. The pain must have given it a new energy, as it flopped in place and fluttered its wings but came to rest again, its small chest heaving. The noises it made sounded vaguely human, and it made Daniel smile as if he'd just overheard a secret whispered between adults.

The soft gray eyes of the bird snapped to him as its beak opened and shut with a meek chirp. He tugged on the wing and it chirped again, louder, almost like a human moan. With a curious smile, Daniel spread his dirt-covered fingers over the wing and stretched it out until it popped and the muscles began to tear loose. This time, it screamed like a boy.

DANIEL'S EYES OPENED SLOWLY. He was instantly grateful to escape the horrors in his dream, but the scream persisted. Musky, stale air filled his lungs with each deep breath as he looked around the room, his eyes adjusting to the beams of light that cut through the window. The screams quickly became an echo and were forgotten—such was the way of his dreams.

"Oh, you're awake!" Jenna rose from her seat across from him, placing a magazine to the side. "You had us mighty worried, actin' the way you did."

"What?" Daniel mumbled as he blinked hard.

"You were talking in your sleep, sayin' your boy's name over and over. We'd have woken you if we thought the sleep would've done more harm than good." She came in to pat his arm. "He's up!" she called down the hallway in her soft voice.

The loud thud of heavy steps came toward the door. Greg pushed his way in, and the light from the window illuminated the gruff, stout man. He wore a sleeveless shirt that exposed his muscular, freckled arms, and he had the thick stubble of a beard.

"We got you something cooking," Greg said with much less hostility than he'd had before. "Figured since you spilled yourself before, you'd be needing something to keep you going."

With a little help from Jenna, Daniel rose to unsteady feet. He looked down to see clothes that weren't his own; apparently someone had stripped away his soiled shirt and dressed him in another that was worn out and a few sizes too big. He moved down the hallway with them and found himself planted on a seat at their table.

Maker sat at the table, dressed in a clean white shirt, no doubt from business attended to after Daniel had left. From there, he could see the living room. It didn't have a television or carpeting, just an old wooden floor and some faded rugs along with a couch that looked like someone had dragged it in from the barn. Someone had opened the blinds too; he could see the dust dancing in the beams of sunlight.

"Still with us, I see?" That was as friendly as the old retired detective could be.

Daniel didn't respond. He slouched into his chair and stared down at the table as someone slid a plate of spaghetti before him. Still, he felt Maker's lingering gaze.

"You overslept breakfast," the German woman said from behind him. "We are having lunch now."

Daniel nodded and stared down at it.

"Well, we don't know this community very well," Maker started. "You do know the—"

"I want in," Daniel interjected, looking up from the plate. "What can I do? That's what you brought me out here for, right? Show me one of them. I'm in. If one of those things took him—" he cut off, unable to continue that line of thought.

"Easiest sale I've ever made." The older man nodded, and pointed at the food. "Finish your food and we'll talk about what happens next."

The rest joined, but no one bothered him. Instead, they talked amongst themselves, accepting Daniel as a fly on the wall. What struck him wasn't when Rebekah discussed how many of the schoolchildren they would have to inspect, or how Jenna talked about the family of the missing boy in the basement crying at church; no, it was the normalcy of it. It was easy for them.

"They think he ran off," Jenna said. "They're sayin' he was actin' all strange just before." That seemed to please them all.

That was their plan. It's business.

No one looked spooked or worried, not even sweet old Jenna; the words hadn't even dampened her smile for more than a moment or two. From their discussion, it seemed

Jenna had found the boy while interacting with the local families.

Professionals. Or lunatics.

He was sure it was one or the other, but he wasn't quite sure which. He knew that these were the only people that offered any answer for Sam, as insane as it might be. He could feel it in his stomach, an instinct that this was the truth.

Or am I just insane? Am I just reaching for anything that can make sense of how my life fell apart?

When the meal was done, Jenna stood up to make coffee. Daniel remained silent, but he looked up, signaling that he was ready to listen.

The old detective's chair groaned as he leaned back. "Mr. Tanner, what I'm going to tell you sounds ridiculous. It sounds like the hallucinations of a madman, but I suggest that you remember what you saw in that basement, and let what you bore witness to expand your understanding. As I said before, these are brood parasites. More specifically, this breed of parasite is a changeling, fairy folk, a fetch. Have you heard any of the old tales, Mr. Tanner? Do you know what a fetch is?"

Fairy folk.

The thought brought colors, wings, and cartoons to mind. Hardly monsters that stole children in the night.

"No, I haven't." It felt strange how he was finding his words now. He took a sip of the coffee that sat in front of him. The cup no longer shook in his hands. "I've never heard of anything like that."

"Most haven't," Greg said, hunched over the table and cleaning his second plate.

"Monsters are real, Mr. Tanner," Maker continued, "and some of them do live under your bed or outside your window. Changelings, for example, are a rare breed, and not always easy to find. The best I could tell you is that they're mythical—magical even. Like I said, they are fairy folk, and they're not all evil. Some care just to be left alone, won't bother you if you don't bother them."

"But some *are* evil," Rebekah said, her German accent clicking with each word. "We hunt the wicked ones. They are not the things of cartoons. They are serious creatures, and powerful. Dark magic."

Magic?

Hadn't Daniel dreamed of magic when he was young? Hadn't he read the stories of boys with power, or watched the movies about child magicians? But magic? He couldn't believe, wouldn't believe.

Except for that thing in the basement.

The thing that grew in size and burned at the touch of iron. The thing with split eyes that laughed at his misery. And the nightmares that seemed more real than life these days.

"No, sir," Jenna said, bringing the last cup of coffee over. "They aren't magic. They're demons. Monsters for sure, but they're demons. Crawled straight out of Hell, of that I'm sure."

Rebekah scoffed. "The old tales are clear, Jenna. They are magic." She spoke to Daniel now, her words clicking with a certain precision. "Magic is a thing to be feared. We have several tomes from the Old World, spent the better portion of our savings to get to Germany and acquire them."

"There's an older book that says otherwise—the Good Book tells it true. There isn't any magic, only Hell's wicked ways." Jenna's smile never faded.

"Magic or demons, who gives a horse's shit?" Greg said.

"We know how to kill them. If they burn in Hell after or fade into the dark, either is fine by me."

"How?" Daniel asked. "How do you kill them? How do you hurt them?"

He looked around the table and couldn't find an answer. Maker finally took it up. "The old stories told of something called Cold Iron. It burns them, kills them, too. They can withstand it for a time, but when they're hurt or tired, they can't resist the burn. Has to be pure iron, though. Can't be a mix. But why does it hurt them, and why doesn't regular metal? Because it does. It's strange like that. You take some iron and form it into a blade. It'll cut 'em. You make it into a bullet and it doesn't seem to do more than a normal bullet would, which isn't much."

"It's the burn from the gun, the power that sends the bullet," Rebekah said. "Fire is something like magic. It burns the metal and it's not *Cold Iron* anymore. Besides, these are creatures of tradition from an ancient world. It is the weapons of our fathers that can kill them."

"Or maybe it's just not enough iron." Maker shook his head. "We don't know. We only have theories."

"Well, fire might fuck with Cold Iron, but it works pretty well on them," Greg said. "Fire's what man used to beat back the dark, yeah? Works on all things crawled from the night. Silver is disagreeable to them too, but it doesn't seem to hurt them like Cold Iron does."

"It told me that there were six in its brood. That's a large brood, assuming the little bastard had it all right. The largest we've ever seen." Maker spoke again. "Minus it and Sam, that leaves four more still hidden away in your town, Mr. Tanner. Now, we are all good at what we do. We could probably locate them without your help, but you could make it a fair bit easier and probably save a few lives. They'd all likely be around the same age as your boy, though it isn't certain. We've seen them anywhere between six and fourteen, usually all around the same age."

Hunting monsters.

Was this the control he had craved? Monsters not of disease but of magic, that crawled around and could be cut?

Am I losing my mind?

Part of him knew it was real. He nodded, imagining the ways he could help. They were right; he would likely know all the parents. But a thought intruded, one that tightened his throat:

"What would you have done if I had said no?"

Jenna's smile slipped away. Greg stared at the table, and Rebekah idly stirred her coffee. Only Maker didn't look away. "This is serious business, Mr. Tanner. We've all lost loved ones, and it's up to us to see as many of the monsters gone as we can. Each one we kill saves countless other children. We won't let anything interfere with that. There's too many things creeping out there, and too few willing and capable to do anything about it."

Daniel let the implications twist inside his mind. "What else is out there? What other things?"

"There are more things out there than just changelings, Mr. Tanner. Many things outside the world of man—some are evil, and some not. We stick to what we know, even if we only know little. The fey, fairy folk—there are stories of them, old stories from all over the world. Each culture has its own. They come from a time when people feared the world, rather than always attempting to understand it."

"Each of the fey is peculiar in its own way, Mr. Tanner," Rebekah's said. "Some fade with the dark, while others have a third or fourth eye that can see something in the beyond. Each brood carries certain unique characteristics. The only thing that is the same is iron; it kills them all. Beyond that, there are few tricks of the trade that can be relied on."

"Better bury the boy out in the woods before he starts to smell," Greg said between bites. Daniel had to wonder if there was a plot of dirt out there planned for him too, had things gone differently.

With that, the meeting was over, and all but Maker got up to attend to other work. Greg could be heard stomping down the steps to the basement and then coming back up, a *thump-thump* with each step now. Rebekah and Jenna had left to go into town for supplies. It left just the two of them, just Daniel and Maker.

And the boy.

His thoughts drifted back to the dead thing dragged up from the basement, the thing Greg now so carelessly dragged out to the woods. Something struck him when he first saw it, but it was lost in the shuffle and the madness of the moment. Lost in the sight of chains and locks and blindfolds.

Lost in those yellow eyes.

I remember him now. He was at one of Sam's T-ball games. Sheryl and Tom's son. I remember the boy playing, talking with the others. He was no different from any other boy out there. How long ago did they take him? How long was he gone? What was his name?

If a boy had gone missing, that would certainly be news in the town. But Daniel had been swallowed up in thoughts of his own son, and couldn't hear any noise from the outside world.

But now another family is out there looking for their son, and praying for him at night, and desperately crying themselves into a restless sleep.

He knew their pain, or rather, he understood it. He had

hoped that Sam would get better, which he knew could be something like the family hoping that their child would be found.

But he won't. Their son is buried out in the woods, where they can never visit. My son has a tombstone and a plot of dirt and . . .

No.

It's not my son. His body is gone, and I will never see him again. That is something else buried out there in my son's place. Something else, something that pretended to be him, something that stole Sam's life from me.

Daniel sat there, considering everything in silence, while Maker drank his coffee and stared out a window. A primitive thought came to him, something that made him shudder, but he was certain that it had to be done.

"I have to go dig that thing out of my son's grave," said Daniel, unsure what to expect in response.

"Okay," Maker said and returned to his coffee.

With that done, Daniel had other questions. "Why do you all do this? I mean, Jenna. She doesn't seem like the right fit."

"Why's that?" Maker asked coolly. "Because she's old, black, religious, or country?"

Daniel shrugged.

"She's smart, smarter than the country twang might imply, and more ruthless than her smile lets on. She's a killer. They're all killers, Mr. Tanner. Don't let anything fool you. Jenna's a chameleon. She can blend in; go places where an old white man with hard eyes might be noticed. A sweet, little old lady won't be seen so harshly on a playground."

Playground.

The word made him shudder. Thankfully, Maker didn't elaborate.

A smile grew on the old detective's face. "She had this

slick idea once, too. Gathered some iron shavings and mixed them into some pancake batter." His smile melted away then. "Of course, the thing figured out what was going on after that first bite. Not enough to really hurt it, but enough to set it off. Ripped the mask right off and got things moving." His gaze intensified as it drifted to an empty corner of the room. "Yeah, that turned out to be a hard one."

It was several long moments before Maker spoke again. "There were seven of us once. Four, now. We're all inheritors of this cause, or crusade, or whatever the hell it is. It's bigger than any one of us."

"What do you mean by inheritors?"

"Just that. None of us were part of the original group. Hell, I don't know who was. I joined a while after . . . Well, we're all here because we're smart. Anyone who wasn't got trimmed away pretty quickly. I don't know what you're going to do. I don't know if you're going to want to go with us after this or not. Prove yourself now, and we'll have a spot for you. But you'll have to be smart—we've all grown old for a reason, Mr. Tanner."

"Daniel. You can call me Daniel."

Maker tipped his head and extended his hand. "Larry would work for me, but everyone calls me Maker anyways." Daniel grasped his rough hand, feeling as if they've just met.

"Without Sam, I don't have anything. Everything is gone. My son, my wife, my career. If something did this to him, then I want to be there when you find it. I want to make sure it can't do it again," he lied. He wasn't concerned with what it might do to anyone else. He wasn't thinking too hard about the family waiting for a son who'd never return.

He hated this thing that moved unseen, this thing that had stolen his child and left its own. He hated it, and he wanted to hurt it the way it had hurt him.

But there was something else, some part that was familiar, like he had always been sleeping and was just now awake. Something had been snaking around in his dreams, slipping into his home each night to plague him while he slept. He'd known it for some time. Only now, did he have a name for it:

Changeling. Fetch. Brood parasite.

"They're not hard to find if you know where to look." Maker stopped when the door opened. Greg walked in and washed the dirt from his hands in the sink, then took a seat.

Maker continued. "Killing them isn't hard either, not if you're ready. It's what you have to do in between the finding and the killing that'll keep you up at night."

"They're tough motherfuckers, so you've got to be smart," Greg said with a voice like sandpaper. "We had one of ours go down a few years back. That's what happens the minute you let your guard down." Greg grabbed his now cold coffee and poured some of the contents of his flask into it.

"He was a fool," Maker said without remorse. "Anyone that stands their ground and locks eyes with one of them is a damn fool and a liability."

That quieted the table for a moment. Then Greg spoke. "You tell 'im yet?"

"Haven't quite gotten there."

"Tell me what?" Daniel asked, looking between the two, a sense of dread rising.

"What the boss hasn't quite told you yet is that the hunt is more important than any one of us." He took a drink from his cup and rubbed a spill from his lip. "We'll all watch your back, but if the time comes, we'll cut you loose if we need to. And we'll expect the same in return."

"I don't think I would have approached that so bluntly," Maker said with some irritation.

Greg shrugged his thick arms. "You find yourself stuck in a room with one of 'em? You beating feet and one's on your tail? You already lost. Game's already done. Ain't nobody else going to toss their ass into the fire to try and get yours out. Same goes for me, for him, for everyone. I ain't going to feel bad if anyone has to cut me loose. The hunt's more important than that." He didn't blink, and his hand was steady.

Daniel nodded. He understood. This was all new to him, this whole thing, but he got it.

Professional.

6

FIVE DAYS AGO, THE GROUP HAD BEEN UNSURE WHEN MAKER told them he wanted to bring in a new member, a thirty-something that wrote comedy novels.

They act like there's a type for this job. There isn't a type for the kind of people we are.

Maker had sniffed around and uncovered some of the accolades and achievements in Daniel's career. The author was big shit in some circles. Maker had even picked up the last two novels and read them in a few days' time. They weren't to his tastes.

Maker knew him now. Without so much as having spoken a word to him, he knew him. That was Maker's gift —he knew people. Understood them and their instincts. He knew Daniel, could see the moving parts in the man like a truck with the hood up. Maker knew a wolf when he saw one, even one that thought it was a sheep.

Daniel was a wolf.

"What makes you think he's got the guts for it?" Greg asked from across the table with a scowl etched across his face.

"He does. He will. I can smell it on him."

"I saw him," Rebekah said as she held Daniel's picture before her. "I saw him in a vision. But, for good or for ill, I do not know."

"You saw Daniel Tanner in your dreams?" Maker said with a stiff voice. He feared and respected what she saw in her dreams. Only a fool wouldn't.

Rebekah held the picture before her, her aged eyes inspecting it one last time. Her back straight and stiff, she tipped her head once. "There was a man in my dreams, searching, but not finding. It was this man."

"Then he's a help or a heart attack. Either way, I'd like to keep an eye on him." Maker laid down a newspaper, the date and location of Daniel's son's burial circled in red. "He's connected."

"Aww, poor boy," Jenna said with wet eyes and utter sincerity. "My heart aches."

Greg scoffed. "Ain't so sure 'bout no new blood. Could get someone killed like last time."

Like last time.

The memory began filling Maker's head, but he shut it out. He had learned to trust his own judgment long ago. "He'll do fine. If not, I'll take care of him." No further explanation was needed.

"There was another," Rebekah continued as if she'd only just remembered. "A man clothed in black, with a narrow, pale face, black eyes, and long white hair to match his skin; a pale man. I saw him coming to the city, as if to claim it. I think he's the one we've been following. However, I cannot be certain what it means, or if it means anything at all."

Her visions were valuable, but sometimes dreams were simply that: dreams. They sifted through them, but nothing was certain.

"Doesn't do us any good to ignore anything. We'll keep our eyes open," Maker insisted. "Until then, we play the cards we're dealt."

The plan was set. Maker would go to the funeral and set eyes on the man. He moved like Maker thought he'd move —not the dull droning expected at a funeral, but something else. Maybe it was something the eye can't see, but the brain noticed. Yes, something was definitely behind Daniel's eyes, something that had been caged and taught to walk upright. If he hadn't seen it, he would have turned away.

He's not just a man in grief—he's hungry for something real.

Maker approached Daniel and gave him his card, even made a call when the man didn't respond. In the meantime, the group was making headway toward their target, but it was clear that a local could be useful.

New Athens. Bigger than the cities they had been in. A long time ago it was a growing city, but that all drained when the coal mines went under, leaving the city fat and diseased. It started to rot from the inside out, until new money found it as an alternative to Atlanta. Some said that saved New Athens; others said it conquered it. The wealth divide widened, and long-time residents found that they were soon clustered in the same rotted section of the city.

All of which would have concerned Maker and his group little if it hadn't complicated things. A lot of signs that the brood normally left behind blended into the mess.

They needed Daniel. Maker knew that, even if the others didn't.

When he brought Daniel in, the man threw up at the first sign of a fiend, even passed out. That hadn't surprised Maker, though, because Daniel was burned out, teetering on the edge. No one really takes well to their first sighting, at least no one Maker ever met.

"I told you," Greg said. "He's weak in the knees. I can see it on him."

"Stow it, Greg. He's in for now."

Later, when Daniel woke up, he needed little prompting, little convincing to join in their insanity. Even Maker was surprised at how easily the man had taken to it.

He's hungry. He's borne it for some time now, that phantom disease that spread its hands over his son. He could only watch as death so slowly and too quickly drained him.

He has something now. Something he can focus on, turn his rage against. Something tangible that he can punish. We gave him purpose, a gift.

That was a lie too, Maker knew. A lie he sometimes had to tell himself. This life was no gift; there was no end to it. There was no victory, only this hunt and then the next, and the next after that, until you found the one you were looking for, the one that kills you. But if it was so miserable, why was someone else always willing to stand up? Why did they always continue?

Because while some people broke, others wanted to break. His instincts told him which one Daniel was.

Not long after his talk with Daniel and Greg at the kitchen table, the women returned. Jenna embraced Daniel and planted a kiss on his cheek as though reuniting with a distant family member. Sometimes, the rest of the group acted annoyed with her persistence and cheeriness. Maker knew better, though.

Jenna's the light that keeps us from going dark.

The woman would never turn her back on another. She might leave someone to die, sure, but that's a risk they all agreed on, and it had been put into practice on occasion. Lose an arm, but the body lives. That was their philosophy.

Jenna had faith, and Greg had the bottle. Rebekah just

had a hard soul, like Maker's. But as long as none of it got in the way, Maker didn't care how they dealt with it. Besides, he knew them all well. None of them would crack. Anyone that would have cracked would have done so long ago.

"Why did it get weak after taking Sam?" Daniel questioned.

Not an unreasonable question, and one that Maker had expected.

"Couldn't tell you," he said flatly. "There's a lot we don't know about them. Where exactly they come from, why they do it."

"That's not completely true," Rebekah remarked. "The old stories tell us some. They lead us to believe they crawl out from the woods, wells, or bridges. Possibly from a place beyond, where we can't travel—like dreams."

"In short," Greg said, much to Rebekah's irritation, "we got no fucking idea. Hell is a good possibility, too. Whatever it is though, it don't matter. They look like kids. Like *your* kid. You learn how to live with that, and the other questions don't matter."

"There's a rarer kind. Older, we think. We haven't seen much of them," Maker finally put forward. "Followed one into the town, though. But he jumps."

There was something in those words, something that quieted the table. The truth was they didn't know much about the man they were following, just what they could get by cutting the things he left behind.

Shortly after, Greg finished his drink and went to collect some firewood. It was only autumn, but the house was unheated, save what a generator could supply. Jenna stepped out to talk with Daniel and get some fresh air. Maker gave a single huff, and cracked a smile when he saw the old woman loop her arms around the younger man's. He never stopped being surprised at how quickly she opened up, how quickly she'd let another person into her circle. Even if that man might soon be dead.

Maker turned to Rebekah, who was busying herself with putting things into the cupboard. "Daniel says he wants to dig that thing out of his son's grave." Maker's voice was flat and informative.

"And you told him?" Rebekah asked as she placed the last of the glasses on its shelf.

"I told him it's fine. Not really necessary, but I can understand it." Maker watched Rebekah as she gave him a flat look. "It'll be a bitch for sure, but we'll wait until we're done."

She finally spoke. "Larry, you surprise me. There is so little that escapes you these days." She turned back to the sink and began to scrub a plate.

Maker took a step forward, unsure. What had he missed? "Spit it out, Rebekah. You know I don't like crosswords, cards, or a woman's games."

"The fairy folk die by Cold Iron," she said while taking a soapy brush to another plate. "Not by disease or natural causes—I expected you to know that. Whatever has occurred to that thing in his son's grave, it's not dead. Perhaps it's stirring even now. The man teeters on the edge, and a fanged yellow-eyed demon in the visage of his child might be enough to make him to slit his wrists."

Shit, she's right. How'd that slip past me?

Without a hint of cruelty, Rebekah said, "Age dulls us all, darling."

I want in.

The words sifted around again in Daniel's head as Jenna looped her arm around his and took him on a stroll. The thought of Sam hurt by some monster played havoc in his mind, and now he was signing up for more. He was joining this insane group that kidnapped things that looked like children. He said he'd join before he had really considered it. He just wanted to get at whatever it was that had taken Sam.

But children?

Could I do that? Could I hurt something that looked like a child, even if it was something that hurt Sam?

Tugging at his arm, Jenna pointed at a bird feeder and kept speaking, but her words fell on deaf ears. Daniel couldn't listen even if he wanted to. The nightmares had him strained and exhausted, and then there was the other thought: that something lay in the bottom of his son's grave, some sinister imitation of the child he loved. It was maddening. He gritted his teeth.

"It doesn't get easier," Jenna said, letting the topic of birds and feed slip. "It stays just as sharp as it always did— you just get harder. That's the secret."

"What?" Daniel finally pulled himself out of his own thoughts.

"They took from you, Daniel, and they're never giving back." Her eyes were wet with tears while she spoke, but her lips still had a wide, sad smile. "There's no way you're going to forget about your son, or make it whole. You can't, and why would you even want to? We're all tryin' to move on. No, the best you can do is say no more. You say these tears are going to be your last, but you know that isn't true either, so then you say you'll make them pay. Save some other little boy or girl out there. And she'll live, and he'll grow, because of you. The children'll never know, but you did right. That means you saved them. That means God will smile on you when you come to meet your boy again."

"I don't believe in God," Daniel said, trying to pull free from Jenna, but her arm was somehow too light to pull from, too soft to break. "What kind of God is going to let my son get taken in the middle of the night, let things like those live?"

"It isn't God that did that, Daniel. It's the devil. He's the one behind this wickedness, the one playin' games with you and me. God is here, waitin' for you. He'll help you if you ask."

No.

Daniel knew better. But no matter how much he wanted to lash out, he knew that Jenna was only trying to help. "God let one of those things take Sam's place in the bottom of my son's grave."

She let a moment of silence pass before she spoke again. "Was your son baptized?"

Daniel shook his head. "None of us were."

Jenna nodded, but frowned with confusion. "I lost my daughter. Lost my husband, too." Her eyes fixed on the woods, as if waiting for something to crawl from it. "I lived with it for a few years. It was strange, so strange. My girl, she had always been so nice, so polite. Then she changed. *It* changed." A single tear dripped down her cheek. This was an old wound, one that had scarred with age, but still sometimes bled. "We thought she was just changin', just how little girls do. But this wasn't like a girl. They get more wicked the older they get."

For a moment, it looked like she was going to continue, but then she cut the story short. He didn't know what to say. What could you say? There was no answer; Daniel knew that as well as anyone.

"Maker lost a grown sister. A baby, too, from one that looked his nephew. Rebekah lost a younger brother when she was small, back in Germany."

The pain in her words cleared Daniel's mind, but he didn't know why. Somehow, they made him feel less alone.

"What about Greg?" he finally asked. "He lost somebody?"

She pulled her gaze from the woods and smiled at Daniel. "He did. But don't ask him about it. He doesn't like to talk about it. He's lost, Daniel—we're all lost. We just got each other, and we got the Lord's work to do."

He wondered then if his story would be the same. He wondered if there'd come a time when he would tell his story, would help another cope with the nightmare that had taken someone of theirs to a terror unknown.

I'm lost.

He couldn't think of a better way to describe it. But there was some comfort in knowing he was with others who understood the way he felt, who knew how he could get back at the thing that took from him. Calmness was spreading over him, changing his emptiness to purpose.

Jenna seemed to read his mind. "You can't do it, Daniel. None of us ever could. The trick is, you don't do it. You make yourself into a new person and you take a piece of your old self with you. But that's all it is, that old self. You aren't the same person anymore; you can't be. When the blind see, it changes them. You'll change, too. You must."

There was rhythm in her words, a sense of wisdom. A thought howled and clawed through his mind: The world has changed.

No. The world didn't change. I did.

"Now, see that one?" Jenna pointed at a red bird, as if

they'd been talking about it the whole time. "He's been showing up lately, funny little thing!"

"Yeah." He let himself smile for the first time in days. "Weird little streak there in his feathers."

Something else was stirring in him. He barely felt it, but he knew it was there. It felt like he was dead, and something else came to wear his skin.

7

"YOU'RE GOING TO GO HOME AND TRY TO GET A FEW NIGHTS' sleep. I'm going to come get you in two days. It'll take us at least that long to get a plan together. Take these." Maker held out a small prescription bottle. Daniel took it and looked at the label: Prazosin. It was prescribed for some woman he didn't know. "It's sleep medication. You won't dream. You're no good to us if you're tripping on your feet. It might knock you on your ass, but keep on it until you're not looking so burned out."

"And eat something, for fuck's sake." Greg's heavy hand slapped his shoulder, sending him lurching forward a step. "You look like a sack of shit, if sacks of shit were anorexic."

Maker then drove him home, leaving him to get ready for what was to come. But other than sleeping and eating, Daniel wasn't sure what he could do. He wondered if being alone would just make everything worse. The idea of sleeping without dreams was appealing, however.

A stack of mail was stuffed into his mailbox. Mostly bills that he had neglected in his desire to shut the world out. He ran through them and paid them off, if only to keep them from disturbing him further.

Not twenty minutes after he turned his phone back on, it came back to life. He grabbed it to see the caller: his mother. Fifteen minutes of frantic conversation later, he was able to convince her he had just needed some time alone. She told him his father had gone to check on him, even used a spare key to get inside, and his father found the revolver near Daniel's bed.

He told her it was Julia's, and that he never wanted it. Then he lied and told her that he only had it out because he was considering getting rid of it. She seemed relieved at that, likely because any alternative would have been too much. In the end, she advised him to keep the gun. She told him of the recent disappearances of a child and the mutilated animal carcasses strewn along the roads. He hadn't heard of that last part, but it was apparently the talk of the town, and his mother had always been cued in to the latest gossip. Strange things are happening these days, she told him.

Strange things, indeed.

When he hung up, he was at a loss. Sitting in front of the TV carried little interest, and old books seemed pointless now. He began pacing the house, thinking, unsure of what to do or how to prepare himself. He found himself staring into Sam's room, staring at the window near his bed, the portal where the creature lurked when he shut his eyes.

He stood in Sam's doorway, wondering if it was like his dream, if a thing that looked like Sam had crawled in. He wondered whether Sam had been awake or dreaming, if he even knew what was happening.

Did it hurt?

Tears dripped from his face, bringing him back to the present. He brushed them away—now was not the time to cry. Now was not the time to lose it all again, not if he was going to finish things.

But when I'm done . . . when it's dead . . . I'll finish things. I'll go to be with Sam.

His thoughts drifted toward the revolver once more.

"Why'd you send him off like that?" Jenna asked as bitterly as she could manage. "It isn't right for that boy to be sitting at home all alone just as he is now. You going to make him sit in the house where they took his boy, now?"

"He needs to get his head straight, Jenna," Greg answered for Maker. "We ain't a damn daycare. Either he'll work his shit out, or he'll eat a bullet."

Jenna frowned at him. "You don't have to be like that!"

"He's right, though," Maker pulled his attention from a newspaper. "He's just learned about everything, he knows what's happened. He's got to live with it, and he's got to move past it."

"He needs a little love, that's all!" Jenna shook her head at the two men.

"Love?" Greg scoffed. "Love will leave you cold, but hate will keep you warm at night. Ain't that right, Maker? That's what you smelled on the boy—he's a hateful bastard, I can see it, too."

"The hell are yammering about, Greg?" Maker asked in a huff as he put the paper down.

"You think someone filled with love is going to sign up with a bunch of lunatics like us? Nobody that ain't a little crazy would listen to what we're saying. You smelled the hate on him. That's why he isn't going to call the cops. That's why you brought him in. You smelled the hunt on that boy."

"Now that ain't so," Jenna protested, shaking her head. "I wasn't all filled with hate when I came in!"

"Well, you compensated with the crazy, didn't you?" Greg asked with a sarcastic snort.

The two continued bickering. Whereas Maker and Rebekah would leave Jenna to her optimism, Greg was much colder, always provoking her.

Maker went back to his paper. They cared enough for each other that their arguments never escalated beyond words, but in truth, Maker found them both to be right.

Maker was a more complicated man than either of them, and he certainly knew people better. Some needed a guiding hand and a loving heart; others needed a push and a clear line of sight to the enemy. Daniel might need a little of both. And despite Jenna's reservations, he was sure that Daniel also needed time alone.

I sure as hell did, didn't I?

The young writer had brought up his son's burial again on their way back into town.

"I just don't like it," Daniel said without tearing his gaze from the car window. "This thing down there pretending to be my son? My parents have already visited there, already laid down flowers for that fucking thing. I want to dig it up. I want to go do it right now."

"It's not that easy," Maker said. "Exhuming something requires a lot of time and machinery. It's not a job for amateurs. We'll get it done but for now, you need to focus on the shit that's out there in the world of the living, not something under six feet of dirt. When the job is done, we'll work on that, I promise you."

That seemed to keep Daniel content, but none of that was the real reason. Maker was sure that Rebekah was right, that Daniel wouldn't find any closure in seeing the

changeling in Sam's mask once more. With the right prod-
ding, it might even reanimate. Something like that could
break a man's mind, especially a man who's already showing
his edges.

They needed him sharp. A brood of six changelings was
a rare occurrence. They'd stumbled into a town with a nest
of three of them once, and thought that was unusual.
But six?

The hell is so special about New Athens?

After he dropped Daniel off, Maker called the group
together in their kitchen war room and floated the idea of
playing it safe and leaving. No one liked the idea, himself
included.

"Well, hell, I like it when the little bastards group
together like this. Means less leg work," Greg said with
conviction. "Besides, damn things got me all curious now."

"Don't get arrogant. It's risky, and one of us is worth a
hundred of them." Perhaps Maker had inflated the
numbers. "Besides, no one's keeping score."

"Shit, I'm keeping score." Greg rose to his feet and raised
his shirt, showing his belt. The old, brown leather had
fifteen grooves cut into it. "I remember each one of the
bastards and I'd gladly notch another four after I dig a
groove for the thing buried out back. Give me an even
twenty."

"Nein," Rebekah cut in. "What is this talk of leaving?
Wasted breath."

Jenna nodded her agreement. "What do your books say,
Rebekah? We've never seen more than three in a town."

Rebekah nodded. "Nothing very helpful. There is some
discussion of broods that size terrorizing the towns of long
past. But, there is no clear reason or predictable behavior to
it. Just more of the same. They would feed more, so we

could expect more damage to the local population, but I suspect they were simply more abundant in the old days."

"Damn. This isn't *that* big of town. We're going to stir up our own mess when those four other kids go missing. If others go missing . . ." Maker shook his head. "We're going to have to work fast."

"Midnight run?" Greg's voice held a hint of dread, but the son of a bitch was always the first to suggest it.

The Midnight run. A full night of home invasion and body snatching before rolling out of town. But with four left? Hell.

"No, heavens no." Jenna shuddered. "What if that plan spoils like last time?"

"Spoils?" Greg said with wide-open arms. "We spared the man a worse fate. Those things reach maturity and they'll kill them anyways. Better for him to have gotten it fast. Better for him to—"

"Scheisse! Are we so low as to talk so easily of a man's death?" Rebekah spat the words at Greg in a fury. "Are we as bad as the monster?"

"As bad as I got to be," Greg said with a snort.

"Enough," Maker said, silencing everyone. "We're not going on any midnight runs—not now, anyway. We're going to put our ears to the ground and identify our targets. Then, we're going to get them as safely as we can."

"Yeah?" Greg nodded his head, agreeing, "And if that all goes south?"

"Then," Maker relented. "It's a midnight run."

THE DAYS STRETCHED ON. Only two days, but what was there to do? Two days seemed like ten with so much running through his head. Two days seemed like forever.

He was sleeping—the pills made sure of that. There were no dreams either, but there was a strange sense of *almost* dreaming when he was awake. Daydreams that seemed like memories from when he was young. He remembered a solid, round rock in his hand—strange, how all those details were so clear now. He remembered the way it felt when he cracked it across the neighbor's kid's head, and the screams that followed; they echoed in his ear like it was still happening.

He had an urge to write it all down, something he used to do to cope before he got married, before Sam. He used to have such strange thoughts; he'd write them out, planning horror novels and gruesome tales. They were never published, never even submitted, though he was sure he had them all on a thumb drive somewhere.

But all that came to end when he had married Julia; he'd felt settled then. All those dark feelings faded, and he hadn't even thought of the rock, the boy, or the bird in years.

The bird. I remember it now. I cried so much after; I don't even know why I did it. But was it even real? It feels like it was. I remember it fluttering on the ground and I remember grabbing it by the wing. . . But it didn't scream like that, did it? It couldn't have. . .

The dreams felt real. Just as real as when he was young and would wake up, unable to tell what was real and what wasn't. It was starting to drive him crazy. He had to do something.

For years as a writer, he'd combed the Internet in his research. Words like *fey* and *changeling* brought up cartoons and comic books in search engines.

Click-click.

The comforting sound of his keyboard and mouse. The

soft clicking felt normal to him, despite what he was looking through.

"Fuck me." He rubbed his eyes as he clicked past an illustration of a beautiful fairy girl staring lustfully, barely hiding her body behind long wings. "Who the hell looks at this?"

Click-click.

One search led to the next, and he found old drawings from ancient books. He then began to find message boards, though they were mostly filled with role-playing games and the ravings of lunatics.

Or is it?

So went the days and the wash of information he peered through.

Two days in the house, and then a knock on the door that brought him to his feet. The hairs on his neck stood up —he peeked through a side window before he went to open the door.

Idiot. Like a monster is going to knock on the fucking door.

Maker inspected him carefully before stepping inside. "You look better. You've been eating?"

"Yeah, but I've been on the Internet, too. I've found something."

"Listen, we've looked before. There's nothing out there, and if there is, it's obscured by fifty layers of bullshit. You try to find something on fairy folk, and you're going to get video games and some really weird pornography."

"Yeah, there was definitely . . . Well, anyway, I found an article here written by a B. Sanders, a reporter. She wrote about a guy she says is a hunter, like you. I looked into it more, and apparently, the article ruined her whole damn career. I did some more tracking and found the guy that others on the message board claim the article is about."

Daniel snatched a stapled stack of papers sitting on the kitchen counter and handed them to Maker. "Figured you'd want a hard copy."

Maker took the paper and took a seat at the kitchen table. He skimmed over it, reading lines here and there. "Hmmm. Well, this is about witches," he said, as if it dismissed everything.

"Yeah, it is. But this guy, his name is Fitcher. He might know something. I sent him a message and he wrote back. It's on that last sheet."

Maker flipped the paper over. "What the hell does this say?"

"That's his username." He pointed at the word: *Boogey-mancomes4u*. "Everyone has a stupid username."

Maker looked up into Daniel's eyes, clearly unsure if he should be taking him seriously. "Coffee?"

Three cups of coffee later and Maker had worked his way through the papers. It was a series of questions and discussions between the two, where Fitcher had gone through his source materials with Daniel to try his best to help.

Pacing the room, Daniel was unsure if Maker thought any of it was factual or helpful. The older man just sat there, drinking and reading silently. His fixed posture was only occasionally broken by a quieted huff or a shake of his head.

"He's saying there's something big here, bigger than just a nest. He says six is a lot," Maker said without looking up as he shuffled through the papers.

Daniel nodded and licked his lips. "He calls it a Shallow. A weak spot between our world and theirs. He thinks it's here in New Athens."

Maker agreed. "I'm going to be frank with you, Daniel. We've never dealt with a brood this size before. It's certainly concerning. We were discussing our options yesterday. But we're here for the long haul." He tapped his finger against the paper and drew a line under the word *Shallow*. "But if this guy isn't entirely full of shit, then that means he's got better access to information than we do, and this is going to be a lot more dangerous than we anticipated. I've never heard of anything called a Shallow, but it fits the bill."

"Yeah," Daniel said. "I know. And he called everything else. He mentioned the Iron and the silver, talked about it cutting away the guise. He said—"

Maker held up a hand, silencing him, before turning back to the paper. "Yeah, I got it. It's the only reason I'm even considering what he has to say. He sounds pretty damn goofy, but I learned long ago to be open-minded about this stuff. Let's bring this back to the others and see what they have to say on the matter. Everyone gets a voice."

Daniel agreed and went to grab his things. They didn't discuss the question that sat at the bottom of the printed pages, the one that Fitcher was unable to answer, but the one that Daniel wanted to know most of all:

Why did the changeling that took Sam wither away?

8

———

ORANGE RAYS FROM THE MORNING SUN CUT THROUGH THE window blinds and shone against the decaying walls of the makeshift kitchen war room. Daniel wasn't sure if the others had slept at all or were instead, fueled by coffee, booze, and cigarettes. He fought through a yawn as he poured a second cup of coffee.

The table was cluttered with material, books, and papers. A single dim light hung from the ceiling, casting a flickering glow down on them. Connected to it were wires that ran across the ceiling and out a crack in the window to a generator that Greg had set up outside.

"Well, don't this just make it all the sweeter? I was getting tired of all these damn repeats anyways." Greg sloshed his drink as he swung his arm in a wide gesture. It might have been an early morning for some, but it was a late night for Greg. "The fuck is a Shallow? I'd like to know and take a hand at bleeding it."

"Sounds to me like nothin' good," Jenna said as she poked her head up from the printed papers, a pair of reading glasses sitting on the tip of her nose. "Sounds like a gate to Hell, and it needs to be closed."

Rebekah turned her chin up. "I doubt that this buffoon would have access to resources greater than ours."

"And it's twice as foolish to think that no one else has anything to offer," Maker said as he pointed at the papers Jenna held. "If this sounded like bullshit or a madman's ravings, I would have tossed it out. But we're working outside the bounds of our experience. We knew it was bad —turns out it's worse. I know you're all committed to it, and so am I. So, we're going to find out all we can, so we're not running around with our flies down."

"Sure, of course. But I don't think this Shallow bullshit and a half-dozen brood is the one to break our boy in on. I say he sits this one out," Greg said as if Daniel wasn't at the table.

Maker sat silent and still in his chair, considering, only moving to loosen the collar that was snug against his throat.

"Wait, what? Are you kidding?" Daniel asked with real surprise. "I just got here, and you want bench me?"

"Ain't a matter of want, it's what we need," Greg said from across the table.

Daniel felt fire rise up his throat. "This shit is in *my* town, it took *my* son. *I* bought into all this insane bullshit, and you're going to cut me out? Maybe a new set of eyes and ideas is what you all need. I'm the one that contacted this Fitcher guy who said it was a Shallow. None of you had any idea."

"Indeed, and I am not so certain still that it is. But we do not make decisions so carelessly, Daniel," Rebekah said. "Each of us has a skill, each of us a role. We do not yet know yours, and a chain breaks with its weakest link."

Jenna reached over to pat Daniel's arm. "They're right,

darling. Maybe it isn't the right time to be jumpin' in on it all. But there's other ways you can help. Don't you worry."

Other ways? They're going to make me sit at the kid's table.

Maker sat stiffly, with his fingers laced together in front of him, and watched Daniel with the calculating gaze of a poker player.

No.

"Are you fucking kidding me? I need this. I'll lose my fucking mind otherwise! I can't even sleep without those pills. And the fucking dreams!"

"Yes, the nightmares," Rebekah said, stone-faced. "Like the one with the monster that looked like your son? Or the one where you were him and felt his pain? Or the one where it comes for you? These, yes?"

Daniel felt as if icy fingers had come up his back and around to his chest, pulling away his clothes and leaving him bare, while Rebekah dug through his head and placed his thoughts on the table for all to see.

"Do you know you have other dreams? Of course, you don't. You forget them before you wake, as most do. I saw those dreams, though. Dreams where you watch it pull Sam apart. These are why you can't eat. There's another where you speak with an apparition, something that is you and not you at the same time. It leaves me unsure which one is real, or if they both are." She tapped her cigarette over an ashtray and left it to smolder on the ceramic edge. "I saw another dream, one where you pressed a pistol to your temple. But that one wasn't a dream, was it? Only an echoing memory, I suspect?"

"What the hell are you?"

Rebekah crossed one leg over the other and sat rigidly. "I am a seer, Mr. Tanner. In my visions, I see the contents of a man as easily as you see his clothes. But that is not the point. The point is, that I know your pain and your motivations. They are not lost to me or to the others. We take risks, but they are calculated. This world is a strange place indeed, Mr. Tanner. That is why decisions are made carefully."

"What the hell was the point in telling me any of this?" Daniel asked as he stood up, nearly shouting. "Why the hell didn't you just let me shoot myself in the fucking head, then?"

"We didn't know there were six of them when we brought you in. Now sit your ass down, boy, or I'll put it down!" Greg shouted back at Daniel, rising from the table like a bull excited by the threat of violence.

"He's coming with us." Maker didn't raise his voice; he didn't need to. Everyone listened. "He's right. It was his son and his choice. It isn't right to open his eyes and then tell him to close them again."

"Right's not got a damn thing to do with it," Greg said with a huff. "The only consideration is if this new guy will get us killed, Maker. We were thinking we had a big nest of three here, and we got to find four more of those motherfuckers in town. We got to be sharp—can't have no dull edge on us. He can cut his teeth on the next one. Hell, we can even let him cut one if he wants, but he can't go out on the hunt with us."

Maker sat quietly, letting the heat roll off Greg before meeting Greg's gaze with his own. "Would you let us tell you to sit out on the one that took Carol?"

Greg's lip curled up against his coffee-stained teeth. A purple vein popped in his unshaven neck and for a second, Daniel thought Greg might hit someone. Instead, he turned and flung his cup against the wall, turning it into a rain of broken pieces and booze. The floorboards shook as he stormed out and slammed the door, nearly ripping it off its hinges.

Jenna took a deep breath, but sat quietly. Rebekah didn't move; she hadn't even turned to look up at Greg. Maker hadn't flinched.

"He's in, and that's the last we hear of it," Maker said as coolly as he had before, then shifted his attention directly to Daniel. "But you're going to follow orders. You're going to do what you're told, when you're told to do it. And you're going to get ready. You're going to go with Rebekah and let her tell you the old stories, and then when Greg cools down, he's going to show you how we kill them. You do what you're told, when you're told."

The words fit like bricks inside Daniel's mind, neatly placed and unable to bend. "Yeah. Yes. Got it." Only now did he realize his nails were cutting into his palms and drops of sweat were rolling down his neck. While the rest seemed unbothered by Greg, Daniel's body was shaking.

Maker watched him, making sure the words sank in, then looked at Jenna. "Give Greg an hour, then go see how he is. I'm going into town. Got a lead." With that, he stood up and dusted off his hands. Broken pieces of the mug crunched under his feet as he made his way out.

Jenna reached over to pat Daniel's hand. "Don't mind Greg, he'll be all right. He always is. He just has his own way, like we all do." She gave him that same comforting smile, and went to get a dustpan.

"Well, Mr. Tanner," Rebekah said as she turned her stony eyes to him. "You are to come with me, it seems." Daniel felt her gaze touch him and flow into him like an onion that she was peeling back.

Can she really see me? Can she see my dreams, how I feel? Does she know how afraid I am?

He watched her as she moved gracefully down the hallway, past the boarded-up windows with only faint traces of light piercing through, illuminating the dust that danced in the air and the stains on the wall. Only after she was gone and Jenna went to get a broom, did he pull his hands up to his face to see how much they shook.

He'll kill himself.

Maker knew that much when he saw how Daniel had reacted when Greg told him he couldn't go with them, couldn't confront the evil that had snuck into his house while he slept. Greg didn't give a shit, though; he'd grown hard.

They all had.

Maker knew the Irishman, knew him like a carpenter knows his tools. Greg was sharp. Though perhaps, that wasn't the right way to describe him.

More like heavy and strong, like a hammer.

But some jobs don't need a hammer; sometimes they need a needle, and that's where Greg failed. He knew how to hunt and kill better than anyone else, but he couldn't see the finer side of things. Unlike Jenna, he couldn't see how a man could unravel, or how to sniff out the creatures in a crowd like Maker. That's why Greg couldn't see the value in Daniel.

I've got plans for him.

Maker pulled out onto the dirt road and pulled the visor down to block the sun. He yawned and rubbed his eyes, the effects of too many early mornings, too many late nights, and too few cups of coffee. Years ago, he seemed to be able stay awake for days with only a few hours of sleep here and there. Those days were past. He was starting to feel the aches now, starting to feel like an old man.

Starting? Hell, I've been feeling it for a while now.

He turned onto the main road, careful not to approach the town the same way, for fear of the neighbors seeing his car any more than necessary. People talk, and they're going to have a lot to talk about soon. He couldn't eliminate risks, but he could reduce them. That's where people got caught: in the details.

New Athens. What hides in you? What in the hell is a Shallow, and why is it here? What's so damn special about you?

It wasn't long before he was back in town and then driving out the opposite side of it, back to the mountain clearings that overlooked New Athens. He passed the old cemetery, not the one where the thing that wore Sam's face rested, but the old Lutheran yard, with its old, abandoned church that oversaw the long-buried dead. For a moment, he wanted to stop and walk over to the graves, but he put that thought away. He wasn't here for that memory, but another one entirely. He had a tip, a lead he wanted to look into, sure, but that wasn't his first stop. He was here for something else.

Parking the car and cutting the lights, Maker left the car running as he stepped out. The morning chill still hung in the air and breathed onto him. He zipped his jacket up and pulled out his flashlight, thumbing it on. There weren't many things that made the old man's heart race these days, fewer things still that made those fingers of fear crawl down his neck. The old moldering sign that read "New Athens Haven," however, always did.

The old lunatic asylum.

He shined his light on the still-standing sign. It was an unwelcome greeting to the fortress of torment behind it, the sprawling compound of brick and pillars that housed nothing save rats and old memories.

He ran his light over the sign and shook his head. The whole rotten place hadn't collapsed or been bulldozed to the ground. Instead, it had been left to fester like an open wound.

I hate this damn place. I hate everything about it. I should burn it down right here and just pick up and leave. Leave this whole stinking business behind. It's no good walking into something blind, no good not knowing what you're dealing with. Someone's going to die here. Greg, or Jenna, or Rebekah. Daniel for damn sure, but I don't think he has a problem with that. Someone's going to die here in New Athens. I know it. And instead of packing my bags, I'm staring at this fucking sign and thinking about burning it down.

He was afraid of this place. Not in a way that made him want to run—he didn't feel that kind of fear anymore. It was something else, something he couldn't explain. He felt like the sign and the building were smiling at him, that some part of it was whispering to him. The winds, the chirp of the bugs, even the hum of his car all had something to say.

Welcome home.

9

REBEKAH STEPPED SOFTLY INTO THE ROOM SHE HAD CLAIMED as her own, a quaint little area in the corner of the house without too much dust, though the floorboards did have a nasty habit of groaning if she didn't step carefully. It sat mostly as she had found it, save the layer of filth she removed from the surface, her bed, and the bookshelves that Greg had put on the wall. They were clean and organized, as was every book stacked upon them.

She'd taken great care with the collection: priceless books passed down through decades and centuries, tales ancient in ancient times. Notes of inquisitors and hunters, old fables. Some were copied and jacketed with newer paper and hardcovers, while others had fragile, yellowed pages, with hard plastic sleeves to protect the precious content from the elements. There was a time when tomes on these topics might have been more numerous, but religious book burnings had reduced the supply. It was a priceless collection for which museums would have bid millions of dollars, but with time and luck they were able to secure it all through connections and people in businesses like theirs.

And the dreams. The books called me there, leading us.

These were old friends, familiar in ways that the people closest to her couldn't be. Most were writ in old German and were difficult for even native speakers to understand; only the few who were intimate with the writings could understand them.

Running a finger down the spine of a faded blue book, she carefully pulled it loose. It wasn't quite old enough or rare enough to deserve a plastic sleeve, but she was always drawn to it regardless. It was a tale of fables, and it was filled with more truth than men would care to believe now. Most of the stories had been created long ago as tales of caution and to account for the extraordinary, but they existed now in their modern forms only to entertain. And it is these episodes of entertainment that filled the minds of children now.

My, how quickly we've all forgotten. How quickly we've bled these sources of value to entertain ourselves with stories of magic, as if magic was a thing not to be feared.

It was true now, and why shouldn't it be? The average man or woman didn't have to be concerned with otherkin, fairy folk, or magic. Those were things of a long-lost age, things now hidden from prying eyes in a world unknown, no longer taking refuge in a cave just outside town.

I wonder if that makes them more or less dangerous?

She opened the blue book and came across a page with a penciled drawing scrawled across it. Long ago, someone had painted with watercolors that left only a faint trace in these times. It showed a woman lying in her labor-bed with her husband nearby. Their babe's cradle had been placed to the side of their bed and just out of their view, a stout creature with dark, leathery skin, rows of fangs, and wide haunting eyes, had their babe in its cruel, hooked hands, with a claw drawn across the babe's mouth. Its own offspring had been placed neatly into the cradle.

She stared at the page, not knowing why this drawing always made her think of her brother and her parents, or why she always found reason to stare at it.

Was it as quiet as this when it took him? Was I in the room? Had it considered me instead?

Hard steps sounded on the wooden floor down the hallway. The steps, Daniel's, were as distinct as fingerprints. She knew what they all sounded like, knew virtually everything about each of them. Such was a necessity in her work.

He was a plain man by her standard, if not over-eager. But there was something mysterious about Daniel. Not his motivations or his intentions—those were all clear. His dreams, his fears, were certainly interesting, perhaps even unique, but that wasn't what concerned her at the moment.

Why does Larry want him so badly?

Larry Maker, their leader. She never could read him, and that's what intrigued her so much about him. Greg was an open book, Jenna, too, but Larry never gave anything away that he didn't intend. It's why she followed him, why she trusted him. When she had asked what was so special about this broken man, Larry had replied simply: "I have an eye for talent."

She pushed him no further.

Rebekah's trust for him went a step further than any of that. Her mind never reached out for his like it did for Daniel's. Her gifts always did seem to have a mind of their own. She'd touched Jenna's and Greg's dreams, and countless others', but never Larry's. She had always wondered why her mind wouldn't touch his.

Is it because I'm scared of what I might find?

The door opened and Daniel stepped in—he looked

flushed, drained even. It was to be expected for one so close to the edge. They had seen countless other men like him and had passed them over, leaving them to whatever tortures their minds constructed. The broken and the staggering were a liability, had only one apparent function: dying.

"I guess I'm ready," said Daniel as he slid his hands inside his pockets and made brief eye contact with Rebekah. His eyes were a touch green, and he was certainly handsome or rather, he had been in better days.

"Good. Now shut the door," she said, closing the book and picture, along with any thoughts of her brother and Larry. She placed it on the shelf and plucked another. "Have a seat, Mr. Tanner."

Daniel took the seat by the desk. "What are we supposed to talk about? The old stories? You've all made it abundantly clear that you don't have many facts about all this."

"No," she said flatly. "Larry told you that he was uncertain. We each have our own theories and conjectures. Jenna found hers in the old book."

"The Bible? I read parts when I was a kid. I don't remember anything about changelings."

"Certainly, but she sees them that way. Perhaps she is right. Perhaps they are demons. I suspect not, though. These stories are ancient. They detail people who fought them, when whole towns might succumb. When real measures needed to be taken to ensure the survival of you and your children. I do not think they are demons, only monsters."

"Yeah, well . . ." Daniel hesitated before speaking again. "How can any of this be real? How can *you* even be real?" He didn't look up to meet her gaze.

"Do I scare you, Mr. Tanner?" Sitting near the

windowsill, Rebekah pushed the window up and lit a
cigarette.

"Yeah, I guess you do. This is all very unnerving."

"Unnerving? You seem to be doing quite well, all things
considered." She put the cigarette to her lips, inhaled, and
turned to blow the smoke out the window. "I would be
concerned if you weren't afraid." She was not a warm
person; she offered no smile or pleasantries. "I am afraid of
the night, Mr. Tanner, not because I do not know what is
there, but because I know what is. I know what lies in
waiting for a moment's weakness, and I know its intentions."

"But not its motivations?"

"Correct. Perhaps in that regard, Jenna has a clearer
understanding. A demon needs no purpose beyond our
torment, though she believes them to be a tithe to Hell."

"A tithe?"

Be careful now.

She nodded and chose her next words deliberately. "Jenna
believes they take the children to be sacrifices. A tithe." She
blew smoke out the window. "I do not believe this."

A careful word could do only so much, and the wet gloss
in Daniel's eyes told her she might not have been careful
enough. Some things, however, simply needed to be said.
"We do not know. No child has ever come back, no one ever
rescued. They do not come back. Ever. They are simply lost.
So, we do not know what it is they experience."

Daniel sat quietly for a moment, then said in a hushed
voice, "What do you think?"

"It doesn't matter what I think. It has little importance."

"I'd still like to hear it."

She watched him, knowing that her words had cut him.
But she never softened the blow for anyone who asked for it.

"I suspect they're twisted into something nefarious, or simply eaten."

He knew as much anyway.

A crack spiraled across Daniel's face and threatened a flood. Instead, he posed a question. "Now what about you, Rebekah? You looked into my head. How did you do that? *Why* did you do that?"

Her back stiffened, and though she expected this question, she never found it terribly easy to explain. "I have what could be described as *second sight*. I have had it since I was young, shortly before my family fled East Germany. It first occurred after an event that can only be described as traumatic, the particulars of which I will not detail here." Her tone did not fluctuate. She broke eye contact only to breathe out another lungful of smoke.

"Since those times, I can, on particular occasions, glimpse things and places. My visions often lend me insight to the future and what may be, though more often, I walk in dreams. While I sleep, my mind wanders, sometimes to invade the dreams of others, such as yourself, and sometimes to search things that I could not explain to you if I desired. Strong emotions tied to places or things can be drawn out, or at times, forced upon me." Her gaze broke from him, and she shuddered as a memory climbed up her back, a memory from behind the Berlin Wall.

She had been nearly catatonic then; the pain, the suffering, flowed like water and gripped like nails. The memories would claw into her brain—thousands suffering, thousands crying, thousands dying. She touched each one, and sometimes, they came to visit while she slept. They pulled at her —not spirits but their memories, the memories of all the suffering, dying people.

"Why do you think I have those dreams?" Daniel broke her line of thought.

"All wars have fronts, Mr. Tanner. This one is no different. There is your body, and there is your soul. They invade your thoughts to probe you, test you, torment you. You wonder why? So, do I. Another question left unanswered. Undoubtedly, some of those dreams are honest nightmares. Others are beings that plague you. Perhaps they are just as I am, and they have little control over such things. Or perhaps they have a taste for it." Daniel's hand shook, and Rebekah paid him the courtesy of pretending not to notice.

"How do I stop them?" he asked.

"Larry gave you the medications, yes? One a day seems to keep the dreams away."

"And that's it? The best I can do is hide?"

"No, no. It is simply the smartest thing to do." She sucked on the cigarette again and blew the smoke out. "How rude of me! Would you like a cigarette, Mr. Tanner?" she asked, holding the pack out to him.

He held up a hand. "I don't smoke."

"Would you believe that I quit some time ago? I was deathly afraid of cancer. It is how my mother went." She took another puff. "Had a scare from it myself a time ago."

"Why'd you start back up?"

"Perhaps at some point you consider, why restrain oneself? If the cancer returns, then it returns."

Daniel watched her closely. "Do you enjoy this line of work, Rebekah?"

"Mr. Tanner, no one enjoys this line of work."

"Then maybe you're just hoping the cancer would give you a reason to quit. A reason to turn your back on all of this."

My, maybe he is a bit more interesting than I expected.

She gave him a light smile as she sucked down the last of the cigarette and snuffed it in the ashtray. "Or perhaps, I'm just hoping the cancer kills me before something else does."

———

THEY TALKED for what might have been hours, but felt like minutes, as Daniel soaked it all in. Rebekah translated the stories for him. Written in a tongue of Old World German, there was no hope for Daniel to understand them without a guide.

"They are not human," Rebekah read to him. "They are beast. Strong sense of smell, their fingers can grow to claws and their teeth into fangs. Many are known to have a vicious bite, a paralytic. That is how they take their prey. There is nothing natural about it, nothing the world could understand or explain. And like the old stories, they are cruel and merciless, though sometimes selfish and easily tricked."

Daniel saw how some of the messages had become blurred throughout the ages. The most recent iterations of these stories told tales of wicked children who were punished for their acts, but they rarely met with such horrible fates as the originals: beheadings, torture, burning. The true messages were lost, and the old tales were told differently.

We always had it wrong. These things were the effects, not the cause. These monsters crept into these towns and stole away the young blood. Children turned wicked after a brush with the changelings.

Some stories chilled Daniel to the bone, like the stories of transformation, the tales of children taken and twisted by fairy folk for their nefarious purposes, made anew as slaves or other things.

Wicked things.

One story was aptly named *The Goat Girl*. Still in bed when they came for her, she was dragged out of her home and into the woods. They stretched her neck and face until it neared breaking, and they buckled her knees, forcing her to bleat. Driven to madness, the villagers killed her with fire.

"We burned one like that. Just as the story told," Rebekah said.

Daniel had to pull himself from his own thoughts, to be there and not there at the same time, or he was sure he'd break. Had Sam been subjected to such tortures? He couldn't think about that—not now, not while there was work to be done.

I'll let myself break when it's finished.

The Jackanapes, another tale, told of a boy who played tricks and laughed joyfully with each jape. His family enjoyed them, harmless things that they were, until they began to turn violent. Broken glass left where others would step, boiling water poured across the parents' bed as they slept. In the end, he drowned his sister and left her body for his parents to find in one of his "japes", then fled into the woods. A hunting party caught him and strung him from a tree, but still he japed. Only with the head of an iron axe did his jokes come to an end.

"Here we see the signs, the cruelties." She tapped a finger on a sketch. It was a black, scrawled drawing of men with torches fearfully looking at the boy, who swung from his neck with maddening glee still in his eyes. "And the usefulness of iron."

There were more tales. In one, a boy who drank blood from cattle through a straw, in another, a boy who showed his "scary face" around town and was found the next day with his face removed; others were seen wearing the boy's stripped face like some mutilated artifact when committing their heinous crimes. There were even tales of adults, such as a man who went from town to town bartering in mysticisms for the price of blood and a soul, or a man whose very existence brought plague.

"The old stories tell of such men," Rebekah said. "And though we've never encountered their like, I have little reason to doubt that such things walk among us."

Other stories described the eating of children, told of things whose hunger could only be sated by the flesh of younglings. Rebekah's eyes held his when she talked about it, when Daniel looked away from the pictures.

Could this be worse than another fate? Is it worse to be eaten than mutilated and enslaved? How can any of this be real? How can no one know about this? If someone knows, why not do something about it?

"These are all stories, though," Daniel said in frustration. "How can we know any of it is true?"

Rebekah closed the book and sat idly, studying Daniel. Was she insulted? He didn't know.

Daniel nodded. Worrying that he might have upset her, he remained quiet.

"Then perhaps, a new story." She stood up and slid the tome back into its place with gentle hands that seemed kinder than her words, and only when it was carefully placed did she turn back to him. "The story I am about to tell you is not inked in any book, and only few know it. I know only the essentials. It is of a boy who lived in this very same town, long ago."

"So, this is a true story?" Daniel asked.

"All stories hold some truth, Mr. Tanner," she said with a bit of irritation, as if he hadn't been listening. "As a wordsmith, you should know that as much as anyone. But yes, he lived here in New Athens quite some time ago. This town, it used to be a coaling town, yes?"

Daniel gave a half shrug. "I suppose. I don't know much about it."

"Yes, it's often too much to ask the young to remember history," she said stiffly. "There was a boy with a mother who was quite mad. The town sent her to the asylum, leaving the boy to fend for himself."

"The old asylum here?"

"Yes, unless there is more than one. This does seem to be a strange enough place to warrant a second asylum. Now may I continue, or will you be questioning all my information?"

Daniel nodded, but kept quiet.

"Now. The mother saw things as I do. She could see faces in shadows, the spirits that walked outside our world, but always wanted in. She became mad, of course. Such things could certainly break you. But that was not the worst of it. She was untrained, you see, and uncontrolled. When her mind wandered into the abyss, her mind would grab her boy and suck him in. This mother was dragged into an asylum and the boy spirited away, but her mind saw no distance between them when they slept. She pulled him in with her. He saw things that broke his mother, but he stayed strong, resilient, and he is still here."

He could hold his silence no more. "Who?" he asked, though he felt he already knew the answer.

"Whom do you think?" she asked as she stood up and returned to the bookcase. "Show me you're not useless and have at least a bit of intuition."

"Maker?"

"Gold star." She ran her finger down a leather spine. "And why did I tell you this story?"

"Because he's real. The stories are real."

"I am happy to have not wasted my time, then." She held out a book, showing the cover to Daniel—*Malleus Malefi-carum.* "Now we will read *Hammer of Witches, which destroyeth Witches and their heresy as with a two-edged sword,*" she said, translating the title. "A guide to witch burnings."

10

After turning through the pages of the *Malleus Maleficarum* and reading an inquisitor's account, Rebekah took the time to dispel rumors and outline themes common throughout the stories.

After a time, Rebekah told him to go, saying that there would certainly be more to come but for now, she had work to do. Daniel could hear the strain in her voice.

"This life wears on you," she told him. "This is not a job —it is a life. It is a road, and from here to there, you may not recognize yourself, Daniel. You will be changed."

There was nothing else to say. With that, he left to find Greg, hoping that the old bastard had calmed down.

He's going to show you how to kill them.

That's what Maker told him. How do you kill something like that? They said Cold Iron, but they also said it was strong, terrifying.

And it looks like a child.

Shoving that thought back, he made his way outside and saw Jenna rocking in a chair.

"How are you feeling?" she asked with a gleaming smile.

He shook his head. "You think they're demons?"

"And Jesus asked him," she said, "What is your name? And he said, 'Legion, for we are many'. They're demons, Daniel. They are many, and we are few, but we have the Good Book, and we have the Lord. That's all you'll ever need."

They sat in silence, her soft hands patting his, with only the squeak of Jenna's rocking chair to accompany them on the cooling day. "Greg's in the barn. He'll be okay to talk to now. That thing before, that's just his way. Don't think less of him, Daniel. We've all been through a lot, but Greg was with us all the way."

Daniel made his way over the gravel and soft grass. A breeze blew from the direction of the road toward the back of the house and the woods. Daniel breathed in some of the cool air, in an effort to untie the knots in his stomach.

You were afraid of Rebekah, and you're going to be afraid of Greg, too? Get your shit together.

He decided not to think any more about it, and continued on the weedy, gravel road to the cracked and fading barn door. He rapped his knuckles on it twice and stepped in.

"You here, Greg?" he asked, poking his head inside to see a maze of decaying junk. A tractor covered in shades of rust sat nearby, parts of it stripped away and hanging loose. Piles of collapsed boxes had been thrown into another corner, along with metal farm implements that had been left to age.

"Yeah, come here," Greg said from the one small corner that showed any signs of organization. His truck was there, with the hood up and some of the parts taken out. He was rubbing an oil rag over a part that Daniel didn't recognize, and his voice was much calmer, like someone had let the air out of him.

Littered with sharp metal, the entire barn looked as if it could collapse at any moment. A large hole in the side of the barn allowed a beam of light to shine through it, right where Greg had set up shop.

"Maker send you to talk to me?" Greg asked, wiping the grease from his hands with a towel. He tossed it on the side of the truck.

"Yeah, he did." Something whined from behind the truck and moved underneath a tarp.

What the hell was that?

"You know, we don't do this. Bring in someone new like this," Greg said. "Come here a second."

Greg pulled the tarp up, showing Daniel that it had been hung in a way to form a shelter. A mutt with brown, white, and black fur was curled up in a soft bed of hay beneath the tarp with a young pup nestling at her side. The dog's eyes instantly fixed on Daniel, its lip pulling up as it let out a low, guttural growl.

"Shh, s'okay girl." Greg bent down and rubbed the dog behind its ear. It stretched its head out as he rubbed underneath its chin and patted its side. The thick man had a pencil-thin grin now. Calmed, the dog kept its focus on Daniel. "She trusts me, but you best stay away. She even tried to take a bite out of Jenna, if you can believe that shit. She's ain't the trusting type, I guess."

"I was always more of a cat person. It's a pretty dog, though. What's her name?"

"Yeah, you look more like a cat person." Greg shook his head. "No idea what her name is. Found her in that field behind the barn. Had some puppies, but this was the only one that survived. She was pretty weak, but I've been getting her back on her feet. Thought about finishing her off myself, but decided I'd let her have a go at it. I was sure she was going to bite it, but she's a tough bitch. Keeps me company out here when I work on the truck. Figured I'd take her with me when we head out. If she wants to go, that is." He let out a breath, and the old Greg came back, the one that was hard. The killer. "Maker told you I'd show you how to kill 'em, right? That's all I'm really good at, killing the sons of bitches."

"Yeah, he did. But you want me to come back later?" He gestured to the truck and the dog.

"No, it's all right." Greg straightened up and adjusted his belt. "You ever been hunting? Ever track anything? I'd guess not—it's a dying art. The real thing, that is, not the weekend warrior that uses all his bullshit to trick it into coming out, or the pussy that sits in a tree and shoots what comes out to feed. Not that I'm against plugging these fuckers in the back of the head when they're not looking. Just saying, it ain't sporting, don't give you no skill. Not against an animal. But these damn things? You take what you can get, sport or not."

Greg grabbed a heavy toolbox from the ground and lifted it with ease, setting it in the bed of the truck. "I spent time up in the Yukon with my pa. You ever hear about a fucking Irishman heading up there?" He laughed and shook his head. "Freeze your balls off up there. Plenty of things ready to take a bite out of you, too. Wolves, bears, moose."

"Moose?"

He nodded his head. "Wouldn't think much about them, would you? They're mean sons of bitches, let me tell you," he said with a laugh under his breath. "Well, killing a moose ain't all that important. What I'm saying is hunting anything like that will likely leave you dry . . . or dead. You go after a wolf and don't know what you're doing, you won't find shit.

Same with bears, or anything. You won't find a damn thing, and there's a good chance you're going to get mauled or killed. These fucking things, the brood, they are much worse. You got to know what you're doing. Got to know how to spot it, how to trap it, how to kill it, but it ain't just that." Greg stopped for a moment, his hands resting on the tool-box. "You ever kill anything?"

"No. Nothing important."

"What, you some fucking vegetarian? I thought maybe you would have shot a deer, maybe put a house pet out of its misery. Nothing? Christ." He pulled a key from his pocket and popped open the tool chest. "Don't matter none. Shooting a deer," he said, half-snorting a laugh. "Hell, shooting a bear, or even a man . . . It's not the same." He reached in and pulled out a stack of Polaroids, then tossed them down in front of Daniel, spilling them in the back of the truck. Faded pictures collected over the years—blood, black ink, children's faces, their eyes closed.

Dead. They look like Sam.

"You think you can kill that?" Greg asked in a huff. "Now, I don't know what you think about me, Dan. Don't give a shit, either. I might be your best friend here, since I'm the only one feeding it to you straight. This ain't a fucking hobby. Ain't a job, neither. It's a lifestyle. You hunt monsters the only way you can." He slammed a finger down on one of the pictures and pulled it up. "By being a fucking monster, 'cause only a monster could kill something that looks like this."

The picture showed a freckled young girl with long red hair. She looked like any other kid; there was nothing peculiar or monstrous about her—except that her teeth had been knocked in and one eyelid was pulled high and tight.

Still alive.

"That ain't all the pictures," Greg said.

Greg pulled out another stack and handed it to Daniel. No children here, only monsters with pointed ears and black-green skin. The first photo focused on a dead boy in a tar-filled bathtub, fingers hooked like claws and eyes a shade of yellow that caught the flash of the camera. The next photo showed a girl, chain around her neck, screaming and swinging a blurred hand at the camera, with a mouthful of needles and bald spots on her head.

There were more.

Daniel could almost hear the painful screech of nails across a chalkboard. Sharp teeth jutted from mouths, fingernails were barbed with hooks of bone. Hunched, curved spines and eyes plucked from nightmares, visible even in the pictures.

"That's what you're killing," Greg said, pointing at the girl chained at the neck. "But here's what's going to happen. You're going to get out there, and it's going to be your turn, and then you're going to see it. They're going to get into your head, those doll eyes. It'll creep on in there and you won't even know it, and then you're dead. Or someone else is. That's how they fuck with you."

Greg gathered the pictures and stacked them neatly in the center of the toolbox. "Or maybe you won't. You won't get dead, nobody else will, and it's not death that haunts your dreams. Instead, it's this little girl's eyes." He held the picture up again. Her wet eyes stared into Daniel's, pleading for help. Greg pulled it away and locked it all in the box again. "She's going to be with you until the day you die. I guarantee it."

Whatever buttons Greg was trying to push, things were changing in Daniel. He could picture himself with the blade and the girl's eyes staring at him.

Did Sam's eyes look like that when they took him?

"Sam's going to be with me every day." He snapped the response before he could think otherwise. "Fuck, Greg, they snuck into my house and took my boy. I cried over that thing that slept in his bed, and I buried it. But Sam . . ." Tears started to drip down his face. "Sam was out there, dying. They killed him. They fucking took my son!" He slammed a hand against the side of the truck as the tears kept coming.

Greg watched as Daniel huffed in air and tried to calm himself. "I get you. I understand. Believe me. You know what Maker said about Carol, yeah?"

"Yeah," Daniel said as he tried to catch himself. "That was your daughter?"

For a moment, it looked like Greg wouldn't say anything at all. "No, my wife. We had our nephew staying with us for a bit. Don't know how the motherfuckers knew it. Don't know how they pick their people, neither. But they knew we had the boy, and they came for him at night. Wife woke up and went in there. Nephew lived." He turned and spat a glob of mucus before grabbing a bottle from the ground. He pulled off the top and took a drink without a wince, then offered it to Daniel.

"Thanks." Daniel took a sip, coughed, and handed the bottle back.

Greg inspected the label carefully. "I was there, too. Passed out drunk. Carol always asked me to drink less." He put the lid back on and set the bottle on the counter. "But she ain't around to ask no more."

Silence filled the barn for a time. Daniel knew what Greg was thinking. He had those same thoughts.

What if I'd listened?

The bigger man shook out of it and broke the silence. "Let's get back to how you kill 'em. So, you really never killed anything, right? Christ Almighty, come on back. I'm going to show you how to hold a shotgun."

———

GREG HATED them almost as much as he hated himself. That's why he drank—it made him forget.

Well, at least it dulled the edges.

Every time they held a meeting, Maker made it clear that they were playing things safe, making sure everyone would get out.

But what if I don't want to get out?

For Greg, that was the truth of it. Each time, part of him hoped the next one would rip it all out of his stomach and make the end a nice clean one, then he could rest and burn in Hell like the good Lord intended. He had no real illusions about what the afterlife might be. There was either no God, or he was going to burn in Hell. Sometimes, he wished he could be like Jenna, praising God Almighty, but then he'd remember that night when God took his sweet wife and left him here alone.

Why the fuck wasn't it me? It'd be better if it had been me. No one would give a shit with me gone. If it just wasn't for that fucking bottle on that fucking night . . .

He still always kept one handy—a bottle, that is. Every day is a good day to get drunk and peel the paint off the inside of your brain, one shot at a time.

He wished he were dead, and he probably would be if it weren't for the rest of them. They needed him. No matter how much he abused them, how many things he broke, or how much shit he talked, they needed him. Truth was, no one could kill like Greg.

No one.

And, although he didn't give a shit about himself, he worried about the others. He didn't much care about letting just one more into the group with Daniel but now, he found himself half-piss drunk and trying to explain to a fucking ninny how to march, how to use a shotgun, and how to bleed them. It'd take some time before he could turn this turd into something with teeth, but hell, got to start somewhere.

Well, it wasn't all bad. Killing them was, after all, one of his favorite topics of discussion.

"You can drown them. You see, all that magic pumping through their black hearts counts for shit when water fills their lungs," he said with a hearty, pleased laugh as Daniel loaded the shotgun.

That was his favorite way: watching them drown. That's when they were at their most desperate, and it wasn't like it was anything special, either. Plain water kills them the same way it kills anything else.

But hell, I love watching the lights go out.

He sat on that thought for a minute while Daniel fumbled with the shotgun. "Fire works, too, but, eh . . . Too damn unruly, fire. Burn your own ass up. You can kill 'em other ways, too. But they're durable. Shoot one in the head and it might just wince. You got to put enough rounds into their heads to make it count. Shoot anything in the head enough times, and it'll die."

Daniel was all right, it seemed. Came off like a prick at first, some little, small-dick liberal. But Greg had to admit, he wasn't so bad.

He's got a taste for the blood, too. You can smell it on him. He'll like the way they bleed too before this is all over.

Greg hated himself, but some part of him liked seeing Daniel walk right down that same path he did. Of course,

Daniel wasn't passed-out drunk when the brood came to his house.

I wasn't either, though.

That was a lie he'd told them all: that he was passed out. The way Rebekah looked at him, though, told him she knew otherwise.

Fucking witch can look right on into your soul.

He went in after his wife screamed and their nephew came racing out of the room, shrieking like a wounded animal. He was drunk, sure; but then, he always was.

Hunched to keep its gray head from scraping the ceiling, it clutched Carol between its long, twig-like fingers. A single hand wrapped around her like she was just a toy to be fucked with. He remembered it clearly. He remembered the extra joint or two in each finger. He remembered the cracked grooves in its dry flesh and those yellow teeth.

I'll never forget.

Its thick spine pierced through the skin, and it had no cock to speak of, despite being completely bare-ass naked. It turned to Greg when he came in. It didn't have eyes, just two pitch-black holes and a wider one for a mouth to match. Carol was already halfway down its throat, still screaming.

Still alive.

In Greg's dreams, he grabbed his shotgun out of the room and fired at it, and it spewed Carol out, slick with muddy spit. She was dead, of course; even the dreams wouldn't give him that. It killed him right afterward—that much was fine.

But that was only in his dreams, only what he wished had happened. No—the reality was that he turned and ran like a goddamn coward, let her screams chase him out. He didn't even pause to think of her. How precious a thing his life had become, in that moment when she'd needed him. More precious than his self-respect.

More precious than her.

And he hated himself for it. He'd hate himself for the rest of his days. Maybe it had been the bottle after all. Booze had never turned him into a coward before, but he'd never lost his damn mind like that, either.

Rebekah came to him one night after one of the nightmares. She told him of a madness that infects the brain, that these *Wechselkinder* strike with, using it like any other weapon.

"They break a man's mind, flood him with horror, and he'll lose himself. At times, he can have no control. The old stories tell it so," she had said, with those piercing eyes that can't help but dig where they fucking shouldn't. Was she judging him? Did she know? Had she fetched his memories while he slept?

He would have killed her for that if he didn't know it was something she couldn't control. After he'd found his wife's body, he'd decided that he would never lose control again, and Rebekah's insight, or warning, didn't help. Not one bit. His wife was still dead, and he'd still run.

I remember how it felt, I remember being afraid for myself. I remember the coward I was.

But just in case she was right, just in case one of those motherfuckers was ever going to try that again, Greg had put enough callouses on his mind that they couldn't break it. When he caught them, he'd hold them, cut them. Sure, it was part of the job, to get information. That's what he told the others, anyway. He took it as his cross to bear; but truth was, he liked it. Not at first, but he did later.

You have to like something like that to keep doing it.

And he felt the little sons of bitches crawl inside his

mind. With a nice, snug, Iron necklace, he kept them weak, made sure they couldn't wrench that cowardice out of him. But they tried, and every time they tried, he made them hurt. He did it so much he got a taste for it, enough of a taste that he could hate himself, but still hate them more.

And he loved to hate them.

That's where he was when he came to New Athens. Right there, right in that sweet spot of enjoying it enough to keep going. He liked the others just fine, Jenna and Maker anyway, but that was it. He had no one else to be accountable to, no one else to write letters to or apologize to. If he had to leave someone to die here, he could do it. They'd all talked about it and everyone knew the score.

It was fine. Everything was fine.

Then this stupid fucking dog found him at the house. He almost shot the damn thing. It wasn't like a normal dog, didn't bark at him until he was close—a low, rough bark, like someone had ripped its vocal cords straight out. It startled the hell out of him, and he wasn't easily startled. It kept growling and he thought he'd just end it there—had the shotgun in the pocket of his shoulder, a load in the breech, and two barrels aimed at its mangy face. But the bitch kept snarling, and he didn't have time for that kind of shit.

Then he heard the whimpering. There, in the weeds, was the puppy, with several others lying dead. Then his gun was down on the ground, and the mother just came up and licked him. Fangs out just seconds before, and now she licked him.

God damn you.

He almost shot it anyway. He had built himself a nice cold place in his heart, and yet this mongrel and her pup had gotten him to lay down his weapon, not to mention the tears welling up in his eyes. Almost shot it, but took it inside instead.

He was all right before New Athens, or this brood, or this Shallow bullshit. Now he had a dog, and some stupid asshole to show how to shoot a gun.

"Tuck it into your shoulder," he said. "I'll rip your fucking head off if you hold it like an asshole again."

11

"Not a damn thing. Got a few ideas in mind for tomorrow, though. You hear anything from Jenna?"

"Nein," Rebekah said as she pulled a cigarette from her lips. "She will be going to the church tomorrow."

"That old trick always needs some time to percolate."

"Indeed," Rebekah said. "Are we now to concern ourselves with the speed of things, Larry?"

"I don't like any of it, Rebekah. It all smells bad. Too many factors, too many variables. I feel like I'm walking around without my damn pants on." Reaching over the counter and pulling back the drapes, he looked out the kitchen window. Daniel was out in the fields with Greg, a shotgun tucked into his shoulder and aimed up. Maker was glad to have another man who knew how to use a gun, and Daniel was taking to it quickly enough. "There's a shitstorm blowing in. I can smell it."

While Daniel had been working with Greg, the others had been searching; Jenna and Maker out on their feet and Rebekah through her books. These things took time to establish, time to sniff out.

But Maker couldn't shake the feeling that something bad was about to happen. He didn't feel like he was hunting.

I feel like I'm being hunted.

"It is not only New Athens that is strange. . ." Rebekah let the cigarette dangling between her lips burn.

"Well, don't make me write you an invitation. Let's hear it."

"It's you." Smoke snaked from her nostrils as she took another puff. "You've been off since we've arrived and everyone knows it, but no one will say. I am not here to question your authority, Larry." She snuffed out the cigarette on the kitchen table, a thin, dying layer of smoke smoldering from it.

"Then why even ask the question?"

Rebekah crossed her arms and remained silent.

"You're relentless, woman. I'm fine. It's just a bigger nest than we've ever hit. And this Shallow business, whatever the hell it is, is unfamiliar territory. It's got me at a disadvantage, and I'm not keen on being in the unknown."

"And Daniel? I admit, the boy is quite interesting. He seems a quick learner, and his ability to draw in all of this is the fastest I've ever seen. He seems like he may fit, but you've been particularly forceful regarding his admittance."

"Yeah, he's come quick. He didn't need that much convincing, even seems to have won over Greg. I have a nose for talent, and a feeling that we'll need him. That's how I got you in, wasn't it?"

But something is definitely fucking wrong here. Something that might kill us.

She sighed, creating a thin trail of smoke. "Perhaps you're right. He certainly seems willing, but whether he's capable is another thing entirely. Though, as you say, he is different from the others. Perhaps under these peculiar circumstances, we must take unusual actions."

She stared at him with cold eyes, and he knew what she was going to say.

She means to go inside. Reach out to them.

Maker scoffed. "I appreciate the effort, but we don't need to go there. At least, not yet."

"Are you not the one suggesting that time is an issue? I trust your instincts, Larry."

"And what if things go south again? You think shit is going to be any easier if we're down by one? I'm not going to throw a slow pitch to you, Rebekah. You were a fucking mess before."

"Larry, come now," she said, stone-faced. "I expected you to be more cordial than that. I am, however, an old, frail, and delicate woman."

"Oh, don't get sarcastic with me. I know you can pull your weight. No one ever questioned that."

"Then why must you carry it all on your shoulders? I know my limits, Larry—there's no need to be concerned about me crossing them. And you won't for a moment convince me that all that has you worried is a few more parasites than usual. It's better to make the move now than to wait and make it in desperation."

Maker stared at the wall, tracing the dancing lines of the wallpaper with his gaze. She was right, of course—she usually was. But he still remembered the last time she'd let them in, the last time her mind had reached out.

When you look into it, it looks into you.

"I'd say no, if I didn't have this damn itch crawling around inside my head. I don't know what it is, Rebekah. If you think you can do it, then do it. But don't you go losing yourself. We can't get along without you."

"Tonight, I'll forego even the smallest dosage of medication and reach out for them. Then what happens, will be what happens."

"Don't let them too deep into your head, woman. It's not worth it. I'd rather ditch and let New Athens burn," he said, and meant it. It was no easy thing to abandon a hunt, but he'd done it before and would do it again.

"Of course, Larry." Her posture and expression didn't change.

Larry relaxed and poured himself a cup of coffee. "I've been to the old asylum out there a few times."

"And why is that?"

"Not sure, to be honest."

"You want me to come with you, see if I can feel anything?"

"Yeah, maybe. Hell, *I* almost feel something there." He downed the coffee in a single gulp; he enjoyed the way it burned. "Let's wait a day or two. See how your dreams go, and if we catch a break with the church, we might not need to go poking around in a place like that at all."

He knew that was all wrong, though. He was certain that the old asylum had a role to play, and that he'd be inside the rusted gates and walking down the rotted halls before long. He had a nose for such things, a sense of direction, instincts that had served him well over the years.

But the thought scared him. Not a childlike fear that turned him away or made him shake. A fear deeper than dying, something that went beyond death. A feeling less like a threat and more like a premonition, a welcoming, with watchful eyes and hooked smiles.

Like Hell is calling me.

THE STRUCK MATCH TOOK FLAME. Flipping off the lights, Rebekah watched the tiny flame dance in the dark before she held it to the candle's wick. The relaxing, fragrant smell of lavender rolled off the candle and greeted the coming chill. Candles were one of the few indulgences she allowed herself.

"I'm going to sit with you," Jenna insisted, and took her place in the chair. "Don't mind me. I won't make a peep until you're ready."

Rebekah shut the window and pulled a blanket over her shoulders. "Yes, please do not wake me under any circumstances. But, whisper to me when the time comes."

Jenna nodded. "I know, I know. I'll be praying for you."

"Lovely," Rebekah said dryly. She lay down on the bed and placed her head on the soft, cool pillow. "Will you turn off the hallway lights, too, please?"

"Of course, dear." Jenna flicked the switch off and the flickering candle flame shifted across the darkness on the walls.

Closing her eyes, she waited for sleep to take her. A chill stretched across her flesh, but it wasn't from the cool air.

I let them get too far inside my head last time. I won't do that this time. I know myself better now. I know what is real and what isn't.

But she remembered those eyes, those teeth that scratched into her mind. She remembered the face they had taken: her young brother. She always thought it strange; she couldn't remember what he looked like, or pick his picture from a pile—it had been so long, and she had been so young—but in the dreams, she knew him. In the dreams, even when she couldn't see his face, she knew him.

Dreams were strange things that few could ever truly comprehend. In dreams, Rebekah knew how to fly, knew how to just lift her feet off the ground and take flight, bending the world to her desires. Only in dreams was she so free.

Is it that I can fly only in dreams or that I forget how when I wake?

A preposterous idea, but one she couldn't help but entertain every time she woke. She remembered most of what happened in a dream, but not everything. It was as though she had deep impressions of it, but the fine details were lost. She was still among the best of the Dreamers—it's what she had trained herself to do. Despite all of that, it was as though she was another person in another state of being that she couldn't completely comprehend. People could tell you that they flew, even show you how, and while they might find it simple to understand, you never would.

Is that what it is? A conversation? Am I the same person there as I am here, or is it something else entirely? Do I dream like normal people?

She didn't know, and knew no way to find out. She had read about similar experiences and plenty of theories. But she wasn't certain. Sometimes, she felt like she was outside the dream, watching something else act. Like a director, issuing commands that were usually, but not always, obeyed. She felt as though another mind lived inside her own. And sometimes, she felt that she was the dream and the waking world was the lie.

It won't be long now.

She sighed. When her thoughts played too quickly or too deeply, she found it hard to sleep. Instead, she imagined herself flying, lifting one foot from the ground and then the other.

How could it be so easy? How could I think it so natural?

She pictured her feet, one next to the other, in her

mind's eye. She thought about what it would take to fly—how could it even be done? How would she even know she was flying? How would she know which foot came up, and which came next? Did it push off by some unseen force, or did the other just lift with it? Was it like swimming? She remembered how she moved her arms, but did she kick her legs as well? Or was it enough just to decide that she would go forward?

She imagined it now: raising her foot, the other coming with it. Then, she was in the air and remembered how. She remembered how to pull up, into the abysses of her mind and through the recesses of another. She didn't try to remember or try to detail it. It was the simplest thing, so easy and natural, that there was no other point to consider at all.

She remembered now because she dreamed and floated. There was no air and no turmoil here, no pain that had come with age. She was the master of everything. But she was here for a purpose, wasn't she?

What did I come here for?

Nothing, surely. Why do anything rather than nothing? Nothing was all there was. Why do anything when she could leave everything behind? She floated there for some time, then steered away from the darkened images and things of the past that held her. Instead, she flew past them, kept herself from their reach.

A whisper came, a whisper that boomed throughout her entire world. "Find them for us. Find them for us," it said, twice and twice again.

Who? Who should I find?

"Find the ones that steal children. Find where they nest and where they lay. Find them, but be careful. Be careful that they don't find you."

Don't let them find you.

The whispers died. She remembered now how the cold world sat on top of this one, the terror that threatened and even broke into this world. She wished she could leave it all, could die in that world and live on here.

But there was duty. She felt the pain that demanded an answer, even if it had been answered dozens of times before. She clung to the matting of the void and used that to pull herself forward. She wondered how she could find them, how she could possibly reach them, before she remembered the one and only truth of this world:

I need only want, and I will.

She wouldn't remember that when she woke up. She knew it here, though, even knew that she'd forget until she was here once more—such was the way of this world and the rules of it.

Renewed with truth and purpose, she delved into the void in search of the dark edges of nightmares beyond the shapeless dreamscape. She glided as a visitor soon forgotten, or as an oddity half-remembered.

Her fingers found a ragged tearful mess of imagination: a shoeless boy crying as classmates and teacher pointed, eyes sharp with judgment. She cast only one glance before leaving.

"I've got you now," said a man with a white-knuckled grip around another man's baldhead. In his other hand, he held a blade. She knew them both in this place—one a husband, the other a wife's lover. So bare were most minds that she knew all there was when looking at them. After a few seconds of consideration, she turned from it as the husband began to work the blade on the lover's screaming face.

Dark things filled the dreams of men—but rarely, were

they unnatural things. New Athens, however, had more darkness than most. More hate and pain, more self-loathing and regret.

This city bleeds.

She saw it then: a heart that flowed with poison as each beat sent another painful, searing wave into dreams; a tumor with snaking legs that choked the dreams around it and fed on the misery of the world.

Wechselkinder.

It burned hot, hotter than usual. This one was ripe, but that also meant strong.

Part of her held back, the part that wanted neither to be inside them, nor have them inside her. It was only a moment's hesitation before she willed herself forward.

Duty.

In an instant, the flight was gone and she stepped from the void into a place she knew to be dangerous. It was a place filled with twisted toys and colorful walls that seemed to stretch infinitely long and at odd angles.

A child's playroom.

With only the tips of her fingers touching the wall, she felt the jutting angles that breathed beneath her. Strange colors—blues, reds, greens, and yellows—striped and dotted the walls without pattern. She rubbed her palm flat across the wall, which flinched like a living thing and sucked in ever so slightly at her touch.

The dull eyes of a toy clown rolled in their sockets, as its head shifted to follow Rebekah.

Is that a sentry? I must be close.

"Where are you?" she whispered as she peeked through the doorways into the rooms. "Are you hiding from me?"

Was it now the creature's will against hers? If it was, then so shall it be. It was of no consequence to her. There was no

pain here, after all. Here, she couldn't remember what pain
felt like, or even why she should fear it, only that she did.
She wondered whether in the waking world, she feared
other strange things, too.

The floors stretched up over her feet like thick mud, so
she started swimming through the air. They gurgled up and
reached for her with slow, thin fingers, but she paid them
little mind. Following the twisting hallways through the
maze of the house, she had no fear of not finding her way
back. The dreams were always simple to her. She always
knew how to get where she was going, never a moment late
or a second early.

The hallway emptied into a brightly lit kitchen. There,
sitting on a table, was a three-layered birthday cake adorned
with tiny, sparkling candles. The candles waved and
breathed with the walls, buzzing with flames that never
grew smaller. Rebekah saw something beneath the icing of
the cake that crawled like an insect, a dot beneath the icing
that zigged and zagged.

Are you in there? Are you hiding from me?

A knife, which glimmered no matter how the light hit it,
took form in Rebekah's hand because she willed it so. She
forced the knife into the cake, and the bump hurried to the
edge of her blade, slowly growing as it closed in.

Peculiar.

A sudden eruption of gooey chunks splattered Rebekah
as something burst from the cake. It was not a bug at all, but
a three-fingered hand, opening and spreading and latching
icily onto Rebekah's wrist.

Rebekah gasped as she was pulled forward from the air.
The hand began to suck her into the cake, the layers now
open wide in a gaping mouth, metal teeth like broken knife
tips. It chomped down on Rebekah's hand, sending burning

pain rushing up her arm, and hot blood flowed from the wounds.

She remembered hurt now.

Rebekah instinctively grasped the edge of the table and pulled back with as much strength as she could muster; her body was far stronger here than in the waking world.

Terror spread like poison through her veins as she struggled to survive. With her feet pressed against the bottom of the table, she wrenched back, feeling new pain as her skin tore against the sharp teeth. The cake slopped from the table, tearing away like wet glue with a sickening pop as Rebekah's arm came free. She struggled like a child from the womb, shrieking for its first gasps of air.

The layers of the cake quaked and opened, presenting a folded dimension. In the distance, a tar-black creature with yellow cat-eyes and horns stared back at her.

"Get out of there, you little bastard!" she yelled, pressing her hand to her wound to staunch the bleeding. The pain fueled her anger, and it was always better to be angry than afraid.

The cake's quaking quieted to a tremble. Seizing the initiative, Rebekah scrambled forward. "Give me your name, dammit!"

The creature grew smaller as it hurried back into its pocket, but Rebekah's mind reached out and snatched it. It shrilled and gripped its black head with sharp talons dipping into its dark flesh. Red ink oozed from its ears and dripped toward Rebekah. The drips speckled in front of her against an unseen shield and spelled a name:

Ben Harris.

I have you, you bastard.

As the final drip fell, the creature regained its self and

turned back to her. "We'll eat you! Hollow out your bones to be our toys!" its horrible voice shrieked.

It rushed forward on all fours, clawing the ground, its tail snaking behind it. Its talons gripped the outside of the cake and began to pull itself free.

Its energy and violence surprised her. This was a strong one, likely the pinnacle of its brood. Rebekah snatched the carving knife from the floor and slashed at the air as she frantically searched the room. She saw no exits, no hallways. Everything had closed, sealing her in.

Get out! Get out now!

Hands reached from the walls behind her, grabbing her and pulling her back against it.

"No!" She knew she didn't have the strength to win. But, hadn't she broken its will when she toppled the cake and ripped away its name?

The creature came at her, its eyes filled with wanting. The creature's gaping, toothless mouth opened in front of her, its pink center contrasting with its dark, naked skin.

"No! No! Stay away from me!" Fear and pain were coming thickly now as the fingers squeezed her so tightly that her bones cracked; it all threatened to overwhelm her and break her focus.

The creature came closer. Its fat, wet tongue stretched out and licked at her head, dragging across her face with dozens of pointed, fleshy spines that grated her flesh and left a burning smear of blood. The creature's wet gums were touching her head as the creature began to suck, its jaws growing wider and wider.

Rebekah was losing focus, and the monster was getting inside her, taking her. She dropped the knife and quivered as she struggled for control. Her finger extended and sunk into the shredded wound on her arm. Grunting from the torment, her hand fell to the floor and began to write in blood.

She pulled out from herself; she was there and not there at the same time, watching and living all at once. She saw her eyelids spasm open and shut, and the creature's eyes hungrily watching her finger form the letters:

TE

What is it getting?

TER

No, no, no! Terrace Drive. It's trying to get where we live!

TERR

With all the strength she had left, Rebekah pulled herself back into her own body and clenched her hand. Struggling against the pain that racked her mind, she reached up and pressed her thumbnail into the creature's eye. It popped, and a sticky liquid trickled down her arm.

The creature ripped back and howled with a child's voice. Rebekah snatched the knife from the ground, and with as much speed and strength as her fading mind still had, she turned to the wall and slashed it open. It ripped to the sides like a sprung curtain and she leaped, diving through the opening.

A dim light showed itself as a speck in the distance. The creature roared behind her as she swam and kicked, utterly maddened as the world grew cold. Her fingers grabbed onto the speck of light and she pulled it close.

She gasped, inhaling real, cold air as she awoke. Sweat dripped down her face as she looked at her arm and found it whole and unhurt. She shivered as she rubbed where the wound had been.

Jenna rushed from her chair and grasped Rebekah's hand. "Don't worry! You're okay now, you're okay!" She hushed Rebekah and wrapped an arm around her.

Rebekah's eyes shut tightly as she gasped for air and fought back the urge to scream. "I saw something, Jenna. I saw something there."

"One of the creatures?"

"Yes, but something else, too. It was hiding something. Inside its mind. It had a door locked away tightly, with chains." Rebekah strained, trying to remember, even with the fog setting in, but when their minds had touched, she'd received only a glimpse. "I almost didn't see it."

What was it? There was a door with chains and cries. It had something. Something it didn't want me to see.

"It was horrible, so horrible," Rebekah said in a burst. "It got inside my head again."

"Oh, honey." Jenna wrapped her arm around Rebekah's shoulders and pulled her close. "You're done. You won't go back, you're all done. The worst part is over."

"No, no." Tears dripped down Rebekah's face as she shook her head. She wished Jenna was right, but knew she wasn't. "It's going to get worse."

I have to go back.

12

BEN HARRIS. A SNOT-NOSED LITTLE SHIT THAT ONCE THREW A baseball at Sam, but other than being a bit of a whiner, he wasn't too bad. His dad was all right, too; Daniel had a drink with him a couple of times. The Harris family had even come to Sam's funeral. He liked them.

Now he's dead. Don't forget that.

Rebekah had torn that name out of a monster's head—as insane as that sounded—and she'd paid a price for it. She was a wraith-like thing now, with her skin taut against her face and the circles under her eyes growing ever darker. Maker said that when she goes inside to look for them, they sink their roots into her. They peel her and run fingers through the layers of her mind, pulling up old memories of pain and torment. The roots snap when she wakes up, but it leaves little pieces of itself rotting inside her mind.

She sleeps most the time now.

"You're going up to bat on this one, Daniel," Maker said, interrupting Daniel's thoughts. "We need you to go to Harris and confirm. Talk with the family, make sure we're not confused. Check for any drastic mood changes."

"But only a mood change? Couldn't that be any kid?"

"A point not missed," Greg said from across the table. "We're not a gaggle of fucking morons. We are well aware of the behavior of children. He's talking about a little son of a bitch that's taken a particular fancy to blades, maybe one that seems interested in hurting people. *Really* hurting people. Or maybe they're just acting all fucked up, shitting all over themselves on a regular basis, out in the mud eating a dead cat. Ain't that hard to spot when you're looking in the right direction."

"We trust Rebekah," Maker continued, "but we play it safe. We want to confirm the target before we move. We're on a clock, though. We can't be sure what they scooped out of Rebekah's mind. She says they were rooting for our address, but she doesn't think they got it. Maybe only the street."

"Terrace Drive is long as hell. Without an exact address, they won't know where we're at," Daniel said with a bit of desperation.

Jenna had been sitting silently, listening to them all. "We need be careful, whatever we do," she finally said. "We do the Lord's work. We'll need to know what they know, and if Daniel can help us find one . . ." Her smile left her face for hardly a moment before it returned, offering only a glimpse of what she held beneath it all.

"Agreed. We've got too much at stake here to get spooked. Better to just leave than lose. Everyone, get your shit packed into your bug-out bags, in case we need to move quickly."

"Bug out? You mean just pick up and leave?" Daniel asked with a little disbelief. "So, what then, we just relocate?"

Greg huffed. "If we bug out, we leave it all, son. If it gets hot, you don't sit in the water until it boils. Live to kill again another day."

"My parents live here. My friends live here. I can't just fucking bug out."

Maker nodded. "Keep them in mind, your parents and your friends, when you're checking out the Harris house. Remember what's at stake. You ready?"

Daniel took a deep breath and nodded.

I'd better be.

DANIEL CRAMMED the hot dog into his mouth. The trembling in his hands concerned him far more than the rumble in his stomach, though. Hunger had little effect on him these days. But if he wanted to look like he wasn't having a nervous breakdown, then he had to make sure his hands wouldn't shake when he talked.

"You have to pull on the wolfskin," Maker had told him before he set out. "You've got a wolf in you, Daniel. You're a hunter. It's in your blood—I can tell. You pull that wolfskin on, and it's not you anymore."

"For fuck's sake, Maker, I don't know how to lie," he said. "I've never done this shit before."

"That's because you're going about it all wrong," Maker replied. "The key isn't to get the other guy to believe you; the key is to believe it yourself. You have to believe the lies and half-truths. You have to convince yourself that you're worried for him, and he'll believe you. Convince yourself until it hurts when you think about it, and use that to get the job done. That's why you need the wolfskin. You pull that on, and you're a wolf."

The wolfskin? What the hell does he mean?

"You're a writer, aren't you?" Maker continued. "You feel sad when you write? You hurt when you lose a character? That's you lying to yourself. That's you convincing yourself it's real. Do that."

The next evening, Daniel was sitting in his car alone, finishing off the last of a drive-thru hot dog. He had lost himself earlier in the day and cried away the morning. For what in particular, he wasn't sure, but he was glad he decided to sleep at home alone rather than face the others. It wasn't until late in the afternoon that he managed to work up the nerve to head over to the *Guns and Ammo* store where Jim Harris was a manager. But then, he became aware of the shaking. He squeezed his hand into a fist to stop the trembling.

Get your shit together, Daniel. You might be losing your mind, but you can't go around looking like a fucking lunatic.

It was darker now, and he found some comfort in that. Something about the sun made him think he'd fail, like the rays would expose his lies. He knew now that the world was different, and with his eyes wide open, everything seemed more dangerous—even walking in to talk with Jim seemed like a confrontation. Daniel hoped to catch him and strike up a conversation about his son, but he wasn't sure how to go about it.

Hey, is your son being an asshole lately? Do you worry about him eating your face at night? Does he do anything disgusting like paint with his vomit or shit in the living room regularly? Has he ever tried to stab his little brother?

How could he bring up any of that? He'd known Jim Harris for years, watched his son grow up alongside Sam. Why was it any different now?

Because you know that his son is one of them. You know you have to look him in the eye. And you have to be the one to end it.

Daniel pulled out his phone and flipped through his photos. He'd saved his favorites as a reminder for each time he started to doubt himself, a reminder of what they had taken from him. He paused on one that showed Sam with his grandparents; Daniel's parents. That was his favorite, one of the good ones that didn't have his wife in it.

As he stepped out of his car, Daniel slid his phone back into his pocket, ignoring the little red numbers that indicated missed calls from friends and family. He filled his lungs with the cool air and buried his balled fists in his jacket pockets.

He walked up to the door quickly, before he could change his mind. A jingling bell alerted everyone when he arrived. The place was nice, the air clean, and the floor spotless. The walls were lined with guns inside glass cases, along with an assortment of hunting equipment, storage gear, and lock safes.

"Can I help you?" Jim Harris asked from behind the counter.

Daniel looked up with a counterfeit smile.

"Hey, Jim."

13

THE SHAKING IN DANIEL'S HANDS STOPPED AND HIS WORDS came smoothly. He nodded solemnly when Jim mentioned Sam and his smile returned when they talked about their children's last baseball game. He played it out, the lie, as smoothly as the truth.

He was the lie.

Or maybe, I just like to pretend that my life is horrible in a way that makes sense again.

Whatever the reason, the gears in his mind were turning fluidly. Even when the question came up that Daniel should have considered, but hadn't.

"Why are you shopping for a firearm?" Jim betrayed more than he probably meant to. It was a simple question, but Daniel could taste the concern in the words:

Are you going to kill yourself?

"Well," Daniel began, "my dad has taken all this pretty hard, too. We used to go hunting when I was young, and he wants me to go out with him again. I have a revolver back home, but no rifle."

The lie poured out of his mouth like water. Daniel had

never hunted before, but it was passable, and seemed to relieve Jim.

People want to be lied to if it makes things more comfortable.

"Well, they say nothing clears your head like getting out there in the woods and getting a scent for something."

More than you'd believe.

In the end, he didn't buy a rifle, but he found it easy to ask Jim if he wanted to catch a beer after work, and though the man seemed momentarily concerned, it passed.

At the bar, a quaint little place right down the street, they talked about Sam, and Daniel ensured him that he was okay, despite the funeral being only a few weeks ago. They even talked about Julia.

"Well, you know, everyone has to grieve in their own way," Daniel said.

But the conversations about Sam, and Julia, and hunting, and baseball, all made him itch beneath his skin. All of it was feigned concern. They had agreed on one beer, but the more they talked, the looser Jim got and then one turned into many. Only after the second beer did Daniel ask Jim about his son, how little Ben Harris was doing with the loss of his friend, and it was with the third beer that Jim started to talk.

Before the words even came out, Daniel's suspicions were confirmed. He saw the shine in Jim's eye, the shine that told him everything he needed to know.

It's him.

Jim told him of the knife—a thin blade his wife used for slicing tomatoes. He told him how it found its way into Ben's hand and then across his sister's leg.

"Spent the night in the hospital," Jim said, his eyes tired.

"Well, like I said, everyone grieves in their own way. I'm sure he didn't really know what he was doing."

Jim took another long sip of beer. "Found the window open the other day. Ben was outside, sleeping on the dirt. I mean, what the hell is that? He's done this a few times, and my wife's all worried. I had to nail the window shut."

"He's been climbing out at night?"

"That, or sometimes when he's outside he just runs the fuck off. Christ almighty, Dan. First there was your son, and then Sheryl and Tom's son, and now Ben. What the hell is going on?"

"That's horrible, Jim."

But was that real empathy? For now, he wasn't there. He was only watching it play out, as though someone else or some*thing* else, was in the driver's seat. Whatever it was, it must have worked. Jim kept talking.

"That's . . ." He looked like he was ready to stop, but Daniel nodded his head, pushing the buttons to keep him talking. "I found him outside, with a cat, neighbor's cat. He had a knife and he was cutting it and . . ."

Jim's eyes were growing wet, and though he didn't say it, Daniel knew what he was thinking. He'd had those same desperate eyes and those same useless thoughts of trying to find the solution to a problem that had none.

You poor bastard. Your son's already dead, and you don't know it.

"A FUCKING CAT, eh? What'd I tell you?" Greg's eyes were cold as he spoke. "And he's a cutter? Sounds like the fucking brood."

Greg had picked Daniel up from his house and they were now heading back to the clubhouse.

"What should we do next?" Daniel had peeled away the

wolfskin, losing the confidence that came with it. "We're not just going to grab him out of his bed, are we?"

"Of course not. You think we're fucking savages? We'll grab the little bastard when he's out, see if he bleeds the right color."

"Are you fucking serious?"

"Oh, relax, you nancy. I'm just taking you for a turn. You know it's Maker who comes up with the plans. We ain't never bled a kid to see if he was one, why the hell would we want to start now?"

Daniel breathed out a sigh of relief and let his head fall against the headrest. The hum of Greg's truck sang a lullaby as his mind stretched out. In his dream, he touched the edges of oblivion and heard whispers in the dark, but a slap on the shoulder brought him back.

"We're here."

Daniel rubbed the back of his head and walked in as the fog cleared from his mind. Whatever dreams he had were quickly fading—only brief images of claws and teeth remained. The terror of his dreams had eased, though something still waited in the dark of his mind every night that he didn't medicate.

They didn't deliberate long. It was just the three men, with Rebekah still in recovery and Jenna out at the church — "digging", as Greg put it. The old man, Maker, seemed content with the information.

"Sounds like we've got one," he said. "We'll build a plan, but don't concern yourself with that, Daniel. You're our scout. Go back out there, get your feet wet, and we'll pull you in soon enough."

"Don't go dragging your feet none, either," the Irishman chimed in. "Once we make a move, it'll make everything 'lot more difficult for you."

"You mean, I'll be with you when you grab him?" Daniel slid his hand beneath the table when the trembles started.

"You don't think you're up for it?" Maker asked stiffly. "We need a third. Rebekah still needs time to recover, and Jenna doesn't ship out with us. That leaves you."

"Yeah." Daniel hoped the quake in his hand wasn't visible at the shoulder. "Yeah, I can do it."

There was something primal in him, a part of him that enjoyed the hunt. It was the new skin, the wolfskin. It wasn't until he had to sit back and think about that look in Jim's eyes, and how Jim would suffer just like he had when Sam died that he started to reconsider.

Is that why you're scared, Daniel? You're scared because of how it might hurt Jim? You're a fucking liar.

He knew it.

"What's step two, Dan?" Greg asked. "Where you looking next?"

Daniel hesitated, considering. "My mom works at the school. There's a football game coming up, and we used to go watch. I'm thinking about heading there with her and my dad, see if she mentions anything strange."

Maker leaned forward—his powerful gaze held Daniel. "Be careful, though. You look suspicious, and you could be the first person they start eyeballing the minute someone else goes missing. They're already on edge after the first kid. But we'll need you when we put things into motion. You just stick with your job."

Greg and Maker picked up and left, leaving Daniel to his thoughts. Everyone here was so different. Maker was meticulous, precise, and detail oriented, whereas Greg had grease under his nails and seemed ready to scream or laugh at any moment. All they had that tied them together was the hunt, this endless task that seemed to take so much more than it gave. Daniel had to wonder if all of them would make the same choices, if they could go back and show their younger selves what they had become. Would they still do it all the same way?

After we're done here, I'm through. I'm not going to end up like this. I'm going to dig that thing out of his grave, finish this for Sam . . . and I'm done.

"The others have left?" Rebekah asked from a few feet away. She hobbled down the hallway to sit with him, a quilt wrapped around her shoulders, her eyes a bleached white. "Pour me some of that coffee, will you?"

He did, and was sorry that it was no longer hot, though Rebekah didn't seem to mind. He was thinking about leaving, but then she spoke again. "I heard you from the other room. It seems my body is aged, but my ears are just as sharp as they ever were. You've confirmed the boy."

"As best I could, I suppose. How are you feeling?" he asked, for he had nothing else to say.

"Horrid." She took a sip of coffee. "And I'm out of cigarettes."

"Can I, uh . . . I'm heading out. You need me to get you some?"

"Do you feel bad about killing your friend's son?" Rebekah asked without looking at him.

Daniel mumbled something incoherent.

Rebekah's eyes focused on the cold coffee. "It's not his son."

"I know. I guess, I just . . . I know how it's going to be for him. Losing his son."

"Do you think you've suffered?" Rebekah finally turned, her gaze sinking into him like hooks. "You haven't suffered."

"What the hell are you talking about?"

"Your child is dead, and you loved him. Others have that

love drained and end up hating even the memories of their children for the twisted things they become. These creatures took everything, even their love. You have not suffered."

"What the hell is wrong with you?" Daniel spat back.

"I hunt the darkness. I see things no person should see, things that have no right to exist. They haunt my every waking moment, the eyes of the monsters and the dead. They are all with me. I smell their blood on my fingers and feel their tongues lash my mind." Her face contorted into disgust. "I suffer. And you wallow here. I can smell the self-pity and weakness on you."

"You don't know shit!"

"I know you better than you know yourself. You beg intrusion with your wallowing. The fairy folk will play their games in your mind because you are neither hot nor cold. You believe, but reject. Your mind will be a playground for them. They will intrude onto your thoughts, wreak havoc upon you, and twist you into what they want. This is what they are. This is what they do to weak minds."

"What the fuck do you want me to do, then?" Daniel knew she was exhausted, knew she was hurt, but so was he.

"Burn your son's photographs. Push him from your mind. You have no time to grow, no time to change. This isn't a war—it is a killing field, where chaff is reaped from the wheat. You must swallow yourself, or you will endanger us all with your . . . weakness." She spat the last word.

Fuck you!

He wanted to say it, but bit his tongue. She was drained, defeated, had something raw and corrupted clawing its way through her brain. Instead, he stood up and stormed out, the floorboards rattling with each step.

His heart beat like a drum and drowned out the words

Rebekah yelled at his back. His hands balled into fists and he wanted to hurt something. There was a madness there that both enraged and calmed him, the primal side had returned. The wolfskin was pulled atop his flesh and he was the hunter once again.

He was in the woods then, his feet carrying him faster than his mind could work. He filled his lungs and roared. He breathed fire from his lungs, spewing out the anger and fear, the desperation that had gripped him for so long. Like a river that overflowed or a dam that burst, the anger erupted.

Tears came next, but not from pain or sadness. He started to regain control of himself, but he felt different. Something in him was fulfilled and hungry at the same, something that had always been there, something unseen. It was hot, unafraid. It wasn't fear.

He liked it.

14

"HE NEEDED THE PUSH," REBEKAH SAID FORCEFULLY. "YOU know just as well as I do that he's not ready. We've never seen anything like this before and we have *him*." She stirred her coffee needlessly and then repeated: "He needed the push."

Rebekah poured a cup from the fresh pot and sat down in her favorite chair in her room. Jenna had burst in, asking what was wrong before she even knew anything was wrong at all.

That damn woman can smell it.

"Mmhmm," Jenna said, bobbing her head. "And you were just the one to give him what he needed, hmm? I think you needed a punchin' bag, and that boy worked just fine."

"Please. I'm hardly the type that needs an outlet. And he's hardly a boy. It does him no good for you to treat him as such."

"We all have an outlet, Rebekah, even you. You were feelin' vulnerable and hurt. So, you hurt him. I understand."

Rebekah could taste the holier-than-thou attitude in

Jenna's words. "Did you come here to bother me? If so, I would rather sleep. I am very tired still."

"About that . . ." Jenna took a seat at Rebekah's desk.

"Larry told you everything, didn't he?" She hoped that would placate Jenna, but she knew better. The old woman wouldn't leave—of that much, Rebekah was sure. Jenna could be as stubborn as a stone when she wanted to be.

"He told me some, but I told him I'd hear the rest from you," Jenna said with the honey-sweet smile of hers. "Everyone needs to talk 'bout it all, every now and then."

Rebekah sighed. "Maker told you about the boy, the address, yes?"

"I suppose if you were wantin' to save time, you could just tell me about what the boy did to you and what else you saw."

"He cut me deep, Jenna. Stuck his twisted little fingers into me." She shuddered. "He—it—was trying to get our address. It wanted to find us. Worse, when it raked me, it stirred a lot of things loose. I've been thinking about the old days."

Jenna said nothing and made no effort to touch or hug Rebekah. She knew Rebekah better than that. Regardless, Rebekah did find some relief in opening up.

"There was something else there, hiding. It had something chained and locked away in its mind."

"What do you mean?" Jenna asked with a curious look. Of course, she wasn't plagued with the abilities that Rebekah had. She could never fully understand.

"We all have things in our minds, some things hidden even from ourselves. I've seen rooms inside the mind with doors that had to be opened, but none ever locked like this, with chains and bolts. What could something like that have hidden?"

"Nothin' good." Jenna's smile slipped. "Sounds dangerous."

Rebekah nodded. "Indeed, it is very curious. These are dangerous times, for sure."

"That's why you've been so hard on Daniel."

"How do you mean?" Rebekah asked.

"You're worried about how dangerous it is, and he reminds you of your brother."

"What?"

"Well, he does, don't he?" Jenna asked, folding her hands over her knees.

Damn you, Jenna.

BEFORE THE NIGHT had even begun, Daniel prowled the streets of New Athens, a hunt that composed itself in sorrow, lies, and smiles. Whispers of the beast beneath his skin set his hair on end. Each conversation had a theme: "I'm sorry about Sam," they would say, sometimes without words but in actions or with their eyes.

I'm sorry, too.

Daniel could see the gears that turned beneath their flesh, the way their emotions and words clicked into place to play this same tune to him over and over again. It was the same play with a different stage and different actors each time, over and over again, a maddening rhythm to it all. And it wasn't long until he knew his part in the act—the part that would twist them, reveal them, and expose them.

It all came so easily to Daniel that he felt he could have been doing it his entire life, like it had always been a part of him, though unknown, a stranger to himself. The wolfskin whispered, told him what to say, and in those moments, he wasn't himself, but someone else entirely.

"My daughter has been throwing up in class each day— the doctors don't know what it is." "My son started hitting the side of the house with his baseball bat." "Did you hear the Hallowell's son cut his friend?" They rolled out, and a list formed in his mind. He wrote them all out in longhand on a neat, clean sheet of paper that folded perfectly down the middle and then again. He kept it in his coat pocket.

A list of names. Children's names.

Which of these are just children, and which are the brood? Have we always been so weird? Have we always accepted so much of our nature? Are all these little bastards on the list, or am I just insane?

Am I insane?

That question came up. A lie, part of his mind told him —he knew better now. He wasn't insane. He was a sane man living in an insane world. Insanity would be to close the shades and pretend it wasn't real. To put that barrel back in his mouth before his work was done.

Insanity is doing this more than you need to. Living this.

Of that, he was sure. The rest—Maker, Greg, Jenna, Rebekah—they all held it together, but they hated themselves, hated what they'd become and what they had to do.

I'm not like them. I'm going to do this one thing, and I'm done. Let them hunt this shit until it kills them if they want. I'm not like them.

He returned with eight names. Their descriptions, their addresses, the causes for concern scrawled on the paper in black ink, with a red star next to the names that drew particular interest. He was nothing if not deliberate and concise. Maker looked it over and passed it around; each took a moment to inspect it.

"Heaven help us," Jenna said, "I've heard a few of these names. I'll have more soon."

Daniel told them what Jim had said about his kid sneaking out at night. "We can use that," Maker said. "They're nocturnal by nature. We just need to pull it out."

"Bring it here," Rebekah said between puffs of her stale cigarette. "If we subdue it here, weaken its shell, I'll cut into the cage. See what spills out."

Greg snorted. "Don't need that. I can cut the damn thing and get it just as good."

"Nein. Not this one," Rebekah said. "He's a strong one. I've seen him." Her face was stretched ever more tautly over her cheekbones. She looked five pounds lighter, and seemed not at all eager to go back at it again. Daniel pitied her.

I'm not the only one at war with my dreams.

"WE NEED THIS TO BE QUIET," Maker told them. "It can't look like an abduction. There's too much heat already. Daniel said this one likes to slink off, so we're going to fish him out."

"Like Kentucky?" Greg asked. Maker gave him a nod. "Grab your shit," Greg said to Daniel. "We're heading out."

The hunt began, and the things between and before blurred as Daniel's mind focused on the scent. The evening passed quickly, as most things seem to do when one is simply a visitor inside one's mind, a witness to events beyond your control. Suddenly, things slowed down and the details came into focus.

The night began. They were in the car, Maker and Greg up front and Daniel in the back, parked on the street— Harris's street.

For the first time in his life, Daniel could feel the world

in a way he couldn't possibly describe. He knew where to go, what slept inside the house; he felt it stirring behind the wall. His mind calculated with a cold, blade-like precision that he had never had before. But more than even that, he *wanted*. And only one thing could sate him.

"That one."

He tipped his head to the modest home on the corner of the street. He glanced at his watch—a little after three in the morning. Just like when he'd checked it the minute before, and the minute before that.

His hands shook in anticipation or fear—he wasn't sure which. They felt cold, stiff. He opened and closed them in a fist, trying to work the tension out. It didn't help.

Sitting in the cold with the minutes ticking by, the edge in his mind began to dull, and old memories trickled in. He blinked hard and tried to grab at the strands as they unraveled, tried to push from the driver's seat and allow the visitor to take over, to pull the wolfskin on again. He desperately needed someone else to be in control.

"Keep your fucking pants on back there, Dan," Greg said without peeling his eyes from the house. "We're just going to have a sit here." He held a pair of binoculars up to his eyes. Maker remained silent.

Daniel tried to keep quiet. He squeezed his hands together between his knees. But something kept nagging at Daniel, scratching at the back of his mind, repeating itself over and over again:

I had to nail the window shut.

That's what Jim had said. Why the hell that thought was lurking there, he didn't know, but it kept coming back. They were going to fish Ben out, but he couldn't come through the window—was that it? Greg and Maker seemed content to try something else.

So why the hell is it bothering me?

"There," Greg said with a grunt. "The little son of a bitch is on the move."

There was a soft glow inside the room—a nightlight, Daniel guessed. Sam had used one in his room. Shadows crept around inside the room, dancing in the twinkling light. A slender hand slapped up against the window and dragged its thin fingers down the glass.

I had to nail the window shut.

"Now what?" Daniel asked, addressing no one in particular.

"You've been inside the house before, right?" asked Maker. "You sure they don't have a security system?"

"What, like on the window?" Daniel rubbed his head. "No. No, I don't think so. Not when I picked Sam up there last time. Jim doesn't make a lot of money."

I had to nail the window shut.

"Good," Maker said in his flat, professional tone. "Give it a little more time. I want to see if anyone wakes up."

With a shaking voice, Daniel said, "The window is nailed shut. How do you plan to get him out?"

Greg grunted. "Just keep your eyes open, kid. You'll see."

Silence filled the car as Greg returned to the binoculars. Daniel thought about the look in Jim's eyes when he'd told him about the window—desperation. Jim doesn't have much money; he takes his two boys to the park instead of the movies. Ben and Sam played ball together—Jim was the first-base coach.

Oh, my God.

Jim didn't know what to do, didn't know how to fix the situation. Something was wrong with his son, so he nailed the window shut. He couldn't afford a therapist. This was all he had. His son is just like mine. This is just like Sam.

Daniel's hand began to quake again. Was he going to steal a child out of the night? Was he really going kill Jim's son?

Am I some kind of fucking monster?

He tried to stifle the thought, but more came, quicker than he could possibly choke them back. What's going to happen to Jim?

Would he kill himself?

Daniel had to force his mouth shut as those thoughts played out. If he said anything, he might break down, and he couldn't let that happen. He had a job to do. Even as the minutes ticked by, he couldn't shake the memory of the look in Jim's eyes, that same look he once saw in the mirror. That same look he had when Sam was dying.

"Thirty minutes in," Maker said. "No movement. I think we're good."

They're going to get Ben. They're going to fucking kill Ben.

"You sit here, Dan," Greg said as he pulled the binoculars down and gripped the door handle.

"No," Maker said. "We need this quick and quiet. Are you good?" He turned back to lock eyes with Daniel.

"What?" he asked meekly.

"Are. You. Good?"

Just like Sam. No. They killed Sam.

"Yeah." Daniel croaked.

"The first one you saw looked weak." Maker's gaze drew Daniel in, locking him into place. "But they're not. They're vicious. They can be tricked, fooled, but they can also rip you open if you give them a chance. It's going to fuck with your mind. Make you see things that aren't there. There's no cure for that but exposure. Keep that in mind. Fight it. Don't be stupid."

"How are we going to get him out, though?"

"The father told you he likes fucking with animals, yeah?" Greg asked with an almost-proud smirk. "I've got a couple of dead rabbits in the back. Going to let that stink get in the air, entice him out. They're fast, vicious motherfuckers. We're going to have to distract the little son of a bitch. Keeping him quiet out here will be the hard part. Greg's going to get close to the window, spill a little rabbit blood, and heat it up." Maker looked behind him and pointed at a bend in the road. "We're going to take the car back there, behind the tree line. We'll coax it, trap it. You just keep your eyes open, and do exactly what we tell you to."

It began. Greg stepped out of the car and retrieved a large duffle bag from the trunk, along with a thick leather jacket that he put on and zipped up, with gloves to match. Maker turned the car around and parked it behind the trees —there was no line of sight now, and nothing to see them, either. Maker killed the engine and stepped out silently. Daniel followed instinctively.

It was hard to see anything in the dark; each shadow seemed to loom and threaten. Greg strolled up, the bag hoisted over his thick shoulder.

Greg leaned over and unzipped the heavy bag and did something just out of Daniel's view. Maker nudged him, and he nearly jumped—the tension of the hunt was thick.

"Here."

Maker handed Daniel the binoculars. Though it was difficult in the low light, Daniel brought them up just long enough to see Greg's hand emerge from the bag with a bloody rabbit. He wiped his bloodied fingers on his jeans and moved behind a tree not far from them. Greg seemed thrilled—giddy even.

"Keep your eyes on the window," Maker told him. "I want you to learn from this. See how they move, walk, and breathe. You get good enough, and you'll be able to spot one in a crowd."

The nightlight twinkled in the bedroom, and a minute or more drained from the night. Daniel felt his heart beating in his throat, choking each breath. Short, shallow sips of air were enough to keep him calm.

There, in the window, four slender fingers came into view again, sliding up and down the glass. A face rose into view, with shadows slipping down his face from the nightlight at his back.

A boy's face.

Did he look so different from any other boy? No—he looked like any out of a hundred or a thousand other kids. Was he a monster?

The boy's shaggy hair swayed as he turned his head, looking around his own room before he turned back to the window and pressed his face to it. His face squished against the glass and he studied the darkness.

Fuck, he sees us.

Daniel stopped breathing and his body stopped shaking. But the boy's gaze flickered by.

Thank God . . .

The boy put his palms on the window and tried to push it up, but it wouldn't budge.

"How's he going to get out?" Daniel whispered, his lungs just now letting in air. "If he breaks the window, Jim will hear."

"They're cunning in their own way, Daniel. Just watch."

It pushed and strained with its thin arms, but still the window wouldn't go up. It gave up and inspected the window more closely. Reaching up for the top of the windowsill, it brought its head to the corner. It paused, then drew its face up, slowly at first, and then with a sudden jerk.

What the fuck is he doing?

With so little light in the room, Daniel could only see it turn to the other corner and press its head to it, again rising slowly and finishing with another sudden jerk. Something glinted in the spinning nightlight.

He's prying the nails out with his fucking teeth!

The boy spat the nail out and went back to pushing the window up, this time with ease. He only looked back for a moment to see if he had been heard. Content, he slinked out the window with a sense of balance and quickness that no child could possibly have, jumping out and landing like an ape, walking forward with its hands hanging low and brushing the ground, intent on being silent.

Daniel licked his parched lips and whispered, "He's out."

"Greg's going to draw him over and snatch him up. You just be ready." Maker opened his jacket and slid a knife out of a sheath on his hip.

After snapping his head left and right, the boy crept to the blood-smeared ground and dipped his fingers into it without hesitation. He brought his thin, red fingers to his nose, sniffing and enjoying the scent before licking them clean. With one look back toward the open window, he stalked along the bloody trail.

"They're cunning," Maker whispered. "But they're greedy."

Daniel's grip tightened on the binoculars hard enough that his fingers hurt. He watched as the boy stopped by the rabbit. Still crouched like some wild beast, the boy picked up the carcass and let the blood run down his hand. He rubbed it between his fingers and found the wound in the rabbit's side, a small hole where Greg had shot it. The boy sunk a finger into the wound and pulled out a bloody chunk, smiling from ear to ear.

A chill rose up Daniel's back as the boy dug more fingers into the wound, tearing it open with morbid glee. He twisted the rabbit's neck and pulled at its ears before dipping his fingers into the wound again, enjoying the hole he had opened. Daniel imagined the snapping noise the neck would have made when it twisted and tore the skin. He could almost hear the bird from his dreams cracking its wing.

The boy dug his fingernails into the rabbit's eye. Daniel pulled away as his stomach turned, threatening to spill his lunch.

"Get your eyes back on it, dammit. Hold it together," Maker said through gritted teeth.

Looking again, he saw its greasy fingers squeeze an eye until it popped with a burst of milky juice. A bloody fist smashed against the rabbit's soft ribs while the boy sat, amused by how the small bones broke.

The boy's head snapped up just as something rustled off in the weeds. Something in the trees moaned like a wounded animal—a frightened, tortured moan that seemed to set the boy ablaze.

With a sudden burst of speed, the boy skittered toward the sound, only stopping a few feet short of the trees, his instincts judging the danger against the hunger that drove it.

"It'll bite. They always do. They're greedy," Maker whispered. "Get ready to move. As soon as it passes the tree, get the car and I'll help Greg."

"No," Daniel shot back as he put the binoculars down. "I need to go there. I need to see it."

Maker hesitated. "Fine. When he makes his move, go quick. This one feeds on pain, maybe even its own. Be careful, and as silent as the grave."

Two dogs pulled inside Daniel, one of fear and the

other of anticipation; one wishing to cower, the other wanting a taste of blood. He didn't want to go, but he needed to.

The boy's hunger won over and he jolted forward. There was no choice now. Daniel was up, following as quietly and quickly as his feet allowed. Rounding a corner, he pressed his back against a wide tree and glanced around it as carefully as he could.

Shit!

Daniel sank back when the boy looked in his direction. After a few choked breaths, Daniel leaned away from the tree to peek again. The boy was already fixed on another rabbit, this one was also slick with blood.

Where the hell is Greg?

Bending down and grabbing the rabbit's head, the boy scratched its eye and played with what leaked from it. He snorted a laugh and smashed his hand against the rabbit's head and body, once, twice.

Thump-thump.

Like steam hissing from a kettle, he fell back onto the grass and put his hand up to his face. Black blood leaked from a gash on his hand as he moaned like a dying cat.

What the fuck is going on?

The rest happened quickly. A thick chain net shot out from the darkness, spreading wide and falling on the boy, pinning him to the ground.

"Couldn't help yourself, could you?" Greg jeered as he stepped out from the dark. "You knew we were looking for you. Saw it all yourself. But you were still so fucking stupid. You had to go for it, didn't you?"

Pain turned to anger as the boy thrashed beneath the net, but each bit of movement weighed him down more. Smoke rose from where the metal touched bare skin. He struggled to get one sizzling hand out from beneath the chain and onto the grass.

Greg strode over and stomped a heavy boot down onto the hand. It hissed in pain as the small bones crunched and wounds flared open under the chains.

"Is that . . ." Daniel said, finally stepping forward.

"You made it too easy," Greg said and stifled a laugh as the boy whined. The boy locked eyes with Daniel and tried to speak but could only whimper. There was no monster, only a boy with wet eyes and a trembling chin, bleeding and broken.

"Help . . ." The boy managed.

He looks just like Sam.

Stinging memories poured into Daniel's mind like water. T-ball games with Sam and Ben, the beers with Jim. They were hurting Sam's friend, Jim's son. This wasn't a monster. This was a boy. This was someone's son. Overwhelming guilt wrapped around Daniel's chest and made it hard to breath.

But Greg smiled. The son of a bitch was enjoying it.

"Smooth as silk, right?" Greg stepped off the boy. "Help me grab the little fucker. Have to do this fast."

"Fuck you!" Daniel closed in and shoved Greg.

"Hey!" Greg said in a muted tone. "Keep your fucking voice down. What the hell's a matter with you?"

"You didn't fucking tell me anything! You and Maker, you didn't tell me shit! We have to . . ." Daniel's gaze was drawn down to the boy's eyes, the boy who looked just like the one who had played on Sam's T-ball team. There was still that slick red blood on his fingers, but his eyes—a child's eyes—were filled with doubt and fear. He was terrified.

Oh God, I can't do this. I can't hurt that kid.

"You're fucking useless," Greg hissed at him. "Go get in the car."

"We can't . . . we can't hurt him. We have to do something else."

This isn't a hunt. This isn't a creature. This is Sam. Oh God, Jim. Jim, I'm so sorry.

Maker grabbed the back of Daniel's arm and squeezed. "Go get in the car."

Maker let go, and Daniel turned around, stumbling like a drunk, his head swirling as he got into the car.

His body shook and begged him not to look back, but his instincts made him turn back. He saw them wrap the boy up in chains, saw Greg pick him up with ease and dump him into the open trunk of the car. Maker pulled on a pair of gloves and picked the dead rabbit up from the ground. He threw the wet mess in the back with the changeling. Then he reached to where the rabbit had been and pulled up a metal spike.

What the hell am I doing? This isn't me. I'm not a killer. I can't do this.

Everyone got in the car and pulled silently away, no lights or sounds in the neighborhood to trouble them. There wasn't as much as a shuffle in the trunk.

Daniel took in a breath as though he was about to say something, but Greg spoke without even looking back.

"You keep your fucking mouth shut."

I've got to stop the car. I've got to let him out.

Daniel clenched his jaw so much that it hurt. He wanted to scream. He wanted to help the dying boy in the trunk.

No. It's getting to me. It's the thing.

"Keep it together, Daniel," Maker said, his gaze meeting Daniel's in the rearview mirror. "It's in your head."

It is. It's toying with me. It's inside my mind, like they told me it would. But, God, I can't help it. It looked so much like Sam.

Daniel clenched his eyes shut as hard as he could and bit into the meat of his hand. The pain was sharp, but it helped him focus.

It was several long moments before he could feel it moving—the searching fingers of the creature in the back, reaching out to press into his mind. And though Daniel had nothing to see, only feel, he could sense its shape: long black tendrils with hooking tips that squirmed into his soul. It weaved into his mind and pulled up more memories, and the emotions tied to them.

His teeth cut skin and blood filled his mouth.

15

THE STENCH OF SIZZLING FLESH CREPT FROM THE TRUNK AND clawed into Daniel's nose. He imagined the way Iron burned, and how the blisters on the changelings' skin popped open with a festering smell. He rolled down the window and sucked in fresh air. Greg snorted a laugh.

The creature, which had been silent for nearly the entire ride, suddenly kicked at the back of the seat.

Thump.

A shrill, pained laugh erupted from the trunk—maddening laughter—that stopped only long enough for the boy to breath and start again.

"Motherfucker!" Greg said. "Rebekah was right—this is a strong one. Let's get it home a little faster, eh?" Maker agreed and sped up.

The jackal-like laughter, which might drive them all insane, seemed to grow louder with each passing minute. Greg's face flushed and burned with anger, and Daniel was sure that if Greg had his way, he would pull the car over and stomp its head in until there was nothing left to laugh.

When they pulled onto their gravel lot, Daniel was

happy for the isolation. Greg opened the trunk, and the creature's laughter surged with new vigor as they pulled it out and dragged it across the yard. It howled with laughter, even as its face sizzled beneath the iron chain, howling even as its head bounced down the wooden steps.

Greg locked its limbs down with spiked iron rods and thick shackles. When they pulled the burning net away, pieces of flesh tugged off like a snake shedding skin, exposing pink flesh beneath it. The boy let out a yelp of pain before laughing again.

But he was no boy—that was clear now. Its wicked eyes had become pools of red under yellow, webbed veins. Its teeth were broken shards, decayed with black rot. The iron had done its job in unmasking him.

Now the thing cackled and thrashed in the basement, enjoying every moment of its own torment. Even sharp blades did nothing to quiet him.

Oily puss oozed from its open wounds and released a stench that choked the air and crawled up the walls. Daniel buckled over and gagged, struggling not to throw up.

There was no disguise now, no intrusions into Daniel's mind. This thing, that looked like a boy just hours before, was changing. Snapping and cracking limbs protruded like spider-legs before Daniel's eyes.

Impossible.

But it wasn't. This was something Daniel could believe in, a thing from old days that hunted the woods for the taste of man, a thing of nightmares.

"Lord, be with us! Lord, help us!" Jenna shouted over the noise.

"Be with us!" the creature screamed between fits of hysteria, thrashing its chains again the metal bedposts. "Lord help us!" it mocked.

"Shut your damn mouth or I'll cleave your fucking skull in!" Greg threatened and gave it a taste of the back of his hand.

It quieted, but only long enough to spit a shard of tooth. It laughed even harder, beginning with a single, loud howl. Barely able to hold the creature, Greg grabbed the axe that leaned against the wall. Maker stopped him.

"Laugh all you want!" Maker bellowed over the creature's hooting. "You're ours!"

"I'm yours! Ha-ha!" it laughed, straining forward against its chains. "Lord, help us!" It mocked again when it saw Jenna praying. "You're ours!"

"Daniel, get Rebekah," Maker said as he sneered at the creature.

Daniel froze in place, unable to enforce his will on his body. The creature held him fixed, this abomination, here, in the world of men. This thing that enjoyed being cut and threatened.

This ate Sam.

He didn't have the anger he thought he would, the anger he felt before. Now, only terror filled him, or something more—the mockery of a cruel world, an insane world. This was insanity; this was reality.

And he couldn't move.

"Daniel! Dammit!" Maker turned around and shoved his arm, but he stayed frozen and fixed.

The hysteria quieted, save for Jenna's prayers, as the monster stopped shaking its chains. It whipped its head around to look at Daniel, and its glaring red eyes found that weakness in him that it could manipulate. Its forked tongue licked out across its face to catch a drip of its own blackened blood, its awful grin unceasing.

"You must be new here."

Heavy hands shook Daniel's shoulder before ripping him back and throwing him to the floor. Greg stepped over him just as the creature began to shout with laughter again.

"Get the fuck out of here! Go get Rebekah, goddammit!"

Daniel was on his feet and rushing up the wooden stairs. His head spun and his body threatened to collapse, but he kept himself up.

Not this time. Not this time.

He swore the madness wouldn't take him. The gripping pangs of lunacy slashed at him, but he wouldn't let it control him or break him. Not again. Not ever again. But all the swearing put little strength in his knees, little courage in his soul.

Get Rebekah. Focus on that.

The howling laughter followed him up the stairs and through the house. Like a drunk, he stumbled down the hall and fell against Rebekah's door, finally trying the handle, nearly crashing through it with his weight.

"You lunatic," Rebekah said while pulling a jacket on. "I had only just buttoned my shirt."

Daniel huffed. "Maker . . ."

"Yes, Larry needs me. I am well aware." She held out her arm as she picked up her bag with the other. "Quickly, now. I am still a bit under the weather."

Daniel took one more deep breath and grabbed at her arm, then tried to hurry her down the hallway.

"Careful now! No need to rip my arm off!"

"Yeah, yeah."

"My God, man, you seem like you're about to have a heart attack. You act like you've never seen a demon. Well, I've been inside your dreams and I know that isn't true."

Daniel nodded, but could say nothing. The howling from the basement pierced through the floorboards.

"Maker is worried that our chains might not be enough for this one's mind," Rebekah said as they hobbled to the basement. "We've seen those of its ilk before. We need to pierce it and let the air out. I was in its mind before—it is a strong one."

Daniel nodded and sucked in another breath.

"No, Daniel. *We* must do it. I'm so sorry, I didn't know. I couldn't prepare you." Her fingers tightly gripped his arm. "You must go with me into the madness."

THE BOTTLE of prescription medication had been sitting on Rebekah's nightstand for the past several days, undisturbed and gathering dust. She always had to forgo taking the pills after reaching out through the dreams. There was once a time she'd tried to take them directly after a dream, but all it did was delay the inevitable. They always came right back, and worse, if they had been denied.

Some things just need to smolder.

Still, it had always left her weakened, physically drained. *Hollow.*

That was how she'd describe it to others: hollow. Empty. Other emotions would sometimes fill the void. She'd been through it before and knew what to expect—her soul had become calloused.

But Larry hated seeing her weakened like that or at least, he was courteous enough to pretend to. Her ability was an asset, after all. And assets must be used.

"This is why I hate it. You look like you've aged ten years," he said.

"Larry, you know it's rude to address a woman's looks like that." She waved him off. "Go now. I need rest."

He left her, on to more important business, of course—things that needed killing. She felt something for Larry. In another time, and in another life, she might have called it love. Neither of them had room for love now.

Lying on her bed and content to let the dreams take her, she let that flicker of love burn a moment before she snuffed it.

Focus. Get better.

Some years back, she'd read that sleeping is the brain's way of cleaning up a mess, disposing of chemical waste. It wasn't hard to imagine it worked in the other world too, and she certainly had waste to dispose of. The thick, plaguing stems of hate that the changeling had left in her mind needed to be cleansed, need to be torn up at the root, and the only cure she'd ever found was sleep. But the roots stretched deep, and oh, the things they dragged with them when uprooted!

What horrors would the dreams hold this night? What pain and misery would slip across her mind? She didn't know, and she couldn't predict or evade it, only endure.

Sleep wasn't long in coming. Larry, Daniel, and Greg had all gone out on the hunt. There was little she could do but rest and prepare.

With her head on the soft pillow and a flickering candle for company, the hand of dreams took her. She was herself no more, but another.

She floated and moved; for how long, she didn't know. Without willing it so, she reached out to the minds of New Athens and played across them, joining with dreams as guest or intruder. She wouldn't remember them all—she never did—but some of the dreams were kind to her, inviting her in to experience their lives. Others revealed the horrors that plagued them; she was happy to forget those.

But then, there were the hateful roots of the changeling, slurping through the canals of her dreams. They lashed at her and drew her back in. Leeching onto the nightmares that Rebekah had pressed into the recesses of her mind, it squeezed until the juice pulped out and flowed over her like rotten fruit.

"No!" Rebekah shuddered as a new wash of misery overcame her.

Her brother. Death. Things cutting at his skin. Misery. He's lost. Confusion. What's happening? Desperation. Uselessness. Fault. Hollow.

Hollow.

Old memories, feelings that filled and drained her simultaneously. Some weren't true in the real world, but in dreams there was no truth or fiction—only *was* and *is*. She didn't know what happened to her brother in the waking world, but here she did. Here, he died a thousand times, and so did she. But she also lived. Lived forever. That was the most horrible.

Did it go on for hours? Days? When she wakes, she might guess how long she slept, but minutes and hours had no meaning here.

A light burned, throwing back the shrieking dark and the diseased roots of the changeling. It surged and touched everything, and then it spoke, without words but in feeling.

This was something she'd never seen before in her dreams. Rebekah quaked before it, and then she was not there to witness but there to speak, to voice and to listen. Her entire being—the waking and the dreaming self—joined. A great fire burned: In the flames, she heard what was to come. As she spoke, the light took the shape of visions of what will or may be.

A shallow pit was shown to her, a hole in this world that

led to lands beyond—the birthing grounds of monsters—from which hooked talons and insane gibberish spewed. Pale fingers reached from it and pulled.

Another vision followed. Five lights came together and went out, one by one, until only the brightest remained. She knew each of those lights by name and knew what they could do. Then came the truth of what was to come or may be, and she knew.

Roaring howls awoke her. The fog and haze of awakening from dreams came like a thief and took the details of the vision, leaving only feeling and direction. The mist returned, but she didn't fear it. Everything was as it should be. Her body groaned as she pulled on her clothes, preparing for the war to come. She filled a small bag with her tape player, candles, and the other tools of her trade.

It wasn't long until she heard footsteps stumbling down the hallway. Daniel burst through the door.

"You lunatic," she hissed.

16

Rebekah stopped Daniel and forced eye contact with him. "I had a vision and I know what must come. The Iron chain around its neck, it won't work this time. This one is too strong—he'll still be connected to his brood. I cannot do it on my own. I am weakened. You must go with me."

"What?" Daniel asked. "I can't . . . I don't know how."

"The other world spoke to me, Daniel. I can't explain it to you, but try to understand. In dreams, we know things that we don't know here. I've brought part of it back with me this time, and I know I can bring you with me. I must."

Someone came stomping up the stairs and ripped the door open. "Dammit, Tanner!" Greg shouted. "Why are you moving like you have a broken hip? We need you down there!"

Rebekah turned to him. "A moment, Greg."

"We don't have no fucking moment! We got the Iron on it, but it's not enough. We need to get the fucking chains on this thing!"

"You will wait for as long as we need!" she hissed.

Greg huffed and went back down into the basement, a string of curses following him.

"This won't be like anything you've seen before," Rebekah said to Daniel. "I've had a lifetime to hone myself, to prepare for the mysteries and the oddities of that other world and still, it remains unknown to me. It is a dangerous place; it was horrible for me before, and it'll be worse now. It's ready this time. But you must trust me, and trust yourself. This will change you. You will not be the same person again."

Be the same? That's something long gone.

"All right. I trust you." He tried to mask the tremble in his voice.

"You must follow and listen closely, or you may be lost." Squeezing his hands hard, she leaned in close and whispered, "Daniel. You do not want to be lost there."

"I'll follow you."

"Quickly now, into the basement. There is little time left."

The creature's insane laughter greeted them as they hurried down the steps. Greg was at the bottom of the steps, scowling.

Maker shrugged at them. "The hell is this all about?"

"There is more here than what appears," Rebekah said, still clutching Daniel's arm. "Daniel must go with me into its mind."

"Ha-ha!" The creature laughed in response. Its fangs had grown sharper and longer.

Maker shrugged again. "What the hell are you talking about, Rebekah?"

"Larry," she said, pulling away from Daniel and approaching Maker. "He has to go with me."

"Come on in! Come on in! I've got enough for *eeevery-body*!" the monster hooted.

"Greg, gag that fucking thing, so I can think," Maker said, thumbing toward the creature. "Okay, Rebekah. Okay. I don't know what the fuck you're doing, though, so you better be careful. Both of you."

"We will." She nodded.

Greg picked up a crowbar from the ground and turned the blunt side up. Like a woodsman cutting logs, he cracked it down twice on the creature's face, the first blow quieting it and the second buying them a minute of silence.

"Heh . . . Heh . . ." The creature muttered, even as the skin began to close. Greg grabbed a locking bit and wrapped it around its head.

Jenna grabbed Daniel's hands and head and pulled him close. "Come here, quickly," she said, and began to pray.

The creature continued to slam its cuffs against the metal frames, desperate to create as much chaos as it could to drown out Jenna's whispered prayers.

"We'll need it to be quieter than that," Rebekah said, tipping her head to Greg.

"Hey, I was just waiting for you to say that." Greg grabbed a small plastic tube sitting on top of an old drawer and popped off the top. He dumped a handful of iron shavings into his cupped hand, finally putting fear in the creature's eyes.

"This is going to hurt like a real motherfucker." Greg laughed. The creature groaned and stopped its commotion with the chains. Greg dumped the handful over its nose. It resisted, but Greg held his thick hands over its face, forcing it to breathe the pieces in. It thrashed uselessly before it finally went still, and its eyes rolled back in its head as black tar seeped from its ears.

"That won't hold it for long," Greg said, dusting off his hands. "Better not spend too much time fucking around."

With the beast finally quieted, Jenna laid out several thick quilts and pillows. Rebekah opened her bag and handed the candles to Maker, directing him where to lay them, and then pulled out the tape player.

She handed it to Daniel. "This will sooth you, and help you get to sleep faster. I'm practiced at this, so I'll slip into the dream before you and wait."

Daniel pulled on the headphones and let them rest on his neck. "How can I get there, to be with you?"

"I don't know. But I will, and so will you. This is another world, another state of being. What we know there, we may not know here. I'll find you there and bring you. It won't be easy for you to fall asleep, but be patient, listen to the tape, and try to relax."

Try to relax. Like that's a fucking option right now.

"I'll help you," said Jenna. "I've helped Rebekah before, too. You'll do fine, sweetie. God will be with you. He's always with the good ones."

Rebekah and Daniel both lay flat on the quilts, which were thick enough to be comfortable. The cool air in the basement would help Daniel sleep, but he couldn't slow his breathing.

"Here, try this." Jenna handed him a small white pill and a glass of water. He took it without hesitation, desperate for anything that could help.

"Try to calm down now," Jenna said.

How can I do any of this if I can't control myself? Does any of this ever get easier?

He pulled the headphones on and pressed the plastic play button on the tape deck. A soothing ocean wash came over it with the sounds of seagulls in the background. He felt warm, but not enough to sleep, not enough to push out the thoughts of the monster lying near him.

This is impossible. This is insane. How can I sleep down here? I won't sleep for days . . .

Minutes ticked by as he waited with his eyes closed. He wondered if Rebekah had fallen asleep yet, but didn't want to open his eyes to look. He was exhausted, as he always seemed to be these days, but his chest kept thumping and the questions kept coming.

How long will we be able to hold that thing? What will happen in the dream? How will it change me? God, I hope that pill starts to work soon.

He took deep breaths.

How long has it been? An hour? How long until the battery runs dead on this tape recorder?

He tried to imagine himself with his Sam. He remembered the time it had rained and Sam stayed home from school, sick. It was just the two of them, and Daniel had taught him a new card game.

That was a good day.

At the time it was fun, but it wasn't until Sam was gone that Daniel would look back at those memories and realize their value. It was a stupid card game, something Daniel used to play, but Sam loved it. He remembered Sam's face, the way he squinted his eyes while he laughed, laughed so hard that he cried.

In Daniel's memory, Sam laughed so loud, so very loud. But was it as loud as Daniel now remembered? Sam's laughter grew to a high-pitched wail as he opened his eyes, and blood drained from the empty sockets. Three-fingered hands reached out from the couch and grabbed Sam, dragging him into its depths.

No. No, this wasn't how it was.

Daniel jumped at the couch and ripped the cushions away, revealing only the dirty springs beneath.

"No, dammit! No, don't take him!"

He got up and looked through the house, his house, the walls stretched and bent as if breathing. Red rain pattered against the windows, leaving oily streaks that spelled words:

Dead. Gone. Kill Yourself.

Daniel went back down to the couch and ripped at it, feeling—*knowing*—that his son was still there. The fabric tore open to an endless well filled with the bodies of demons, each waiting to uncoil into Daniel's house. Sneering faces and glowing eyes came ripping up the walls of the well, threatening to drown Daniel with their sheer numbers. A voice came from behind Daniel:

"I can help you."

But he wanted no help. He wanted only his son. He paid the voice no mind as he struggled against the clawed hands and into the clutch of the demons.

"Daniel. Remember. Remember why you are here." The voice came from everywhere at once.

Rebekah.

He was no longer in a house, but in a place that was no place at all. There was only his voice and her voice.

"Rebekah? Where are we?"

A beautiful girl stepped out of the nothingness. Her skin was smooth and her hair short. She was young and athletic, not at all like the old woman he knew her to be. Not at all like Rebekah.

"Inside your mind, Daniel. Only your mind could have been so vicious," she said. "Our own thoughts are always the worst."

"I thought it was real. . ."

"And it was. It was real. Everything here is real, and it can kill you just the same."

He knew that, too. He knew this world—he'd been here before.

"Then we're off to find the changeling and disconnect it from the brood?"

How strange that had sounded before, how alien. Now he understood it. Now it all made sense. Everything made sense here.

"Yes, follow me," she said.

He wanted to turn, to follow her, but he felt another presence nearby that sucked in the world around him. It grated on him, angered him, to know that it was close, that it was watching, that it was whispering to him.

"That." Daniel pointed at a man-shaped thing that sat hugging its legs and sobbing, a pool of tears streaking down its arms. "He is me, isn't he?"

"Yes, Daniel. He is you. But quickly, we must go."

A cold thought came to Daniel.

"How do I kill him?"

REBEKAH WAS THERE only minutes before Daniel. She didn't know how much time had passed in the waking world, but time had no meaning here. The moment she saw him, she wanted to leave. His mind was broken, bleeding, painful to be around, with its jagged edges that cut when her mind reached out to it.

She had no interest in him, but she had to remember.

There was something, wasn't there? Something I had to do.

And then there was the sweet voice again: "Remember, Rebekah. Remember that you are there for him and he for you. Remember who you are and what you do. Remember."

It was always such a struggle to remember her purpose when she was here. Why should she force such pain on herself when she could just sleep here forever?

Duty. That is why we torture ourselves. Duty . . . and something more. Hate? Maybe it's hate. Yes, hate. I hate them.

Hate burned stronger than duty. That was something that carried over between worlds, a light that guided the way. Her light was a black torch burning with hate. She looked at Daniel, saw his cruel imagination and the self-inflicted tortures; it felt crowded there when she slipped in.

She watched him stare into that demon-filled pit. And though he might not realize it, she was sure he had a name for each one.

Regret. Conflict. Depression. Suicide.

These were among the names of the many demons she had for her own. Her demons were chained and subdued though, each one neatly contained in its own room, with only infrequent troubles arising. But Daniel's were left to run amok and abuse him at their whim.

She said what was needed to remind him why they were there. They were there for duty, for hate. But Daniel seemed to hate only himself.

After she had finally talked him into pulling away, his mind took one more gambit to torment him, and Daniel found another side of himself. One that was crying and broken, even more than he was now; Rebekah could taste that much.

Daniel said, "That. He is me, isn't he?"

"Yes, Daniel. He is you. But quickly, we must go."

Rebekah felt as if the darkness around her took a breath. "How do I kill him?"

Daniel knew how—she was sure of it. He was seeking permission. Here, nothing imagined was impossible if you had the will to power it. But, like a child with matches and a fascination with fire, Daniel didn't know the effects of the forces he could manipulate.

"No, Daniel. We can't do that. You don't know what it could do to you."

"Yes, I do," he said, his eyes burning hot. "I know exactly what it'll do."

The world faded to black and all that existed was the choice. Rebekah watched as Daniel glared at his weakness. She could try to stop him, pit her mind against his and force him to stop, but she wasn't here for that. She needed him, and he needed her. She couldn't weaken herself now.

"Give me time, Daniel, and I'll show you how to build the best of cages in your mind, how to take control but not lose yourself in the process."

Carelessly, he grabbed the weakness by the chin and lifted its face. It had no eyes or mouth, only a blank slate that leaked tears from the pores of its skin. It quaked, ready to crumble into nothing and give up the ghost.

Daniel's hand held a blade then—a sharp thing with a razor's edge, perfect for cutting the soul. It was slick with blood—such was the reality and wanting of this world. It bled because it anticipated bleeding. It desired it. The pathetic, faceless thing splayed on the floor waited without resistance.

"Cut pieces off yourself, Daniel, and you'll never be whole again," she warned. "Look at it—it's not just your fears. It's your love for Sam, your memories of him. It's what weakens you, what holds you back. But it can fuel you, too, Daniel. Cut that love away, and you'll lose him forever. And then what?"

"Then I'll finish this."

The blade rose quickly, slinging blood, and sank into the blank face. A mouth ripped open and moaned in pain. Daniel's blade rose and fell, again and again, cutting new pits into the face. His hand, mad with fury, clenched at its throat, intent on ripping the pain and sorrow from his mind.

He'll leave himself an emotionless killer.

Rebekah raised her hand and bricks snapped into place between Daniel and his target, forming a cage of brick and mortar.

"What the hell are you doing?" Daniel turned to her, his face that of a beast, with fangs and yellow eyes.

"I'm giving you a chance, Daniel. It's caged now. Its weakened, but it still breathes. Come with me, and when everything is finished, if you still desire it, I'll rip the walls down."

His voice boomed, raking her like claws. "You will do it now, or I'll kill you!"

His threats were hollow. Her mind may have been weakened, wounded from the blooding of the creature several nights before, but those things are native to this realm, and Daniel was still only an inexperienced visitor. She was more than strong enough to subdue him and break him if necessary, but that would only weaken them both.

"Look at what you have become, Daniel. Is this what you want to be? Is this how you honor your son? By being like the things that killed him?"

As subtly as she could, she reached into the winds and grabbed Daniel's thoughts of Sam. She pressed them into Daniel's mind, and he bowed his head.

"You're right," he said. He looked at the cage, a faint sobbing noise coming through it. "I'll leave it here, walled inside. Later, we'll decide what to do."

"Yes, Daniel, that is wise."

They'd be back here one day. She hoped she could stop him from becoming a monster then, too.

I know what stirs in the belly of that man. And I know it's something to be afraid of.

17

WITH EACH STEP, HE CHANGED. COILS OF MUSCLE WRAPPED farther up his arms. He became a thing that could hunt and kill and eat the dead, with only the softest of voices to quell the hunger.

He became the wolf.

Daniel stalked forward—not a smooth glide like Rebekah's, but the brutish movements of a predator on a warpath.

"Be careful, Daniel," Rebekah said, swimming through the air. "I dealt with this creature before, but it's ready for us now. It's very dangerous. We must cut it from its brood."

And then, they were inside its mind. They knew it well, as if they had crossed some border into enemy lands, past heraldry flags identifying it—such was the tone and color of it. The deeper they pressed, the stronger the changeling's mind pressed back. Like a cloud that swallowed him, Daniel felt the reins of power lifting. The control he felt was gone, given to another to be used against him.

They stepped into the valley between tall, looming mountains that penetrated the sky, rising higher than anything natural could. The shadows at the edges of the rock took the forms of men, and an insane gibbering echoed as they bled in and out of one another.

Claws ripped painlessly through the flesh of Daniel's fingertips, sprouting for want of the beasts.

"There," said Rebekah.

Unconcerned with the echoes, she glided to the base of a mountain. She came to a small cottage, no bigger than a single room, with a stone chimney that spewed black, choking smoke into the sky.

"Follow me, Daniel."

The house squirmed, stretching up and down with living breath. The windows were smashed in and the smell of burnt flesh seeped out. A battered door opened as they neared, welcoming them inside.

"The creature plays games. Its reality is our lie—our truth is the only truth. Be mindful of that, and be willing to make it so." Rebekah moved in without hesitation.

The inside opened into a maze of stairs and corridors that snaked off in different directions.

"How do you know where we're going?" Daniel asked as Rebekah moved to take the first left.

"I can feel it, Daniel," she said. "In time, you will, too. You have to reach out and feel with your mind. This is all a lie, meant to confuse you. I insist I know the way."

He felt the *knowing* of everything in his mind, the instinctual knowledge of the world. But he wasn't strong enough to resist the reins of the changeling's mind, reins that clouded his control and pressed the creature's will against his own. He could only follow, and he did so quietly.

They weaved through the cold, wooden tunnels, the labyrinth of unending darkness that Daniel could somehow pierce with his will. Rebekah never looked back and only occasionally, reached out to rub her fingers against the rough, stony walls. Rebekah and Daniel pressed on until the narrow tunnels unloaded to the heart of the cottage, a large room of rock, carved with ancient words that he couldn't read but understood all the same: threats and warnings, words of disgust and blasphemous names, words of power.

And there, in the center of it all, were large cords, thick as men, that jutted out of the ceiling and into the floor. They pulsed, as if sending blood to a beating heart.

"There." Rebekah slowed her glide as her feet met the ground. "That's what connects it to the brood."

"Then let's rip it out."

Rebekah hesitated. "Don't you feel it, Daniel? It's watching."

It came, crawling on all fours, wearing shadows like a cloak, its body long and thin, and its head a shaggy mess of hair with twisted horns stretching out. Only its glowing, silver eyes pierced the dark.

"You've come again! Such interesting visitors," it said in a purring voice. "Welcome. Won't you stay?"

Daniel saw the two eyes turn into six as the changeling broke into a fit of laughter, joined by the shadows stretching off the wall and becoming whole.

But where fear once nestled in Daniel, there was now only his animal side, the part that children are taught from a young age to hide and cage, only to reveal itself in fits of rage and fury. Only the crazed and insane let that part of themselves out, only monsters indulged.

I'll kill them all.

The beast took root and Daniel was the intruder, intent on taking from another. He was the monster.

"Come out here, you son of a bitch!" Daniel challenged. "I'll kill you!"

The silver gaze of the changeling followed Daniel as the creature crept forward, the persistent coat of shadows following it.

"It was a mistake to come here," it said, standing up on its hind legs to make itself taller and flaunt the curved horns atop its head. It stepped from the darkness to reveal lidless eyes and black-green skin.

"I'm going to keep you."

THE HEAT RADIATING off Daniel made it difficult for Rebekah to focus.

No wonder they found us so quickly. His hate burns like a signal flare.

Daniel's body was unconsciously transforming into something neither human nor beast. Pounds of muscle and mats of hair erupted from Daniel's arms, engulfing his skin, and his eyes had narrowed to yellow, cat-like slits. He was more beast than man now.

It wasn't that Daniel was a lunatic or a monster on the inside—she knew better. It's that they all were. Everyone. Under the right circumstances, anyone could fall into that ancestral barbarism. But Daniel did this to himself when he started cutting off pieces of himself.

Was this why I needed to bring Daniel? So he could become this, and face the enemy? What have I done to him?

"I'm going to keep you."

Her focus came back just long enough to hear the changeling's threat. Its shadow-men, rippling things that bent and swayed like scarecrows in the wind, stalked forward.

"Go, Daniel." Rebekah said and pulled a torch from the

ground, her will making it true, and its fiery glow pushing the shadows back. "I'll hold them. You cut the strands and let's be gone."

"He doesn't want to go," one of the shadow-men whispered through the wind. "He wants to play with us," another said with the same voice. It tested itself against the flame's glow, and drew back burned fingers.

"Yes," the changeling said as it stalked at the edges of the flame, its shadows pushing against the light in an unnatural struggle. "He wants to be here. Don't you?"

"Don't listen, Daniel!" Rebekah said. She held the flame even higher and strained to stay focused. "They'll toy with you! I can hold them, but you must go quickly!"

With a grunt, Daniel turned and moved to the strands, ready to rip them from the ground without a word, but the changeling spoke again.

"Did we kill one of yours?" Its piercing, silver eyes focused on Daniel, the flames dancing within it. "Tell me which one was yours, and I'll tell you if he screamed. I'll tell you how much we hurt him."

The hate bubbled over.

Oh no.

With feet pounding against stone and an echoing roar Daniel tore past the edge of the flame's light and met the eager and gibbering shadow-men.

A snap in her focus caused the flames to dim. Something burst from the floor, like a man of clay, with a doleful face pained by its own existence. It stretched up and grabbed her from the air. The room itself was now an enemy.

She could spare only one last glance at Daniel, who was lashing at the enemies dancing around him. Molding arms latched around her and reached for her mouth. She tried to scream, but it filled her mouth and seeped down her throat.

No!

She yelled inside, feeling her strength wane. She dug her fingers into the arm reaching down her throat and pulled it loose with a wet snap, throwing it at the ground, only to watch it squirm back to the base of the clay. The clay man reached up for the flame and tried to snuff it out with its body.

Craning her neck, Rebekah saw Daniel tearing at a shadow, ripping his hand through it and throwing black stew against the wall. The changeling howled with laughter.

"Daniel!" she yelled. "Burn them! Burn the shadows!"

She heard a pained moan, and then the clay man shoved its hand into the flame, choking it out, sending the room into darkness. Rebekah felt the rest of it tighten against her and topple to the ground, slamming her against the rock and choking the life from her. She was surprised at how strong this changeling had become; it was unlike any she had seen before.

"Daniel!" She looked toward him once again. "Burn them, Daniel! Burn them!"

She wasn't sure if he heard, and she was growing weak beneath the clay. She felt her bones threatening to snap.

The flames began to catch against the stone ground as if it were dry grass. Daniel was in the center of it. His hate was an inferno that consumed the shadows, burning everything, and snared the changeling like ropes.

The flames didn't stop. They stretched farther up, and the clay man, squealing, threatened to take Rebekah down with him. Her bare skin felt pain more intense than she'd ever experienced in the dream world.

"Daniel!" she yelled as the clay man melted and hardened around her. "Enough!"

But Daniel didn't hear her. His claws were wrapped around the changeling's throat and he screamed as it burned to a husk, even as the flames burned his own skin and turned it a charred black. His hate consumed him.

No. No, not like this!

"Stop it! Stop it!"

The changeling's arms were swinging wildly, looking for something to grab, something to climb to escape the flame, but finding nothing. Daniel wouldn't stop. Rebekah felt it— he was enjoying it too much.

No! No, it can't end like this! We can't be lost here inside its mind! We can't die here!

As the flames climbed Rebekah's leg, she sent her mind out to the wall beyond this thing and into Daniel. With hammer and sledge, she pounded against the brick and concrete cage until it cracked. The weakness inside bellowed and rose to the hole, sticking its white, bleeding hand out and pouring its sorrow and pain back onto Daniel.

Rebekah began to fade. This was how she would die. But she always wanted that, didn't she?

Didn't I always hope it would end?

18

THE FIRE, A MANIFESTATION OF DANIEL'S HATE FOR THE world and everything in it, burned hot. Madness fueled the flames with a desire to burn everything, including himself. But the faceless torment, jutting its hand through the cracks of the brick cage, touched Daniel's mind and dragged him out of his raging inferno.

The chills of doubt, sorrow, and fear ran their fingers up his back and across his neck—still less than what they were, but enough for him to find focus.

Oh my God, what did I do?

He looked around and saw the once-surging veins of the changeling's hive-mind burned to cinders and collapsing. The husk of the changeling itself was curled into a ball and the jackals were only a memory. The world shifted around him, and the changeling, with no power to hold its domain, let it crumble into pieces.

An old woman lay where Rebekah had fallen—a broken, burned body that looked unable to stand or breathe. There was only a dying light there, quieting more with each passing second.

Is she dead?

"Rebekah? I'm sorry, I'm so sorry."

Exposed red muscle peeked from beneath the charred skin that stretched to her face. There was no movement, and her mind only faintly stirred.

"Rebekah, don't leave. I'm so sorry." He clutched her hand. "It's not time for you."

His untrained mind reached for hers and entered, tracing through the canals and locked rooms; even in the throes of death, she kept part of herself locked away. Only one room was open: its faded brown door was cracked open and let out a dim light. The door creaked open and he found it empty, save a single glowing candle that was fading. Then there was no more around them, and only the candle existed, growing fainter by the moment. Taking it in his hand, he begged it not to die.

What can I do? How can I save you?

"I'm so sorry. Please don't leave, Rebekah," he pleaded, but still the candle faded. He placed it on the dark floor, which rippled out like water.

In desperation, he reached further and found a room with heavy locks and a door that had not been opened in some time. The locks were popped, and the door was ajar.

Memories and a want of death circled the room. Pictures of her brother lined the walls. Her brother had died young, but these were pictures from her imagination of the kind of man he could have been. He looked like Daniel, had the same eyes and the same hair color.

Desire was there, too—clear in ways the eye couldn't see but the mind could feel. Daniel was the hope she wanted, the one who could fill the void for her. The one thing she had left:

Duty.

It was everywhere, across pictures and through her thoughts and desires, hidden in ways that were becoming clear. It was duty that drove her to keep these things at bay, to save whom she could because only she could.

And she had been the only one, until Daniel arrived.

The room disappeared, and the candle flickered before him once more. "The fight isn't over, Rebekah," he whispered. "Your duty isn't finished. The war continues."

He shared his memories with her, his thoughts and his imagination, opening rooms that had been closed and lost. They mixed together in strange colored patterns. And then he let his mind speak to her. It told her he was weak, that he wasn't strong like her, that he would break, that he was too brittle to bend.

Not all of her wanted to die—only part. He showed her that he would fail, what they would do to him when he did —or worse, what he would do to the others.

"We need you."

That was enough. The candle flickered and began to grow, slowly, until it fully illuminated the stone room. The candle took the form of Rebekah once more.

"You couldn't leave me a moment's peace, could you? I was content with this end."

"No, you weren't," he said with a smirk.

"I suppose I don't like the idea of anything other than myself killing me, even you." She was weak, but her energy was returning. "You hold great power, Daniel, but you're useless to us if you can't control yourself."

It was all burning inside him, this fuel that drove him to hunt and to kill, to want it. But he also knew it would kill him if he wasn't careful.

"You were right to cage that part of me."

"In time, I'll show you how to build a powerful room

for yourself, how to keep everything nice and tucked away in a place where it can breathe and move, but be controlled."

The two moved to the husk of the changeling. It had shriveled to the size of a small child and its burned limbs curled in on each other.

"Is this fucking thing dead?" Daniel asked, nudging it with his foot.

"No, it's not." She reached out and pulled Daniel back. "If it was, there'd be nothing here. It can't possibly take much more, though, so the kicking must cease."

"Well, what is there to do now?"

She stared silently at it. "We meant only to sever it from the hive mind. But, if it's weakened now, we could try to peek further inside, to see what secrets it might hold. But we cannot be sure what we may find."

"Let's do it."

"Now, we will see what tall tales this devil spins." Rebekah pulled all the answers that she could out of the husk. Wounded and damaged, it couldn't defend itself or direct their invasion of its consciousness. She grabbed ahold of its memories and stretched them open.

A pale man, seen through the eyes of the memory, spoke. "Go out there and have fun." His lips were gray and corpse-like, with frizzled, bleached hair to match his white skin. His eyes were black pits, much like the solid colors of the changelings Daniel had seen.

"What the hell is he?" Daniel whispered to Rebekah.

"He? It? Them? I imagine those are the words we would use, as there are no names for a thing like this. Reach out, Daniel. Touch this creature's memory and you will see. There is no name for this pale man."

In the memory, they saw through the changeling's eyes.

A full grin stretched across the pale man's face. "It's time, little one," he said. "Our time. Go now. Feed."

The memories stretched further. Thoughts of the families the changeling had tormented, the night it had taken the child's bed as his own. The most revisited memories popped into Daniel's mind in no particular order or consistency, no cataloging, and spread like flames over an oil-soaked towel—not things simply to be viewed, but participated in. They became a part of him as they slithered down into the trenches of his being.

Teeth. Claws. Blood. Pain. Excitement.

When he saw it come out from under the bed to stare at young Ben Harris, the changeling's surging sense of anticipation formed a hunger in its stomach and now, Daniel's stomach also ached. It forced Daniel to pull away.

Oh God, I can't do it.

He snapped the connection, unable to bear it anymore. He found it hard to draw the line from where these new memories and sensations ended and his own began. "Fuck!" He clutched his mind, trying to squeeze himself together, but found himself pouring out, melting into puddles and blurring with the insides of the monster. He remembered the taste of young Ben Harris. He remembered the squeals the boy made when he died.

It was all he could do to stop it from taking him.

Rebekah didn't pull away. She snuck into it, suffered through it. Daniel knew then why she hated herself, why she wanted death more than anything, why she was so stern and strict and uncaring.

He knew the voices that whispered in her head, and how loud they must be, for he had only a taste, but she drank from it.

REBEKAH DREW in a breath of real air. Her eyes flickered open, and she had to fight not to fall again into the dark embrace of sleep.

"Help . . ." It was all she could manage as she lifted her fingers inches from the ground. Her mind had recovered easily enough from the dream world, but Daniel had done his damage to her here in the waking world.

"For fuck's sake, girl. You were seizing like a son of a bitch there. Thought we might lose you." Greg reached down and grabbed her while Maker scooped her up from the other side.

Gasping and unable to speak, Rebekah searched for Daniel. She found him crumpled against a wall, fighting sleep like her. The changeling was still chained to the bed, but no longer thrashing or resisting. Now, it only hissed in air like its lungs were full of gravel.

"Did you do it?" Maker asked. "Cut the strands?"

Rebekah tipped her chin and flicked her gaze toward Daniel.

Maker shook his head, "He hasn't told us anything. He says he doesn't remember much."

Rebekah tried to nod her head, but her eyes betrayed her and slipped closed. They stayed closed until the sun's rays cut through the blinds.

"Morning." Jenna said with a smile. After she finished opening the blinds, she sat down in her rocking chair. "You were starting to stir again, so I got you up."

Rebekah licked her sore lips. She blinked hard from the light and groaned, "How long?"

"Been three days. Took the Good Lord three days and

three nights to rise, I figured that'd be good enough for you, too."

Rebekah tried to sit up but found an IV in her arm. She glanced at it and then at Jenna.

"You were real exhausted. I was making sure you were getting the good stuff to keep the nightmares away. Best to let the body recover, and then we can see what happens next. You want me to get you something to drink?"

"Nein." Rebekah squeezed her hand into a fist to test her strength. She was drained, but still had work to do. Breathing in the stale air, she spoke with a hoarse voice. "But a cigarette would be nice. And open the window. The smell of that thing is coming up through the floorboards."

Jenna frowned. "How about a glass of water, and then a cigarette?" Without waiting for a reply, Jenna was already out the door. There was no use in arguing with her—she was too stubborn. A short time later, she returned and offered the glass to Rebekah.

"What kind of woman forces her will on a weak patient?" Rebekah intended it to be a joke, but it came out with a snap. She took the glass and drank. The water went down easily.

"The kind that supposes she'd like to keep you around."

"Then give me the cigarette, so I don't kill myself."

Jenna shook her head. She grabbed the cigarettes from the table and handed them to Rebekah. "You've got a mean streak, you do."

Rebekah lit it and took a puff. She closed her eyes as she inhaled and then breathed out a snaking smoke trail.

"How's our fledgling killer? He nearly murdered me."

"Did he, now?" Jenna asked with a raised eyebrow. "He's doing all right. He slept most of a day, but he's been up. He's foggy 'bout it all, don't remember much. He's out with the boys now. How'd he almost kill you?"

Rebekah took another puff. "His mind is wild, and his emotions are out of control. He's a danger to himself and all of us." She lingered.

"But ..."

She snuffed the cigarette and rolled her eyes. "But he's strong, stronger than I ever was. And he's young. And we're all so old and ..."

Her thoughts went to the locked room. She knew now why the changeling had kept the precious thought so tightly locked. She had opened that vault and seen what spilled out.

Jenna, always so calm, waited patiently for Rebekah to find the words.

They don't come back. They never come back.

"Sam." The name creaked out of her dry throat.

"What?" Jenna insisted.

"He's not dead."

Jenna gasped and rose to her feet. "Are you sure?"

"As certain as I can be." Rebekah sighed. "Now you know why I needed this cigarette."

19

THIS WAS A DREAM; DANIEL KNEW IT BY THE WAY THE MIRROR rippled like water when he touched it. He knew it was a dream, but he still had to act in it, still had to play his part. He even had to pretend that it was real. And it was, in its own way.

My dreams have been fucked like this ever since I came out of that monster's head.

"Your dreams have always been fucked like this," his reflection told him.

"No," Daniel said, shaking his head. "They haven't always been this strange."

"Tanner." It called him by his last name like his college friends had. "You're a fucking basket case. You should just kill yourself. Seriously, remember the Glock you have at home? Push that shit to your head and take the pain away. This bullshit is crazy, man. Why put yourself through that?"

"Well, it's a revolver, actually. We thought about the Glock, but went with the revolver instead," Daniel said to his reflection. "But, yeah. I was thinking about doing that, but I still have things to do. I need to help them kill those things."

"You're going to help them kill?" It snorted. "You about fucking murdered Rebekah."

Daniel rubbed his head. "What?" He didn't quite remember that, but there was something there, something fuzzy.

Could I have done that?

"Yeah, you don't remember that? You were going to burn the fucking consciousness out of everyone, even yourself. You're a damn lunatic."

"I don't know." Daniel shook his head. "That doesn't sound like me."

"Of course it doesn't fucking sound like you. It sounds like me." The reflection pointed at itself. "We're two sides of a coin, but it's still one fucking coin. Shit just has two sides."

"Eh." Daniel waved him off. "This isn't making a lot of sense."

"And who the hell put you in charge? You don't even know what's going on. I mean, fuck, man. Do you even like to see them bleed?"

"See them bleed? No! Why would I like that? They're terrifying. I just want to kill the damn things."

"I know, Tanner, I know. But here's the thing." The reflection stepped closer, its eyes wide and body thick with dark hair. "I like to see them bleed. I like it when they hurt." It reached through the glass and straightened Daniel's collar. "Don't you think I should drive the boat for a while? Just, you know, so I can bleed them? You don't like it, anyway."

"I don't know. Do you think that's a good idea? How about I just let you watch a little more?"

"No." It growled and curled its lips to expose a row of

teeth. "It's a fucking terrific idea, and you know it. Quit being such a little bitch."

"No," Daniel said, stepping back from the mirror. "I think I'm going to wake up now. You better stay here."

"Get back here, goddammit! I'm tired of this fucking cage!" The reflection pounded against the glass. "I'm not finished here! Get in this fucking mirror!"

The words rang through Daniel's head as his eyes flickered open. The dream lingered only a few seconds before it left him entirely. Sweat was dripping down his face despite the cool air of the room. He fanned himself and stood up.

He couldn't sleep more than a few hours at a time since that night, and the truth was, he couldn't even remember much of what had happened.

"I don't know," he had said to Maker that night. "It's all a blur. I just remember shapes, colors. Hell, and I remember, it hurt really bad. I can't fucking think."

Maker sent Daniel to rest in his own bed, but it didn't feel like his anymore. He'd left the cozy bed back in his old life; this was a stranger's house now.

He ordered a blade made of iron from the Internet. It was a lot harder to find one than he had expected. Even after paying triple the cost to get it as soon as possible, he had to wait the better part of a week.

It seemed like dust coated everything, in ways he hadn't noticed before. It smelled weird and itched like this was a place to fear.

Is it fear? Or is it just that I feel so fucking uncomfortable here?

Whatever it was, it didn't feel right. He didn't feel comfortable. The TV, the newspaper, the Internet—none of it was real anymore. It was all a lie. He used to live inside this lie, used to close his eyes and pretend, like everyone else: Like everything wasn't so fragile; like everything couldn't break so easily; like the world wasn't evil.

But there wasn't good or evil in the world. Daniel knew that now—there were only the takers and the taken. He'd woken from the lie and now he couldn't close his eyes again —even if he wanted to.

He talked with his parents; maybe that was just one last attempt to see if he could feel normal again. They wanted to go out to eat with him, so he slipped into the wolfskin. He smiled, despite no one seeing him, and told them he was fine—sad, but fine, and he had a lot of work to catch up on. That last part was true. He ignored all the other emails and phone calls.

Days later, the knife arrived in the mail, in a small brown box as normal as anything. It was smaller than he'd hoped, but it'd do. He immediately decided the handle wasn't suitable for him and took it apart. Years of hobbies in art and construction were finally useful as he rebuilt the handle with a tight leather grip.

This'll hold if I stick something with it.

Thoughts of the knife were all that kept him sane. He stepped out to buy a sheath for it, one that would run along the length of his belt and tuck neatly into the small of his back.

One last day of restless sleep and uneasy conversations with the whispers in his head, and he was driving back to the house on Terrace Drive. Somehow his foot felt heavier, leaning itself on the gas just a bit more, as though it were as eager to get there as the rest of his body.

The moment his car was parked, he was out and grabbing his duffle bag from the back. He heard a whistle and looked up to see Greg coming from the barn.

Son of a bitch is still walking around in a T- shirt even though the temperature is dropping.

"You moving in?" Greg asked with a hint of irritation in his voice.

Daniel hefted the heavy bag onto his back. "Yeah, figured I'd better do it."

"I thought you'd have figured otherwise, you know, like waiting until Maker came back to get you." Greg stopped short of the car and stared, one foot up a little like an animal ready to mark its turf.

He might have just been taking a piss along the perimeter when I showed up.

"Yeah, well, I'm fine. In fact, I'm fucking better than fine."

Like that feeling I get right before a guard dog barks. It's sizing you up.

"We have rules here, *Dan*." Greg's eyes didn't falter. "You come in when we tell you that you can come in. Get it?"

"The fuck do you care?" Daniel dropped his bag and leveled his shoulders.

Now Greg laughed and took a step closer. "I like you, Dan. I do. But you know I've killed a lot of 'em, right? Lots and lots, different shapes and sizes. You probably didn't hear about the cop back in Dallas. No one tell you that story? He got too close to us, sniffing around our shit. Maybe it was our fault, maybe we were a little sloppy. I ended it. Didn't like it, but I did."

"Now, you know why no one told you about that cop?" Greg continued. "Because it's fucking understood that I'm the one watching you. If you go fucking driving around and letting anyone notice that you've got a clubhouse out here, or people wonder where your car is and start looking . . ." He let the last part drop. "Now, get your shit inside." He spat and turned back toward the barn.

"You killed a fucking cop? You're a real piece of shit, Greg."

"Take a look in the mirror. You're almost there yourself." Greg didn't bother turning around.

A choked scream climbed up Daniel's throat. He stifled it, grabbed his bag, and carried it inside. He had spied an empty room in the place before; he intended to take it before anyone could tell him not to.

The room was cluttered with old furniture that he thought would surely suit the fireplace, and the floorboards groaned annoyingly with each step. It'd work fine, though. He dropped his bag on the floor and immediately regretted doing so as an ocean of dust was thrown into the air; he fanned it away and began to clean.

"Good Lord!" Jenna said as she poked her head into the room, a plastic container of cleaning supplies in hand. "Let me give you a hand here. This looks all kinds of dirty."

"Thanks," Daniel said, managing a smile—the first in days. "I appreciate it."

"Daniel?" she asked, a tremble in her voice when she saw his face.

Is she afraid of me?

"Yeah?"

She reached out and grabbed his hand, then gave him a warm hug. "I'm just glad to have you around, s'all."

He nodded, confused, and then went about cleaning.

What the hell was that all about?

It didn't take them long to clean everything—it wasn't a big room, after all. He made a few mental notes of things he needed, next time he went home. Jenna left him and headed to the chapel in town.

Alone now in an empty room, Daniel felt at a loss. He sat back against a wall and tried to think about how to pass the time. Maker was out, Jenna had told him that Rebekah was asleep, and he sure as hell didn't want to talk with Greg right now.

Take a look in the mirror. You're almost there.

What the hell was he talking about? I'm not a fucking monster like him.

Daniel found his way to the bathroom. He stepped onto the grimy yellow tiles and stared into the cracked mirror, shattered lines crawling through it like webs. This wasn't what Greg meant, but he was surprised; his hair had grown too long, and his beard was thick.

"Shit." He ran a hand through his hair; he always hated it when it got too long. For years he'd had biweekly haircuts but now, it was hanging over his ears.

How long has it been now? A month? Two?

He got the trimmers out of his bag. They were for keeping his face nice and smooth, the way Julia liked it, but now he just popped the clip off and ran it over his head, shaving down to the scalp.

A swipe of pale scalp revealed an old scar—a thin, barely visible line about an inch and half long. He'd opened his head in a fight with another kid when he was eleven or twelve years old.

It had been some time since he'd thought about that. It was clear now, like the scar had opened the door to yesterday. He remembered his finger coming back, slick with blood, and the pounding in his head—it didn't hurt. No, it wasn't pain; it was something like a calling, his instincts telling him what to do next. He remembered picking up the rock and dashing it against the other kid's head. Once. Twice. Three times.

Wait. No. That didn't happen, did it? I didn't hit the kid.

Something was moving in his head, like a hand shifting beneath a blanket, as he questioned the memory.

No, it didn't happen like that. I can't remember. . . It doesn't matter.

Stifling the thought, he dusted off the blades and shortened his beard, content that he at least looked better on the outside.

"I prefer that a man keep a head of hair."

Rebekah had crept up behind him. For an old and tired woman, she was remarkably quiet on her feet.

"Yeah, well." He shrugged at her. "You need something?"

"Was going to use the bathroom. But you finish. Make sure you sweep that mess up, though."

"Wait, Rebekah," he said. "I wanted to talk with you about what happened. I . . . I can't really remember anything."

"This is not uncommon. You should not be concerned."

"What did we do? What happened?"

"We beat it. We pierced it and brought it under submission. It is in the basement still." She tried to turn again, but she was hiding something. He felt it.

"What aren't you telling me?"

Her pale blue eyes accosted him, and had they been weapons, she might have killed him with them. "You take your damn hand off me and never touch me like that again," she spat.

Only now, did he realize he had grabbed her. She felt so frail, so different. He let go.

"Sorry, I just . . ." He shook his head.

"I'm exhausted," Rebekah said with a tired sigh. "But if you wait one or two more days, I will try to have a deep discussion with you about it. Until then, I want you to just rest, open your mind. Try to clear your thoughts. It'll be easier to remember later. You've packed too much trash into your mind. It clutters and distracts you. Now, let an old woman sleep, for the love of God."

Rebekah left. Daniel felt it in his bones—this place was where he needed to be. But there was nothing he could do right now. He still had no place in their group.

He stepped out into the cold air, heading to the barn. Greg's dog started growling at him the moment he pulled the door open. Greg glanced up from the engine, and then went back to it.

"What? You come here to settle some shit?"

"Why do you keep the pictures?" Daniel ignored the growling dog and stepped closer.

Greg sighed and leaned back. "What's this now?" He wiped the oil from his hands and tossed the rag aside. The dog calmed, but kept her eyes on Daniel.

"Why would you keep pictures of dead children in your toolbox? What the fuck is wrong with you?" His words came out stronger than he had intended.

"I like you, kid." Greg squared his shoulders and looked squarely at him. "But don't think I won't cut you to teach you a lesson about running your fucking mouth."

"Why?" Daniel insisted.

Greg rolled his eyes, then relaxed some. "You ever see a lion kill a zebra? It's raw. It's art. We don't look and think the fucking thing is a monster, do we? That's just what it is. It's a killer. Ain't nothing unnatural about it."

"These are children . . ."

"Wrong!" Greg yelled, loud enough to shake Daniel and start the dog growling again. Greg stormed forward, making Daniel fight to hold his ground without stumbling back. "They're not fucking kids, Dan. That's where you're wrong. That's where you're dangerous."

Shaking his head, Daniel suddenly felt weak in the knees. He turned to find a chair to sit in while Greg calmed down.

Greg snorted. "Fuck you. You're not here to argue with me—you're here to argue with yourself. What, you think it's disrespectful that I keep the pictures? You're going to do it too, or you're going to lose the other half of your mind. Hell, only part of the fight is out there—the rest of it is in here." He tapped his temple. "You're just like me, Tanner. I can smell it all over you. You're going to need to start taking your own pictures, putting notches in your belt, or you're going to fucking break."

Daniel studied Greg and then stared at the floor. "How can I do it? How the Hell can I get it straight in my head?"

"Well, shaving your head didn't help. You still look like an ugly cunt, just less Unabomber and more skinhead."

"Can you show me your knife?" Daniel asked, looking up to meet Greg's eyes. "Show me how to use it?"

"Kid." Greg knew what was coming. "That's not what you want. Everyone has a part to play, and cutting them ain't for you. I told you to stick a toe in, not jump in the fucking deep end."

"You make them talk with that?" His gaze shifted to the knife atop the tool case—an aged thing, but clean and deadly sharp.

"I can. It'd turn your stomach raw, though."

"So would a slaughterhouse, but I still eat meat."

"All right, then. You want to get your hands dirty, I won't stop you." Greg turned back to pat his dog on the head and grabbed his knife. "Thing's still in the basement. Let's roll."

A STINK WAS in the air now, the one that comes with cutting. Adrenaline, blood, and fear: they mix into a cocktail that stinks in a way that few can appreciate—an acquired taste. Greg was one of those few.

Not because it was fun—well, not the first time, at least. The first time, the stupid thing was squawking and throwing a hissy fit about its own life like it wasn't already a forgone conclusion.

"You keep quiet, dammit!" Greg said through gritted teeth. "The best you can hope for is a quick end, fucking cunt. So start talking." He cut the deal with the sharp end of a knife.

It didn't get it quickly either, not after it told him how many it killed, how many it ate. Greg figured he owed it to somebody to make it hurt. He hoped that if there was a Hell, the creature had his name etched into its hide, just so it'd never forget.

Greg told himself he had to do it, but he wasn't sure why. Later, he did it to dig out more information. Given enough time, even a torturer can see art in form. He was good in a way that only a man who enjoys his work could be. But that took time. It was years before he saw the art in the blade—he didn't stumble into it. Besides, he was careful how much he'd let himself do; he'd seen other men fall into that pit. He tried to keep only half a leg in himself. But, there was something scary about the eagerness that filled Daniel's eyes. Greg had seen eyes like that before in half-starved coyotes looking for a taste of something that was still moving. It wasn't that long ago that he had bitch-legs when the blood started rolling, but now he wanted a front row seat.

Something in him had turned rotten.

Greg hadn't gotten a chance to take his knife to the changeling quite yet; he had been planning to for some time now, but he found it best to let the thing get ripe with a few days of waiting before starting the work—one of the tricks of the trade. But the fucker had come out even worse than Rebekah, so it needed to recover enough to care about being tortured, to get that full feeling back in its bones. They mend quickly, sometimes in just hours. The iron was there to keep it nice and slow, and it was a few days before it was up to full speed.

Heading down the steps, Greg and Daniel found it pawing at the chains, writhing around, trying to escape. It hissed at them beneath its gag and flashed its eyes at Greg, like he was some child afraid of such things.

Cute.

He let out a laugh to let the creature know how futile it all was. It got that panicked look in its eyes again, like a cornered animal.

No. Like a cow in the butcher's line.

"Man, I bet you're strong," Greg said as he opened his arms wide. He watched its gaze move to his throat. He knew what it was thinking, and he knew there was nothing it could do.

Predictable.

Greg couldn't guess what they lived on: meat, or actual fear, like Rebekah suspected, but the bastard sure as hell hadn't gotten either for the last few days. So, it was all nice and pliable.

Greg sat down next to it, intentionally close, to put it on edge and give it a little hope of what it could do if only those chains were just a little looser. Greg had put the chains on the creature. There was an art to that too—just enough slack to let it breath, but not enough to let it hurt you. Daniel stayed back and watched.

"You'd just love to get a piece of me, wouldn't you?"

It responded with a throaty growl, but it said enough with its gaze.

"Is that where we're at now? You were all laughs, threats, and promises before. Looks like you're still here, though. Looks like you ain't gone nowhere."

The chains rattled and shook, but it still couldn't conjure anything beyond a hiss. Greg pulled out a blade and tested his thumb against it, drawing a bead of blood. He sucked it from this thumb.

And then his work began.

He always found it hilarious to turn viewers' stomachs as they watched—sometimes they'd even puke. Not even Maker, who's had a hand or two at cutting, watches unless he has to. Daniel didn't break though, not this time, He only sat there with watchful eyes, even as Greg cut the venom glands out of the screaming changeling's bony chest and showed them to him.

"That's what puts you to sleep when they bite."

He held up the two organs. They looked like tiny brown kidneys colored with red veins. Daniel shook a little, but continued to watch.

No, he's not just watching. He's enjoying it.

That was unsettling, a strange feeling for a man like Greg. He decided not to butter this one up so much. He reached down to remove the gag.

"Wait," Daniel said. "Let me."

20

THERE HAD BEEN A LOT OF CHATTER ON THE POLICE SCANNERS for the past few days, and there were a lot of eyes out there looking for little Ben Harris. They were planning on sweeping the woods soon, so they were asking for volunteers.

No one saw anything. No Amber Alert. We're still good.

Maker knew that meant they had room to breathe, but not much. Things would start cracking soon, and he liked the idea of a midnight run more and more. Still, he felt a twinge of pain for the Harris family—not quite guilt, but an echo of it.

New Athens was pushing Maker's finely tuned detective skills to the limit, and he kept coming up dry. A brood this size required a mixture of discretion, quickness, and instincts; he certainly had those in good supply, but he'd never needed to make use of them so broadly. The city looked like a monster itself, each corner and alleyway holding shadows in which the brood could lurk.

Jenna told them of Jenny Robinson. There was some chatter that said the girl had thrown up in class. It wasn't particularly noteworthy, except that she'd aimed for other students and painted the wall with it afterward. Apparently, she had been slopping elbow-deep in it and laughing like a lunatic through the whole thing.

What the hell is so funny?

Maker had run into a few of them that laughed like that —acting insane and enjoying it—but nothing like this.

Runs in their blood.

With Rebekah sleeping more hours than not and Daniel unsure of what even happened, Maker had few avenues to investigate. Still, he made the best of his time and made one pass through Jenny Robinson's neighborhood. That was all he'd risk. The damn house didn't sit on the corner like the Harris's—her little haven was nestled right in the middle of a neighborhood. That complicated things.

Three down, three to go.

Maker tried to stay positive, but they'd already be long gone in any other hunt.

From the outside of the house, he saw what damage a changeling could do: a long scratch down the side of the Robinson's car, a broken window, and a cracked mailbox. There was no chance it was anything but a changeling. He could spot their signs the way an expert deer hunter could pull a dry track off the ground on a summer's day. That was made by a changeling's clawed fingers.

Looks like a violent one.

It made him happy to see it because truth was that Maker was starting to feel out of his element. His particular set of skills weren't up for the task, and he regretted that.

Or maybe I'm just getting slow.

He felt like there were loose strands that he just couldn't tie together. That kind of thing could drive a man like Maker insane, little monsters or no.

It's all right. You identified that claw mark. We'll confirm it and we're good.

He had just parked the car at home when Jenna stuck her head outside and told him that he needed to talk to Rebekah. He followed Jenna in, and heard Rebekah's raspy breathing before he could see her. The poor woman could hardly hold her eyes open.

"Larry, I could barely see anything." She squeezed her eyes shut and then forced them open. "When I looked inside it, it was like I was carrying a candle, only able to see a few feet in front of me at a time. Everything is still confusing and blurry."

"You need to rest," Jenna insisted. "You're exhausted."

"No." She shook her head at Jenna and then looked back at Maker. "There's a body. One, maybe more." She drew a sharp, painful breath. "It's on the ridge outside of town."

"Where?" he asked, leaning in.

She shook her head. "I don't know exactly. I saw a dirt road. And . . . and a water tower in the distance to my right." Her eyes searched the wall, looking for something only she could see as she drew in another deep breath. "The sun, it was rising, or setting, I don't know." She blinked hard.

Maker gently squeezed her hand. "What else?"

"I felt the asylum. It was nearby. I . . . I didn't see it, but I could feel it."

I knew I should have burned that fucking place down.

"That's . . ." she said, her voice dry. "That's all I can remember. Just the nest . . . She held a hand up to her head. "It comes and goes. I'm fine sometimes, and then it's so painful other times."

He patted her arm as she trailed off again. "You're cold. You just sleep, all right? We'll handle it without you. You're nearing the edge."

With one last tip of her head, she closed her eyes and immediately fell asleep. He shook his head tiredly at Jenna as he stood up and stepped out of the room.

I've never seen her in that kind of pain.

"What do you think?" Jenna waited until they hit the kitchen to speak.

"I think I got a nest to find." He tried to shield any other thoughts from his mind.

"No." Jenna shook her head. "About Rebekah." She spoke in whispers, afraid Rebekah might hear, even though the door was closed and she was asleep.

Maker shook his head. "I know what you meant. But we can't think about that."

"Maker . . . Larry," Jenna said, shaking her head with tears in her eyes. "I think the cancer is back. I think what she's doing is making it get here all the quicker. She's gotten even worse since that night. We were talking before, now she's barely awake. I found blood . . ."

Maker felt like icy fingers had gripped his heart and squeezed. He shook his head. "We've seen this before, Jenna. She comes and goes in waves as she clears that shit out of her head. We've got a job, Jenna, and so does she. Rebekah knows that. She knows her place."

"I know that, Maker, I know that. But this is worse. All I'm saying is that we can't let her keep doing this. It's going to kill her."

He tilted his head. "You think she doesn't know that? You think she wants to quit? What'd she say when you told her about the cancer?"

"Well, I told her we needed to start getting treatment and testing—"

"What did she say, Jenna?"

"She told me to leave it alone."

"Then leave the damn thing alone. She's a soldier, Jenna. Soldiers fight. Sometimes they die." He hated the words that poured out of his mouth. He changed the conversation then; he knew if Jenna kept talking she'd convince him otherwise. "Where's Daniel? I saw his car out there."

Jenna sighed and flicked her eyes to the basement door.

"He's down there?" he asked. "With Greg?"

"Yeah. Greg's making him a right fine soldier for you." She crossed her arms and stared back at Maker. "It was making all kinds of noise earlier when you was out. Been quiet some time now."

"I'll check on them."

Jenna went back to Rebekah as Maker turned away. He opened the door to the basement, surprised that Daniel had found it in him to stomach Greg's games.

How the hell long has he been down here?

Maker didn't suspect there was anything to rip out of the thing that hadn't already been taken. It wasn't uncommon for Greg to vent on one of them, though. It wasn't something Maker was particular happy with, but he'd learned to leave a man like Greg to his own devices, so long as he was pointed in the right direction.

He saw Daniel first, sitting on the floor and drinking a beer, with Greg slumped in a chair near him. Sweat dripped down their faces. Maker was thankful for the curtain that hid the creature and the mess it surely was now.

"What the hell is going on?"

"Greg is showing me how to cut them. To make them talk." There wasn't quite a smile on his face, but a hint of one.

Maker glanced at Greg; there was no joy there, however. Greg smirked, but it was feigned, and Maker could read a face like others read a newspaper.

"Yeah? And what'd it say?" Maker asked, staring hard at Daniel. "Tell you about all its little brothers and sisters running around? Tell you about this pale man?"

"Just seemed like it was talking bullshit."

"Oh, really? You cut something, and it tells you whatever the fuck it thinks you want to hear." He glared daggers at Greg. "Kill it, bury it. Daniel's going out with me."

"Sure," Greg said as he rose to his feet.

"Wait," Daniel said, standing up. "Should we just kill it? We can work on these things. Do more to see how to hurt them. Greg showed me where the venom glands are. We should dissect it more. I need to know this kind of shit." No one paid him any mind. Greg was already going behind the curtain.

"Daniel, go upstairs, and wash your face. We're heading out."

"Wait a minute—"

Maker stopped him with a look. "Go wash your fucking face and grab your shit. You're going to help me find a body."

———

HEAVY CHAINS WRAPPED around her arms and pulled her down, keeping her in this world—Rebekah knew them to be the chains of sleep and exhaustion.

Something akin to a root was growing through the base of her mind. It stretched around and its sharp edges jutted out, scratching each groove of her mind as she moved. She tried to grab it and rip it out, but the spines sank into her flesh, lashing her arms like vines, growing yards by the second. She cried out, there in the hollow of her mind, against this thing that wouldn't stop spreading.

"I can't . . ." The blood dripped down her arms and pooled in her palms. "I can't stop it," she said to no one.

There was more there, more rooms and places she'd taken from the creature, but its spiny roots were too strong, too thick, and kept the whole place closed off.

How is it so strong?

She pulled herself together and grabbed at the roots. With a painful strain, she pulled them loose, but their spines took her flesh with them, leaving bloody grooves. She summoned her will and forced the wounds closed, sealing all but a drip of blood.

I can't stop.

Behind those doors were the memories of children who once lived. One of those doors held Sam.

Is he dead now? Why did they keep him alive? Why did his changeling grow sick?

She had to know, had to find it, but it was so hard and so painful. She couldn't tell anyone other than Jenna until she found out more. Jenna, with whom she had shared so many burdens, was the only one who could know. Daniel certainly couldn't take it—she'd only tell him if she found something better, but it hurt her so much to keep going.

Jenna wouldn't stop because it hurt. Jenna would keep going if there was any chance of finding that boy.

Jenna had cried when she'd told her that the boy might still be alive. She'd broken down in a way that Rebekah had never seen before.

But we've never heard of that—a child who lived. Could it be real?

It hurt, but it had to be done. She stripped another bloody vine from her mind, and more came to her, little by little, more vines and more information that she dug out.

She saw the body, felt the asylum, but there was more to be done, and more to dig.

She had duty though, didn't she? Did duty die with pain? Did her suffering exclude her from it?

No. A boy may live if an old woman hurts. That is all that must be said.

She went back to attacking the roots.

21

MAKER HADN'T SAID A WORD OR EVEN GLANCED AT DANIEL, since he got in the car. Something about his posture made Daniel keep his mouth shut, but even that lasted only so long.

"So, a body?" Daniel finally asked.

"Yeah." Maker kept his eyes on the road. "Not exactly sure where, but I've got a guess."

Daniel shrugged his shoulders, trying to prompt more. "Yeah?"

"Rebekah. She was up for a bit today. Told me she's still unpacking some of the shit she took out of that thing back there. She saw a body of some consequence, but she wasn't sure where. She told me a few things, though. It's on a ridge looking into town. There was a dirt road, and she could spy the water tower."

Daniel itched with excitement. "How did she see any of it?"

"She lives in its memories. Grabbed pieces out of the thing's head. You should have been able to see things, too. Why you couldn't, I don't know. Maybe you just need a little more practice. She's knocking on death's door, and you're up walking around fine."

"Well, certainly not by choice. It's not like I *want* to forget what happened there."

"No, you don't seem to have any problem dealing with that," he said, his gaze sharpening. "Rebekah also said she saw the sun setting or rising, so I think it's on the east or west side of town."

"So, where are we headed?"

"You tell me. Dirt road. Water tower. What's that tell you?"

Daniel rubbed his head. "Well, there's an old water tower on Lincoln drive, I think."

"Yeah? And?"

Daniel sighed and closed his eyes, trying to picture it. "Well . . ." He opened the window, glanced out, and saw the setting sun. "I guess, if she could see the tower, and the sun was setting, it must be on the east side of town, over there. The old asylum is out there. You knew that, though, didn't you?"

Maker tipped his head. "Rebekah also said she felt the asylum nearby."

"The asylum—I've never been out there before. No one really goes out there anymore."

"No one, eh? Well, lucky us, we still have an hour or two of daylight."

"Is this a good idea, to be out there while it's getting dark?"

"Maybe not. But I wanted to get you out of the damn house."

That's what this was all about.

"What about it?" Daniel shot back.

"You like to hurt them? What's that say about you?"

"Says a lot, I suspect." Daniel fought back a sneer. "Says I don't want to think about them as human anymore, and I think it'll get easier after cutting a few pieces off of them."

"There's a better way. Take it slow—it's not a damn race." Maker pulled the car onto the long road leading out of town and up the mountainside. "You have to walk the edge, or you'll fall."

They sat the rest of the way in silence. As they curled up the mountainside and neared the ridge, they saw the asylum —a menacing wound on New Athens, halls like a grinning mouth, with two wide front windows for eyes and dozens of weathered pockmarks. Daniel had never seen it himself. Never close up anyway, always from a distance or in a picture, where it wasn't so inviting, or threatening, or real. It didn't have a face until you saw it in person.

There were stories of kids heading up here, screwing around and getting themselves cut on rusted metal, which was enough to keep most people out. Those still curious would find large wooden planks nailed to the sides and broken glass lying on the ground.

"Well, this looks terrifying," Daniel said as Maker brought the car to a stop and flipped the headlights off. "Why the hell didn't they ever tear it down?"

"Researched that myself." Maker's eyes scanned the darkness. "There had been talk of renovations and preservation. No way in hell now."

Maker glared at the asylum like he could see through the walls. A few heartbeats ticked before he spoke again.

"You bring your gun?"

"Yeah, I'm getting in the habit of keeping the damn thing on me. Why?"

Maker cocked his head to one side; he waited in silence for a few moments. "I was here the other day." He popped his door open, stepped out, and pointed. "That streak of blood wasn't." He grabbed a kit from the back seat, opened it, and retrieved two flashlights. "Here," he said and handed one to Daniel.

The orange rays of the sun pulled back from the ground, stretching shadows out like pointed fingers ready to drag them all to an early grave. Despite the darkness, Daniel could still see, though it gave him no relief to see the bloodstains.

"The hell is that?" Daniel asked as he followed Maker.

Maker kept his eyes on the gaping door as he neared it; the trail of blood led inside. "Could be an animal." Maker opened his jacket and pulled out his own revolver, then thumbed on the flashlight. The beam of light shone against the blood, a red smear that slicked its way into the darkness of the asylum. "But I don't think so." Maker shined the light across the front of the building, a shimmer catching the broken windows.

"How can you tell?"

"Because Rebekah told us to come to the fucking asylum, and there's a streak of blood here."

"A fair point." Daniel nodded, and licked his lips. "We going in?"

Maker dipped his finger in the blood. He held up two red fingers to Daniel.

Still wet? It's here.

That thought twisted inside Daniel. His revolver gave a solid *click* as he pulled the hammer back.

"Ease up, there. We're not going inside." Maker eyed Daniel and pushed his pistol down with one hand. "It's not worth it. They trick people like that."

But the beast was already stirring in Daniel, calling out

for prey. "What if it's still in here?" His vision seemed to sharpen in the darkness as his throat went dry.

"That's what I'm concerned about, you idiot," Maker said. "We don't even have the right weapons. Bullets won't do anything but slow it down."

I've got the knife.

A moan rattled from the second floor.

Daniel rubbed his tongue over his front teeth, the itch driving him forward as the wolfskin climbed over his own and a voice whispered. Without words, it spoke to him of blood and pain, vengeance due. Something snapped, and there was no choice.

The hunt had him.

He stepped inside as carefully as he could, and scanned the corners of the asylum. Broken mud-streaked tiles littered the floor, and plaster had peeled from the collapsing walls. The hall stretched farther down and took a bend; a set of stairs led up. Daniel couldn't hear Maker speak over the thumping pulse in his ears, but he felt the man behind him.

The bloody streaks led him up the stairs as his light guided the way. He stopped every few feet to listen, just as Greg had taught him. There was a low whistle of air through the building, and something in the distance dripped. Then there was the moan again, something sucking in a dying breath. It was just around the corner. He could almost see it, almost smell the blood in its wounds.

Maker slammed a hand down on his shoulder before he could move again. In silent warning, Maker held up a hand, demanding that he wait. Silently, he leaned just around the corner, glanced, then motioned for Daniel to look. The blood dragged right into the mouth of an open door. Maker held up two fingers between them and pointed again. Daniel nodded.

Slowly, they moved together, scanning either side of the hallway with their lights. If something was here, it certainly knew they were here, too.

I can feel it watching me.

His body spoke to him, but was it a lie? Maker had told him to trust his instincts, trust the feelings beneath the skin that come with age and transformation into a different type of man. They stopped short of the door; Maker nodded once and the two pushed in quickly.

Lying on the floor and sucking in breath was a deer, one of its hind legs torn off and bleeding everywhere. Something had cracked its front legs at odd angles. The tortured thing wheezed, but the light had already gone from its eyes.

Maker didn't hesitate. He started to check the room, glancing out of each window, but Daniel's eyes were drawn to the deer. Its chest rose and lowered in labored breath, alive, despite having no reason to be. Daniel couldn't stop his gaze from gliding down to the gorge of open meat in its chest and belly. He could see the varying shades of red that made up its insides, dark red to almost pink, and the bloody tips of broken bones sticking out. The gnawed parts were across its leg. Sharp teeth must have sawn through it.

It gasped in one last time and then its chest stopped.

They kept it alive while they ate it.

"God, do they keep it alive just for fun?"

"Probably." Maker used his light to scan the ceiling and checked the closets. He glanced at Daniel, whose nervous eyes said he was unsure.

Daniel felt pinpricks against his skin as the hair raised on the back of his neck. He turned around, started out the door, and listened.

I feel like it's watching me.

He waited several long moments before he heard it.

"Ha-ha-ha!" Something burst out in laughter from deep within the asylum.

THE BONE CRACKED in a way that sounded almost musical. They groan first, and then creak before they snap in a twisted symphony that the pale man enjoyed before a meal. He licked and slurped the meat from the bones with his pointed tongue, dragging the slop into his mouth. Red juices squeezed down his face as he chewed—he preferred it that way. The meat moaned painfully for the loss of its leg. He preferred it that way, too.

"Shh." He patted his soaked fingers against its thigh the way one might pet a cat. "It's okay, you're fine." He slurped another piece of wet meat from the bone. "You're fine."

The deer's gaze stayed on him, watching him lick its muscle from the stolen bones. That was fun in its own way —watching it watch him. It had cried a lot more as he'd dragged it through the forest, but he'd beaten some silence into it, and the loss of blood was probably quieting it. He had to crack each of its legs to get the fight out of it, though careful not to kill it too quickly.

Such things require a deft hand and patience.

The pale man turned his black eyes up to a pair of head-lights that shone in the distance, intruding on his lair. The deer moaned again.

"Shh," he insisted again, holding a finger to his narrow chin and gray lips. He sucked another piece of juicy meat from the bone. He was nearly done with this one, but perhaps more meat had come.

Men certainly taste better.

He ran a red hand through his hair, leaving a greasy

streak in the long white curls. He crept up to the windows and his ears sharpened. The car pulled in close to the asylum. He watched as two men stepped from it, but despite his sharper ears, he couldn't quite hear what they were saying, only a few words here and there.

Gun. Greg. Blood.

"Curious," he whispered to the moaning deer. "Who do you think they are?"

They flashed a light against the blood and then up at the windows. He ducked as the light pierced the glass, and then went back to watching.

Hunters? Here?

"Very curious. Do you think they found me?" he asked, continuing the conversation with the dying meat. "I was told there were some here, but I have yet to see them. My children have been looking—shh, here they come!"

He bid the meat goodbye as he skittered to the wall and climbed it like a spider—the laws of nature meant little to him. Soft echoes told him of their quiet steps coming up the stairs. He found a shadow and sank into it like an alligator in a swamp.

The two came with their guns drawn, pointing them around as if they would help. The gray-haired one shined his light across the room. The light passed over the pale man's shadow, and he was blind and shut off to the world until the shadows returned. He curled his lip in irritation.

The younger one, with the bald head, focused on the deer, concerned with the noises it made.

It's funny, the things they care about.

"God, did they keep it alive just for fun?" The bald one finally pulled his eyes away and looked around.

"Probably." Gray checked inside the dusty closets. "I can feel it watching me."

The pale man had to stifle a laugh. It was all he could do to keep from bursting out in laughter and giving himself away. He wasn't afraid of that, though; he just wanted to enjoy this a little longer. He breathed deeply to capture the sweet smell of confusion, fear, and . . .

No.

Something else was there, a familiar scent.

His gray lips formed a sneer again. He shifted in the shadows, from one to another, and came down by their feet. He considered pulling the younger one in, digging his fingers into his neck to see if he bled the same color as every other man. Instead, he took a cautious breath, preferring to keep the game up rather than let his anger spoil it.

He knew that smell: his offspring. They'd taken one of his. He had felt his offspring break from him before, snapped loose from his hold in their delicate minds. Such things were not uncommon. His children were always so vigorous and independent, a danger to others and themselves. It was fine that they died—it was the natural order of things. They were quite durable, but still might drown or burn, or just hurl themselves in front of a train to see what it felt like. But his son had been hunted.

They killed one of mine. I can smell my child's blood on the younger one. He hurt my child.

He shifted again in the shadows, near the old man's feet.

I'll pull the old one in first, tear out his throat, and leave him. Then the younger. I'll hold him and hurt him until he tells me what he's done.

Claws split through the tips of his fingers and his teeth took on a sharpness. His claws came up from the dark gloom of his world, ready to pull the old man in.

But the younger one turned. There was something about

how he moved, something different about it. The pale man shifted and took another breath.

The boy. I can smell him. I have his boy.

The pale man shifted further away, to a shadow down the hall, and climbed out of it. He couldn't hold his laughter. "Pfft! Heh-heh-heh." It burst out of him. "Ha-ha-ha!"

I have his son!

"Ha-ha-ha!"

22

DANIEL'S LUNGS BURNED FOR AIR, BUT HE KEPT RUNNING. Even Maker's shouts couldn't slow him as he tore through the asylum. Something was here, and he wanted it. He wanted to hurt it. He hated it. He hated that laugh, hated what it did to that deer. Not because of the deer's pain, but because it had done it.

It set his blood on fire; there was no fear, only anticipation and want. He searched, but he couldn't find the origin of the voice. Maker tried to keep up with him at first, but eventually fell behind, screaming meaningless words.

Dank, empty rooms, one after another. All silent, other than that cackling that echoed through his brain. "Fuck you! You fucking coward!" Daniel screamed curses into the darkness.

With the world silent, madness started to grip him. His revolver felt heavy in his hand, so he let it drop to the ground with a dull *clunk*, and then his whole body followed, sliding down the wall. It wasn't here anymore; he knew that in his bones. This was the thing that had taken his son—he was sure of it—so close but so easily gone. This thing he hated had a face, and it laughed at him. It joked that he couldn't do anything but fail. He was the joke.

He pulled at his hair and the beast inside him screamed, "Where the fuck are you?"

"It's not here." Maker's words finally found meaning to Daniel. "And why would it be? Why would it fight you and not just kill you? You damn idiot!" Maker shouted, then stopped to take a few deep breaths. "I told you before, anyone who stands their ground and locks eyes with them is a damn fool. They trap idiots like this. You fell right for it."

"Then why didn't it kill me?" he asked, looking up at Maker, his eyes still burning red. "Why the fuck wouldn't it kill me if this was a trap?"

Maker grunted. "Maybe it hasn't quite had its fun yet. Maybe you're too good to fuck with. Or maybe you just got lucky, and howling like a mad man actually scared it off. But if you have a fucking death wish, say it right now, and I'll put one in your goddamn head right here!" He jerked his gun up to show he meant it. "Otherwise, you don't fucking kill yourself without a good reason."

"Why do you even care?" The energy drained from Daniel and he slumped against the wall.

Maker's face stiffened. "Because you'd be useful if you weren't so damn stupid. Now get up before I shoot you myself, and I still have half a mind to do it anyway."

"He was right here," Daniel said, standing up. "It was . . . I don't know."

"Yeah, I got that, too. But what the hell were you going to do if you found him? Shoot him? Punch him in the jaw?"

With an exhausted sigh, Daniel rose to his feet and reached for the blade sheathed behind his back. He slid it out and handed it to Maker. "Stick him with this?"

Maker eyed Daniel, then took the blade and tested its

weight and edge. "Not bad. Could have maybe nicked him before he ripped your damn throat out." He handed it back to Daniel.

Daniel slid the blade back into the sheath and then followed Maker out, laboring to breathe with each step.

"Lost a lot of daylight," Maker said, irritated. "Just shut the hell up now and follow me."

They found the tire tracks that Rebekah had mentioned and followed them with their lights. The tracks, which led to a ridge that overlooked the city, were fairly easy to follow, even in the dark. It would have been a pleasant view of the night sky and city, if not for the smell.

That's fucking terrible.

Daniel pressed his nose into his arm as he surveyed the ridge. Maker didn't seem bothered as he searched the darkness with his flashlight.

"There," Maker said.

"Well." The smell made Daniel's eyes water. "What the hell is that?" He pointed at a bloody heap that had been mauled beyond recognition.

"No idea. But that's a man." He pointed to another mess —a body splayed out in a tree. It still had recognizable flesh on it—a bloody hand hung loose, dangling from a branch, with red smears that had dripped and dried. A head of matted, blood-soaked hair was tucked into the branch. Gray sludge leaked out from its open skull and slopped down into a pile at the base of the tree. Hundreds of ants crawled over the leaked brain matter.

Daniel's stomach tied itself into knots; he had to step back and turn away. He had nearly walked off the edge of the ridge before he felt like could breathe again. He gulped and tried to focus on the blinking city lights, but the stench of the dead still clung to his nostrils.

"What the hell good is all that going to do us?" he asked with a half-glance over his shoulder at Maker.

"Greg is better at these kinds of things," said Maker, "especially when it comes to animals. But I know a thing or two about people, and I know how a brood works." He took two steps deeper into the grass and leaned down.

Son of a bitch.

Daniel turned and crept back over; he saw that even Maker had his jacket over his nose now. He did the same.

"This body. It looks a few months old." Maker pointed at several decaying parts.

"Are you sure it's even a body?" Daniel pinched his nose shut through the jacket.

"Yes." Maker didn't elaborate. "This one up here? It's much fresher. That tells us a lot."

Daniel sat quietly, without anything to add.

"Tells us they've been here for a while," continued Maker, "that they're eating meat and being careful to hide it. Might even be going out of town. Haven't heard anything about missing people here, other than the kids. Maybe the progenitor is bringing in the meat."

They gather here.

"Certainly, someone will come back. Which may have been a hell of a lot more useful, had you not tipped our hand back there with the laughter. We could have staked this place out better. That was just too damn risky."

"Fine, you were right. What do you want?"

"I want you to listen next time. Think with your head, not with your ... feet."

Daniel nodded and sighed. "So, they need to eat meat like this?"

Maker shook his head. "Maybe. Or maybe they just like it. We have kept them penned up before. They get weaker, but they never starve to death." He waved his hand back toward the car. "Come on, let's get out of here. We'll come back with Greg tomorrow."

When they neared their car, Maker flashed his light in the back seat and looked out once more. Daniel gave him a curious look.

"In this job, it pays to be paranoid."

THE TWO MEN WALKED OFF, their lights glowing in the dark. The pale man shifted through the shadows and climbed out from under a tree. He wrapped a long bony finger under his sharp chin. "Could it be?" he asked with amusement.

Oh, this game! I remember it so well!

He pressed a hand to his chest and began to sway like a dancer in the night. "So many I have had, so many have tried, and so long it has been." A sharp grin spread across his face. "I thought all the true professionals had died! But they were able to find me here." He squeezed his mouth shut to keep from laughing too loudly.

Such a pleasant thought. He knew that some were looking for him, but he thought them a simple annoyance. But these men brought some skill to the game—the gray one did, anyway.

Their scent lingered in the air. "Oh, they smell so wonderful! So different!" He turned and plunged into a shadow, then whispered to the dark. He connected with another and bade it to open a door to him and show him the way into the world.

A smiling face came in the darkness; it said nothing, but its mind burned bright like a signal. The pale man was in its shadow and with disjointed arms, he pulled himself from beneath it and into a room. A doll-faced girl sat in her bed, her plump hands pressed against her red cheeks, giggling loudly as the slender pale man drew itself up from the floor.

"You called me?" the doll-faced girl asked.

"Little one?" he whispered. "We have a game to play!"

"A game!" She clapped loudly. "I love games! What kind of game?" Her hazel eyes shone in a way no real child's would.

"The best kind! Though it's been so long that I've forgotten some of the rules."

"That's okay, we can make our own rules." She grinned widely and bobbed her head up and down.

"Caroline Lee?" a voice called from down the hallway. "You go to sleep, now. We're not going to do this again, you hear?"

"How about my daddy? Do we play with him?"

The pale man's grin stretched from ear to ear. He shook his head. "No, we have new friends to play with."

"Caroline? Are you talking to someone?"

"So, we're not going to play with daddy anymore?" the girl asked, her eyes wide and curious.

The pale man shook his head. "We don't need to play with him anymore." He ran a tongue across his sharp teeth.

"Caroline!" Steps stormed down the hall and pulled the door open, flooding the dark room with light. "Caroline, now you answer me when I'm speaking to you! I've had it up to here with you these days!"

The pale man slunk up from behind the door, silently climbing up the wall with only his fingertips. He smiled at the girl and held a finger to his lips.

Shh.

The girl looked sad. "Oh, please! Just one more game?" she asked, looking up.

"Game? What in the world are you talking about?" her father asked.

The pale man frowned, but let it change into a smile. He nodded sharply, eager for what would come next.

"No games now, Caroline. You had better go to bed or there will be hell to pay. Now. Do you hear me?"

Her mouth stretched wide and fanned open to display dozens of sharp teeth; her hideous laugh came before the screams.

23

DANIEL'S BREATH LEFT A FOG ON THE CAR WINDOW. HE WIPED it off idly, intently watching the trees hurry past, while wallowing in what was done and what had been lost.

I fucked everything up. We could have had them all, but I didn't listen. What the hell is wrong with me?

He felt as if he had no control, like he had been split down the middle, and the two sides fought each other. How could he even trust himself?

"Fuck me," Daniel said, breaking the silence. "What if I broke our only chance, Maker?"

"No, we're still fine. Just take it as a lesson. Truth is, I've been rusty. We should have gone in better prepared. I don't know where the hell my head has been."

"Maker, listen, I'm sor—"

Ripping away from the shadows behind Daniel, a clawed hand sank its pointed nails into the meat of Daniel's shoulder as it climbed from the back seat. It had horns and let out a deafening shriek.

"Fuck!" Maker yelled and jerked the car into a spin, tires screeching against the road.

The thin nails ripped at Daniel's muscles, trying to find something strong to hold onto as the car lost control. Daniel screamed as a sharp burning pain twisted in his arm while the car jerked from side to side, skidding across the road. In a blind panic, he grabbed at the claw and tried to pull it out. Instead, the sharp nails cut into his hand, and he clenched tighter. The horned changeling lashed at Maker with its free hand, catching him on the side of the face twice, exposing the muscle beneath the skin.

The car went off the road and into a ditch, bobbing them all up and down in the car. It slammed to a halt; somehow, Maker had the pistol in his hand.

Bam! Bam!

In a flash of deafening sound and blinding light, Maker fired two shots into the creature's body. It sailed backward, ripping its fingers from Daniel and taking some of his arm with it.

"Fuck!" Daniel yelled.

The world turned up and then down, spinning in Daniel's head. The blasts were disorienting, and blood leaked from his scalp. He wasn't sure, but he might have hit his skull against the inside of the car—it all happened so quickly. With clumsy hands, he fumbled with his seat belt and eventually found the door handle. The door opened, spilling him onto the grass.

"Son of a bitch!"

Clawed fingers reached up and scratched at the inside of the back window, leaving a dark smear on the glass.

"Maker?" Daniel yelled. He tried to focus, but could only hear something ringing. "Maker!"

The door opened and the horned head of the girl poked out. Two large uneven horns sprang from her forehead; thick brown wisps of bristling hair came from her chin and beneath her high cheekbones. And the two bullet holes still smoked in her face, one through a ruined eye that she seemed less than concerned about. He might not have known her to be a girl at all if not for the pink pajamas, now colored with fresh blood.

As she crept forward, the large, off-center horns shook like a rattle. "You'll be so fun to play with!" The words were fuzzy in Daniel's ear as he tried to steady himself.

"Maker!" Daniel yelled as he scampered back, the ringing dying down to a whimper now.

"Who is that? The old man? He tastes good, mmm!" She licked the blood from her fingers, and a wet chunk dripped from her mouth.

"Do it then!" The torn shoulder burned and made it hard for Daniel to move. He felt for the gun but couldn't find it, so he rolled to his side, pulled out the knife, and held it in front of him with a shaky hand. "Come on! Do it, you bitch! Fucking do it!"

The girl came down onto her hands and feet with her back curved into an arch. She giggled as she scooted forward, waving one claw in the air. "I'm going to getcha! I'm going to getcha!" she taunted as she inched forward. "I'm going to getcha, then I'm going to peel you! Peel you all the way down!" She burst into hysterical laughter.

Bam!

A blast hit the girl in the side, knocking her off her feet and stopping her mid-laugh. Maker had come around the car with his pistol trained on her. Daniel didn't hesitate. With all that he had left, he sprang onto her small frame and pounded the blade down into her chest. It went in with a loud thud, and came out with a tearing grind and her agonized scream. He grabbed at her wrist and tried to pin it, then slammed the knife down again.

She screeched like a dying cat as he brought the knife up, then down again into her head. It went in easier than Daniel expected, like when he used to carve pumpkins as a kid. If he was blindfolded, he might have thought he was carving a new smile across her face. The first stab into her head was all she needed—the strikes after that were just for him. Her body shook under him in the throes of death, twisting and needling him, but still dying.

Black blood slipped and sprayed with each strike. Daniel hit her again and again, until nothing recognizable remained.

"That's enough!" Maker yelled. "Get it in the car, we have to go!" Maker left. There was no time to argue with him, as a car had stopped close by and someone was stepping out.

"Are you okay?" the voice called.

Maker leveled his gun at him and fired twice, purposefully missing him with both shots. The man sprang back into his car and raced off. Daniel watched it for only a moment before he stood up. He grabbed the girl; her hand still shuddered with tiny movements.

She's so light and small. . .

He put her in the back. Maker opened the trunk and came back with a small gasoline container. Blood was still oozing down his head as he poured gasoline on the grass where Daniel and the girl had been. He put the container back and returned with a match; he struck it against the car and threw it at the grass. It went up quickly.

Daniel shut the girl in the back and fell against the side of the car with a groan. Maker came up alongside him and the damage became visible: several long claw marks scratched down his face, and one corner of his face hung loose.

"Shit, Maker!" Daniel groaned out. "We need to get you to the fucking hospital!"

Maker only grunted, stumbled to the car, and pulled himself into the passenger's seat. "Can you drive? I can't see."

Daniel got into the driver's seat, but his left arm hurt too much to even grab the wheel. He pressed the gas, but it felt like the car might not get out of the ditch. Finally, he found solid ground and the car pulled out. Daniel spared one glance back and saw the fire spreading through the grass.

"No goddamned hospital. Get me to Jenna." Maker took off his jacket and held it to his face, even as more blood leaked out.

They didn't talk; Maker was losing too much blood. Daniel gunned it and prayed there were no police out.

He should have been afraid. He should have been terrified, worried about Maker, or ready to lose his mind. But another thought cooked in his head.

Four down, two to go.

A HAIL of splinters burst into the air; Daniel was having trouble pulling the car in, and the mailbox paid for it. The car slammed to a halt near the house, leaving tire tracks across the yard. He hit the horn three times before he opened the door and yelled.

"Maker needs help!"

Moving faster than Daniel thought she could, Jenna came running out of the house and Greg ran up from the barn.

"Jesus, God!" Jenna said as she came to Maker's door. "What happened?"

Greg opened the door and Maker slumped out, one hand pressing against the still-bleeding wound. Blood had soaked his white shirt and turned the seat dark red.

"Daniel knocked one off," Maker said with some pride. "It's in the back, leaking all over the damn seat."

"Well, fuck me, looks like it got you too, Maker," Greg said, inspecting the wound. "Shit, yeah. Long as you don't bleed to death, this looks like a good 'un."

"Lord Almighty!" Jenna peeked into the back and then at the others. "Get inside, get inside! I'll fetch a needle!"

"Ain't so bad," Maker said, but struggled to keep on his feet. "Head wounds always bleed."

Greg all but carried Maker in, while Jenna snatched one of Daniel's arms and supported him like a crutch. In the kitchen, Greg knocked everything from the table, and with a mighty heave, put Maker onto it.

Jenna shot into the dark of the hallway and returned with a towel and medical kit. "Hold this to you arm." With steady hands, she pressed the clean white towel to the wound.

Steady hands.

Jenna had looked shocked and worried outside but now, she was focused and not at all unprepared or incapable.

New waves of pain stabbed Daniel's arm when he pressed the towel to it, but Maker looked near death. The old man might have lost an eye. Daniel couldn't take his eyes off him, even as blood soaked his arm and dripped from his fingers.

Greg poured a shot from a bottle marked with a black *x*. He helped Maker down it, then helped himself to one. He then poured some into a small square pan where Jenna put her needles.

"Don't look so fucking concerned, Dan," Greg said with

a feigned smile. "Jenna can sew a shotgun wound. Why the hell do you think we keep her around? The hag sure as hell can't fight for shit."

"Yeah," Daniel said with a nod, but he could read the lines of doubt written in Greg's eyes.

"He'll pull through," Jenna said without making eye contact. The smile and the concern she typically wore had faded, replaced with a new focus. She pinched a suture needle between her two calloused fingers and went to work stitching up the seeping tears on Maker's face. "You just hold 'em steady!" she shouted. Greg pressed his weight down on Maker.

"Fuck." Maker grimaced as Jenna sewed his flesh and pulled the flaps together.

"Now you sit still!" She stopped momentarily to stare at Maker eye to eye. She then glanced at Greg. "We're going to need to top 'em off."

"See? He's fine," Greg said with fading lines of stress. "And this is why they keep me around—universal donor. She's the stitcher, I'm the blood bag."

When it came to Daniel's turn, he took a long swill of Greg's bottle and let Jenna get to sewing. He groaned, but was glad for Greg's poison to soften the edge.

"First war wound, you pussy," Greg said with a hearty grin and got a sharp look from Jenna. "Don't worry none. It adds character."

Jenna pulled out a small red vial from her kit and shook it up.

"What's that?" Daniel said.

"Antivenom we milked from those glands I took." Greg answered.

"He didn't get bit, only scratched."

"Mmhmm, but best to be safe. They've surprised us

before. You're getting a dose, too." Jenna looked at Daniel for only a moment before she pulled a syringe and loaded it from the vial.

Maker passed out before he even got his dose, leaving Daniel to explain everything. "The damn thing just came out of the back seat. Maker even checked back there. Have you ever seen that? Heard about something like that happening?"

Greg was readying to say something, but a hoarse voice came from the hallway.

"Yes." Her voice came like nails on glass. "In the old stories, though I've never seen them." Rebekah was there with a cane, hunched over as she spoke.

"Me either." Greg shook his head.

"This is somethin' much darker than we've ever had to deal with, Daniel," Jenna said from her seat, exhausted and fanning herself with an empty hand. "And you should be asleep."

"Like I could sleep through this noise." Rebekah stood silently for a moment, as she looked Maker over. "You two found something at the asylum?"

"Yeah. Something was there, inside the asylum, not sure what. Two bodies that looked gnawed-on were outside."

"Well, we're going to have to go check it out again. In the meanwhile, I'm going to go see how the bitch you carved up looks." Greg said, and left the room.

Daniel sat with Jenna and Rebekah, neither saying a word, but Rebekah's eyes said all that was needed as she watched Maker.

She loves him.

There wasn't long to reflect on that before Greg was back, dragging the dead changeling. The thing's dead eyes and cold skin weren't nearly as terrifying now. In death, she looked unreal, with her sharp, crooked teeth and jutting horns, like a latex toy. Nothing was terrifying about her anymore. In a way, he pitied her, but he wasn't sure why. Was it the long blonde hair or the pink pajamas with the smiling cartoon characters? She might have been pretty if her hair wasn't tangled and matted with blood.

It's not pity for the creature—it's for the girl she killed and the family that'll mourn her. You can't help but imagine what that girl looks like.

Daniel only watched her, deaf to the others, as they went about their business. Greg tried to say something to him, but Daniel just shook him off and kept his eyes on the girl.

Who were you? Why did you do this?

Those questions and more came, but questions for the dead always went unanswered.

"He's waking up!" Jenna said from the kitchen.

Maker had stirred awake and was rubbing his arm when they came back. He found the needle and tubing leading to an IV bag, and he lifted his hand to the patch across his head. "Now here I was hoping that was just some shitty nightmare."

"Oh, it's a nightmare, all right, just one you don't wake up from," Greg said as he leaned forward. "You good enough to talk?"

"I don't reckon it matters much if I'm good or not." Maker licked his lips, and Jenna handed him some water. He downed half the cup. "We need to get packed and leave. We're compromised. I'm sorry, Daniel, but we can't stay."

"I get it." Daniel hung his head. "They're coming after us and we lost our shot. We barely made it through that."

Before Daniel could tell them that he was going to stay behind, Rebekah cleared her throat. Daniel saw her glance at Jenna. "We can't leave. I saw more in the memories I ripped from the last parasite. We can't run from this one. The one we tracked to the town, he's old. Very old."

"Which is why we have to be more than careful." Maker pressed a hand to his head and groaned. "We don't know what we're dealing with here. We'll have to contact another cell to take this one."

"No. He's not important." A tear dripped from Rebekah's hard eyes, like water from a stone. "Daniel's son . . ."

Sam?

"He's not dead."

24

THE PALE MAN STUFFED A KNUCKLE INTO HIS MOUTH TO STIFLE a laugh while watching the car swerve off the road. His teeth cut the skin, and black blood filled his mouth. He lapped at the cut, but didn't take his eyes from the car.

He grew giddy and shook with muffled laughter as the younger man stumbled from the car with the pale man's daughter slinking out after him. She was toying with him, her hand held high as she taunted him.

Oh, it's so funny!

Something akin to pride flooded the pale man, and he longed to watch his daughter eat her fill of the hunters. He hoped there'd be enough of them left to ply answers from later, but that was only a minor concern.

"Here it comes!" he said to no one, with speckles of blood flying from his lips with each word.

The younger man pulled out a blade and waved it around like it would actually be of some use. The pale man's grin widened—he liked it when they were afraid.

But then the gray-haired man came around the car. Two blasts from the old man's pistol knocked her off balance, and then the younger man pounced. A flash as the knife went up and down, driving it into her head over and over until she went surprisingly limp.

Dead?

There was no laughter now; his glossy black eyes blinked rapidly, confused and unbelieving. Falling to his hands and feet, he scampered forward, elbows bent inward, to get a better look.

There was still no laughter when another man stopped, and the old man fired at him. Still nothing when they loaded his brood into their car, bloody and mangled, and set fire to her blood.

Dead.

The thought was shocking, enraging even. Not for reasons people would understand—there was no love between him and his brood—but because she was his and not for any other to take.

Beneath his bitten knuckle that was still held to his lips, his teeth cracked and ground enough that a shard broke into his throat. After they drove away, he scurried over to where the fire burned. It singed the grass, burning off the traces of his offspring's blood. The shadows of the flame danced over him, and he lost track of time while considering what had happened.

Cold Iron. They have Cold Iron.

A curse from God, laid upon his kind since the old days. So powerful was he, that he could dance between shadows, and he had even found a hole to move freely between his world and theirs.

But fucking Cold Iron still hurts.

His child would never grow, never continue the line. It was dead. So many of his died—they always did, one way or another. So self-destructive was his kind that few reached maturity.

He had felt another of his pass just this day. Such a thing wasn't startling; there was a madness in their blood, such that they would sometimes kill themselves or let the mask slip too far off and risk turning into one of the beasts that can't leave the shadows. These things happen, and so was the way of their existence. When dead, the bodies would quickly slip the mask back on. Nature had a way of keeping secrets.

But Cold Iron exposed it all.

Cold Iron burned the mask away, and they might never return. He saw them ravage his girl with it, and now he had to consider that they might have done the same to his boy.

I'll tear their fucking faces off and pick my teeth with their bones!

Some time may have passed; he didn't know or care. So focused was he on playing these thoughts through his head —*hunter, Cold Iron, dead*—that he only just now noticed the light.

"Are you okay?" a voice asked from behind. "Sir, what are you doing? Did you set the fire?"

His curly white locks blew in the cool breeze as his head swiveled toward the uniformed man. The man shined his flashing electric torch at the pale man.

Quite irritating.

The man's instincts must have been sharp; he already had his pistol in his hand, probably sensing that this thing before him was from the pit. His voice was not so strong. He didn't run, however—surely a credit to his species.

"Stay where you are!" He aimed the pistol at the pale man. "Hands up! Hands up, dammit!"

The laughter came back then, a bellow so strong that it

shook his whole body from head to toe. Throwing his head back, he roared, and let his laugh carry through the night.

Instinct seized the police officer, and he fired two rounds into the pale man's chest. The bullets rocked him back, but didn't take him from his feet like the man surely had hoped. Instead, the pale man strode forward, slowly, as another round slammed into his chest.

With a snap, he grabbed the gun and twisted it out of the man's hand, hard enough that it broke his fingers with a loud *pop*. The man's screams now came even louder than the laughter.

The pale man took him from his feet like one might snatch an insolent child, and dragged him to the shadows of the woods, content to enjoy himself.

"Ha-ha! Ha-ha!"

The man struggled for his life, kicking and hammering his fists against the monster. "Get off me! Get the fuck off me!" The pale man grabbed the man by the face; claws dug into flesh. He dragged the man to a place beyond; when they entered, a hundred hungry eyes came to life to greet them.

THERE WAS ice in Daniel's blood, and his limbs were like hollow trees.

He's not dead?

Nothing made sense; nothing could make him move. Hadn't he heard them say before that no one ever came back? They were dead, never to return.

Sam isn't dead?

"What?" Maker spat out, leaning up from the table.

"He's not dead," Rebekah said again, and Jenna took her

arm when she wobbled. "I saw it when we were first there. I just didn't know it at first. And I had to wait."

"Wait for what?" Greg asked with a huff.

"Before, I knew only that they hadn't killed him when we thought. Now, I know they still have him, but I don't know why." She settled into a chair.

"Sam." Daniel's blood began to thaw. "How is he still alive?"

She turned her gaze to Daniel and in that moment, only she and he existed. "I don't know, exactly. I suspect it's connected to his parasite's sickness and apparent death." She chose her words carefully. "They didn't eat him, and I believe it grew sick for it."

"Where can I find him?" In a burst, he was on his feet and inches from Rebekah.

"I don't know," Rebekah said, turning her face to stone. "I wish I did. By God, I wish I did!"

"They had him this entire fucking time and you didn't tell me!" He slammed his fist into the old cabinet, cracking the wood.

"Tell you? How could I?" She rose to her feet, fragile and weak, but staring into Daniel's eyes. "You're a maniac! You've almost lost your mind, and what good would you be to us if I had told you he lived, only to now be dead? But that is of no consequence now. There is no more time to wait. The game is changed, and now our moves are forced."

Fire burned in Daniel's lungs; his fingers cracked as they curled into white-knuckled fists. Another scream was readying in his lungs when Jenna's soft hands touched his.

"Daniel. We're going to get your boy back," she said.

The wind left him, and he took his seat. Blood was dripping down his shoulder again, but he didn't care. He slipped his head into his hands and sobbed.

Something broke inside him. Fears flooded out, washing over him and pouring exhaustion into him. He felt like his heart might give out, or like he might just collapse into a coma.

At first, there was something beyond the fear, something to hope for. But the eyes around him told him that no one knew what to do. No one could tell him how to save his son, only that he still breathed.

But for how long? What kind of hell do they have him in? What are they doing to him? Wouldn't he be better off dead?

"What can we do?" he managed to say, but he didn't look up. He couldn't meet their empty eyes, couldn't bear to see that they had nothing left to give him, no way to help Sam.

Their silence only confirmed that.

"We're going to save him." Jenna said again, the only one of them optimistic or foolish enough to say anything. "God saved your boy once, Daniel. And he brought you here to us, put you in this room with these people at this time. There's a plan here bigger than our eyes can see, and we have all the tools we need, Daniel. God will be with us."

He looked up. Her silken eyes poured cool water over Daniel's soul; she meant every word. They would do everything they could to get Sam back.

Greg huffed. "Might be suicide, Tanner, but I ain't never saved no damn kid before." He gave a frank nod to Daniel.

"Yeah, Dan." Maker said, drawing in a raspy breath. "We'll do what we can. We'll get him."

"We're going to get your boy back, Daniel," Jenna said with a wide smile and utter belief in it. "I see the gears moving. I see that God built me, and us, the way we are for this moment, for your boy. We're going to kill this devil, and we're going to save your son."

25

BROKEN GLASS CHURNED IN REBEKAH'S LUNGS WITH EACH breath, threatening that each could be her last. Her hand shook, and though she needed rest—she had to be ready for what came next—she couldn't sleep. But Daniel went out quickly. They all agreed that Daniel needed to rest, so they gave him a sedative, though he refused any medication that might alter his dreams.

Still, he went so easily.

Rebekah was startled by the fervor in Daniel, how quickly he had become engrossed in everything. It was only a scant few months ago that they had come to the town of New Athens, chasing after Rebekah's visions—since then, fall had turned the leaves orange, and winter was starting, bringing the first snowfall of the year.

Rebekah held her fingers against the cold glass the way she did when she was a girl, and watched the flakes fall from the sky. The chill of the night whistled through a crack in the frame and made her breath visible.

She thought of old times, simpler times: first, when she was a girl and winter was a thing to fear. In East

Germany, the cold brought a chill from which some didn't wake.

I wish that all there was to fear were winter and death.

Life had carried her beyond that, beyond fear of death. Now, she feared hope. It was a dangerous thing that shook her bones and quickened her heart in ways she hadn't felt in years. She saw Sam in those visions. Sam, who looked so much like her own younger brother.

Does he? His hair isn't the same, nor his eyes. But do I remember what my little brother even looked like? I see him in both Sam and Daniel, somehow.

There was no direction or vision to tell her where Sam was, only that he still breathed. She felt it in the memory. There was something about the boy, something the *Wechselkinder* had that kept him alive.

She wasn't ready for any of this, to even tell anyone that he was still alive. There was nothing to gain from it, and she knew that if he died, it would have been better for Daniel never to have known. But what could she do besides tell the others that they couldn't leave, that there might be a chance to save this boy?

She had nothing, only hope.

Hope can kill a person who is already low and used to the taste of mud in his mouth, who doesn't want to keep going, who only waits for the end. Hope can drive you mad chasing it or kill you when it breaks. There was no place for hope in a heart as cold as Rebekah's.

Hope will kill me.

Her cheeks grew wet. How long had it been since she'd last cried? How long had it been since she'd really been afraid? She had the scars, both mental and physical, to show how calloused she'd become. She'd watched family members die, seen friends torn apart, failed, and known that others paid the price. But now she had hope, and it hurt more than anything she'd ever experienced.

"Rebekah," Jenna said as she stepped into the bedroom. "You best lay down and cover up! You'll catch a chill that way!"

Rebekah turned to her, her eyes still puffy and slick with tears. She didn't know what she wanted. The chill was the least of her concerns.

"Oh, Rebekah," Jenna said softly and wrapped her arms around Rebekah.

"Jenna," Rebekah said as she hugged the woman. "How could this happen? How could God do this to me? How could He ask this of me? I can't save this boy. I can't save anyone. I don't know where he is! I don't know what to do! Jenna, I can't do it."

Rebekah didn't believe in God. How could she, with all she'd seen and all she'd experienced? But now, in the most frightening moment of her life, she couldn't help but think of Him.

"Rebekah." Jenna squeezed her tight. "He spoke to you because you're the only one who *can* help. You're the only one with the gifts, girl. And God loves you; that's why He came to you. That's why He gave you these gifts, Rebekah. You're the only one who can do it."

She's right. I have to stay strong. Without me, there's no chance.

"Thank you, Jenna," she said, pulling away and smiling at the woman she knew to be one of her only true friends in life. She wiped away the tears. "I know what to do."

She had a reason to go on now, a reason not to break or to die, a reason to keep fighting.

She had hope.

SLEEP CAME for Daniel like he was already dead. It sank its fingers into him and pulled him into the land of dreams. He hadn't fought it. He didn't know this world when he was awake, but something in the back of his mind told him to go there, welcomed him, to the land of dreams.

And soon he was there.

"I know it's fucking maddening. That's what I've been saying from day one."

The conversation was already halfway done before it had begun—such was the strangeness of the dream world.

"Sam? How can he be alive? It doesn't make any sense."

"Sure, it does. They want to fuck with you. So how do you get back? You cut them. You hurt them. Little pain, little blood—it picks their games apart. But you have to do more than that. You have to enjoy it. You have to show them that you can play their games too, and that you *like* it." He pressed his hand flat against the glass of the mirror. He only vaguely looked like Daniel, with nails grown into claws and eyes like a cat's, black shards in pools of yellow. "You have to *like* to hurt them."

Outside the glass, Daniel sat on his bed. The dream-haze stretched a faded boundary around a vision of what Daniel's room had looked like in his youth. Things lurked there, dark things that reached for you when you got too close. His fears and pain, some bred anew just by being told that Sam was still alive. Each was ugly, scarred, and in cease-less torment.

The conversation moved from one to the other, but they were all one, just the same. Each side of him spoke, each was a voice in his head. Each knew what the other would say, but let him say it anyway, for the sake of theater.

"I think you're right." His voice quaked, and his fingers squeezed the sheets of his childhood bed. "I don't want to be like them, but I want Sam. Oh God, I want Sam back."

A new chorus of howls came from the fears that reached out for him, each seeking to pull him into the darkness. They had howled to the point where he couldn't hear or understand anything; the fears were all-consuming. He had beaten them, pushed them back, and Rebekah had blocked it all up in a room. He'd left his insecurities and pains caged in a stone prison to rot.

It had grown too strong with new thoughts of Sam, and moaned so loudly Daniel thought it might finally break him. It didn't bend like a person, only like something with soft, flexible bones. It reached through the prison and howled as it pushed through, leaving a slick layer of red puss as it pulsed through the gaps it had broken in the rock. Red and slicked with a yellow sheen, it had no eyes, no direction or senses; it moaned and slopped around the floors of Daniel's mind. It was the madness that threatened to break him, that told him to kill himself, or collapse.

Fear had turned into something blind and aimless that lashed out at whatever it could hold. Even now, it still joined its screaming howl with those of the other fears.

"What do you think it is?" Daniel asked, already knowing, watching it wail and pull closer to him. "Why do you think it won't die?"

"Because you feed it," the one with sharp teeth said and pushed harder on the glass. "You keep it here, and you feed it by pretending you're something you're not. You let it breathe." He stretched a hand through the glass, bending like water, as it motioned for the other to come closer.

"You're right."

The fear wailed and slapped a wet hand down. It dug its fingers in and pulled closer.

"I feed it; I hold onto it. Why would I do that?" He stood and moved closer to the glass; tears ran down his cheeks, tears that burned and dripped to the floor, leaving a spatter of bruises wherever they hit.

"Because." He stretched his head through the glass, sending ripples through it. "You think it makes you human to be afraid. But I live in this world. I know the rules and the games. I'll eat the motherfucker. *Just let me out.*"

Daniel's red fear slapped a wet hand down into his room and pulled itself into the light, leaving a greasy streak through his mind. It reared its head back so far that its neck might snap, and it screeched loudly enough that the glass cracked. It was close enough that Daniel could see the red veins running through its pink flesh.

He turned from it and looked back into the splintered eyes of the other. He took the other's hand. One's hands were cold, the other's hot. One was desperate to be set loose, the other wanting nothing more than to collapse into nothingness.

"Dan. You're doing the right thing." He smiled wide with a mouthful of gleaming fangs.

Then their places were changed, and another stood out of the mirror and the other rested within its cage. Daniel took a deep breath, feeling for the first time in his life, uncaged and in control. His gaze settled on the screaming fears and the wallowing misery that reached up from the ground.

He cracked its wet neck with the heel of his boot.

"Let's clean this shit up."

26

———

THE BANDAGE ON MAKER'S HEAD HAD GROWN WET AGAIN; HE sighed and thought of how close he'd come to losing an eye. Those claws were sharp enough to cut through skin and muscle and scratch the bone beneath, and it hurt like hell.

"Son of a bitch," he said and pressed his hand to his head.

The damn thing's stink was still in his nose, a smell like a wild animal that had shit all over itself. This one had been fresh off the kill; Maker had seen the blood all over its pink pajamas.

Fucking strange that it came after us like that.

"Why do you reckon it did that?" Greg asked, like he had read Maker's mind.

"Well," Maker began, "the damn things are more like beasts than men—that's your area. I got a theory, but I'd like to hear yours first." He took a gulp of cold water; it stung his dry throat.

After a hearty laugh, Greg shook his head. "Well, I think you got a little too close to the den and it sent one out to push you back. About did the job, till Dan back there gigged the little bitch with his knife."

Maker tipped his head, his eyes heavy with exhaustion. "Yeah, glad he had the damn thing. And I think you're right." He let his hand drop and eased his eyes closed. "Never had one of them ambush me like that. I thought I knew all their tricks. Coming out of the back seat like that? Shit."

"You don't ever really know a wild animal, sure as fuck don't know one that ain't got no right to exist. Ain't the first time we saw a new trick."

The old man nodded and felt the weight of his years like bricks on his back. "Well, if we were close, then it's that fucking asylum." He shook his head and groaned as another stab of pain came. "I hate that God-forsaken place."

"Well, hell, all you had to do was tell me 'abandoned mental ward' and I'd hate the fucking place, too." Greg stood up from his chair and rubbed the stubble on his chin, something Maker knew meant he had the itch. "We have to get our asses back there. Give it a little time to get comfortable, and we'll see what we can shake up."

"Mmhmm. It's reasonable to assume that the thing laughing at us was that pale man that Rebekah saw in her vision."

"You hear a damn laugh in the dark and you get all that?" Greg asked with smirk that showed his bad teeth.

Maker looked up and opened his eyes again. "I felt it in my bones. That's the son of a bitch. I knew he was there all along—part of me did, anyway."

"Okay. Good enough for me. So, we know where this bastard lives but not what he wants, why he's here, or what he's capable of. Sounds like a shit show to grab a seat in, frankly."

"And we don't know where he has the boy, or why."

"Yeah." Greg took a kick from his flask. He'd been taking it easy on the drink, so Maker wouldn't begrudge him a little. A little did always seem to get the gears churning in Greg's mind. "Fuck me, though, Maker, the only plan I got is a shit one."

"Like you said, it's a shit show. Lay it on me."

Greg shook his head as if he hated it even while he said it. "Midnight run. We grab the rest of his nest, bring 'em back here, and put the work on them, see what we can get. Then we drag what's left of them to your asylum, get those bleeders calling out. Momma will come runnin', that's for damn sure."

"You want to kick the nest?"

"Don't think '*want to*' are the right words." He swilled his flask and took another shot. "My imagination says it's playing out one of two ways over there with this pale fucker. Either he's looking for us, or looking at how to get on down the road. Either one ain't no good for us. The way I'm seeing it, though?" he waved his hand flat out in front of him. "I think I can cut us twenty-eighty odds. That's about as good as we can get. I've had a good run, though, and I ain't never saved no damn kid. I can think of worse causes to sell my life to."

"Well, that sure isn't bullshit. This looks like a death-trap." Maker agreed. None of it was good. Any other day in his life, he'd walk away and watch New Athens burn in his rearview mirror.

But the boy. We might be able to bring one back. That was worth gambling an old man's life. That's worth gambling every-one's lives.

They were going to play this game, shit odds or not.

"I guess you're right. Better to bring the fight to him. We

have one more confirmed; I drove by the house and say it's about as close to certain as can be. Think you can go check out the other name on Jenna's list? See if you can get us a confirmation? Take Daniel with you. If he sits here, he's going to lose his mind."

"Kid's already lost his fucking mind, Maker. That much is clear. I'll do it, though."

"We're going to need your tools. I hope they're sharp."

"They are. I got them out in the barn, tarp and lock on 'em." Greg said in a voice filled with pride. "Got your present in there, too, nice and dry."

"Greg, this might be it for us, you know. Even if everything goes right, we're going to have to get the hell out of Dodge, fast." He lazily waved his hand toward the barn. "I saw you with the dog. I know you like it. What you do with it is your business, but you need to do something."

"Yeah, you're right," Greg said. "I suppose it's time to go drop her off somewhere."

"She looks healthy. She's a fighter." Maker gave him a nod and with that, Greg set off.

Maker watched him leave and the room grew silent, leaving him with only his thoughts. He looked out the back window at the woods; he was afraid of them, but more than that, he was afraid he wasn't up for this. He was old, hurt, and tired, more so than he could ever remember. He could practically feel the dust on his bones.

But now, he only watched the snowfall, a haze in the sky like it was blocking the eye of God.

I suppose it's best God not see what's coming next.

GREG WASN'T A HAPPY PERSON. Sometimes, he figured he

only lived, breathed, shit, and ate out of habit. He didn't like himself, didn't like what he did either, but he was good at it, so there must be a reason. There had to be some reason for it all.

Maybe it's the boy. Maybe he's the reason for it all?

He let the idea roll around his head like the bottles on the floor of his truck. It was a nice thought, but he'd grown out of a need for a reason long ago. What reason is there in a world where an old drunk lives to hurt things, things that scream when an iron knife cuts them, but a bullet doesn't do much but annoy them? He wished there was a reason, but he didn't expect to find one.

He barely took notice of the snow falling on his bare shoulders and clinging to his shirt, not with so much focus on that tarp and what was beneath it in the back of the barn. He paused only when the dog moaned at him as he came in. Her tail started wagging when she saw it was Greg. Damn thing never barked—must have been hurt pretty badly before, and the scars around its throat suggested as much. Some old asshole must not have liked her much, but he did.

Never even named her.

He rubbed under her chin. It was suitable that she didn't have a name; she was only passing through his life, no point in getting attached. His life might not last much longer anyway, and besides, the dog was only here because it had the rotten luck of having a litter of pups outside in the fall.

Shit luck, girl, just like me.

He rubbed her soft ears; she seemed to like that. She closed her eyes and the pup came yawning and stretching from its nest of blankets before it shot to Greg, its tail flicking back and forth. Its hair fuzzed up when Greg rubbed his thumb over its head; he could nearly fit the entire damn thing in one hand. He reached into the bed of his truck and grabbed a coffee can full of dog food. They shot to the bowl when he popped the top off and poured it out; he rubbed the mother's back while she ate.

Rotten luck, you finding me now. Year or two ago would have been better.

Now, he turned to the heavy gray tarp slung over his workbench. He pulled it off and slapped it to the ground, sending dust into the air and exposing the small boxes and the bench beneath it, along with several propane tanks rigged for a good time. It was all kept clean, more clean than necessary. It was important to respect the things you killed with.

"You treat your tools like you treat your lovers. Keep 'em pretty, groomed, and don't let any other motherfuckers touch 'em."

That's what his father had told him. A man's tools were his life out in the woods, in the jungle. Out there, men live and die by the sharpness of a blade and the reliability of a gun.

This was his jungle, and these were his tools.

Bear traps, enlarged and bladed with iron points. Spear tips with screw-on inserts—some with hooks, others barbed. Knives, arranged according to their varying purposes. Iron axe-heads. His metal net, used just a short time before on a thing buried out back. And boxes of hand-pressed shotgun shells filled with iron—not enough to kill, but he liked to think it made it hurt more. All of it filled or tipped with iron, and all of it useless except for hunting a brood.

Greg picked up one of the knives. He'd never used it before, never had to. He'd hunted changelings for a long time, but never like this, never going straight at it to get something back. He'd always wondered how he'd do with one close up. That certainly wasn't the plan; that's what you did when a plan failed. But part of him still hoped he'd get the chance.

I bet I could cut one of those big motherfuckers down, given half a chance.

He appraised it all like, he imagined, a father watched his son play ball. A small part of him twisted, the part that told him this was all he had, and he'd never have more. He swallowed that; now wasn't the time to get emotional.

The dog pressed her wet nose into his hand. He turned with a smile and ran his rough hand through her coat again; it had a nice, healthy sheen to it.

"We're going to get you dropped off somewhere nice, girl. I'll make sure we get you somewhere good. Snow's falling now, so don't think I'd just kick your rotten ass out on the side of the road." He rubbed her ears when she licked his hands. "Maybe tomorrow, when I have a drive through town, I'll keep an eye out for you."

Yeah, if only she'd come a year earlier. Rotten luck.

27

"THAT'S THE HOUSE," DANIEL SAID WITH A TIP OF HIS HEAD. Something growled inside him, echoed from a hollow point inside his soul where he'd carved out a piece.

"You sure, now?" Greg asked, leaning forward and peering from the driver's seat of his truck.

"It's in there."

"How the fuck do you know it's in there? You don't know shit."

Daniel didn't tear his eyes from the house—he couldn't. "I know it. I can feel it in there."

"Fuck, come on now. Don't start pulling Maker's shit on me. You ain't got his instincts."

Daniel turned his burning eyes on Greg. "It's in that fucking house."

"Well." Greg tensed up. "Maybe you're right and maybe you're not. But we've got three other potentials. We only came to this one first because it best fits the bill. Jenna heard the birds squawking that this one was lighting things on fire, and Maker caught that the police were out here, and—hey wait, get the fuck back in here!"

Already two steps out the door and slamming it behind him, Daniel heard Greg's curses, but his feet were moving too quickly to stop, leaving prints in the thin layer of snow as he neared the porch. The air was too chilly for his thin jacket, but something in his core warmed him, as though the wolfskin actually held the heat that burned in his chest.

Paul and Sara Montgomery.

This was their home, out here on the improper end of New Athens, where lawns weren't always mowed and bank foreclosure signs lined the street, which had been filled with some of the descendants of the coal miners before the mine closed. Most of them were good people, even if they couldn't pay the bank.

Not these assholes.

Paul had a reputation as a loudmouth and shit-starter. One story went that he broke a man's jaw during one of his older son's football games. Sara didn't fare much better— Daniel only knew her from a PTA meeting, when she came in drunk after screaming at a teacher in another room. He didn't stick around to find out why.

While his gaze swept from side to side to watch for any movement, Daniel walked alongside Paul's pickup, pulled out his keys, and gouged the door on the passenger's side a good two inches. The pickup had a nice cherry-red coat and looked only a few years old. Paul's priorities were clear.

Shouldn't leave it out in the snow if you love it so damn much.

Next, he was up at the front door and pushing the bell. When it didn't ring, he knocked. Someone yelled from inside and a few moments later, a college-age man wearing a faded football jersey that matched a fading black eye opened the door.

"What?" was all the kid said.

Daniel smiled, the wolfskin purring in his ear. "This is the Montgomery house, right? Your dad home? I'm afraid I scratched his car the other day, but had to run. The supermarket told me he lived here."

"You dented my dad's car?" the kid said. Without another word, he turned and stepped away, letting the door swing shut with a loud crack on its frame.

Daniel took a breath; something stank in the house, but he wasn't sure what. Looking back, he glanced at Greg idling not far away. A string of curses came from inside the house, followed by stomping.

The door swung open with a crack as the hinges caught. "What the fuck? You scratched my car?" Paul Montgomery wore shorts tucked under a belly that hung over his waistband. Blurry stretched-out tattoos covered his arms, and a thick beard peppered with spots of gray stretched up his face. The scent of bottom-shelf alcohol clung to his breath.

"Yeah, sorry about that." Daniel stepped back from the glass door just as Paul shoved it open. "I scratched it with my cart. Shit, man, real careless, I'm sorry. Was going to see if I could settle out-of-pocket with you."

"Show me where you fucking hit it." Paul scowled as he grabbed a coat and zipped it up over his hairy chest. He stormed outside, rudely shoving Daniel out of the way. He found the scratch and ran his finger over it as his face turned a shade of red. "Son of a bitch! Just got this motherfucker paid off. What the fuck were you doing?"

Paul tensed up—a night of boozing made him all the more belligerent. In another time, Daniel might have been afraid; now he only faked it. "Aw, man, I'm real sorry. I hit it at Save-A-Lot, but I had to get going. I came back the next day and asked if anyone knew whose car it was, and they told me you live out here."

"Save-A-Lot? That Jew store?" He spit the words through yellow teeth. "I don't shop at that cunt's place."

"Oh, maybe it was Roger's? Sorry, my mind's a damn blank right now." Daniel pulled out his wallet, fanning it open to show the crisp fifty-dollar bills tucked in. "Shit, man, I'd prefer not to get insurance in on this. How much you think I owe you?" He watched the tightness leave Paul's jaw and shoulders when he flashed the money.

"Yeah, we could work something out." Paul's eyes, now soft, rolled up to meet Daniel's.

Everyone has buttons. You only have to find the right ones to push to win the game.

GREG FELT his stomach tighten and his throat ache for a drink. An itch crawled up the back of his neck and came to rest behind his eye, making it twitch. Usually, only a drink could scratch it, but he had to stay focused on the task at hand.

This idiot is going to get me killed.

He saw the kid answer the door and the old man show up. The son of a bitch looked like he'd spent the night on a bender and was ready to twist Daniel's head off from the get-go.

You'd think someone named Montgomery would be more respectable. He's definitely the son of a coal miner, though. Did more than his fair share of work outside too, by the look of his arms.

The slob planted a hand on Daniel and shoved him back, clearly ready to lose his shit for half a reason.

Fuck me.

Greg put his truck into park and wondered if he'd have to get out and stop the man from killing Daniel, and with the man's face getting redder as he squared his shoulders up, Greg already had his hand on the door handle. Daniel inched back like a coward, the type of reaction that only goaded men like this Montgomery; Greg knew that for damn sure. But then Daniel's wallet flashed out and the man changed. He still looked pissed, but his eyes flicked to the wallet like it had a picture of Angelina Jolie's tits in it.

Now, the redneck looked almost friendly. Ten or so minutes later, and Daniel was walking back to the truck.

"That's him," Daniel said, slamming the door behind him.

What an idiot.

"What is this, fucking bush league? I oughta slap you upside your damn head," Greg growled as he put the car into drive. "That was damn foolish. We still don't know shit, and now people saw us out here. Didn't you *just* have a fucking talk with Maker about listening? He told us how you ran your stupid ass off and ruined everything. You wasted a bunch of time."

"Yeah? And I'd do it again," Daniel shot back. "Sam is out there, Greg. We don't have time to dick around. I just asked the asshole back there, and he confirmed it. It was the right move. Besides, after that damn thing attacked us in the car and I heard about Sam—I think Maker was wrong. We need to push. He knows it now, too."

"How?" Greg asked. "I saw you gouge the fucker's car and butter him up with some money, but what else did you do?"

"I told him I saw his son play Englewood a few years back when he sacked their quarterback, blew another kid's helmet off. I wasn't there but it was the talk of the town for a good week or so. That put a smile on his face. I asked him if he thought his younger son would play ball, too."

"All right, then, what'd he say?"

"Told me that he might play ball if he didn't kill him first. He said the boy's been burning things and even hit his brother Kevin in the face when he was sleeping, giving him a shiner. Said he's been acting up for a few months now, but it only got bad these last few weeks."

Greg huffed. "And *that* son of a bitch back there was so forthcoming with the information? You got all that in a ten-minute conversation?"

Daniel looked at the clock on the truck dash. "Looks like fourteen minutes to me."

"Smart-ass."

"We're going to have to hit them tonight," Daniel said. "Paul's going to go out and spend a lot of that money on booze. He'll make it easy for us."

"Maybe," Greg said with a nod of his head. "But what about his boy, that blockhead motherfucker? What if he shows up when we're getting the kid? Then what?"

"Then what, Greg? I'm getting my son back anyway I can; *you* should understand that."

"What? You think because I nailed someone when I had to, that I'd just up and shoot some fucking kid because your ass is sloppy? That I'd let *you* shoot some kid? Get the fuck out of here."

"Jesus Christ." Daniel shook his head and turned to gaze out the window. "I'm not going to go shoot any fucking kid, Greg. But he sure as hell wouldn't stop me."

"Good. You go ahead and stow that shit right now," Greg grumbled and scratched his head—still had that itch.

Man, I need a damn drink.

"Well," Greg said, "if we need it, I got a Taser."

Daniel didn't turn to look at him; he only kept his eyes out the window.

Somebody flipped on the fucking switch in that boy.

28

Stepping from the shadows and into the bend of his world, the pale man was greeted by the wet sounds of tearing muscles and the crunch of bones beneath jaws.

The police officer hadn't screamed long—they never did. An unfortunate thing, here in his world: there was little opportunity to enjoy his work before his children found it. So focused were they on pain and hurt that they made no effort to enjoy it, only got their share as quickly and greedily as they could. And of course, to feed, but that was clearly secondary, judging by the mess of stinking flesh still on the floor.

Breathing deeply, he filled his nostrils with the dead man's stink. Then, bending down to look at the corpse's mutilated face, he drank in the man's hollow gaze. His children scattered the moment he leaned toward the body— they were afraid of the pale man and what cruelties he was known to visit upon them for enjoyment, if one happened to be too slow to get out of his way.

Those eyes. What a bright shade of green they must have

been. Were those for someone else to enjoy? Was there a ring on your finger? I don't remember.

White fingers reached down between the dead man's lips and pulled them open; a stream of blood leaked out.

Clean teeth—you took care of yourself. But what is this?

Between his slender fingers, he squeezed the man's jaw and leveraged his fingers on his teeth. The jaw cracked under his palm and a gold tooth came loose.

They still do this, hmm?

He palmed the tooth and stood up; the smallest of his children raced back to the body the moment he left. As he walked, the shadows of the world sucked at his shoes like a thin layer of mud.

With a joyful whistle, he squeezed the tooth between two fingers until it mushed like a ball of dough. The nail on his index finger stretched to a needle-sharp point, and he etched lines into the gold orb, the whistling tune still on his lips. He neared a heavy door with chains and a padlock that came undone at his presence. The chains uncoiled like snakes and slithered back into the wall, dragging the open lock with them.

Like a faithful servant, the door opened to reveal a sleeping boy—he'd been sleeping since the night they'd taken him. There was a smell on him, a unique smell that gathered the interests of the pale man. But now, the boy slept and waited for the nightmares to end.

Usually, things of the real world were consumed by this world. But the boy was still here, still sleeping—an oddity in an odd time.

The pale man laid the gold ball, a smile dug crudely across it, down by the boy's head. The golden orb watched the boy with a ceaseless gaze and a perpetual smile. The pale man's gray lips formed a smile.

"We're going to see your daddy soon."

———

"Did you hear that?" Maker asked, pointing a finger at the radio. "The missing cop? They found his car right out there where Daniel and I were last night."

"Heaven help that poor boy. Lord rest his soul," Jenna said, flashing her eyes to the heavens.

"A husband and wife, along with two children, were butchered inside a house, too. One of the kids is missing. A description of the kid matches the one that attacked us. This is going to set the town on fire. We're going to have one of hell of a time moving now. You don't go to the church anymore, all right? We have to wrap this all up, one way or the other. Someone saw us that night, too. I fired a few rounds to put some fire on his ass, but who knows what he saw. I'll bet that's why that poor bastard cop went out there and got grabbed."

Maker felt a pang of guilt in his chest. He folded it and tucked it away with the rest; it didn't pay to be concerned with the dead.

"I don't imagine that will be an issue," Rebekah said as she stirred her coffee. "The end is coming soon. You can feel it, yes?"

Maker grunted. "No doubt about that. Hope you got enough cigarettes. I don't think we can send Greg out for any more. That's for damn sure."

"I've given them up."

Maker nodded—he understood. This boy changed the game. It was rattling everyone, for better or for worse. He didn't like the idea of everyone not being completely on their game when the rules were changing.

You go to war with the army you have.

"When Greg and Daniel get back and tell us what they got, we're going to set up for the midnight run. Two houses in one night." Maker didn't like the way that tasted in his mouth. "That is, if you got us another confirmation?"

"As confirmed as my hazy gutter magic can be. I found her face in the other's memory, and I reached out for it. It wasn't hard to find—like a torch, burning brighter than the others. She seems to be another particularly nasty creature."

They all seemed particularly nasty.

He remembered the last time Rebekah said one of them burned bright: they lost a man then. Rebekah had told him that the brightest ones were twice as vicious and twice as insane.

"Good. I wouldn't move unless we had it confirmed," he lied; it still wasn't as concrete as he liked.

"What do you want me to do?" Jenna asked as sweetly as she always did.

"You're going to stay here and wait, in case we bring in a bleeder."

"And you?" Jenna tipped her head and let the smile slip. "You, with your half-good eye and pain meds shooting through your arm? Maker, I know you always said your right eye was your good one, but you ain't going to be seeing through that for a while. I'm going to have to drive."

"Like hell, Jenna, I've seen you drive. With only half an eye, I'm still twice as good as you."

"And when it gets dark, Maker? You're going to see fine out there in the dark? Or are you going to be blind?"

It was a good point, though he was loath to admit it.

"Okay. You're going to drive, and I'll ride shotgun. That'll leave you here all alone. Rebekah. You going to be okay?"

"Me, all alone in the house, with the rest of you out there crawling in the dark? I'll be fine. I need to rest anyway."

"Good. We're going to need you as ready as you can be, Rebekah. We're going to need everyone soon."

The years just kept getting heavier on his shoulders, along with every scar and ache. A half-blind man leading a near-crippled woman who walks through dreams, and a retired nurse who's never killed anything. He had to remind himself again.

You go to war with the soldiers you have.

29

"THAT'S THE ONE," MAKER SAID WITH A CHILL IN HIS VOICE.

He's worried. Probably the first time he's had to sit the bench in a long time.

Daniel wasn't. He was hungry.

This neighborhood was dark. Streetlights lined the road and should have come to life hours ago, but the few streetlights still working only flickered weakly, while the others just gave a dull buzz of electricity. That was fine. Dark was better.

"Wrap around the back," Daniel said. "Drop us off here and take it around to the backstreet there. It's a dead end, but we'll have more cover there in the dark. Most of those houses looked foreclosed when Greg and I went by."

"Works for me." Greg's face had been locked in a perpetual grimace since they'd left. He was trying to work himself up.

Three's the team.

That's what Maker had told him the first time. They never went out with fewer than three, but here they were, going in with two.

We're going in shorthanded, but it doesn't matter. Nothing matters. I'm going to kill them all. Nothing is going to stop me from getting Sam back.

There was no need to pull the wolfskin on; it was already there, craving the teeth and the blood, and whispering in his ear.

Nothing is going to stop me.

Greg knocked Daniel's shoulder. "Get your fucking head in the game, I'm talking to you."

"What?" Daniel asked flatly.

"I said, looks like you were right." Greg pointed out the window to the driveway. The red truck was gone. "He's out tying one on."

Daniel nodded—such was the reputation of Mr. Montgomery. His wife's car wasn't there, either. Daniel knew she worked third shift and would be out for at least the next few hours, which he had already discussed with the group.

"That leaves us the older brother and the changeling," Maker said and glanced toward the back seat. "Keep your damn head on a swivel, and make it fast. I can smell the lead from here; those rednecks probably have a dozen guns laying around there."

"S'okay. I got the Taser." Greg tapped his hip holster.

Greg had a heavy-looking Kevlar vest strapped on. It matched Daniel's, which was Maker's vest, adjusted to fit Daniel's smaller frame. He liked the feel of it. Strong.

They made one pass around the house and were coming around for a second pass to drop them off. They had made the plan back at the house: go in through the front door if it's unlocked, head into the kid's room, which was clearly marked with a firefighter sticker on the window; if the front door was locked, go in through the kid's window. Smash and grab, knife him with Iron and get out.

This can go wrong.

The weak part of Daniel whimpered. He ignored it as he pulled on his black knit mask.

You're wearing a mask and breaking into a house to snatch a kid. That's what the monsters do. That's what you're doing. That's what you are. You're the monster.

The whisper grew sharper even as Jenna took a wide turn around and started heading back.

You're the monster, the voice said again, over and over. *You're the monster.*

I'll be the fucking monster.

There was no more debate when Jenna stopped the car.

"Go," was all Maker said.

Greg was out first, hulked over and low, a black mask snug on his face. The Taser was in his left hand, a hatchet in the other. The chain-metal net was strapped across his back, and a pair of handcuffs was connected to his belt.

The car was pulling away the second Daniel shut the door. Daniel's feet were on the grass, and he hunkered down. Swiftly and quietly, he stalked like a man with a lifetime of hunting meat in the woods.

Greg came up to the side of the front door and eased up just enough to see through the door's window. He clipped his hatchet to his belt and let it hang, giving him a free hand.

"TV's on," Greg whispered. "Looks like we're in luck. Older son is passed out."

His fingers tested the old rusted doorknob; it groaned as the bolt scratched out. Greg turned back to Daniel and gave a silent nod.

Unlocked. Tasting like a peach.

"Make it fast," Greg said and opened the door wide. One squeak and Greg was in, with Daniel after him.

The older son lazily looked up, his eyes red and puffy, several empty beer cans on the table in front of him. Greg was on him; he shoved his hand over the kid's mouth before he could say anything. But the footballer came to life just as fast. He snatched at Greg's wrist, pushed him to the side, and threw a fist against the side of Greg's face, connecting with his jaw.

"Getta fuck off me!" the kid shouted in a drunken slur.

Dropping his weight, Greg threw an elbow into the kid's nose and buried him in the couch. "Don't fuckin' move! Don't make me kill you!" Greg snarled as he pulled his Taser out and stuffed it into the kid's side.

"Kevin? What's going on? Is the TV on?" a woman asked, coming down the hall. Sarah Montgomery.

She's not supposed to be here.

Despite all the courage he'd felt earlier and all the whispers of the wolfskin, Daniel had none of it now. He could only watch as the plan broke.

"Kevin?" she asked again before her eyes went wide.

"Just—" was all Daniel could say before she took off down the hallway.

"Go get her!" Greg screamed.

He shot forward like a dog after a rabbit. The wood floor was slick and with the snow still stuck to his boots, he had trouble keeping his feet beneath him; he stumbled and slammed into the wall and saw only her foot disappear behind a door. He grabbed a small table covered with plates and pulled himself up, sending the plates crashing to the ground. He rounded the door to face her. The barrel of her gun was leveled at his chest.

He didn't say anything; there was no time before the gun went off.

Bam! Bam!

Two blasts, flashing the whole room with light. Slugs hit him in the chest with enough force to throw him back.

Bam!

An explosion blew a hole in the wall near his head. Instinct took control and he snatched his revolver from his holster, the same gun he had planned to kill himself with.

Bam!

The heavy pistol rocked in Daniel's unsteady hand with a powerful blast. Few could have made a shot like that, with an arm that wasn't angled right and a single grip on the pistol throwing everything off.

But Daniel did.

It caught her just below the center of her left breast. He knew because he saw the blood spatter against the wall; the heavy round had done its work well.

Now, she gave only a low hiss as life left her body. She tried to mouth something, but got no words out. Her dying eyes said everything that was needed. They were afraid, terrified of this monster in her home.

There was no courtesy of a quick death. This wasn't how Daniel imagined it; he watched her die, held there in her last moments. This was slow and torturous. Her eyes stayed on him the entire time; although she said nothing, he knew what she was thinking.

What's going to happen to my sons?

The revolver was heavy and nearly slipped from his fingers. "I didn't mean to . . ." he said to the corpse. "I just . . ."

There was no other way. Don't think about it; she's already dead. Get the kid and get out.

The voice in his head pushed him on. Sarah Montgomery's dead eyes watched him as he turned to go find her child.

Greg was coming down the hall. "She dead?"

"Yeah. And the kid?" Daniel replied.

"He'll live. Let's do this." Greg stormed past the room, not bothering to look in at the woman. "Do it fast. If the little fucker was sleeping before, he sure as hell isn't now."

Greg arrived at the door, and with his pistol in one hand and the hatchet in the other, gave Daniel a nod. Daniel nodded back, and Greg squared with the door. After two heavy breaths, Greg kicked the sweet spot on the door. It crashed open, splintering wood and swinging open. The nightmare came to life.

It gripped the ceiling, a hissing sprawl of long, disjointed spider-like legs that jutted from its back. Only the hallway light caught it in the dark room, shining off its glassy eyes as it kept itself in the dark.

Something deeper than fear locked Daniel's muscles; he was eye-to-eye with something that no longer resembled a human being. He froze, his mind unable to process that this nightmare was real.

"Get moving!" Greg yelled and stepped in to face it. He slammed his hand against the light switch. The light came on and Daniel saw its mask sliding off. The wet, loose skin no longer served a purpose. Weak, childlike arms hung loose and swaying as the monster moved.

Then his revolver came up, rocking in Daniel's hands with deafening sound and two brilliant flashes of light. Two blasts caught its side and dropped it from the ceiling. It hit the ground and moved its up-pointed legs in a twisting fury before it could right itself.

"Come here, you little shit!" Greg held the hatchet up with his right hand as he aimed his pistol with the left; two shots went wide as the creature shrieked and leapt.

Daniel shot again. Skittering across the ceiling, it jerked

left and right to shift from each blast of Daniel's gun. The pistol was empty and Daniel dropped it.

Greg fared better, and his next blast caught it in the mouth, blowing a hole out the back of its throat and letting the light of the hallway shine through. Brown claws lashed out as Greg reared back, dodging them. Another leg came at him, but Greg split the tip of it with his hatchet, sending a wet chunk across the room. A painful shriek followed, and Greg howled in laughter.

"Get down here, you little fucker!" Greg swung the hatchet at air just as it shifted away.

"I'll kill you!" It shrilled. "I'll crack your bones and suck them dry!"

Fanged mandibles unfolded from its mouth, dripping with strings of mucus. Greg ground his teeth and slung his hatchet end over end, catching the creature by surprise and tumbling it off the ceiling. Greg's net came loose and swung wide. Spiny legs came up and the claw points pushed the Iron net away while smoke sizzled where the Iron touched its flesh. Its legs were working on the chain, trying to pull itself free again.

With the beat of his heart sounding in his ear, Daniel pounced forward, finding a home for his knife.

"Kill . . . you . . ." it gasped, flicking its long tongue out with each word.

"Shut the fuck up." Greg stomped the back of its head, smashing it like an overripe melon between the metal grooves of the chain.

Daniel pulled away and left it thrashing in the throes of death.

"Son of a bitch," Daniel said.

"Well," Greg said, pulling his hatchet out with a wet pop. "So much for bringing this one in alive."

"I DON'T LIKE IT."

"You never do," Jenna said, still idling the car.

"This is horseshit. Midnight run with two people? We're asking for someone to get killed."

"And if you were out there, you'd get it or somebody else would. Maker, don't go pretending you can see. I've seen a lot of people hurt and on your pain pills. You don't go grabbing a gun and running around. You shouldn't even be here," she said with some bite to her words. "Now you sit there and—"

Bam! Bam!

Two lights flashed through one of the back windows.

Bam!

And then another.

"Son of a bitch!" Maker grabbed at the handle, ready to jump out. His hand was already reaching for his hip.

"Maker!" Jenna grabbed at him. "You sit! We have to wait. You go in there, they might shoot you, or you shoot one of 'em on accident! You can't! We knew there was going to be shooting!"

"Dammit!" He pounded his fist against the dashboard. "Hell, Jenna, I can't just sit here!"

"Have faith," she said.

He ground his teeth, trying to find some measure of control. It had gone silent, and he sat with no idea of what was happening. This wasn't where he was supposed to be, not sitting in the car and wondering whether things went bad. That's not how a good leader leads—they lead from the front.

"Lord, they do have to hurry, though," Jenna said,

turning back to the house. "Someone's going to call the police."

Bang!

Another flash of light.

Bang! Bang!

Two more and Maker could hold himself no longer. He was out the door, with Jenna's yells ringing behind him.

Something had gone wrong. There shouldn't have been that many shots. Bullets hardly scratch a changeling; something must be wrong.

I shouldn't have been sitting in that fucking car.

With fingers numb from the cold, he tried to pull his own black mask on, but stumbled in a pit on the ground and fell into the snow.

Didn't see that.

The ground was covered with fresh snow that crunched under his feet as he got back up. Something dripped down his face from under his bandage.

Son of a bitch, did I tear something?

He got to his feet and pressed one wet hand to his face. As he stumbled out of the ditch, his vision blurred; Jenna was right, he could hardly see what he was doing. If he died because he was half-blind, so be it. He had left people to die before, but this was different.

Daniel's son might still be alive.

Drips of blood peppered down his face and over his hand, dripping on the snow and leaving a thin trail. They sure as hell didn't like blood smeared over a crime scene. He ripped a glove out of his pocket and held that under the bandage as he came up to the sliding glass back door. With the butt of his pistol he pushed at the handle, but it was locked. Through the blinds he could see the TV in the living room.

"Son of a bitch." He cracked his pistol against the door, making a spider's web in the glass. He was readying to bash it again when he saw two figures looming in the hallway.

Greg and Daniel.

Greg had the monster sprawled across his back—a wicked-looking thing, for sure. Daniel came in front of him, rattled the door, and popped the lock.

"You all right?" Maker asked.

"Yeah, let's get the hell out of here." Daniel pushed past Maker.

Something moaned behind them in the living room.

"Older son is cuffed in there," Greg croaked.

The three of them hurried back to the car, Maker having the most trouble, despite Greg lugging the dead changeling. Jenna popped the trunk and Greg stuffed it inside. The car took off the moment Greg closed his door.

Speeding off in silence, Maker clutched his bandage while the other two sat quietly in the back. Jenna was the first to speak.

"So, you got 'em? I was worried."

"Yeah, we got 'em." Greg responded. "She was already dead, Dan. She had one of those things in her house. She's dead, but the older boy'll live."

"I don't fucking care." Daniel said through gritted teeth. "It doesn't matter. We have one more to hit tonight. Let's focus on that."

Jenna sighed quietly at that, but Maker knew better. There was a story there in the cracks of Daniel's voice. He'd just killed someone. It wasn't going to stop him, but it was going to haunt him for the rest of his life.

I should have been in there.

30

THE VEST, NOW HEAVY WITH SWEAT, PEELED OFF. DANIEL'S hands kept shaking as he rubbed the sore spots where the bullets hit, both near his stomach. The vest had done its job. He tossed it onto the floor of the car. There was a twitch in his arm that made him consider just how close he had come to dying and leaving Sam to *them*.

Good thing Sarah Montgomery can't shoot for shit.

That thought crawled its way into him and he felt the crack of glass inside his mind. Had he really grown so cold? Did he really not care about killing that woman? He was a monster.

I'm not a monster. I can't deal with it now. I can't think about it. We have one more. If I get Sam back, it's all worth it. If I get Sam back, nothing else matters; they can kill me.

"One more to go, and this one might be ready." Greg said, and cracked his knuckles. "How much farther to the Robinson's house?"

"Ten minutes," Maker said.

Daniel drew in deep breaths as he tried to imagine all the things they did to those children. A wave of fear was pricking him and growing like a poisonous cloud. Now wasn't the time to be afraid; instead, he raced through the plan in his head, hoping that he would be ready this time.

They'd chosen the Montgomery house first because it was supposed to be empty. Supposed to be easier.

Easier.

Daniel nearly laughed at that thought now.

The Robinson house sat nestled in the middle of the neighborhood, which meant that they couldn't make a plan to go in from the back. It was also just off the side of the main road, meaning people would be driving by, even late in the day. Jenna told them that the girl had been home sick, ever since that puke-painting in class. She had two sisters, and there was no reason to think that the whole family wouldn't be home.

Daniel had seen her picture in a yearbook, which Maker had somehow gathered: a smiling girl with big glasses and a short ponytail.

She was probably dead shortly after the picture was taken.

They didn't know who was going to be home, and they didn't even know what room she was going to be in. They were going in half-cocked.

And I don't even have my damn vest anymore.

Daniel clicked open the cylinder of his revolver and began to pull the empty caps out and drop them on the floor. He watched them roll on the car's floor—empty things that no longer had purpose. Then he took six more from his pocket and planted them in place, wondering if any would be for the girl's parents.

I'm getting Sam back.

"I'm going in this time," Maker said, pulling Daniel from his memories. "It was stupid to send only two. Three's the team, even if I'm half-blind."

"Now, you can't be doing that! I told you, you might just shoot one of them!"

"I won't pull my damn gun unless I have to, but they'll need an extra eye, even if it's only one."

"He's right, Jenna," Greg insisted. "We can use the old warhorse, but we'll keep him in the back, so he's not stumbling around." Greg reached up to pat Maker's shoulder.

"It's fine," Daniel said. "Just don't shoot either one of us."

Jenna finally relented. "Heaven help us. I'll keep the car running." She pulled down a street, closing in on the house.

"We absolutely need this one alive," Maker said, his gaze already fixed on the house. "We cannot kill her. If we're going to use her in the plan at all, we need her alive."

"Got it," Daniel said.

"Son of a bitch." Greg was pointing out the window. "Don't tell me that house with the light on is the one we're going for."

The car slowed down, and Jenna leaned forward in her seat. The lights were clearly on in the living room. "Should we keep going?"

"Look," Daniel said, his eyes sharp in the dark. "The front door looks cracked open."

"Well, this is an invitation if I've ever seen one," Maker said. "But I guess we have to go in anyway."

"Hell, it'd be rude to miss our own party." Greg smiled and flashed his coffee-stained teeth.

"Oh, be quick! Be as quick as you can!" Jenna whispered, even though it was unnecessary.

"Drop us off, head off, and circle around. We'll be fast." Maker said.

When the car stopped, the masks came on and out the door they went, Greg and Daniel first with Maker slow behind them. Daniel felt light, like in a dream, and drawn to the house, unable to stop his feet from moving, even if he wanted. His body was telling him he had no choice.

They got up to the porch. Daniel cast one look back to see Jenna who sat waiting on the road, her eyes filled with concern before she started off.

Greg got in close to the door; it whistled with the cold winter air blowing through the crack. With two gloved fingers, he pushed it open and glanced inside. "The dad's in here," he said, making no effort to lower his voice. "He's dead."

"THEY'RE COMING FOR YOU," he whispered in the dark after his daughter let him in. "They killed one of your brothers today."

"They did?" the girl asked with wide, glassy eyes. "Which one?"

A strange question, he thought. Such occasional surprises happened. Surprises were part of the joy of being a father, after all.

Do any of them even have names?

"Don't be bothered with that right now. You need to get ready."

Her eyes were like large saucers, engulfing her face; here with her father, the mask of humanity was unnecessary. "Can I kill them?" She grinned, her tongue flicking out and running over the edges of her sharp teeth.

"Well . . ." He smiled excitedly and reached out to grasp her chin between his long pale fingers, lifting her head to focus only on him. "First, I want you to finish with your family here. We're done playing with them."

"Okay!" she said greedily and bit her lip. "And then?"

"You wait for them just like we talked about, remember? And when they get here, I have another plan." He made no effort to lower his voice, but his laughter was loud enough to stir the house awake. "And you get to meet another member of the family!"

A light flipped on and shone through the crack at the bottom of the door. The little girl hissed like a snake as her eyes turned from her father to steps coming down the hall.

The pale man watched proudly as her back snapped and stretched, hunching her over, and the skin split to expose muscle beneath as it grew. The growing snout rattled as her teeth sharpened in her mouth.

"Oh, you were always my favorite."

31

THE ROBINSON FAMILY'S COZY HOUSE HAD TURNED RED. ITS fireplace and welcome mat that read "Welcome Y'all!" were wet with chunks of the Robinsons. Blood was streaked across the white walls and caked the furniture. What looked like Mr. Robinson had its purple and red insides slopping out into a pile on the floor, half-split and left to leak. White and red cartilage poked out from his twisted neck, angled as if he had been trying to get a good look down the hallway behind him. Snapped fingers jutted into the air, pointing this way and that. His jaw, snapped in half, sat on top of the TV. No one else was visible.

An animal sound screamed from the other room, where it sounded like skin was being stripped from the bone. Greg was already leading the group back, his hatchet and Taser both in hand with Daniel behind him.

"Be careful," Maker said to both of them. "It could be a trick." His voice was steady, as if he was unconcerned by the footprints he was leaving through Mr. Robinson's insides.

Fire burned in Daniel's chest, boiling his blood. He could smell the jungle, and it smelled like piss, shit, and blood. The wolf was whispering in his ear, and his hands were steady. Greg slowed when Maker said it might be a trap, but Daniel pushed forward. He was going to find it. He was going to end it.

Whimpers were coming from the room as he rounded the corner, and then he saw the creature, much like the one from his nightmares. It was a hairless, pale creature, with a large, misshapen head and a drooping chin that resembled some kind of monstrous elf. Needle-point teeth curved in behind its purple-black lips. It still wore the white night-gown the girl's parents had dressed her in, but it had red on it now; red from her father in the living room, and her mother in pieces on the floor.

And there was the Robinson's other daughter.

"Shh, sister," it whispered in the girl's ear with its claw clasped over her mouth. "Our friends are here." The girl moaned and cried, tears streaming down her face as the changeling watched Daniel, her eyes like black water, reflecting everything. "We've been waiting for you."

"Where's the other kid?" Daniel asked, daring a step forward. The changeling bared her teeth and her claws tightened on the young girl's throat, drawing a bead of blood.

"Hiding under a bed somewhere," the changeling said with a scratchy voice. "Maybe she's dead. I did open her leg."

Daniel shot a glance back at Maker. "Find the girl." Greg was there alongside him with weapons in hand, his eyes intent on the changeling. Daniel didn't look to see if Maker obeyed.

"You want me?" the changeling asked, amused even as it pinched the girl's face and tipped her head back to expose her bare neck. "You want me?" the changeling asked again.

She's going to kill that girl.

"Yes." Daniel said and took a step forward. "I want to cut pieces off of you until you beg me to kill you."

"Not wise to tempt me!" the creature hissed.

"Do it," he said, his eyes flicking to the girl and then back to the changeling.

Be careful.

"I will. Do you think the neck or the cheek would be softer?" The changeling's dark tongue licked the girl's skin. The girl shuddered and cried beneath the monster's hand. Daniel hesitated, and the changeling smiled.

Greg groaned behind him. "Don't talk to it—that girl is already dead. Let's just kill it." Greg pulled his metal net off his shoulder and held it loose.

"Do it, fat man, and I'll tear her throat out!" The changeling hissed again. "No, no, I'm here to talk. He wants you to know something."

Daniel's flesh turned to goose skin as a wave of heat rolled over him. "What, then?"

"He knows." Her heavy white eyelids widened, opening like a baby's mouth as she giggled. "He has your son. He knows who you are."

"What the hell does that mean?" His foot started to shake.

The changeling's smile stretched so far that the corners of its lips nearly touched its ears, its mouth now a gaping hole of teeth that giggled. It giggled again, each laugh akin to needles tapping glass.

"What's that mean?" Daniel repeated, his hand starting to shake. He tightened his grip on the pommel of his knife, still in its sheath. "What's that mean!"

The giggles stopped. "Ready?" It slammed her mouth into the child's soft neck; the girl's scream filled the room.

"No!" Daniel lunged forward, but Greg's net was faster. It

caught them in a tangle. The girl shrieked as the teeth worked at her soft flesh, but the changeling pulled back to bellow from the pain of the net. Daniel pulled the girl away, seeing blood drip down her neck mixed with the black changeling blood.

He leapt and dug his knife in twice before he realized he had drawn it, so strong and fast was the beast inside him. There were no giggles now, only screams and shrieks of pain as he stabbed the creature. Only after he pulled the blade out a third time, did he realize he was screaming. It had stopped fighting beneath the net, but still lived.

Pull it back. Don't kill it.

Forcing himself off, he cursed it. "You're mine now, you little bitch!" Tears stung his eyes as he gripped the blade, not letting himself use it again. "I've got you and you're not getting off so easy. I'm not going to kill you here; I'm going to make it hurt!"

The changeling laughed while smoke sizzled upon its grey, opened flesh. "I can smell the blood in you. You're just like us."

A heavy boot came down onto the changeling's face. "I hate the ones that talk too much," Greg said.

Turning to the girl, Daniel found her gasping with red bubbles popping around her mouth. He pulled her small frail body to his; she felt ready to break apart in his arms. "Maker!" he yelled.

"I can't find her!" he yelled from another room as he made his way back clumsily.

Maker's too off with the painkillers.

"It doesn't matter. We need to get this girl to a hospital," Daniel said between breaths. The girl breathed weakly; her skin was already turning a pale white.

"She's as good as dead, Daniel. That thing put its venom

in her." Greg shook his head and the changeling underneath his boot laughed. "She'll start freezing up soon. The arms and legs first, and the lungs next. Leave her."

"No! Fuck that! We're getting her to a hospital." He stomped past Greg, leaving the broken changeling behind him.

"Leave her!" Greg huffed. "She's too far gone. I don't like it, but we got work to do."

The hell is wrong with him?

"You shut your fucking mouth!" Daniel roared at Greg. "We're not leaving her!"

Maker slammed a hand against the doorframe for support. "Yeah, come on. We'll take her. But she won't go to a hospital. We'll have to take her with us. Hospital doesn't have what she needs."

Greg scoffed, but Daniel was already moving through the house, his shoe coming off the floor with a wet smack as he stepped through Mr. Robinson. Daniel kicked the front door open, leaving a bloody print and rattling it against its frame.

Don't die on me. Don't die on me.

The wolfskin was burning away from him as he ran to the car, now only vaguely aware of Greg and Maker behind him. All of his rage and instincts were melting inside his chest and the fear was coming back, fear that this girl who he didn't even know would die, that he couldn't save her. Fear that Sam was like this girl, her lips turning purple as changeling venom pulsed through her veins.

How long did she have? How long can someone live like this? How much was inside her?

She was going to die; he felt that in his bones. Greg was right. She'd suffered too much, lost too much blood.

But there's a chance.

And any chance that he could save her was enough.

"Oh my God!" Jenna said as Daniel closed in. "Is she alive?"

"It bit her, Jenna, it got her bad! She's lost a lot of blood. We need to get her back."

Maker came down next to him, hitting against the car and out of breath as he climbed into the back.

"Pop the trunk!" Greg hissed, and Jenna did. A loud thump sounded before the trunk slammed closed—Greg was not being gentle.

When Greg was inside, Jenna hit the gas, throwing them all back. Daniel gripped the girl's head close to his chest. Her hair was already soaked with black changeling blood that ran down Daniel's hand.

"Hold in there. Stay with us," Daniel whispered in her ear. "You're going to be fine, you're going to be fine." Tears streaked down his cheeks.

Please don't die.

THE LINES on the papers began to blur, their words becoming incoherent in her mind as they sometimes did when accompanied by exhaustion. Rebekah had been studying, reviewing more of her tomes and putting her tired eyes to some use while the others were gone—out risking their lives.

And I'm just here doing nothing but letting cancer eat my body.

Her books were piled into a tall stack; she had been reading them over and over again, looking for clues. Of course, she'd read them all dozens of times before, but perhaps she had missed something. Hours had gone by. She had planned for more hours yet, but her eyes must have grown too heavy, and she slipped off into the other world, where real and unreal are much the same and the impossible is only a suggestion, where darkness flowed like ink and could be touched.

I hadn't meant to sleep . . . But is this world so bad? Is it so bad to be here and not there? Why do I need to be there? Why can't everyone just come and be here?

For some time now, she had been going into Daniel's dreams. Showing him how to build his cages around his demons. But he wasn't calling to her now, and there was no voice this time to remind her of her purpose, no one to tell her what she should do.

And why should they? Am I that old woman who lives in that house and wishes she were dead? That's not me. I'm a beautiful young thing. I have wings. I can fly.

She looked down at her young hands. There was no old woman here; she was someone else. Maybe that old woman was the dream, and this was real. She took to the air and began to float, this time not caring for the minds of others. She went to an old door, a fantasy she often visited.

There was a young man waiting; his body was warm, as she imagined. The man's life wasn't scarred here like it was in the waking world. Here, they made love, sometimes for hours. Other times, they held hands and talked, but never about monsters or blood, no—they talked about life. They talked about their children, the ones she never had. They even talked about growing old, but it wasn't weakness here; it was life.

How things could have been. How things should have been.

If only she had convinced Larry to leave with her before.

Could she have done that? Why was she in this war? Had she not paid enough?

There was a prick of the old woman, the part of her that didn't live in such fantasies. The old woman had no control here, but the young woman could feel her thoughts bleed over, enough that the fantasy closed, and she was outside the door again.

Why should I care about what she wants? Why should I care about any of them?

"Because of the boy."

Who said that?

"I did." A warm voice came through the ink. It was neither strange nor unusual, only comforting.

There was no need to speak words here, but the voice did anyway. Rebekah responded only with thought.

The boy, yes, I remember now. But he's dead.

"No, Rebekah, he's alive."

How? How can he be alive? No one ever comes back.

"He is like them. He was born of them, like his father, and he was saved. Baptized of his sins."

That's a myth.

"This world is myth," the voice said. "He needs you at the Shallow. It is an entrance to this world, a gate where the darkness has found entry. You must go. Only you and his father may enter. You are a walker, and he has the blood of that world."

I don't want to go there. Let him go without me. He hurt me before. He's stronger than me.

"Strong, but unguided. Powerful, but undisciplined. He needs you to stay with him and help him become what he should be."

Why me? I don't want to be there anymore.

"Remember the boy, Sam. Remember your brother, little Derrick."

She hadn't said her brother's name in years, hadn't heard it spoken or even read it from a page. It hurt too much; and it did now, even from the voice that sounded so warm and pure. It stung like fire to hear it, and after years of not saying his name, years of trying not to think of him, his face came to her now. His hair was the same color as Sam's and Daniel's, and his smile lifted in one corner, the same as their smiles.

Derrick . . .

Her heart ached. She remembered him now, remembered what he meant to her, and that love grew to remind her what Daniel and Sam meant to her, what hope a boy's life could bring.

"Derrick waits for you here with us, with your mother and father. He waits for you."

Let me come then! Choose another! Let me be with my family! I don't want to go back!

"You will see him again. But for now, there is more you must do. What would they all have been without you, Rebekah? What would have happened to them without your guiding hand and your sacrifice? What would the world have against the darkness, if not for those like you with their duty?"

Duty. Yes. I have a duty to Sam and Daniel. I have a duty to them all.

"And hope, Rebekah. Hope lives in you, shepherd of men."

It spoke more, not with words but feeling. In time, she would awake—she knew this—and most of what she knew now would be gone. Most of what she'd heard and seen would be stripped from her. But she would still have that feeling, still carry the echoes of love, and still have the direction provided, if not the reasons why.

But now, she thought of her brother, his face. She reached out and touched that memory. So handsome—she hoped she would remember that, at least.

I'll be with you again.

32

YEARS CARRY WEIGHT AND COME WITH A FOG THAT SOMETIMES sits inside your brain. Maker had once been the best there was at what he did, but sitting in the front seat blind and unsure of himself, he felt about as useful as a wrench on a math test.

"Go, dammit! She's dying!" Daniel screamed from the back seat. Jenna stepped on the gas even more, tearing down the streets, blaring through red lights and stop signs. By the grace of God, they hadn't met any traffic, but if their luck ran short, a cop might see them and pull them over, or follow them back to their house. What then? What would happen? The night would be done, and they could do nothing for Sam. Was this worth it?

It is. And if you ever think that a little girl's life isn't, then you're as evil as they are, you piece of shit. Get your head straight. They need you.

Maker bit his lip as Jenna took a corner, cutting through grass. The car bounced back onto the road and sped onto Terrace Drive, the long winding road that led to their house.

There was no sign of the sister back there. She must be

okay, even if everyone else was dead. Maybe she even got away. Maybe the cops are on their way there right now.

Yeah, and maybe this is all a bad dream and you're not so fucking useless.

For a midnight run, this could have been expected, considering how they went in. They had cased the Robinson house, but hadn't been inside or even known what the family members looked like.

Yeah. A real shit show. Instead, the girl's whole family is dead and she probably will be, too.

"Hold on, just a little more!" Jenna said. She cut down their road and made the engine scream, then stomped on the brakes in front of their house. Maker felt his brain rock inside his head and vomit stir inside his stomach.

"Christ's sake, Jenna! Your driving will kill the girl!" Greg threw the door open.

The changeling howled in the back; no doubt the force of being thrown around was painful with her flesh against the barbed net.

"Go! Just go! Get it ready!" Daniel opened the car door and jumped out with the girl scooped up in his arms.

Maker stumbled out behind him, his head still spinning, and struggled to keep up with the others. He couldn't get the strength into his legs and soon, he had to stop for breath. "Greg! Get the damn thing into the basement, all right?"

If Greg replied, Maker didn't hear it. He was already stepping onto the porch and nearly falling. It had become slick with snow, but he grabbed the railing. Jenna and Daniel were already inside the house, and Maker could hear them rummaging around in the kitchen.

Finally inside, he saw the same table where he had lain, only now the girl was there. Daniel held her hand while Jenna dug out a syringe.

"Lord help me, I hope we have enough," Jenna said as she loaded it.

"If she's still alive," Maker said, before taking a gasp of air. "You can save her, Jenna."

Jenna can save her. She's still sharp.

Daniel sobbed and squeezed the girl's hand. Maker watched him for a moment, but Daniel didn't notice. His eyes were on the girl's face the entire time, even when Jenna put the syringe into her vein and then got out the sewing needles. Daniel's eyes had grown red and puffy, like at Sam's funeral. Maker wondered why this bothered Daniel so much, why it seemed to hurt so badly. He wanted to save the girl too, but Daniel was falling apart.

Because he's not like you. He's not an old, dull, jaded son of a bitch. You've been trying to make him more like you, but you should be more like him.

There was nothing left to do, but wait and watch Jenna work.

Jenna's fingers worked with the precision of a pianist, and sometime later, with sweat on her brow, she said, "I've done all I can." She finished sewing and wiped away the blood. "It's for God now." She sat down and prayed. Daniel bowed his head and prayed, too.

Maker took a seat next to Jenna and her hand reached out for his without stopping the prayer. He bowed his head and prayed, too, hoping an old killer's prayers still had some value.

———

SLOWING DOWN CAN KILL YOU. Your mind gets to work on your sins.

Daniel saw the woman he'd killed. He tried to keep his

eyes on the girl in front of him, like that would somehow even out the scales. But he remembered that look she had when she died trying to protect her children.

I'm not afraid of them anymore. I'm afraid of me.

He was okay with it. He didn't want to kill anyone, but fuck it, he'd do whatever he had to do for Sam. But then he saw this girl, so scared and so innocent, just caught in this fucking mess like everyone else, a victim as much as he was. She was going to die, thinking her sister clawed her throat out after gutting her parents like fish. That's what it looked like—their guts dragged out and left to dry like chum.

And at first, I didn't give a shit.

It might have been for only a moment, but it was true. He'd convinced himself it didn't matter. Her life was spent and there was nothing he could do about it. But when he looked at her, he saw Sam. He thought of the woman he killed, and her son waking up to find his mom dead, and then he knew he couldn't go one step more. Any further into the deep end and he'd break. He needed to save her, not only for her, but for himself, too.

Daniel held the girl's hand until it stopped shaking and her breathing steadied. "You think she's going to be all right?"

Jenna looked up, her face for once too exhausted to hold a smile. "Yeah. Yeah, Daniel, I think she will." It had been a long, rough night for old Jenna, but he'd grown a new respect for the woman.

"Hey, Dan?" Maker said, looking tired and in pain—the medication had worn off. "How about you go check on Rebekah. I'm a little concerned that she didn't come out with all this noise." He licked his lips and slowly blinked. "Can you drag my police scanner in here, too? I might be falling apart, but my ears still work. And can you step out to the barn and take a look at Greg? See how he's holding up?"

Greg. I had to question myself about the girl; but in the end, I turned up the right way. Greg wanted to leave her. And even after we got her in here, he never stepped in. He only went out to sharpen his weapons and load his guns. I might be halfway lost, but he's already two feet in.

Daniel watched the girl's chest rise and fall, and nodded. "Yeah, sure."

He wheeled the police scanner in and plugged it into the wall. Maker gave him a nod of thanks and Jenna flashed him a tired smile. They both turned to watch the girl as he left to see Rebekah.

He knocked once and heard some movement, but nothing else.

"Rebekah?"

He opened the door; he was concerned that something might have happened. She had her face nearly pressed into a book, and glanced up at him with wide, startled eyes.

"Daniel?"

"Yeah? How are you? We were worried about you. We were making a lot of noise out there and you didn't come out."

"No one was screaming, so I assumed you had it under control. I expected as much, after a midnight run." She looked back down into the book.

"What's got you so focused? You find something we didn't know?"

"Yes. Just, I don't know." She shook her head and looked up at him again. "I fell asleep while you were gone. I can't remember what happened, but I remember something. I remember, I had to look at one of my books. I saw it in the dream."

She opened it: a red leather cover with German scrawled across it. "This is the tome—it has a story about a monster that can walk in dreams, which it doesn't have to visit like I do. It's from there. I think it's a type of changeling."

"And you think we're dealing with one now?"

"Yes. Well, no. I do think the pale man may be one. But that's not why I find it interesting." She shook her head and hesitated, choosing her words cautiously before she looked at him once more. "It's why you had to come with me before, into its mind. I'm only a visitor. You're a native. You're one of them."

33

MAKER SAT THERE, WATCHING THE GIRL, HER CHEST RISING and falling steadily like the low ocean waves he remembered from better years.

She's alive.

He had saved someone. Maybe he didn't personally, but his team had. He always told himself that they were out there for the families the monsters stole from. He told himself he was a surgeon, cutting away the disease. There was no doubt that the families would mourn the loss of their children, a pain some might never wake from. But he had to. He was a scalpel, cutting away the infection and the rotted part of their families. It hurt to feel the blade, but they were better for it, even if they didn't know it.

Even if it killed them.

But now, he didn't have to convince himself. Here sat a little girl who wouldn't be here, if not for his people. This girl lived because of them, because Maker put together the best team that he could and sacrificed for it, and asked others to sacrifice for it as well. And here was the reward, a girl who still breathed, and later, there might be a boy, too.

That's worth an old man's life.

But why did he have that itch that said something was about to go wrong? Why were his nerves crawling up his throat? Did he miss something? Or was he just too old now, too confused? He'd been so dull lately, so out of tune, like a musician that forgot his strings.

Ever since we got here, I felt the fog growing, the years catching . . .

Jenna was still sitting in her chair with her eyes closed, dozing. The poor woman was exhausted. He looked at the police scanner and was wary of disturbing her. But that itch . . .

What did I miss?

He reached over and turned the radio on; it buzzed to life, but without chatter.

They must not have found the houses yet.

The ache was coming back to his head. He rubbed the sore spot and decided against another shot of painkillers— best to keep a clear mind. A few years back, he wouldn't have been slow like this, he wouldn't be second guessing himself or making mistakes. But even the sharpest blade grows dull.

We're going to have to go back out again tonight. We're going to have to make this count. But, son of a bitch, I'm too damn old for midnight runs.

He looked at Jenna, who hadn't stirred, so he let it continue. The police scanner buzzed for several minutes— he was surprised to hear it that way, so quiet. With all that was going on, he had expected to have multiple incidents around the city, things catching fire, with a cop gone and children disappearing. The itch stayed there on his neck.

Why's it so damn quiet?

The city should have started to consume itself; he'd seen

it happen before. Multiple accidental shootings, several reports of missing people, and distress calls all over, but instead, silence. He could do nothing but rub his head, pour a glass of water, and listen.

Then he heard the address.

"Dispatch, this is Unit c34 at Baker's Drive."

He knew why they had been on radio silence. A call had been put in to keep all nonessential talk off the radio.

Maybe they did find the house?

The voice continued. "I found two of the children. Jesus Christ, they're dead out here in the back. Face down out on the fucking lawn. The other is still missing. That's four visible victims. Requesting homicide and a K9 unit on scene."

Two children? Jenny Robinson had two sisters.

"Roger that, unit c34," Dispatch said. "Will send officers for a 10-69."

What the fuck is going on?

The itch grew spider legs and walked up Maker's spine, and his instincts pulled his gaze to the girl. A shrill laugh erupted in the room then, and sent a shiver up Maker's back. In that moment, he knew it all as he felt the *snap* of the trap locking around him.

The thin body of the girl sat up on the table.

"I hoped to wait a little longer." Venom dripped from her mouth. "My daddy is on his way now."

"My Lord!" Jenna exclaimed, waking in a startle.

Slow.

His mind worked it out before his body had reacted.

Too damn slow.

Now he was on his feet and reaching for Daniel's knife, the blade sitting just a few feet away on the kitchen counter. The girl sprang up with coiled muscles and lashed his hand with razor-like fingers. Skin split open, sending burning pain up his arm. His body moved on its own now, like he had trained it to do so long ago. He kicked the girl's soft chest, sending her over the table. That kick was strong enough to have killed her if she was anything normal but now, it only knocked her over and threw him off balance. His hand slapped at the counter before catching something to steady himself. Daniel's knife slid off the counter and clattered to the floor. With the knife out of reach, instinct took his hand to the pistol in the holster instead.

"Jenna!" he bellowed as the girl rose from the other side. "Go! Get them out of here!"

Without pause, Jenna went hurrying down the hallway. "We have one in here! There's a demon in here!"

"It's too late," the girl said with her pointed snake-tooth smile. "I already opened the door for him."

The girl was snorting with laughter when Maker fired a round, hitting her in the forehead and rocking her back, painting the wall with a thin spray of black gore. She fell to the ground with hysterical laughter, her skin torn where the bullet had hit. She reached a finger up into the hole and started to peel the skin back, the mask tearing off and shedding away like a dead layer of skin.

Think.

He commanded himself in those split seconds of life and death.

Be calm. Make a plan.

Nothing came.

A pale hand reached out from the shadows under the table, the tips of its fingers digging into the cracking tile like it was loose dirt.

It's him. It's the nightmare.

The gray-lipped and smiling face of the pale man came

up—a haunting look at madness given form. The monster's skin was as white as unblemished paper, but its eyes were black as Hell. His laughter was black too, and cut like an echo through the silence inside Maker's brain. The laughter climbed into his ears and slithered down to his heart, threatening to make it burst, like something was squeezing the pulp from his chest.

You're dead. There's no time.

Maker was already between the pale man and the hallway before he'd finished the thought.

"Maker!" Daniel said, coming from his room and starting down the hallway.

"No, dammit!" he yelled between gasps. "Get Rebekah and Jenna out of here! I'll hold it!"

Daniel started to run to him.

"No, goddammit!" Maker yelled. "Get them out, Daniel, you get them the fuck out of here!"

Maker turned back to the nightmare and locked his gaze onto its eyes, black pools of ink. He was a fool, a damn fool. But, God willing, he was going to sell his life dearly. He was going to hold it until the others got out.

It's your turn to pay the bill, old man.

The pistol was suddenly heavy, but he had it up and firing in a barrage of light. Each blast brought more laughter; each shot rocked the pale man back inches.

When the pistol ran dry, the monster spoke with a sound that scratched the inside of Maker's brain like dozens of hairy legs:

"Go get your sister," the pale man said to the girl with the smoking hole in her head. "And then, kill the others."

He brought another?

With a chirping giggle and the pitter-patter of her bare feet, she skittered toward the basement. Maker dropped to the floor and scraped up Daniel's Iron knife, holding it in front of him while the world pushed him from the back. His chest burned, and he couldn't bring his foot up again.

Just slow him down. That's all you need, old man. That's all I'm asking. Just slow him down.

The pale man was painful to look at—something so unnatural and twisted—as though each breath he took filled the room with toxins. He had no right to exist in this world—nightmares weren't supposed to be real. Each painful moment was an assault against Maker's sanity, a crude insult to reality.

"I wore a black suit for the occasion." The milky pools of his black eyes held Maker, pressing a choking fear into him. "Do you like it? I was excited to meet you." With the back of his hand, he swatted the table from between them, sending it smashing against the wall in a hail of splinters.

Maker gritted his teeth and held the knife up higher. "We're going to kill you," he said, though he had no faith in the words. "We're going to burn your entire fucking brood!"

"I'll make more." Its black lips were lined with amusement. "Want to see?" He reached his hand into the shadow of the wall and created a space where none had been. Dozens of glassy eyes lit up in the darkness.

Hold them. Hold them as long as you can. God, please let this be for something. Please let Daniel get Sam.

Like a dam bursting, the creatures flowed from the wall in a wave of teeth and claws—gruesome things like small dogs and cats, with legs and arms that jutted from their backs and hips and hooked like talons. Each shrieked with the devil's laughter and the evil joy of their brood.

The overwhelming sight of the mass of mouths and teeth turned Maker's blood cold, and he knew there would be no stopping the flood.

Maker slashed the blade at them, the Cold Iron finding home in the back of one of their heads and plunging in with a wet pop. He pulled it free and slashed at another, but they were on him in a torrent of gnashing teeth.

Thin pointed teeth mauled Maker's flesh, injecting burning venom into his blood with dozens of small bites. The fiery pain became too much, and he screamed as their fingers rent muscle from bone.

He only got the one. He might have gotten more when he was younger, but he was just too old now. Too slow, too tired, too stupid.

This was my fault.

Even through the pain he knew that. He knew when he was sharper, this wouldn't have happened. Everyone would die tonight because of him. He'd led them all to slaughter because he had underestimated his enemy and overestimated himself.

He was a failure.

They greedily stuffed their mouths with the bits of matted skin and muscle they'd torn from him. Blood was already filling his lungs while the venom paralyzed his muscles.

"Choke!" he said between gasps of pain. "Choke on it!"

The giddy laughter continued as they dragged him into the shadows, a feast for what lay in wait. He pounded the knife down once more before one latched onto his arm, forcing him to drop it.

"Choke on it, you motherfuckers!" he bellowed as they pulled him into the darkness.

I got only one.

"Choke on it!"

Then Hell embraced him.

"YOU'RE ONE OF THEM," Rebekah told him, completely unsure of how he'd react.

"What the hell are you talking about?"

"I felt it, Daniel, in the dream. I can't remember exactly, but the dream, it told me you have their blood. One of your ancestors was like them, and it's passed down to you."

"Rebekah," he scoffed, "that doesn't make any sense."

"Doesn't it, Daniel?" she asked, closing the book. "You took to this life faster than anyone we've ever seen. You bought into the insanity of it all, even walked into the dreams with me and nearly killed everyone. You're powerful. It's in your blood. And Sam—it's in his blood, too."

Daniel's face turned red. "How could something like this happen?"

"It doesn't happen often," she said with some pity. "Changelings are by nature self-destructive, and most die young. I believe that somewhere along the line, one lived long enough to reach maturity. Probably, it raped one of your ancestors and passed the blood down to you."

Daniel laughed, unsure of what to say. "Well what does any of that mean, and why would it matter?"

She patted the red book. "It means we can kill him. If we find the Shallow, you can open the door and go inside. Not in dreams, but in a physical sense. We can try to find Sam there." Tears welled in her eyes. "Daniel, it means we have hope."

Something screamed from the kitchen, something else got knocked over. "What the hell was that?" Daniel asked, standing up from his seat.

"Sit down. It's probably just Greg coming back. You know how he is."

Daniel hesitated. Then there was a shout, and Jenna was screaming.

"We have one in here! There's a changeling in here!" Jenna came pushing in just as Daniel opened the door. "The girl! She came alive! She said her daddy's on his way!"

My God, it's happening. I felt this in the dream. We have to go.

Daniel stepped to the door, but Rebekah grabbed him by the wrist with her thin fingers, clamped as strongly as they could. "No, Daniel! We must leave!"

"Maker's in there!" He shrugged off her grip, yanking her forward and hurting her arm.

Now is our chance.

"No, there isn't time, Daniel. We must go now, while it's here. We must go to the Shallow. Larry would understand."

Daniel's eyes shot daggers at her, as though some demon had just crawled into her skin. Had she grown so cold that she'd let Larry die?

Yes. Larry would understand. He would want it this way.

But she had no hope of holding Daniel, and didn't try again. He left without another word. With frantic speed, Rebekah grabbed the red book and two others. "Quick, Jenna! The window!" she said, pointing as she pulled her coat on. There was yelling outside—Maker demanding that Daniel leave them—and she heard the jagged voice behind it, the monstrous voice that cut through the air and the walls.

"Want to see?"

She knew whom that voice belonged to, by the way it ran its sharp edges down her ears and through her heart, leaving an infestation of fear. She decided not to listen anymore, to try to dull its voice.

With a grunt of strength, Jenna pushed the window

open. "You go!" Jenna insisted and there was no time to argue.

Rebekah took one last look at her books—priceless things that had survived countless wars and book burnings throughout the centuries. There would be no hope of replacing them. She turned and hesitated only long enough to rip open the top drawer of her desk drawer and grab a small black leather case and the tape recorder sitting on top. Then she said her silent goodbyes to her books and let Jenna help her out the window.

It won't take the monster long to kill Larry.

34

"GET THEM OUT, DANIEL, YOU GET THEM THE FUCK OUT OF here!" Maker roared to him before turning back to the monster, this thing of nightmares and demons. The pale man rose, growing like a shadow in a setting sun, making himself a head taller than Maker. A pencil-thin grin stretched sharply from ear to ear in a V-shape above a pointed chin.

Maker was dead. This man, whom Daniel thought old and slow just twenty minutes earlier, was selling his life as dearly as he could. Daniel turned away. It wasn't so hard after seeing the pale man. Those eyes that hung on Maker flicked to Daniel for only a moment and showed such little concern—they were nothing to the pale man.

Daniel hoped that Maker died quickly, that his pain wouldn't last long. But the screams of torment that followed behind him said otherwise.

I'll kill him, Maker. I swear.

Darting back into the room, he saw Rebekah outside the window and Jenna readying to go through. He slammed the door behind him. "Let's go! Fast!" He grabbed her arm and helped her out.

The skittering of dozens of feet behind the door told him to go faster. Their claws scratched at the door before Jenna was fully through, and they laughed and shrieked in all the horrendous ways he imagined monsters could. Wood cracked and with a glance, he saw a talon puncture the door.

Oh, my God . . .

It was all he could do to not shove Jenna through. Instead, he held himself together until she was done, and then he jumped through the window, slamming onto the snow and popping up a second later.

Rebekah limped forward. "Quickly now, Daniel! While it's occupied, our only chance!"

"We have to get Greg!" Daniel said as he grabbed Rebekah's arm to help her along.

"You go!" Jenna said, coming up alongside them. "Take Daniel's car. I'll get Greg and we'll meet you later!"

She's dead. Greg's dead. They're both going to die.

"No," Daniel said, now looking into Jenna's eyes, this woman who had kept him from insanity, the first one in the group to show him kindness.

"You get your boy, Daniel. You get him and nothin' else matters! You go!" Jenna turned and ran through the dark toward the barn.

"She's right, Daniel." Rebekah clawed at his arm to focus him. "We have to go."

He helped Rebekah to his car and they got inside. With one glance at the porch, he saw the swarm of darkness claw its way out of the house. It was nearly one solid mass, with bodies that occasionally split from it, bodies with wet skin and yellow eyes that cut the dark.

Howls chased him as he got into the driver's seat and started the car. He threw it into reverse as something jumped onto the hood.

"Ha-ha!" The thin frame of the girl he had been carrying now had a flat, white face, as though her nose had fallen off and her skin had turned as pale as snow. Her eyes had sunk back into her head and she roared and slashed at the windshield with long pencil-thin fingers.

Daniel roared back, the beast clawing for his throat as he hit the gas. The changeling went sliding, but dug her fingers into the hood. He jerked the wheel, spinning the car and throwing the girl into the driveway, leaving a bloody finger broken off and stuck in the hood. He watched her yellow eyes light up in his headlights as she bashed her head against the grill.

Iron or not, she had to feel that.

In the rearview mirror, he saw one of the creatures Greg had mentioned stalk from the front door. As heavy as a horse and twice the size of a man, with arms that dragged over the ground and claws the curled in like lions use to kill; nothing about it even feigned humanity.

God help them.

GREG'S STEREO blasted while he worked on his truck. The heap ran just fine before; that wasn't the problem. He simply liked to take pieces of it apart and put them back together. He liked to say he was fixing the old worn parts, but the truth was, that it was a type of therapy to help him think. And he had a lot to think about.

It had been wrong to bring that girl back. He knew it, somehow. His instincts told him to leave her. She was going to die, and it would hurt them all when she did. It would kill the group's moral if she died with them, or just slow them all down trying to figure out what to do with her.

She's probably already dead.

They needed to stay focused on killing this thing and getting Sam. They needed to clear away distractions. But he kept thinking about that girl. Was Daniel right? Had he sunk so deep that he'd leave a little girl because he didn't care, or was there really no way to help her?

Maybe we'll save her. Maybe we'll save Sam, too. Maybe we aren't all as bad as we think we are. Yeah. And maybe I'll start shitting rainbows.

Either way, he knew that having anything around to love was a liability. Anything soft made you weak. Those mother-fuckers used the weak part against him once and now, he'd spent long years making sure every part of him was hard.

But you'd really walk out on a little girl, you piece of shit?

He didn't have time to finish that thought. Jenna burst through the door screaming, "Greg!" Tears streaked down her face. Greg had never seen her that way. "The girl! She . . . she was one of them, Greg! She got the others in here! Maker, he's dead!"

"What?" Greg asked in disbelief. "Maker's dead?"

She started to sob when she saw his truck and the pieces that were disassembled and laid out on a clean towel. "Oh no, Greg, your truck . . . We're dead, too. Greg, I'm sorry! I'm so sorry!" She hugged him tightly.

We're dead?

In an hour, he could get the alternator back in and get the car started, maybe less if he hurried. But he could tell by the look in Jenna's eyes that he didn't have five minutes.

Rotten luck.

He jerked the cord from the stereo loose, sending it

tumbling and smashing against the ground, and then he heard the screaming, the howling laughter, and the horrendous roars of the beasts. He knew this was no joke.

This was death.

This is what you always wanted, didn't you? You wanted to be dead, didn't you? Here's death. It's right outside and coming on in.

Jenna buried her head in his chest; he squeezed her tightly, letting her sob.

"Help me get my gear on," he said, pushing her away.

"What are you going to do?"

"Kill them."

He went to his toolboxes and grabbed his vest. Jenna helped him strap it on and then pull on his heavy work coat. He loved that coat; it had a thick layer of leather protection, but allowed enough mobility to work in. Next, was his Iron hatchet, sharp enough now to shave your balls; he tucked the handle into his belt. Then came the sawed-off shotgun, strap pulled over his shoulders, and his Iron knife tucked into its sheath and clipped to his belt.

They howled outside, telling him they were closing in. He grabbed an Iron-headed spear from the wall; it felt right in his hands. The world made sense.

"Lock yourself in the truck." He pulled on his welding mask; it was hard to see in it, but needed.

Jenna jumped into the truck and hit the locks. She held her hands together and closed her eyes in prayer. He was happy for it.

We're going to need it.

Something slammed into the barn door, cracking it; the thing was apparently too stupid to use the door handle. Greg stormed over with heavy steps that beat in his chest.

Something cracked against the barn door once more,

then twice, but before the next blow, Greg pulled the door open and the creature raked its hand against air. It was a stout, ugly thing, with a mouth carved into its chest and three arms that swung wildly, looking like some nightmarish jack-o'-lantern. He'd never seen one of these, but it didn't matter. The spear tip slammed into its chest-face and threw it back.

No one kills like Greg.

The others all knew it. These fucking things would know it, too.

No one.

The jack-o'-lantern writhed on the ground and the freshly sharpened metal slid from its chest, erupting in a fountain of black blood. But where one died, more came with shrieking fury to take its place. The spear's reach found the first to brave forward and the Iron burned fear into the others. The sharp edge cut through them as if they were barely thicker than shadows, burning away in smoky flames that screamed in torment.

Greg watched the headlights of Daniel's car swing in a semicircle and gun down the driveway with what looked like a four-foot skinned rat hanging from it. He only hoped that Rebekah and Daniel were both in that car.

Jenna, that fucking dumb bitch, she should be in that car.

Then they were on him, and there was no more time to think. Greg was fast. Faster than he knew he could be. Faster than he had any right to be as an old man with too much in the gut. Coals burned in his chest like an old steam engine, churning gears with fires of anger and hate. He had always wanted this, always wanted to test his mettle against them.

He had his chance now as the creatures, a mass of teeth and jaws rallied against him. Their black skin and fleshy mouths stood out against the falling white snow. One howler darted at him, and Greg plunged the spear into its misshapen skull so deep that it stuck on hard bone. He shook the spear and the limp body rolled with it, forcing him to drop it as more circled. Before it hit the snow, the shotgun came up and blasted both barrels into three snapping mouths, blowing meaty chunks from their wailing faces. The shotgun was tossed away, spent, and the hatchet and knife came up next.

"Come on, you fucks!"

Adrenaline burned his muscles; he felt stronger and more alive than he had in years. More answered him, closing in with their snapping teeth and reaching claws. His blades whipped out, severing muscle from bone and rending heads from necks, while the dead formed a burning pile. "Ha-ha!" He let his own bellowing laugh join their frantic cries.

One leapt up from a pile of the dead and bit his arm. With a heavy jerk, Greg shook it off and buried the knife in its chest, feeling like he'd sunk the blade into a heavy sandbag that died in painful jolts. Another took the opportunity to bite him in the leg, pulsing hot venom into his blood. He kicked it loose and swung his axe to meet it in the air when it lunged, splitting its skull open in a hail of splintered bone and opened meat. Another dug at the back of his arm. He sank his knife into it and ripped it off with pieces of his arm. The heel on his heavy boot collapsed its squirming head, pulping dark green and red brains up against his rubber sole.

"Come on now! Come on!" He planted a foot forward and begged them to continue. They swarmed, climbing over their dead, but war was in Greg's blood. There had been a hunger in him for a long time, and even with the venom slowing him, he still fought like a demon. Metal lashed out even before his eyes could see the threat; his body jerked from biting blows and razor hands. He bellowed with each new dead added to his pile.

Only when he found them all dead, and the snow slick with their black burning blood, did he storm to the house.

No one else dies tonight. I hope that pale motherfucker is here. I hope I get my chance with him. I hope he gives me one shot to end it all.

Greg knew fighting them head-on was what you did when a plan failed. It was stupid, suicide, but here he was, and the heaps of dead and his own gore-caked arms said otherwise.

But he felt the venom starting to cripple his arms. He was big and if he pulled it off fast, he hoped he would have time to send a few more back into the pits of Hell.

"Come on! Get out here, you pussies!" he shouted as he thumped toward the house, leaving bloody tracks in the snow.

Something stirred in the shadows of the house, climbing out from the back. It was hard to see in his welder's mask, but he knew what it was just by the shape. One of those large fuckers, just like the one that took his wife so long ago. Neckless and rippled with muscle, it walked on all fours with only a large, gaping mouth, from which heat rose in the cool air. He felt the fear slithering around inside him, just like that night so long ago when he'd broken. He ate the fear and refused to run. He refused to do anything but stand and fight and die there in the snow.

"Come here, you ugly bastard!"

Smaller forms were emerging from the shadows, jabbering like beasts insane with hunger looking for meat to fill their bellies. The largest threw its head back and roared like a wolf that had lungs the size of boulders, echoing through the woods and into the night. The others shrieked as they joined the screaming, but pulled back and no longer pressed the attack against Greg. Instead, they returned to the house like a flood of water running down a bathtub drain.

They think I'm done.

Greg roared back, digging the scream up from a primal spot in his heart. His lungs burned, and he sucked in breath to curse at it. "You think you scare me, you motherfucker? You think I'm afraid of you?" he asked in a spitting rage behind the mask as he gripped his hatchet as hard as he could. "I hope this hurts, you ugly bastard! I hope it fucking burns!"

The large beast's mighty head swung down as it started a heavy gallop. Greg rushed in to meet it halfway, no longer able to wait.

———

A KNUCKLE SNAPPED off in his mouth, and black blood oozed down his lip. He hardly felt the bone crunch under his teeth. He watched them take the girl, the girl he had just planted, into their car and back to their home, not knowing that the real Robinson girls were laid out dead in the backyard.

It was hard to stifle his roaring laughter, so instead, he took the finger off. An annoyance, but it'd grow back in time. He flicked it away.

What if they had just looked around the back? They would have seen the bodies there. Wouldn't that have been hilarious!

This cell had seemed sharp, but it was clear now that they weren't. They came to him at first like they might be worthy of the game, but he saw now that they were dull and easily tricked. They either hadn't dealt with the likes of him before or were simply lucky enough to have survived.

He stepped back into the shadows and waited. His daughter would beckon him to the other side soon. It might be some time—she'd have to heal and concentrate—but they'd give her the chance. They had no reason to suspect. He watched the rippling shadows and time slowly passed. Finally, he saw his girl's face there, a snake-tooth and gleaming smile.

He told her to wait until she got back and could see how many others were there—he wanted to get them all—and he wanted her to wait until all their weapons were gone and they were at their most vulnerable.

That's when it'll be the funniest!

She bade him to come and he came. When he rose up from the shadows, there was some pity there in him, not for any suffering but for the loss of the game. He'd have liked the game to be a *bit* more challenging than it was. But instead, they went running like they always do when he caught them—chickens with their heads twisted off. He took the old man first, the only one to stand against him in the kitchen. His children dragged the man into the shadows with a promise that it wouldn't be fast, that it would be very long and very painful. His children might be apt to finish a meal quickly, but he demanded patience of them this time. His brood had special, painful plans for this one.

The lowest of his children spread out and chased the meat with mindless determination. He sent his daughter to free the other and got the two girls in front of him.

"Find me the hunters. Kill them all, but bring me the man, the one that smells like the boy." They nodded eagerly, mops of hair flapping, and ran off.

One returned quickly to speak to him, a pleasant smile on her thin lips.

"The man is outside," she said giddily, "and heading to his car with the old cunt."

"Slash her throat and bring me the man as alive as he can be."

That one raced off. As he strolled down the hallway, he found the room that they had all been holed up in; his children had broken the door rather than turn the handle— hilarious things, they were. The room was filled with books that smelled of old paper and the scent of lands he'd travelled long ago.

He was sure men found books to be valuable, but he rarely saw the necessity of them, though he supposed things that lived and died as quickly as them, might need to read the words of others. For him, death wasn't a problem.

With long fingers, he plucked one tome and peeled off its plastic case; he cracked it open and tossed it away almost instantly when he saw there were no pictures. He did the same with another, watching the spine crack and the papers flutter out when they collided with the wall or ground. The third had interesting things like drawings of monsters and words like *Wechselbalg.*

Oh, is this one about me?

Skimming through it, reading Old German as easily as any other language, he found it full of falsities and harebrained remedies for changeling hauntings; only a few facts seemed to have any truth. With a grunt, he threw it away, tossing it against the wall and bursting it into a hail of pages.

Growing bored with them, he sunk his claws into the edge of the bookcase, pulled it over, and watched the books spill out. His lowly brood swarmed up, excited with the violence, and tore at the pages as if that might gain them favor with him.

He ignored them and walked to the front of the house to see if they had taken the man. He found him gone, and another man was out fighting with his children—the fat one from the house. With a snicker, he watched the man butcher the lowest of his brood, and then the pale man turned to the shadows.

Come.

He beckoned the largest of his brood and set it upon the man. "Go. Kill." They were not complicated beasts.

"Finish up here," he said, looking at his daughter, and then he bled back into the shadows.

35

DANIEL GRIPPED THE STEERING WHEEL AND TOOK SHORT breaths. "They're not coming to the asylum. They won't be there. They're dead."

"I know," Rebekah said without peeling her gaze from the road.

"I don't have any weapons. My knife and gun are back there. I don't have anything."

Rebekah nodded and said nothing else. Though her face was stiff, Daniel could see the doubt.

"Where's the Shallow?"

"It's in the asylum."

"*Where* in the fucking asylum? I've been there already. The place is a giant rotting corpse."

She sighed and shook her head. "I'm not sure. We're going to have to find it. I just . . . I know we will. We'll find it. I just hope the master stays away long enough for us to get in."

Fire burned in Daniel's chest. He wanted to scream at Rebekah, or smack her, or pound the steering wheel, or rip back to the house and slam the car into as many of them as he could, anything that would give him some control.

It felt good to run that girl over, didn't it? Use that. But get it right. Rebekah isn't the one wrong here. She's not the one who did this to you. She's sacrificing for Sam. They all are. They're all dead. Get your shit together and make it count. You'd sacrifice anything for Sam, but they already have.

He grabbed Rebekah's hand. She looked more startled than if he had smacked her. "I'm with you, Rebekah. Let's get Sam."

Gripping his hand with her delicate fingers, and stopping only to wipe a tear from her eye, she said, "I'm with you too, Daniel." Then she gasped and pointed forward.

Clawed fingers sank into the hood of their car with a horrid, piercing sound, scraping deeper into the metal as the small changeling girl pulled her smashed head from the headlights. Pieces of skull had collapsed, crushing half her face in on itself. One eye had popped loose from its deep socket and smashed flat against her face while her jaw rattled loosely with her hangman's laugh.

Brains leaking from a smashed skull only slowed her down. And even now, with slop leaking down her head, she still wanted them.

"Get . . . you . . ." Her loose jaw rattled, a piece of skin flapping in the air.

"Fucking die!" Daniel savagely jerked the wheel and the car slammed into the guardrail, filling the air with the sounds of grinding metal. The changeling wailed until her leg got caught, ripping her off and sending her under the tires.

Daniel slammed on the brakes, screeching the car to a halt, and watched it through the rearview mirror. Its mangled face was pressed into the asphalt, a horribly disfigured arm was twisted behind it, and one leg looked to be completely gone. It stretched out its good arm and tried to push itself up like an awkward puppet coming up on strings. Black and red sludge oozed from its mouth in the red glow of the car's taillights.

"What are you doing? We should leave!" Rebekah said as she looked back over her shoulder.

"No." Daniel put the car into reverse and gunned it. He hit the changeling just as she was coming to a knee. Throwing the car into forward, he ran over her again until she filled the rearview mirror once more.

"Daniel!" Rebekah screamed. "That won't kill it! You're only toying with it!"

"No." He shook his head. "We need it."

GREG FELL BACK; the venom had turned his left arm into a goddamn log, but he'd planted that Iron axe right into the fucking thing's forehead before he went down. It was writhing on the ground, shaking its head and trying to loosen the Iron from it, moaning loudly, like a stuck pig with death creeping in. The small ones were gone, and he hadn't seen any of the others. It had just been him and this big son of a bitch for the last few minutes.

I killed you, you son of a bitch. I fucking killed you.

That thought warmed him, even if everything else was cold and he was so tired. More would be on him soon—he was sure of it. He didn't know what hole they had crawled into—probably tearing apart their house for anything of use —but they'd be back.

Let them come. I'm too damn tired.

"Ha-ha!" A shrill laugh came from behind him, though

he barely heard it over the bitching from the cow dying next to him. Rolling over, he saw the small changeling girl from the house, the one he had caught in the net. It prowled forward on all fours, its arms now as long as its legs and stitched with thick black hairs, and a tail that it didn't have earlier, swished behind it now.

"Impressive, fat man. But I see you slowing down. I see you about to fall over."

"Come here, you fucking slut. I'll show you how tired I am!" The words slurred out of his mouth as he pointed the tip of his knife at it. "I'll cut your ugly fucking face off!"

They were hollow threats; his arm shook and threatened to give at any moment. It'd be the easiest thing in the world right now to just let the creature have it, to just roll over and let it all go dark.

It knew that, too. It knew how close he was to death, but it had also seen him kill so many others, so the bitch would take its time. The flicking tail waved at Greg as it strolled over to the large beast and grabbed the hatchet by the wooden handle. It pulled the hatchet from the cow's head, tossed it toward the house, and echoed its thud with a laugh. The beast shook its head and pawed around.

Like a big, stupid motherfucker. Do it, then. Be fast.

The next part happened quickly. The creature spread its fingers, showing its talons. Its laughter stopped as it readied to pounce. Greg almost missed the shadow coming up behind it, sprinting at the changeling as quickly as she could.

You stupid dog!

His dog hadn't barked—her old hurt throat might have given her away if she could—but she had come nearly silent under the dying cow's moans. She jumped into the air and slammed into the back of the changeling, taking them both down in a tumble. They thrashed on the ground and he saw the changeling's hand come up and down with sprays of blood.

No! Damn you! Don't you fucking die for me!

Dragging his leg forward, Greg forced it to bend even if it shot shards of pain into his bones. "No!"

The dog whined, and he saw her teeth on the changeling's throat, pinning it down. With all of the power he had left, Greg leapt and sank his blade into the changeling's bony back. The blade dug in three more times before the changeling stopped fighting and died with a hollow look of fright in its eyes.

"No, dammit . . ." Greg grabbed the changeling by the hair, a patch of it coming loose with a wet snap as he did, and pulled its dead body off the dog. The creature's twisted fingers had come off, red with the dog's blood. The dog loosened her jaws and stared up at Greg. She sucked in three more breaths and watched him. What was she thinking? Why did she do that? Why did she come to save Greg? Soon after, she stopped breathing and went limp, her eyes as dead as the monster's.

I didn't even name her.

He snatched the dog's loose body from the ground and stumbled back to the barn, ignoring the burning stab of pain. There were more huffs and snorts from the large beast behind him, not as dead as Greg once thought it, but he didn't care.

The dog's head rolled loosely in his arms as he entered, and Jenna threw open the truck door, rushing to meet him. "Greg!" She wrapped an arm around him and Greg's knee froze up, making him stumble to the ground and drop the dog on the floor.

She died for me! I'm a piece of shit and she died for me. My life isn't worth a dog's! My life isn't worth anything. I'm useless, and she died for me.

"Oh God, Jenna!" he blubbered as hot tears stung his cheeks. "They killed her! They fucking killed her!"

I don't deserve it. You should have let me die, you stupid bitch. You should have let me die, you stupid fucking dog.

Jenna looked out the door, but Greg squeezed his eyes shut. He wanted it all to be a lie; he wanted it all to be a trick played on him. He didn't care if he died. He didn't care if they cut pieces from while he screamed, but he didn't want anything to die for him. He didn't deserve it. He didn't deserve anything like that. He was a hateful old man that didn't love anything. He was a coward at heart, who'd left his wife to die and shot a man dead rather than let himself get caught. He didn't want anything. He never wanted a fucking dog. He didn't want something that could hurt him. He didn't want to breathe. He didn't want to love anything. He should have shot her in the goddamn face when he first saw her. He should have blown her head off and drowned her pup.

She died for me.

"Come on, now!" Jenna said as she tried weakly to pull him, but he didn't move. He didn't care. There was nothing he could do to help Jenna live. There was nothing he could do to save himself or bring that dog back and force her to run in the other direction. Nothing he could do to have dropped her off a day earlier like he planned.

"You should have left with them, you dumb bitch," he mumbled to Jenna. "That was always the plan, you fucking idiot."

If she said something back, he didn't hear it. The soup of the venom was entering his brain. He knew it, but he didn't care. They'd taken everything from him. Not only his wife, but his happiness and every waking moment since her death. There was nothing left to live for but his hate for them. He never wanted anything, even the dog. But she'd grown on him. He should have taken her and dropped her off like he planned, her and her pup. But she was his. The first thing he'd had in a long time that cared about him and breathed.

And they killed her.

"Get ahold of yourself, Greg!" Jenna said and slapped him across the face.

He needed that. He got ahold of his wits. They told him there was nothing left to cry over—better to see it all to the end. He let go of the dog and let her body lay close to his.

He looked up at Jenna. "You're right. Help me over to the propane tanks." He was wheezing now; the toxins were working on his lungs. "We'll take a few more of them with us if we can."

Jenna nodded and closed her eyes.

He heard the hulking monster howl. It had regained its focus.

It won't be long now.

With Jenna under one of his arms, they lurched over to his tool chest. Greg admired it one last time and then fished a key out of his pocket.

"Hurry, now!" Jenna urged. "It's almost here!"

With a weak nod, he went through the key ring until he found the right one. He collapsed to one knee and opened a worn metal box. There were three sticks of dynamite, all neatly taped together. One last gift Maker had acquired for him. Fresh, too; they'd only gotten them just before reaching New Athens.

Going to be the best gift the old bastard ever gave me.

He patted the propane tanks and reached up to turn the

squeaking handle. He held the dynamite out in front of him and cracked off all but the tips of the wicks. "Don't suppose you saw my lighter in the truck, did you?"

Jenna laughed and took a seat next to him. "No need. Rebekah quit smoking and asked me to throw this away. Still had it in my pocket, though." She pulled out Rebekah's old lighter and held it before them like a prize.

Greg smiled and reached for the lighter; she planted it in his hands. "Maybe she knew we'd need it."

Jenna nodded and hugged Greg. "I couldn't leave you, Greg. I just couldn't." Jenna said, almost as an apology.

He squeezed her side. "Jenna?" Tears started to drip one last time. "You think God can forgive me for what I've done? For all the people I've hurt and all the evil I've lived?"

She threw her arm around him and gripped him tightly, just as the howling creature shoved its maw in through the open door.

"I'm so proud of you, Greg. God will forgive you if you ask Him to, honey. He loves you."

Greg struck the lighter and brought the flame to life. And clenched his eyes shut for a moment.

Please forgive me, God.

The monster howled and threw its shoulders into the doorframe, trying to push its way in. Part of the roof collapsed on top of it. The monster shrieked and barreled forward anyway, splintering the wood.

Greg held the flame to the wick.

36

"WE'RE GOING TO HAVE TO LET IT HEAL," REBEKAH HAD TOLD him only a short time before. "It might take a few hours."

Heal enough to feel it when he cuts it.

That's what she said when Daniel scooped the changeling's body out of the street and put it in the back of his car. Daniel's car had smashed its chest and cracked its spine, leaving it a crippled heap of splintered bones, ruptured organs, and torn flesh. It was on the very doorstep of death. Even someone as used to violence and gore as Rebekah found it sickening.

But in a few hours, it'll be up and talking again.

She watched as Daniel sat hunched over his desk, scribbling in his notebook, draining the last drops of alcohol left in his house. Normally, she would have been against that, enraged, even.

He's going to need it.

Daniel would have to hurt it until it told them what they needed. They couldn't risk going inside its head—Rebekah was too weak, and she needed to save everything she had for the night.

Tonight, we go into the belly of the beast. Hell itself.

There was no telling why Daniel felt the need to scribble his thoughts into a book with a shaky hand and a belly full of booze. She could hear Maker's ghost whispering in her ear, telling her that it was a bad idea to leave any evidence. But he had raced to the book after he'd chained the creature up in the basement and started a fire to warm the house. She was concerned about the chains, though; they weren't Cold Iron like the ones back at their place. Nothing in this house was "weapon-quality" to fight changelings.

But why should they be concerned with evidence tonight? Their friends were surely dead and waiting to be found. Evidence and prosecution were secondary concerns, and only a real possibility if they survive the night.

Save Sam, and spit in the devil's face.

Both seemed equally difficult at the moment.

She ached for a cigarette, but instead, decided to head into the basement and watch the creature heal. And it did. Like water rolling off a duck's back, so simple and effortless.

The basement was filled with furniture that felt alien to Rebekah: Daniel's big-screen TV in one corner and a pool table in the opposite, a large leather couch, and drink tables nearby. Over the years, Rebekah had gotten so used to the dank, disgusting places where they performed their work that it was strange to see a place carpeted and clean, or at least one that had been, before they dragged the broken body of the monster through it.

Now, this once-cozy house had a changeling sitting near-dead with occasional snaps of life as it weaved itself back together. Chunks of gore had leaked off and soaked the carpet. Splatters of brain and black juice dripped into a wet pile on the ground where its head hung loose. The chains were around it and laced through a wooden chair. Rebekah sat across from it and watched. Slowly, in ways that eyes couldn't notice, she saw the flesh knit itself together. The only way to see it at all was by marking where the cut was at one point against the creature's clothing, and turning back a minute later to see the cut rising just above the mark.

This entire brood had been made of sterner stuff than she had ever dealt with. None had pressed them so hard or come at them so ruthlessly. None had been so intelligent or quick to heal.

And none had ever killed so many of my friends.

Had she ever seen one in this way? Watched it with such desperation? This was their hope. This thing held the key to the end, and all they had to do was find something sharp and painful enough to reach in and open it up.

I could really use a cigarette.

DANIEL STOPPED and squeezed his eyes tightly shut, wondering again why writing always seemed to make things easier, as if it somehow made them certain, a thing no longer to be questioned. The pen dropped and his head slid into his hands. It felt heavy in his grasp, but surely another drink would make it lighter. It did.

When I've finished this drink, I'll go to that thing in my base-ment and cut it. I'll hurt it until it gives me what I want. What does that make me? When I stared into the abyss . . .

The next drink went down as easily as the others.

Did it stare back into me?

He stopped with a sigh and looked up at his awards hanging around his desk, and then the pictures of him with his wife Julia and their son Sam. They looked so happy then, and they were.

That was a long time ago.

Things were different now. Not too far back, he was scared of those things with claws and teeth that climbed from shadows. He was scared of what they could do to him.

I'm not scared of them anymore. I'm scared of me. What does it say about me that I started enjoying the sounds they make when they die?

I remember that lie I use to live, but now it's less of a memory and more like a conversation I once had with a stranger. I died sometime during these last few months, but it wasn't all at once. Step by step, death crept into me until I was a shell, and something else was born. I'm not that man anymore—that man who could love and write. He's long dead. I'm something new, something that has a taste that I can't shake, and a longing for what a sharp knife can do.

He remembered the dead: Jenna, Greg, and Maker. Each touched by much of the same, but each a different person. Then there was Rebekah, who'd broken every one of her rules to help him get his son back. And lastly, there was him. Was he like them? What was he becoming?

He reread the letter as if he was sending it to and receiving it from himself, then folded it and placed it in his pocket. There would be time to finish it later, if he still breathed.

There was other business to attend to in the basement. He pulled on a leather winter gloves that his wife had bought for him a few years back, the ones he'd never actually worn. He had always preferred the comfort of his knitted wool gloves, even if they didn't hold the heat as well. But the leather gloves would be good for the Iron fire poker that had been sitting in the fire for some time, becoming cherry red. He was sure it'd melt his bare hands to grab it.

He wanted it that way.

"I'VE READ before that torture isn't all that useful," he told Rebekah before he started. "That people will simply lie or tell you whatever you want to hear to make it stop."

"These are not men. Their allegiances break easily when pain is applied and the right questions are asked."

Of course, he would do it anyway, even if it wouldn't have helped. This creature had wormed its way into his head, just like Maker had warned him they could. And it got him to bring it back to the house.

And now three people are dead.

"You've been with him longer than the others, haven't you? The others didn't know about you. You were with him, weren't you?" He pointed the hot poker at the changeling.

It bared its teeth at him and he read its face.

It was with him.

"Where's the Shallow?" Daniel asked it before applying the heat.

"What the fuck is a Shallow?" the thing that played as a little girl asked with a mouth of broken teeth.

He held the Iron up and kissed the heat to its face. "The soft spot in the world where you came in."

It sat, insolent, trying to eat him with its gaze. He was done with questions now and waited only for answers. It held out at the first taste of the heat—a strong monster, apparently. It wavered with the second jab of the Iron poker, but the third melted its resolve.

"In the basement!"

It had been shrieking that same thing for a while.

"In the basement! It's in the fucking basement!"

Daniel kept hurting it to make sure it wasn't lying to

him. And when he was sure it wasn't, he kept hurting it anyway.

The poker had gone cold, the changeling's flesh having sucked all the heat from it. Daniel left the poker to cook in the fire once more and returned when it was blazing hot. He saw the blisters already forming on the changeling's skin and the thin tangles of flesh repairing the scarred burns.

"This is hard work," Daniel said, looking at the hot Iron. "It's tiring me out, going up and down those steps to heat this thing. Tell me, though. Does your skin just keep growing back like that? Can I do this all night?"

"You son of a bitch," the changeling croaked. "You motherfucker, we're going to get you. We're going to get you! We're going to eat your boy for this! We're going to peel his skin off like a pig!"

"About that . . ." He set the heated Iron to it again.

"It's in the basement, under the stairs of the asylum!" it said between gasps.

"No." He pulled the heat off. "Why did you keep my son? Why is he still alive?"

The changeling looked as if it was about to say something snide, so he pressed the Iron down onto its hand. "Ahhh!" It whipped its body from side to side, fruitlessly trying to get away from the Iron. "I don't know! I don't know! Stop it! Stop it, you fucker! I don't know!"

Daniel pulled the Iron off.

The changeling gasped huge mouthfuls of air while its blistered lips quivered. It turned its single good eye to Daniel. "*I don't know!*"

Then I'm done with you.

He pulled back the fire poker and lashed it against the creature's face, splattering black blood from the soft spot that was healing.

The thing's head rocked to the side and bounced off its shoulder. "No!" it gasped. "I told you everything!"

A growl that only he could hear burned in his ear; the wolfskin wanted blood. "And it still wasn't enough." Daniel hit it again and again while Rebekah watched, beating it until his hands ached, but the thing lived. He kicked the chair over and turned the pointed edge of the poker down. With a powerful thrust, he put it through the changeling's soft, healing head, sending it into the quivering throes of death.

Rebekah watched him unflinchingly, her face stony and eyes sharp. "You done with your plaything?"

The wolfskin purred in his ear; the blood sated it for the moment, but it would be hungry again.

"Let's go hunting."

37

"Do you think she knew?"

"Who?" Rebekah asked as she watched the snowflakes fall outside the car window.

Daniel kept to the speed limit this time. "My wife, Julia. She told me it wasn't Sam when he was sick. She knew it somehow."

"Perhaps some part of her knew," Rebekah speculated. "A mother's intuition can be a powerful thing."

Daniel fell silent. There were no more words between them, nothing more to be said as they walked into the mouth of madness. And each minute put more weight onto Rebekah's shoulders, more weight of what it was they were here to do. That alone kept her silent. She could only imagine what it was doing to Daniel.

Only when they'd arrived, did he speak again.

"Here." Daniel turned the headlights onto the haunting sign: *New Athens Haven.*

A chill like a swarm of spiders crawled from the small of Rebekah's back to the nape of her neck. She knew this place. Without having ever seen it, she knew it. Part of her mind was drawn to it each night. This was a dark place that swallowed shadows and drew everything in.

This was the den of evil.

Daniel parked the car and stepped out; his boots crunched against the frozen snow as he held the fire poker in front of him. Rebekah followed him out, letting her gaze run across the decaying building as she pulled the collar of her coat higher.

A man armed with a fire poker and an old woman nearly frozen to death—quite the slayers we make.

She had left everything else at the house, bringing only her coat, her tape player, and the black leather case tucked inside her jacket. She didn't expect she'd make a good warrior, not in the waking world. Neither did she expect to survive the night. That was fine.

Keep me on my feet until we have the boy, and then take what you will.

She wasn't sure whom that prayer was addressed to. Anyone who would listen, she supposed.

Seeing Daniel, his arm and Iron held high in one hand and the light in the other, she remembered the old stories, the tales of knights with torches and swords wading into dens of ghouls. They were always so brave and chivalrous, ready to challenge the impossible to rescue the innocent. In the fairy tales, the knights always won.

But this isn't a fairy tale, is it? And Daniel is no knight. Our hands are caked in blood.

The one truth Rebekah knew about the real world was that there were no happy endings, and the best were only bittersweet. She followed Daniel into the mouth of the asylum, the dank place with long shadows that seemed to move and listen to each step they took. The doors had collapsed inward and the wind and snow blew in freely.

Surely no sane city would keep such a blight nearby, such a reckless hazard within reach of the city, breeding rot and infestation.

It's the evil here. They feel it. They're afraid to come here, afraid to even tear it down. All they can do is hide from it, and tell their children scary stories to keep them away, just like the old tales. A place like this would only serve someone like that pale man.

Something chirped in the distance.

"Did you hear that?" Daniel stiffened.

"Yes." Rebekah's eyes went wide. Their only hope was to have the monsters distracted. "Perhaps it was nothing." She didn't believe that, but what else could they do? If the creatures were here, then they were dead. Hopelessly outmatched, armed with only hope, determination, and a fire poker.

Perhaps more determination than hope.

"Stay close to me." Daniel pointed the light in front of him, cutting away the dark.

"Heh-heh-heh."

What was that?

Rebekah drew as close to Daniel as she could, so close that she could smell the sweat on his neck.

A thing crawled across the wall and into the light, like a lizard unafraid to leave the shadows, believing that it was the apex. It was smaller than a child, but its skin was black as night and the shadows it came from—only its green eyes pierced the darkness. If the thing could form words, it chose not to.

"We must hurry, Daniel," she whispered to his back. "Perhaps it's told him we are here." Could it even do that? She didn't know. Either way, there was no turning back. The thought hadn't even crossed her.

A tail whipped behind the creature as it crawled forward on stubby legs and arms. Daniel flashed his light; it hissed, and steam rose from its pink mouth. Daniel's grip tightened on the cold metal of the fire poker and he charged just as the creature's limbs bowed. He slashed it across the face with the sharp tip of the poker. It swung a claw at him and cut him just below the elbow.

With an angry huff, Daniel swung again and caught it with the hook of the poker, pulling it from the wall. Taking advantage of its exposed belly, Daniel gouged it several times, and after a fit of flailing limbs, it went stiff. It puffed up like an inflated balloon, and then started to leak gas from its wounds, reminding Rebekah of the dead sow she'd found in a creek one summer.

Daniel clenched his teeth and covered his mouth. "Not as strong as the others." Daniel blinked hard and pulled the weapon from the carcass. "He left a weak one back here to guard."

"Why not? He's not afraid of us." Rebekah shook her head, heavier now than it had ever been. "I hope that was the only one."

"Rebekah, can you feel it? I can. I couldn't before, but I can now," he said, looking toward the stairs. "I can feel it down there, waiting for us."

A mouth of darkness, where once-white steps had turned a sickly gray, led only to a black gullet swallowing the night. Neither of them moved toward it.

"You couldn't before?" She could feel it, too, the Shallow, open and calling to them, like this was all a game and they had parts to play. Her bones ached. She reached for his hand and came up to his side.

"Let's go," Daniel said.

As they descended the stairs, letting their flashlights

push back the dark, things seem to skitter out of sight. Rebekah wasn't sure if she imagined it or if they were actually crawling up her legs now. Putrid water had pooled in several areas. The walls were lined with half-torn posters that were mostly rotted off and showing only a faint word or two.

It was unmistakable. Right where the creature had told them, under the stairs in the basement, a black puddle stretched down the wall, rippling and bubbling in some dead wind blowing from the other side.

"How do we get in?" Daniel asked as he watched it closely, not daring to step closer.

"*We* don't, Daniel," Rebekah said. "I'm not a native of that world. The dream told me. You'll be stronger there, Daniel, more powerful than you have been. I have to go in the old way, through dreams. You'll have to go in yourself, but I'll meet you there."

"How can you sleep down here?"

"Please, leave a woman her secrets."

Daniel squeezed her hand. "Will you be safe here?"

"Yes. I'll be waiting for you when you come out. Hurry, now."

"Thank you."

He looked so afraid then, so ready to break into a million pieces. But it wasn't the same kind of fear he'd had when he first met Rebekah. He faced the bubbling Shallow, dropped the poker by Rebekah's feet, and stepped forward without another pause. The pool bowed inward a few inches before swallowing Daniel whole.

Go, Daniel. Save Sam.

She found a dry spot on the ground to rest her head. It was cold, too cold, but that wouldn't matter while she slept. She pulled out the black leather case. Truthfully, even with her focus, she doubted she could sleep in a place like this. Her heart was beating too fast and it was too cold. That's what the case was for. This was her silver bullet. She unzipped it and opened it flat against the ground. A syringe, tubing, and a vial lay strapped inside.

Save him, Daniel.

She would be there soon to help Daniel, but she regretted lying to him. She wouldn't be there to meet him when he came back. She really doubted she'd ever wake up again.

Save him. Save us all.

DANIEL STEPPED into the world between worlds where nothing and everything was real. But before, when he came in a dream, it was all so foggy and soft.

Now, it hurt.

He felt claws raking down his skin. He wanted to scream from the pain, but found he had no mouth and no air to breathe. Unseen fire burned bubbles on his skin and his insides, and he felt he might suffocate. He curled in on himself like a ball, twisting his center end-over-end with no real shape, human or otherwise.

Was this the end? Had Rebekah simply led him to his death?

No. There is no end.

No ends or beginnings. Nothing real or fake. Nothing but the dream, and the will, and the reality over which Daniel had no control.

It all hurts so much. How long have I been here? Days? Weeks? Minutes?

A living body was never meant to go into the Dream

world, and he was being punished for that. He might have died there with no real hope of taking the next step forward, if it hadn't been for the voice.

"I'm here, Daniel," a gorgeous girl said with a voice like honey. Somehow, even without seeing her, he knew she was beautiful.

"You have hands, Daniel. Look at them."

I hurt so much...

"Daniel. Listen to me. Look at your hands."

There were no hands or eyes to look with. There was only hot, searing pain. The pain of being a real thing in an unreal place, the unnatural forces around him seeking to undo him.

There was no reason for anything, no reason at all to exist.

Why am I here? It's cold. What am I? It's hot.

"You're here for Sam."

Sam.

That brought everything back. Just as if he was descending stairs into madness, he turned around and reached up. He found purpose.

Nails scraped at the inside of his head as he willed himself to have eyes, or simply opened them. He looked down and saw his hands, though fire still burned in him.

"I know you hurt—I can feel it, too. But you have hands, Daniel, hands that can bend and break this world. You're strong, and you have the blood of this world."

Her soft, glowing hands reached out and touched his. "Don't hurt anymore," she whispered.

He saw her then, just as she was the last time he saw her: a gorgeous woman with long, braided, blonde hair and eyes that were rich and blue.

Rebekah. She's so beautiful.

"Are you with me now?"

"Yes," he said, now willing himself a voice and pressing the fire in his chest away as he pulled on the wolfskin.

This was his world, his place. The other world was the lie, and this was where he should be. This was the place he always belonged. He was something new here, something awakened.

Rebekah's smile faltered. "You're not Daniel . . ."

"No," he said with a grin stretching across his face. "I'm not."

38

Seconds ticked by, each more irritating than the last. Countless years had done nothing to curb his impatience. Desire was a strange thing for an ageless being such as him. Few things could pique his interest; few things could keep him enthralled. He wanted little. But now he did.

He wanted that fucking man.

His daughter should have gotten to them now, should have been able to tell him something, anything, about what was happening. But he couldn't find her in the shadows. She neither opened herself to him, nor made herself available to be found.

It's possible that they had silver or iron hung around her neck. It's possible she'd decided to just abandon everything and head off—such things happen. It's also possible that she killed herself. Or maybe they killed her.

She was my favorite.

This only roused his irritation. It was rather inconvenient for her to be dead. Nearly all of his brood—all such disappointments—were dead, even his youngest brought to form so shortly ago. Very irritating—it left all the groundwork to him. What was there to do now? Go snatch away another human child to make another of his own, or ...

Wait for the bastards to come here.

But would they be so stupid as to come into the dream, to challenge him? This was a game, one he wanted to win, but not so easily. Would they make it easy? Would they come here? What a bore. Now that he had considered it, he hoped that they ran, gathered themselves, and came to hunt him later. He could take more children tomorrow and just sit right here in his nest, let a new brood grow. Besides, he was starting to like this town, wasn't he?

What was the name again? It eluded him, and he gave it only a moment's consideration. It was nice to have this place, with its Shallow hole in the world, by which he could come and go so easily. For one such as he, so old and so strong with the dreams, it was hard to move between the worlds unless someone opened the door. But the Shallow made it so much easier to come and go throughout this shitty little town. He supposed that was fine. If he couldn't have the man right now, then at least he might make things interesting for later; if they had any salt, they'd know how to find him. But they had been weaving in and out of his children's dreams before, hadn't they? They might still come ...

Would they both be foolish enough to come here and challenge me? What could I do? How can I make it fun?

Something dark and horrible came to him and he rocked with laughter.

"Oh, I've got something. I've got something, and it's *so good.*"

A FEVERED SCREAM howled inside him. It made and unmade

things, bent the world to his liking by forcing his will upon the rest. So, he did. His hands seeped with blood to prove it.

He enjoyed it.

They had crossed the bounds and entered this other world; guided by instinct and an inherent understanding of where to go. Like a candle burning in the dark, they knew where Sam was. The distance to him was merely a construct, a thing made by the pale man when they entered his mind, or his domain; perhaps both were one and the same to his kind.

There was no mountain here, no house inside the pale man's construct. It was instead, a weeping forest of gray trees, each dying an eternal death; endless suffering that seeped into the hearts of those who looked upon it; and such things that a monster would enjoy. There were faces etched upon each tree, tormented things that whispered and moved when you didn't look at them. So many of their voices spoke at once that it was impossible to understand a single one.

Things bled out of the trees like dark sap. They came from the pools and marshes that seemed only now to ooze and bubble out of the ground, laughing grimly, an army with no real formation or unity—only a howling mob of hate and pain laughing wickedly to turn intruders back, or set them off ease.

I love it.

The truth was that the minute Rebekah brought him back—helped him regain himself—everything became clear. Here in this world, the part of Daniel that feared and broke was locked away, allowed to wallow in its own torment and misery. But the animal side, the wolf side, was loose. That was the side that Daniel trusted, the one he put up to fight for him.

It was something that had always been there, something that was in every man, but more so in people like Daniel, who had some trace of the blood of the wicked ones. It had always whispered to him, always suggested or taunted—but only that, only a whisper. Then, over these last few months, it had been stirred awake by the presence of another beast and no longer slept.

Now it stood, ready to be heard.

Daniel didn't say that; he only felt it. Perhaps those thoughts or feelings had formed into words that Rebekah heard because she seemed cautious and worried for him. Of course, she hadn't meant to let him know, but it wasn't hard for Daniel to notice how reluctant she was to turn her back on him.

But now wasn't the time to be concerned with Rebekah's feelings. Now there was only the mob, and the blood to spill.

Daniel had claws because he had no use for hands. He set them upon the first of the creatures to dare him. They went easy, the weakest of the pale man's world. They were the castoff of nightmares taken from other's dreams and pressed into the pale man's service in his world.

No, it's not his anymore. It's mine.

Before he was the wolf, he found it difficult to go to war against them, afraid to fight them, afraid to get lost in the nightmares. It wasn't like that anymore; he felt at home. And when the waves of gnashing teeth fell upon him—and he killed them—he had never felt more alive. He wasn't afraid anymore. He hated them. He loved to hate them. And here, hate was a weapon as sharp as any blade. It rolled off Daniel like whipping chains seeking an enemy to end.

There was no Rebekah, no changeling, not even Sam. Now, there were only the monsters before him and the monster inside him and the craving. He stomped the wet ground and felt the whole world shake, then raked a powerful hand forward and cut three of them down. Their deaths only made him want more.

Some came on long, bowed legs with three-fingered hands tipped like spears and tails lashing behind them; others came on short, jaunty, hoofed feet with jaws that opened as wide as a man and horns that seemed to always bend in Daniel's direction. More still came, in such volume that their movement appeared as one mass of quaking flesh.

"Go!" their master roared behind them. "Drown him in your blood!" he shouted when it saw how uselessly they died.

They hurried to their deaths, more fearful of what the master might do; a grand thing it must be, to provoke something into such a quick death. They rose from the ground and the pools, climbed down from the abyss above and out of the cracked smiles of the trees, hundreds or more of them, each meeting its end before Daniel, who was now more beast than man. And when their numbers thinned at Daniel's claws, the master strode forward on his thick, muscular legs, hefting his heavy bulk forward. A fat, red tongue flicked out of his mouth and over his purple lips as his gaze turned to Daniel.

There was fear there that Daniel could see; but more than that, Daniel could taste it. Whereas the small ones were too stupid to know their fate, this one did. But this one too, must have a master that it feared more than death. It ripped heavy blades up from unseen places and hulked forward.

The creature's fear, and its understanding of what it faced, ignited Daniel even more.

It's so much sweeter when they understand.

Someone screamed; a loud thunderous roar tore

through the imagined forest like a hurricane. It was several long moments before Daniel realized it was he who had screamed. The trees themselves responded, slaves now to a new master; their branches came alive and sharpened to points. They reached out and grabbed at the last of the minions and stuffed them into their gaping mouths as their miserable bark expressions changed to greed and lust.

They had come alive for Daniel. He'd taken them himself without conscious thought, though he knew it the instant it happened, as if all of them were the fingers of his hands, working to play the same tune. They snatched up the fat master before it had closed even half the distance to him. The trees now wailed a gluttonous tune as they fought over the wet chunks they tore from the screaming monster. Daniel watched it, soaking in every bit, with his mouth watering and enjoying the screams and the pain. He hated everything about this place, hated it just as much as he loved it.

Burn it. Burn it all down and take it.

"Daniel!"

Something screamed, but it meant nothing to him. He let the branches dig into the soft center of the fat monster's head and spill its secrets, to be known by all.

"Daniel!" The scream came again and was again ignored.

Reaching inside the pulped head, Daniel dug out the wet, gray mass. His clawed fingers shoveled it into his mouth and each bite exploded with memories and secrets.

He saw what it knew. He tasted the fear that ran through it, the fear of someone like Daniel. It had never felt something like him. Nothing like him had ever come to face its master. He tasted its submission to the pale man, a submission born of pain and misery, and hatred for the master. He tasted its loathing for existence and the pain it suffered moment by moment.

He tasted it all and wanted more.

I'll take this all. I'll take everything they have. I'll kill them and remake them. I'll tear the nightmares from everyone and leash them to my world. I'll be the monster. I'll be the hunter. I'll be the wolf.

I'll be the master.

39

THERE WAS ANOTHER NOW; SHE KNEW IT THE MOMENT DANIEL became lucid. His mind was reaching out defensively, afraid to be here, and it put the other side ahead. Maybe it was for the best, but that thing couldn't love Sam—of that, she was sure. There must still be part of Daniel mixed in to keep driving it; maybe only a whisper in a yelling mob, or a single line in a scribble, but he was still there. She hoped it'd be enough.

It was when it came to war. The wicked things came down and Daniel had taken them.

No. He consumed them.

She had never seen anything like it. Ghastly chains leapt from Daniel's back, ripping apart everything around them, but still the creatures came. Rebekah knew that there was only so long they could last; nothing was staunching the flow of creatures. And when one died, two rose to take its place.

When does a nightmare die?

And that's what these were: nightmares given form and made real in this unreal place.

When does a man's mind break?

But she knew the answer already. Daniel was broken. She had known that for a long time; he was always teetering on the edge, always with something swimming beneath the surface. She might not have known it at the time, but some part of Maker did. Some part of Maker saw the killer in Daniel, and now Rebekah saw it, too.

Then, the horror of it all came to an end, and Daniel stood alone atop a pile of dead, eating.

"Daniel!" Rebekah yelled at him as he ripped pulp from a skull. He shoveled handfuls into his mouth and with each, his arms grew, his eyes darkened, and thick hair coursed down his back.

She yelled his name again and again. Each time, he ignored her.

Anger gripped at her as much as fear. They had to move quickly; they didn't have time for this. "Daniel, what about Sam?! What about your son?!"

A flash of his eyes silenced her, and then he returned to gorging. Any thoughts of his son were lost—lost as much as he was. She could see it in his eyes.

I've seen eyes like that before.

There had been eyes like that in a man who'd worked with them. He too had been lost, and Greg had put him down—a thing not unheard of in their line of work. The madness is an infection; when it takes root, it can eat everything you are.

"There's a beast in each man," Greg had told her. "Always clawing to get out, just waiting for its chance."

He'd be here soon, the pale man. He and whatever else he had to kill them with. Daniel was strong, but he wasn't that strong. Was this the end then? Was Daniel consumed by his madness, and Sam lost forever?

No, I have to try.

Daniel stood hunched over the dead bodies, ripping pieces and eating, sucking meat from the bones. If he was lost, it didn't matter. The Daniel she knew would have said the same.

He'll stay here, burn like a bonfire in the night. The changeling will come for him and I'll have time to get Sam. I'm sorry, Daniel.

I'm sorry I wasn't better for you.

———

COME TO ME. I'm waiting.

The pale man stood with anticipation, forcing himself to wait for the man to finish eating the dead and dig a little deeper. It wasn't hard to follow him in such a burning pit. He was swallowing the very world around him.

He's come so far in such a short time. He'll be so interesting. Daniel, was that his name? I think I'll let this one keep a name!

A claw gouged the fabric of the world and tore a hole into it. The pale man's black eyes grew wide, and his smile beamed from ear to ear as he watched Daniel pull himself through.

He's almost there, almost ripe. Such a beast!

The pale man could hear the whispers trying to take control in the part of Daniel's mind that was still a man. The beast had shoved it all away, enjoying what it could do here.

Creatures bled from the blackness of the dream and threw themselves at this monster of a man. With joyous rage, he snuffed them out. More came to die, and a collection of the dead piled high.

The pale man snickered quietly to avoid revealing himself.

Wait a moment longer... Just a moment longer...

Some of his mindless children hesitated. Daniel ripped one from where it stood, and bit the top of its head off, spilling slush that stank like chum as its arms flailed. Chitters and mews came from the rest: enough of them were dead to buy their submission and fear, but not yet their obedience. They scattered with each step he took. Fear of what he did surpassed fear of what their master might do.

"Ha-ha!"

Barking laughter ripped from the pale man—he could hold it back no more. He spoke from the shadows. "I've never seen one like you before, and I've seen a lot. You've come here, whole body, mind, and soul, and you're still here!"

Like a cornered, stupid beast, Daniel turned around and around, searching for the voice.

As if you could find me. So much potential, but so stupid.

"I can smell the blood on you. And *him*."

There was a blink of a moment when the whispers in Daniel's head grew louder. It was quickly gone.

"Ha-ha! You're about pure English, aren't you? Not your son, though. He's got a mix of that Romanian slut blood. I can smell it all over him."

"Get out here, dammit!"

"Why? So you can kill me?" The pale man stepped from the shadows in front of him. "You're going to tear me apart?"

Daniel dug his feet into the ground and leapt forward without moving any distance toward the pale man.

"This is my nightmare, you fucking idiot. You come here with claws and sharp teeth. Look at you! What are you? Are you so stupid as to think you can climb in here and tear my throat out? Why, because it worked on the others? Hah! That wasn't war or blood. That was your control. But I can kill you in so many more interesting ways." It'd been so long since he'd spoken so much, but he was ever so eager.

"I am the master," Daniel said, summoning his strength of will. "I am—"

"No." The pale man was whispering in his ear now and gingerly pressing his hands on the back of Daniel's shoulders. "No, you're not. And that's fine. Hah! It's fine that you thought you were. You're more like me than any child I've had. But I have something you want."

The pale man opened a room. There was no color, only shades of black and gray, and each edge and corner was sharper than it should have been. It was Daniel's house.

"This was where I took him while you slept."

Daniel struggled not to walk, but the pale man pushed him, spreading his madness over him and compelling him forward. He didn't need claws to end Daniel, not with so many more enjoyable ways here.

"What?" Finally, Daniel found some words.

"It's him," the pale man said, pointing at Sam's room. "It's who you've been looking for. I've kept him for you."

This will pull the man out . . .

The fight was out of him now. Daniel stepped forward on trembling feet toward the door and the pale man followed behind. Sam sat there with his back to them, staring at the wall. More whispers came from Daniel's mind, bringing a smile to the pale man's gray lips.

"Sam? Sam, are you okay?"

Daniel took a step forward, but froze. Sam's head twisted and cracked as if it were on a hinge, turning around to face them. Sharp teeth filled his mouth and yellow eyes burned in his skull.

"No . . ."

"Do you like him?" the pale man asked. "I've been

working on him for some time now. You see, I can do a few things with someone like him. Someone like you. You'll both be together forever now. Aren't you happy?"

"It was better when I thought he was dead." The whispers were in control now.

There's the man. Strangle the man dead, and the beast remains.

"It was, I'm sure. But he's so much more interesting now. It hurts you, though, doesn't it? That was your fault, and you let it get to you. Hope hurts so much. To see him like that, after you've waited so long, fought so hard, and given so much."

The hair and teeth melted away and Daniel was like a man again. It broke like a trench collapsing from a storm flood, a wash of pain. The pale man felt it, too; it burned so bright that it couldn't be missed. Not the kind of pain that cuts, but the only kind that meant anything here: misery and sorrow. They burrowed into Daniel, and he collapsed into a sobbing mess.

It'd been so long since the pale man could play this game. So long since there were players at this level, where he could sew and shape his world in ways to torment them.

Oh, I want to keep him. We're going to do such fun things!

A chain leapt from the ground and tightened around Daniel's neck.

"It must hurt. I can't imagine how much, as I've never loved anything." The pale man wrapped his fingers around the chain and pulled it tight, feeling Daniel choke for breath.

He's almost ready. It's almost done.

"It can be finished," the pale man said and pulled a gleaming razor from the air. With an open hand, he held it before Daniel. With doll eyes and unsteady fingers, Daniel took it.

"Open it. Cut yourself. Finish it."

Turning a dark shade of red and gasping for breath, Daniel opened the blade and turned his bare wrist up.

The pale man's gray lips pulled tighter—it was so much fun. Sam's little body and head shook with laughter at the idea.

"Do it."

40

THIS WAS NOT A WAR THAT COULD BE WON. SOME WERE SIMPLY too powerful to engage, too dangerous to face with any hope of success. Rebekah reached up into the shadows of the world and wrapped them around herself. She made herself small, tucking inside the walls and fabrics of the void to where she barely existed at all.

As careful as a thief in the night, she slunk through the world and into the constructs of the pale man's domain, now simply a gust of wind or a bump crawling across a wall. She felt the powers being thrown about in another place, a forceful boom of energy. There was a small hope that Daniel could keep him focused long enough that an old woman might go unnoticed.

A hallway with countless rooms stretched out, each with misshapen doors that were chained and locked with cords and links that moved and breathed as she watched them. Things cried behinds the doors: memories and victims that the pale man sought to contain.

Though the pale man was distracted, she was in the pit and still needed to tread carefully. Before her was a door of rotted lumber and a brass handle. The cords upon it hissed as she neared it, and there was nothing left to gamble with but her life.

"I am the master who flails and commands. I am the owner of this room and the contents inside." Her will stretched out against the door and it felt like her hand rubbed against broken glass. She clenched it until it broke, and she made it true. The hissing cords uncoiled and the door creaked open.

Oh my God...

For a moment, she forgot where she was. She took a breath and it caught in her throat; she reached up instinctively to feel her heartbeat—all things she would have done in the waking world, which somehow echoed here.

There was Sam, the same boy in Daniel's pictures and dreams, lying on his bed, asleep. Sleeping for months, no doubt. Now she understood why he still lived and why Sam's changeling had grown sick. The room held more than Sam—it held the thoughts and memories of him. It had all come to her the moment it cracked open.

I know now.

She watched as a small golden ball that sat on the floor turned to her, revealing a golden eye. It blinked once.

"We're done with you," Rebekah hissed, then stomped her heel, shattering it into pieces and causing the world to quiver. Turning quickly to Sam, she gathered him from the bed.

He looks so much like Derrick.

"Come on, Sam," she said, stirring him awake.

His eyes stirred open and from the oddness of the dream-world, he began speaking as though she was a familiar friend and all of this was known to him.

"He won't let me leave. He told me while I slept. He

wanted me to wake up, but I was waiting for you. The voice told me to wait for you. He knows you're here. He won't let us leave."

"I know, I know." Rebekah gripped his hand. "Follow me, quickly."

This world hated her—the very rooms themselves revolted, faces screamed from the walls and hands reached for them. Rebekah pulled Sam tightly to her chest.

"Stay close, Sam, stay close! None of this is real—it's only real if we allow it."

She pressed her will against it to keep it only a lie, but she felt the world struggle and knew she would not last long.

"Are you an angel?" Sam asked, staring at her. She had no time or focus to answer him, only to keep the walls at bay. Wings cracked like sprouts from her shoulder blades and folded out. He was willing it, willing her to be his angel.

I'll be whatever he needs me to be.

She flew as quickly as she could, her powerful wings throwing them forward. The ground followed her up, reaching for her feet as she passed. Sam cried and his eyes melded closed—such was his desire to not see anything. "That's good, Sam," she risked saying. "That's good. Keep your eyes closed. This is a bad dream."

They neared the tear in the world where the real and unreal met. She brought Sam to his feet and pointed him to the Shallow.

"Go now, Sam. Don't wait. Go through here and into the world. Get out of here and run back to town as fast as you can."

"What about you?" he whimpered, his eyes wet.

"I can't come that way, Sam. I'm only a dream, a good

dream in a nightmare. This is all just a bad dream for you and you need to wake up. It's time for you to wake up."

He took a step from her and turned around. "I won't forget you when I wake."

She smiled and nodded, watching him as he left. Now, she turned back to the spot that burned, back to Daniel and the pale man at war.

"Hold a little longer, Daniel. I'm coming."

"Do it."

The pale man prompted again. The changeling that had pretended to be Sam watched them with the dull, smiling face of a lunatic. It had been hard to find it; the pale man had nearly forgotten all about it. So weak and strained, it was barely reaching out for him and opening the door. He found it in the casket and drew it through. It was too cold and too drained to do anything but smile and laugh at Daniel's misery.

Why had it been so weak? Why had it felt so drained? These were questions, but questions that interested him little.

The pale man's fingers sank deep into Daniel's mind, twisting and pushing at certain cues, pulling Daniel's love to the forefront and sliding away any doubts that arose.

"Do it," he insisted again, and pulled the chain even tighter on Daniel's neck.

Daniel choked; his face filled with blood because he imagined it would. He took the razor and held it just above his wrist.

"You'll be with him forever this way. I'll make sure of it."

The pale man's mind slithered deeper into the canals of

Daniel's mind. Like a surgeon's blade, he snipped and cut at the strands that resisted. Piece by piece, the man started to break.

That's it.

The dark little fingers twisted and turned inside Daniel, untying knots of emotions and corrupting others. They reached for the doors and dark corners of Daniel's mind, even as the changeling that wore Sam's face giggled and bobbed its head.

Daniel pushed the blade against his skin and a bead of blood formed as the wound wept. The skin split, little by little, unzipping to the red muscle beneath.

Pale fingers found a wall and a thing howling behind it. The fingers grew to a tip and found thin holes in the brick to slither through. A wet, red-skinned, eyeless creature moaned there, slapping its wet palms against the wall relentlessly.

Oh, this is perfect! Blind fear. You caged it! You're so strong! Imagine what I can make with you! Imagine how fun it will be to break and mold you!

The fingers grew in size, cracking the wall and making a hole. The blind fear slapped against it instantly and grabbed at the pale man, sending a shiver through his core.

Oooh, it's terrible! Ha-ha! He'll kill himself for me!

It pulled itself through the wall and wailed, sending sharp, painful echoes. They rattled the pale man, and a dull ache pounded in his skull.

No, wait. It's not that. What was that?

The pale man felt something crack in his mind, and he knew it was not caused by Daniel. So focused was he that he hadn't noticed the woman enter the room. He only felt it when the bitch crushed his golden eye.

It'd been so long since he felt that kind of pain that it

was almost new again. It was frightening, even for a creature born of fear, to be hurt inside his domain, where his will was law.

No, not frightening. Infuriating! She wants to hurt me? Here? I'll skin the bitch!

Blackness oozed from the wet hole where his eye had been when he pulled his hand away. He suddenly noticed that the chain leading from Daniel's neck was loose.

"That's not Sam," Daniel said, turning around and sneering at the pale man with rows of sharp teeth expanding inside his mouth. The beast was in him again.

No, you fucker...

"It's not, Daniel," the woman called as she bent her will to enter the room. "Sam's gone. I took him to the Shallow. He's waiting for you on the other side. That isn't him." She held her hand up and a blue flame took the creature that wore Sam's face, melting him and turning his smile into a waxy drip. It was so weak that it didn't even cry in pain.

"You fucking whore!"

She ruined everything! Fuck it—I'll just kill them all and eat the kid.

"Go, Daniel!" the woman insisted. "Go, leave! I'll hold him!"

"No. Oh, no, no, no." The pale man found it hard to even form words as his thoughts became convoluted. "He's not going *anywhere*. I'm going to tear you both apart, piece by piece. I'm going to go inside you and cut away everything you are and drag it here, so I can watch it bleed forever. I'm not going to let you die, no, not right away, not until I have you staked down, and then I'll go back out there and drag that boy in for how you hurt me, for how you fucking—"

The fury snapped, and now he only feared that he couldn't stop himself from killing them.

41

Every loving father makes a promise to his children when they're born. It's not said aloud or sometimes even consciously thought, but all loving fathers make it.

My life now is to see you grow old. My life is to protect you and keep you safe. My life is to die for you, if you need me to.

That's the covenant of love that all fathers make when they hold their newborn children and stare into their eyes.

My life for yours.

That's what Daniel thought when he saw the pale man shift away. The pale man had been inside his head, toying with his thoughts, pale fingers delved into his mind, twisting, bending, and breaking things that Daniel penned up years ago. A shattering fear ran through Daniel, a fear of what would happen to his son if he failed. But that fear held a promise, that promise he'd made long ago.

My life for yours.

But the connection between Daniel and the pale man didn't run only one way. No, Daniel felt what the monster felt, too. He saw the disturbed images popping up like flashes in the dark. They were things that would turn a man's hair gray and rot his insides. Daniel was certain that these images, real in this world, would seem just as real when he woke, new nightmares to live with for the rest of his life, even if his life would be spent trapped in this dark world.

And the pale man knew it. He ran his fingers across Daniel like a tongue slick with spit. He licked Daniel's insides and knew which parts were rotten, which flavors of pain and hatred hurt the most.

The pale man could barely hold himself together. Immortals wanted for few things, but the things they did want could drive them insane. The pale man was beyond lunacy; he was a symbol of insanity. He was a nightmare. He was unnatural. And he was manic beyond conception.

Daniel saw all this through the images that flickered inside the pale man's mind like an old-time projector running a reel. He saw Sam's arms being pulled until they popped off like a doll's limbs; saw his insides ripped out like red cotton. He saw jagged teeth tearing at his son, hurting him if only to hurt Daniel even more. He saw all this and knew what grisly horrors awaited Sam, who would be dragged back into the pale man's pit should Daniel fail.

He wasn't going to let that happen. He wasn't going anywhere, despite Rebekah's pleas. He was going to make sure this nightmare stayed with him and that it wouldn't threaten his son again.

Claws busted through Daniel's fingers, splitting the flesh like overripe fruit. Fear and the promise to his son now gave him new resolve, a new reserve of will to draw upon. He latched onto the pale man's body and sank his nails into the white flesh until the black tar that pulsed through the pale man oozed up. It hurt because Daniel's will made it hurt, made it burn like fire against the dark.

The pale man's head twisted around and stared at Daniel with an eye like a black pit and a gaze that snapped and threatened to drink his soul. But there was the other, broken eye, which sat in the pale man's skull, crushed like a rotted olive and leaking pink juice. Daniel shoved his clawed thumb into that eye and was rewarded with new and painful screams.

Rebekah was there, with her back ripped by wings and a glow that shoved back the darkness. With a whip of her head, she linked her mind to Daniel's and threw her will behind his. They forced pain upon the monster, injecting their truth into his lies.

The force threw the pale man back and Daniel's claw was ripped from him. But the venomous pain kept burning. It stretched in painful lines from the monster, burning his flesh black. Digging his heels and fingers into the ground, the pale man dragged himself forward against the whirl-wind of pain.

"You can't kill me here! You can't stop me!" he shrieked. Hairy arachnid legs erupted from his back with a sickening crack and clung to the ground.

"I'm going to hollow you out. I'm going to chew on your love." The creature gnashed his fangs in anticipation. "I am the nightmare that cannot die. I am the eyes that watch you through the dark."

With heat bubbling beneath his skin, Daniel yelled, "I am the fire that consumes the dark!"

"The sun that rises to see the night end," Rebekah said, even as she grew weak.

Fire roared around the pale man, blistering his skin and turning it to ash. His powerful legs stabbed into the ground and clawed closer to them. "I am the nightmare you lock away, the one that comes to you even when awake. I am the insanity that drives you." He pulled closer to them, growing larger as he did. They strained against the pale man, feeling the fabric of their minds and joined will start to tear.

Daniel felt his mind buckle, and the pale man sank a claw in front of him and pulled close enough that Daniel could see his reflection in the pale man's black eyes. "I am what your son's dead eyes see as he lays in his casket." A shift in his eyes showed Sam being dragged amid torturous screams.

Sam's pain and dead eyes hit Daniel like a blast from a jet engine. The force riveted through him, bending his bones and bleeding his eyes. Collapsing to the ground, Daniel flailed in a burst of painful emotions that ripped like hooks through his mind. As he struggled to pull the lies from his head, he saw the pale man turn to Rebekah.

A thick tongue licked across the pale man's burnt lips. His one good eye filled with the lust of an animal before the kill. He pressed against Rebekah's assault, and she stood her ground in defiance. But her light did nothing as the pale man slammed one hand out and grabbed her by the neck, pulling her in. She shrieked when his fingers dug grooves into her flesh.

She let out a bloodcurdling wail that echoed through Daniel's mind and ricocheted off his insides like a pinball. Daniel tried to fight it all, tried to stand, but fell to his knees again.

Sam's not dead! Sam's not dead!

But he was here. He was dead and buried, and Daniel was putting the gun back into his mouth, and the phone didn't ring this time. Only the gun rang.

No, no. That's not true!

The pale man's skin started to grow back as his tongue licked across Rebekah's forehead, stealing her thoughts. A gray-lipped smile stretched across his face. "I am the thing that took Derrick—"

"No, no!" Rebekah said, dripping with tears. She tried to resist it, make it not true, but here it was.

The pale man grabbed her by the head and dragged her closer, squeezing her so tightly between his hands that Daniel heard her skull crack. "I am the one that cracked his bones and sucked them dry," the pale man whispered into her ear. "I am the pain he felt when his arm twisted and splintered."

As the pale man kept whispering, spiders climbed from his mouth and into Rebekah's ear.

Daniel turned his eyes from Rebekah and focused with all he could. He slammed his hand into his mouth, hard enough that his teeth ached, and reached down into his insides, going as deep as his elbow. Something squirmed inside him, and he squeezed it between his fingers. With a wet slopping sound, he pulled his arm out and gagged up white mucus. He looked at his hand to see a pale worm thrashing in his closed grip, and he knew it to be the pale man's lies. He squeezed it until it popped.

More words were spilling out. "I am the tears that come from his eyes when he cries for help. I am the thing with teeth that eats his flesh. I am the nightmare you lock into a corner of your mind. I am the key that undoes the lock and the pain that comes out. I am your misery. I am—"

"Get off her, dammit!" Daniel lurched forward and knocked the beast loose. Rebekah collapsed onto the ground; her wings melted away, and she laid on the ground, a broken mess shrieking in madness.

"You're next, ha-ha!" the pale man said, forming up. "I'm going to break your insides and scoop out the wet pieces. And then I'm going to—"

"You want to get inside me? You want to see what I have trapped in here?" Daniel bounded forward and grabbed the monster with such audacity he surprised even himself. "I'll show you!" Daniel's jaw stretched open wide and he sank his teeth into the pale man's head. He bit down, chewing away bites, and the pale man snapped out laughter. With cold, pale hands, he reached inside Daniel and pulled himself in.

Tap-tap-tap.

Fear is the unknown and the waiting, the powerlessness against circumstance and fate.

Tap-tap-tap.

Daniel's foot knocked against the ground as he took deep breaths. Anxiety choked his lungs and the only slight relief he could find was to keep moving his foot, his body's way of telling him it was ready to react, ready to run away if needed. If only running away from your problems solved them.

Julia was in the operating room; something had gone wrong. Someone had tried to explain it to him, but the static in his ears was turned up all the way.

"The doctor is doing everything she can," one of those faceless people said.

Tap-tap-tap.

He stood up and paced before sitting down again. The waiting room was empty.

No, it wasn't.

Yes, it was.

The baby, Sam, was coming early. Too early. And that

look of pain and fear on Julia's face when she doubled over in the kitchen, it choked his brain.

The blood. Don't forget the blood.

Yes, the blood.

Blood had come streaming down her legs. That wasn't supposed to happen. Daniel had gotten her into the car, but he felt so weak, so slow, unable to move fast enough as Julia screamed.

She screamed so much. The blood, was it on my hands?

Yes. It was on your hands. And she was pale.

He barely heard one of the faceless people come in again and speak, "Mr. Tanner, I'm sorry but . . ."

No. That's not what happened. . .

Yes, it is.

"She died on the operating table. The baby, he's here." And then, he was in the nurse's arms. "Do you want to see him?"

Needles stitched through Daniel's flesh and took control of him. Strings pulled him like a puppet as he reached over to the blanketed bundle and took the baby and looked into its eyes: cold, dead eyes. He didn't want to, but the strings controlled him.

"He's dead, too," the faceless woman said. "Strangled, you see. Isn't that funny?"

"No!" Daniel yelled, but couldn't let go of the baby. "That didn't happen!"

Yes, it did.

"No, it didn't!" he screamed to the world.

But did it happen? How could he be sure? Didn't he just see it?

Oh, it did. And it's going to happen again and again and again.

"This isn't you, this is me. I am in control."

Wrong. I am here and I am you. I'm going to hollow you out until there's nothing left and then I'm going to wear you like a pair of old jeans until you fall apart. But I'm going to keep a piece of you here. I want you to watch.

Daniel looked down at his hands; they were empty. He squeezed them tightly, letting the pain seep in as his fingernails dug into his palms.

"I'm not going to let you do this. I'm going to kill you."

You're not going to let me? I don't have to do anything! I can just walk around, open the doors that you've built up, and let you eat yourself. You're twisted—insane, even. I haven't seen one like you. There are two of you in here, one just walking around the edges trying to keep out of sight, but I see you! I see you all! I see how you hurt yourself, and I fucking love it!

But I know it was destiny for you to be here now. I know how beautiful you are, now that I'm here! If I'm inside you, then I can be out there so much more easily, out in the real world. You can walk between them and I can just sit inside you and pull the strings. This is the most amazing thing to have ever happened to me! You've built yourself a room and you keep pieces locked inside. I've never seen such crazy shit, and believe me, I've seen some crazy shit.

"No, you can't do this."

Can't do what? I can do whatever I want. I'm going to start by raping your wife. Then her mother.

"No!" Daniel began to run, racing through the halls of his mind. Shadows stepped off the wall and followed him.

You can't get away from me, Daniel! There's nowhere to run in here! Nowhere that I can't come find you and drag you out. Ha-ha! You've built a fucking fortress for me in here!

The pale man's laughter chased Daniel as he struggled to get away. He grabbed the matting of his mind and used it to pull himself forward. He tried to hide in memories, but the dark ones were up and running loose.

He found a single tree, twice as thick as a man, growing roots into his mind. He came to the dark side of it and stepped in.

HE WAS in the woods now, with a stick, pulling at an injured bird's wing. It pulled off with a disgusting pop as the bird flailed and screeched. It was funny. So funny, the way it twisted and screeched. But it had a sickening feeling behind it, too, something that he felt even today.

"I guess there always were two sides to you," the shadows said as they descended from the sky. "This is the side I understand, the side you always wanted to be. Look at that smile you had. You enjoyed that look in the bird's eyes, the part where something even as stupid as it, could understand it's about to die."

"Get away from me, dammit!" Daniel turned and fled. The shadows stretched out, reaching for him, as the bird screeched out its requiem with a dying gasp. He found a puddle and jumped through it before bothering to look inside.

For a moment, he was soaked and muddy, trudging to the dark water. Then he was in his house, watching, sitting, with the revolver in his hand. Everything was heavy here— the weight of the world pressed against his shoulders, making him slump and struggle to breathe. Only the revolver was light, only it moved freely as it rose and pressed to his temple.

He pulled the trigger and the metal ripped through his head, painting the wall behind him with splashes of red.

No.

Yes.

No!

He reached from the wall and grabbed onto his bed frame. He pulled himself out of the wall, which ripped at him like glue until he snapped loose. "That's not what happened, dammit! The phone rang!" He screamed as powerfully as his lungs would allow. "It rang!"

It rang, and he stepped over his dead body as he ran down the hallway to answer it. The dead hand reached up and grabbed him by the ankle.

"Daniel, you didn't answer the phone," the dead man said. "You shot yourself. You're dead. That was a lie. You're dead. This is Hell. You're in Hell."

He kicked it off and started to run, daring one look back to see the dead man crawling behind him. He answered the phone and saw mirrors in the receiver. He stuck a thumb into one and stretched the mirror, making it big enough to step inside.

RAIN TAPPED against the glass and he and Sam played cards. It had been a gloomy day, but it was so warm now.

"Nope, nope. You have to play the same color or the same number, and only one card at a time!"

"But you said two before!"

"No, I said if you play a joker, then you *get* two more cards."

A shadow stretched through a mirror on the wall, following Daniel in. "What the fuck is this shit? You're going to hide from me in here? Do you know what I'm going to do to him? This isn't going to be a happy memory anymore. I hope you like red, because I'm going to paint the room with your boy's insides."

"This isn't a room," Daniel said, looking up from the game, just as Sam faded away and the world turned dark. "It's a cage."

"Ha-ha!" The pale man took form inside the shadow and his gray lips stretched open over a mouthful of teeth.

"It's true," said another voice from behind the mirror, this one with yellow split eyes. "You were right. We are two and we built this cage long ago. I know, because he put me in there."

"What the fuck are you talking about?"

"It's okay," Daniel said. "It's numb here. Cold and numb. You won't feel anything. That's how we built it. You're going to sit inside here with me."

"No," the pale man said, turning to the mirror and rushing to it. He smashed his hands against the glass. "You can't keep me in here. You can't keep me locked in here! You're not strong enough!"

"Oh, but you're the one that let everything loose, didn't you? I wasn't strong enough to put you in there, but you freed up all that I was, and you chased him right through that mirror into that room. I'm strong now and he and I both agree this time. You're going to stay."

The pale man's eyes were already starting to chill as the calming, dull effects of the cage seeped into him. With rage, he beat against the glass as the yellow-eyed Daniel lowered a blanket over the mirror.

"The other side is going to stay with you," Daniel said from outside the mirror. "He's going to make sure you stay calm while I take care of Sam. That was our deal."

Beneath the blanket, the pale man's words could not be heard, but Daniel was sure he wasn't laughing.

Daniel felt free, freer than he had ever felt. Free of guilt and anxiety, they were here now, but not howling and screaming like before. They didn't have that power anymore. Now, they moaned and dragged themselves around, looking for a way to torment him, and finding none.

He was the beast now. He was in control.

He stepped outside himself and into the dream world; Rebekah was there, still sobbing against the ground. She took no notice of him—her own tortures were unimaginable—as he stepped past her to the Shallow spot in the world.

Cold, painful air entered his lungs as he gasped. His mind scrambled with the sudden rush of reality, as if a multidimensional world had suddenly collapsed into one. The haze of the real world set in and started to cloud his mind, leaving only the briefest understanding of what had happened: only that he had won.

"Daddy?"

A new spark lit inside him when he saw Sam. He knew it was real this time; he knew it by the pain in his arm and the way he shook from the cold. He had broken reality to save his son and chase back a nightmare; he knew that, if nothing else.

My life for yours.

"Sam, I love you. Oh, my God, I love you so much," he said it over and over as tears stung his face. He said the words again and meant it each time, but there was something else there inside him.

Something hollow.

42

————

SOME SCARS NEVER HEAL. REBEKAH KNEW THIS, AND SHE certainly had her share. She rocked back in her chair. She'd been there for some time, and there was little to do but wait.

She was surprised when she woke and found sunlight on her skin. She hadn't expected to see the sun again. The dose she took should have been enough to keep her asleep forever, but she apparently wasn't as feeble as she thought.

That, or the world's just not done with me yet.

She wasn't exactly sure how she'd survived. The nurses told her a man had dropped her off and immediately left. It had been some hassle when Rebekah awoke; she even had to speak with some policemen. Whatever she said had apparently been enough; she always had a few good stories rehearsed and ready, though she wasn't troubling herself with those thoughts now. It seemed they had more important business than to interrogate a poor, confused old woman.

Now, she only wanted to rest and wait, to pull the disease out of her mind and think again. She hadn't talked to Daniel, nor had she done anything to make contact with him. But she felt him in her dreams, timid and scared, looking for her, but afraid to come any closer.

But he got it worse, didn't he? I saw that thing go inside his head. I only had pieces of it, and they're still there. I can't imagine what it did to him.

There was no need to make it easy; she didn't go to him, but left a message in the dreams if he came to look. It told him where he could find her.

Then, she waited.

The days went by, just like today, and now the sun had set and the moon was in the air. She was tired, but she didn't want to sleep.

I've had enough of dreams lately. It's time for something real.

It was nice just to sit in her chair and look out the window at the falling snow. Winter had some finality to it—the death of one season, leading to the beginning of another.

Headlights painted the window of her hotel room, bought with what was left of her dwindling bank account. She continued to rock in the chair as she heard a car door open and close, then steps against crunching snow; her ears were as sharp as ever. A few moments later, there was a knock at the door.

"Come in."

The door rattled open and she saw him standing there, silent and exhausted. He froze for a moment, afraid to come in, as if that somehow would be an end to things. Only when she spoke, did he step inside and close the door.

"I've been expecting you, Daniel."

"I tried," he said, coming in and sitting on the bed. He wasn't so much talking to her as thinking aloud. "I was so happy to get Sam back." Daniel sighed. "I tried to stay, and . . ."

"And?"

"He's gone. He's safe, but he's gone. What the fuck is wrong with me?" he asked with utter sincerity.

"You've seen things, Daniel, things we're not supposed to see. You can't be the same person after that. You're *not* the same person after that."

"I can't be a person at all. I don't know how to live anymore. I don't know what to do. I feel like I'm wearing someone else's skin."

"I think you do. I felt you reaching out for me, Daniel. That's how you knew I was here. You were looking for me."

"I need help."

Rebekah shook her head. "You don't need help, Daniel. You need the hunt. You're like me, and there are others out there like us, others we can find and rebuild with. I'm sorry, Daniel, but this isn't a game you quit, not in a way that leaves you breathing. But you already knew that, didn't you? I know you, Daniel. I know you."

"You're right," he said. "I can't quit this. I have to keep going, or I'm going to kill myself."

"There have always been people like us, Daniel, people to grab the torch and walk into the shadows. We are the shepherds of men."

"You're right, Rebekah. I want this. I *need* this. But I'm not the shepherd." Daniel looked up at her and she could almost see something behind those eyes.

"I'm the wolf."

He tried, he really did.

Coming out of the Shallow, unsure of what even

happened, he was ready to get Sam out of there and to step right over the top of Rebekah's cooling body.

He saw the needle in her arm. He didn't know what it was, but he figured it wouldn't be long until she was done. Besides, she wanted it that way.

Or is it that you just don't care anymore?

Sam wouldn't let him leave her. Sam—still a bright light, even after all that.

"Daddy, we gotta help her!"

He did, but only because Sam wanted it. They got Rebekah and dropped her off at the hospital one town over, then left. He hoped he'd never see her again. Never see any of this again. He was just going to take Sam and leave. Forget the house, forget everything. It wasn't long before they were on the road and nearly out of the state.

Just let it all rot.

Something told him otherwise, that he could never be that again. The things that happened to him in the dream, they were already a blurred haze with brief flashes of clarity. He hoped it would be the same for Sam. He hoped that he would just forget it all and go on to live a regular life, in a new place, with people who didn't know Sam and didn't know he was supposed to be buried out in a cold field.

He's never going to have a life again. Not with you. Not with what you've done and the things you've seen. The police will be looking for you. They'll have a lot of questions about Sam and what you've been doing. You're not his father anymore.

He knew that. There was no need for the voice to tell him. So, what did he have then?

Julia.

That was who he thought of—Julia, the same woman who had abandoned Sam when he was sick.

That wasn't Sam. You know better now. Somehow, she did, too.

Sam was in the front seat, asleep for the first time in days after half of one of Daniel's dream pills—one of the last Daniel had. Daniel watched him, his small chest rising and falling, his brow furrowed. What was he dreaming? Was he thinking about what happened there? Would he be able to live a normal life ever again?

Not with me.

That voice came again. He pulled the car over, sighed and squeezed the steering wheel. He looked once again at Sam, his eyes closed and his head resting against the seat.

My life for yours.

What was there now for the two of them? Could Sam ever go back to school? Did he ever have any hope of having children, or a family of his own? Was there any hope at all?

Not with you.

He stepped out of the car to use the phone. The phone rang several times. He had to lean over the car, suddenly weak at the knees. A soft voice finally answered.

"Hello?"

"Julia? It's me, Dan. We need to talk. . ."

EPILOGUE

BEFORE HE COULD SAY GOODBYE TO NEW ATHENS, HE DECIDED to take one last long trip out to Terrace Drive. He didn't dare pull in, not when he saw the police tape up, not with what he'd heard in town about what they found in that place: ash, his dead friends, and enough ordnance to get the feds interested.

He just had to see. He slowed his car down and let it roll for a moment. That was all he needed, all the time it took to say goodbye.

He turned the car back toward town and flipped on the high beams. There were two glowing eyes in the field. A small, shivering, bundle of fur climbed out onto the road. It sat on the ground and barked at him.

Greg's pup.

He stopped the car and went over to pick it up. He shot a glance either way. There was no telling what happened to its mother, but he could guess.

"How'd you get all the way out there by yourself?"

The dog nuzzled his fingers as he brought it back to his

car, finding it a warm spot on his jacket in the passenger seat.

Later, Daniel sat at his desk; he was sure that this was the last time he ever would. An empty glass sat nearby and a pen rested in his hands. He scratched out his thoughts in a hand that didn't feel like his anymore.

I'm not a father anymore. That person died, and I'm something else, something that can't love and can only see red when I close my eyes.

I took Sam to Julia. I explained everything to her and told her what to do. I told her to blame everything on me, to tell them I had him the entire time. I told her they're going to dig that grave up, and I'm not sure what they're going to find. But it's my fault. I killed whatever's in there.

I just hope it's still dead.

I told her to take him. Go away from here. I told her she had to take Sam and leave, to never come back. And never call me again or anyone here, to just take our son and leave. She did.

Rebekah and I spent one more night at New Athens in the dreams. We went inside Sam's mind and I saw the one who plagues him now. I saw what's inside his head. We built a wall for him and caged it. I put his love for me in a room, one that he can visit when he wants, but not something that will torment him.

That's the last gift I'll ever be able to give to him.

I look at the world and I watch the way it moves. I see the gears turning and a script that no one knows they're reading. I see their lips move as they recite it. I see their faces as they pretend to laugh or feign a frown. I know they're lying; I know they're playing a part in a game they can't see. I know they're all glass and ready to crack.

This world doesn't mean anything. It's a layer of skin laid over the top of the dead, a layer that only moves until the rot finds it.

The rot found me, and it grew inside me. It's still there—I feel it. I feel him. He's not dead. He still shows me things, things with Sam, things I won't write down. He still whispers to me in the back of my head. Sometimes, when I dream, he tries to pull me in.

I can't be anything other than that rot.

Don't judge me. If you saw what I saw, and hear the whispers I hear, you would understand. If you were me, and you were at the end, you would do the same.

You would be the same.

Don't ever try to find me. There isn't anyone to find.

I'm simply lost.

ABOUT THE AUTHOR

J.Z. Foster is an Urban Fantasy / Horror writer originally from Ohio. He spent several years in South Korea where he met and married his wife and together they opened an English school.

Now a first-time father, he's returned to the States—and his hometown roots.

He received the writing bug from his mother, NYTimes best-selling author, Lori Foster.

He is writing a growing universe and exploring all the dark corners of it. Check out his other books and let him know how you like them!

NOTE FROM THE AUTHOR

Did you like this book? Then *please* consider helping me out with a review on *Goodreads*, *Amazon*, or anywhere else!

I am trying to make writing my full time career to give you as many good books as I can, please help me do it!

Reviews help sell books and get the word out for starting authors like me.

Thank you for the help!

FOLLOW THE AUTHOR

Want to know when the next book drops?

You can follow his writing progress on his Facebook page,
https://www.facebook.com/JZFosterAuthor/
Want to know what else is going on in JZ Foster's world,
or write to him directly?

Send an email to **Boogeymancomes4u@gmail.com** or
follow him on *Instagram* / *Twitter* at **@JZFosterAuthor.**

Sign up for his newsletter here:
https://tinyurl.com/JZFosterAuthor

ALSO BY J.Z. FOSTER

Look for these titles on Amazon now!

Witch Hunter: Into the Outside

The Wicked Ones: Children of the Lost

Mind Wreck: Shadow Games

J.Z. Foster. The Wicked Ones: Children of the Lost

❀ Created with Vellum